LUST UNDER LICENCE

by

NOEL AMOS

This work is sold subject to the condition that it shall not, by way of trade or otherwise, be lent, resold, hired out or otherwise circulated without the publisher's prior written consent in any form of binding or cover other than that in which it is published, and without a similar condition being imposed on the subsequent purchaser. The author asserts that all characters depicted in this work of fiction are eighteen years of age or older, and that all characters and situations are entirely imaginary and bear no relation to any real person or actual happening.

Copyright Noel Amos. The right of Noel Amos to be identified as author of this book has been asserted in accordance with section 77 and 78 of the Copyrights Designs and Patents Act 1988.

Cover image by Barbara Jensen.

This novel is fiction - in real life practice safe sex.

The women meet in a sunny conservatory. They sit round a glass table on padded cane chairs and drink iced mineral water from tall glasses. Some make notes on leather-backed pads, one takes minutes on a laptop portable. A female observer would approve of their style, in particular the elegant cut of their summer suits and dresses. A male observer might be tempted to look further than the packaging and imagine exploring the delectable flesh within.

But there are no observers to this meeting. Its concerns are secret and only the palms and ferns swaying in the cool down draught from the ceiling fans are witness to its deliberations. The Corrections Committee of The Primrose Court is going about its weekly business. That business is the regulation of sex. And the prosecution of men.

'What are we going to do about this,' says a willowy brunette as she pushes a thick folder into the middle of the table, 'in the light of recent events?'

'I thought that gentleman might get a mention,' says the chairwoman, a well-preserved blonde of indeterminate years.

'Nail the bastard now,' says a woman in a thin skinny-ribbed top.

'I agree,' says another, her short black hair as stylishly cropped as a French mannequin. 'Let's get him while public opinion's on our side.'

The chairwoman sighs, the mood of the gathering is plain. Very well,' she says. 'Pass the file to Prosecutor Hawk.'

One - A La Recherche Des Bonks Perdus
Chapter 1

The patient woke on the third day. A woman was bending over him and his first impression was of the view down the neck of her candy-striped blouse as she adjusted his pillows. A shaft of sunlight shone from a window onto the pale skin of her cleavage which gaped, milky and warm, inches from his face. The aroma of chocolate and perfume rose from her dimpled flesh. On the sumptuous cupola of her right breast was a name tag.

'Nurse Biscuit,' he said.

The woman leapt backwards as if she'd been stung. A shilling-sized circle of scarlet blazed on each cheek and her blue eyes were wide with alarm.

'Golly!' she cried. 'You're awake!' She giggled and put a band to her mouth. 'I'll just fetch - oh!'

She gave up the struggle to finish the sentence and ran from the room with a squeak of laughter. As she did so the patient couldn't help noticing that, for a nurse, her skirt was distractingly short.

He looked around the room. There were swagged floral curtains on the high windows and Matisse prints on the wall. The carpet was thick. Opposite his bed was a large television set and on top of it a card offering a choice of movies. Next to a writing desk stood a small teak cabinet labelled 'Minibar'. Only the bed on which he lay and the bank of instruments that surrounded it, some with tubes which snaked beneath the sheets, indicated that he was in some kind of medical establishment. From behind his head, in the room next door, came the thump of rock music and raised, cheerful voices.

'Where am I?' he said to the woman in a white coat and granny glasses who now entered the room accompanied by a more composed Nurse Biscuit.

'Partridge Place,' she replied, taking a clipboard of notes from the end of the bed.

The patient thought for a second. The catch phrase from an advert came into his head: 'The Exclusive Care Facility for Exclusive People,' he said.

'You won't get better care elsewhere,' said the woman, failing to add 'or more expensive' - it went without saying.

Her fingers were cool and firm as she took his pulse. Like Nurse Biscuit, she too wore a name tag. She saw the direction of his gaze.

'I'm Madeleine Flint,' she said, 'the consultant in charge of your case.'

'But who am I?' said the patient. 'And what am I doing here?'

This time Nurse Biscuit could not control her laughter.

They brought him the papers to read and left him alone, though he heard plenty of stifled whispering at the door. He had the impression he was being observed. He soon forgot about it as he turned to the front page of the *Daily Dog*.

CITY PLONKER TAKES THE PLUNGE

Mystery of nude tycoon

Millionaire businessman Tom Glass, the City's Mr Cool, fell off his pedestal yesterday when he survived an embarrassing freak accident that landed him in hospital. Theatre-goers emerging from The Gryphon Theatre discovered Glass half naked in a builder's skip in the road outside his office at 10.30 last night. It is assumed that Glass fell from the balcony of his penthouse on the tenth floor.

No trousers

'When I left the theatre I saw a man lying in a pile of rubbish,' said Randolph Sutcliffe, 43. 'At first I thought he was drunk. He was wearing stockings and suspenders but no trousers and he had a pair of ladies' knickers on his head. He looked like he'd been having a high old time. What's more, he was still up for it, if you know what I mean. My wife's in shock.'

On the job

Last night Glass was recovering in a luxury hospital reserved for the nobs. Staff at his company, Glass Mountain, were tight-lipped about the activities of their owner and Chief Executive. 'As far as I know, Tom was working late,' said a company spokesperson. 'We're all praying he'll soon be back on the job.' Mr Glass's fiancée, Marianne Matthews, Badger TV's weather girl, was not available for comment.

The other papers, in their various styles, were no less gleeful. The *Daily Blizzard* made the incident the subject of a centre-page comment:

The Blizzard finds it shameful that one of our best and brightest young entrepreneurs should be guilty of gross impropriety in public on the same day that the business community launches its New Leaf campaign to reinforce moral values in the office environment. Such conduct undermines all the good work put in by right-thinking male executives and is a calculated insult to the increasingly powerful female voice in the business world. Tom Glass has been dead lucky this time but we suggest that he cleans up his act fast - even fat cats can run out of lives.

The patient stared at the pile of newspapers. There were three days' worth and the story even rumbled on in the most recent. It didn't make a lot of sense to him. He couldn't remember any of it. He jabbed his finger onto the red alarm button by his bed. Nurse Biscuit appeared at the door instantly.

'Get me a mirror,' he demanded before she had set foot in the room. His voice was deep and authoritative. The sound comforted him. 'What are you waiting for?' he yelled and the rosy-cheeked nurse vanished, returning with a hand mirror a moment later.

He studied the photographs in the papers and compared them with his reflection: straight nose, cleft chin, a shock of dark hair falling over the brow. It was the same man.

Nurse Biscuit was looking at him closely, fear and curiosity written on her pretty face.

'What's your first name?' he said.

'Eve.'

He held out his hand and took her small one in his grasp. 'It seems mine is Tom. Sit down, Eve, and tell me all you know about me because, believe me, I haven't got a clue.'

She hesitated, her hand still in his. He wouldn't let go.

'It's all right, Eve,' said the voice of Dr Flint as she advanced on the bed holding a hypodermic needle. 'You can stay and chat to Mr Glass after he's had his injection.'

'What's that for?' said Tom, suspicion in his voice, as his sleeve was raised and Madeleine Flint aimed her weapon.

'Relax, Mr Glass, you're not lording it over your business empire now.' And she slid the needle into a vein.

'What business empire?' Tom shouted. 'Don't you understand - I can't remember who I am!'

'Trust me,' said Madeleine, emptying the syringe into his arm. 'I promise you'll soon remember things you never knew you knew.'

4

Chapter 2

Gossamer Hawk rose at six every day to take a leisurely bath. As she luxuriated in the warm soapy water she sometimes heard the screams and bellows of her two toddling offspring as they rampaged on the floor below. If they were too noisy she would reprimand her husband, Peregrine, over breakfast. Gossamer needed tranquillity first thing in the morning to prepare her mind and body for the rigours of the day ahead.

After milkless tea, wholemeal toast and a quick skim of the newspapers she watched Perry herd Annabel and Pasco into the family Volvo to ferry them off to nursery school. Then she made a list of house-husbandly tasks for Perry to accomplish during the day: 'Iron my turquoise blouse, fetch the dryclean, return P's library books, do Sainsbury's and don't forget Blenkinsops are coming for dinner - asparagus soufflé rack of lamb would be nice. I'll try to be back by eight.' At last, with the satisfaction that comes from unselfish delegation, she whisked her scarlet Honda Prelude out of the garage and plunged into the traffic heading for central London. Prosecutor Hawk was ready for business.

Gossamer's appointment to The Primrose Court had taken newspapers by surprise. What was a little-known barrister, a mother-of-two with an inane giggle and a schoolgirl vocabulary, doing at the cutting edge of sexual correction? To outsiders, this rangy English rose with unruly fair hair and disarming milky-blue eyes seemed lightweight. But those who had seen her operate - such as her former colleagues in chambers and her opponents in court - knew that the rose had thorns.

Gossamer was a great believer in the clear-desk policy. First thing in the morning her in-tray groaned with paper; by the end of the day not a scrap would be visible. The rapid assimilation and processing of material was one of her strengths. She had once been the school swot - it was the foundation of her success.

Today she beavered at her in-coming paper pile with customary zeal. She had an interview with a journalist scheduled for eleven and she aimed to clear her desk by then. Soon she was down to just one item, a thick yellow file bulked out with newspaper cuttings. She read the name scrawled in black felt-tip on the cover and settled down to read with glee. For once she was going to take her time.

An hour later Gossamer was interrupted by the arrival of Kelvin Priest of *Nouveau*, a modish magazine for thinking men - or so it claimed. Giving interviews to the press was not Gossamer's favourite task, particularly to such a small-beer publication. But selling the business of The Primrose Court to the thinking man *was* part of her job.

She had no objection to Kelvin, however. She had a soft spot for broody English types - they never gave her any trouble.

'Speaking as a male,' he was saying, 'how do I know when my thoughts need correcting? I mean, if I see an attractive woman in the street and I think to myself, well, something overtly sexist like—'

'"Cor, get a load of the arse on that"?' Gossamer's tinkling tones enunciated every syllable and brought a blush to Kelvin's cheeks.

'Yes, that kind of thing.'

Gossamer beamed at him and pushed a lock of thick honey-hued hair from off her forehead. 'Well, Kelvin, that is an obvious misdemeanour and you should be ashamed of yourself.'

Kelvin looked suitably ashamed but persisted.

'But suppose I'm walking behind this woman, thinking about something else, and I can't help staring at her, um, figure even though my mind is elsewhere.'

'You mean the way you're staring now.'

'I'm sorry?'

'I have no doubt, Mr Priest, that you are a conscientious journalist and that your sole concern in interviewing me is to faithfully interpret my remarks for your readers, however...'

'However?'

'You haven't taken your eyes off my breasts since you sat down.'

Kelvin's face was crimson. It was true that his glance had strayed once or twice to the divide of Gossamer's cleavage, prettily exposed in the vee of her open-necked blouse. He opened his mouth to deny it but no sound emerged. There was a degree of intensity in her big blue eyes that prevented him. They bored into his like a searchlight on a black night. Not many men, in or out of the dock, found it easy to lie to Prosecutor Hawk.

'Don't worry, Mr Priest, I know you are just doing your job as best you can,' she said with a deprecating smile. 'After all, the male of the species is a rudimentary organism at best and it would be unreasonable of me to expect a lusty young man like you to be able to rise above the imperatives of his genitalia. Just so long as you understand that when you contemplate stripping off my blouse and manhandling my breasts then you are simply rising to the siren song of lust that men have answered down the ages. Inside every man in a suit and tie is a shaggy-haired barbarian longing to rape and defile and thrust his hard brutal flesh into a woman's soft and yielding femininity. Believe me, Mr Priest, in my line of work I *know*. Would you like some coffee?'

Kelvin nodded. He couldn't speak, he didn't trust himself to be coherent through the tangle of emotions that currently overwhelmed him. He was intimidated by Gossamer's eloquence and ashamed of his masculine inheritance. Yet the urge to *manhandle* her, now it had been openly acknowledged, had not diminished. Far from it. Somewhere in his mind, he was speculating on the size, the shape, the weight, the actual *feel* of her tits. He couldn't help it.

'Alberto, sweetie,' said Gossamer to a slim Latin fellow who had appeared in the doorway, 'pop out and get us a couple of cappuccinos, there's a love.'

Alberto flashed a toothy smile and swivelled on his Cuban heels. His black trousers were cinched at the waist and pulled as tight as cellophane across the hard round peach of his bum.

'My new assistant,' explained Gossamer. 'He'll run to the Italian cafe over the road. The coffee in this place tastes like pee.'

'He looks like a waiter,' ventured Kelvin.

'He used to be one - his father owns the cafe. Now he's a computer whizz. Can't spell for toffee but can boot up and download all night long, if you get my drift.'

Kelvin didn't think he did but he smiled all the same. Seconds later Alberto was arranging cups on the desk, a gold necklace dangling from the open neck of his sparkling white shirt.

'What kept you, sweetheart?' said Gossamer. 'I suppose you were drooling over Maria's *melanzane* again?'

Alberto's face froze in a pantomime of horror.

'Miss Gossamer, how could you say that? You know there is only one woman in my life,' he paused, his handsome face inches from Gossamer's, 'my mother.'

The pair of them laughed fit to bust and Alberto turned to go. As he did so he looked at Kelvin and rolled his eyes to heaven.

'Alberto, you're a wicked boy,' said Gossamer to his twinkling buttocks as he glided from the room.

Kelvin sipped foam from his cup, quite bemused.

'Lovely man,' said Gossamer. 'A complete pussy-hound, of course. He'll be off as soon as he's piddled on all the lampposts round here, worse luck.'

'But, Prosecutor Hawk—'

'Kelvin, please. Any man who admires my breasts as much as you obviously do, must call me Gossamer.'

'Gossamer, the man's a classic macho male, a gigolo, a pimp - surely he represents everything you wish to change in the male sex?'

Gossamer laughed, a long-drawn-out peal of high-pitched merriment that set her substantial titties atremble.

'Poor Kelvin,' she said at last, 'you really don't understand, do you? Perhaps you'd like to take me to dinner some time and I'll raise your awareness.'

The moment the confused Kelvin had picked up his notes and gone, Gossamer summoned Alberto with an urgency born of pent-up desperation.

'Quick, take them down.'

'But, Miss Gossamer—'

'Shut up. I want your thick dick in my hand in thirty seconds or you're back on the dole queue.'

Alberto shrugged and dropped his pants, he knew there was no point in arguing.

His long curving Latin prong did not share its owner's reluctance. As he stood beside her desk it waved in the Prosecutor's face like a truncheon. She plunged her mouth over the broad brown tip like a starving woman.

'OH!' he groaned in pleasure and pain as sharp fingernails dragged his scrotum downwards.

She took her mouth away and replaced it with her other hand, staring greedily at the tumescent genitals in her grasp.

'You're hung like a horse,' she muttered. 'Put me over the desk and fuck me silly or I'll have you gelded.' She grinned to herself at the prospect.

Alberto took no notice of her last remark, he was already pulling her to her feet and hauling her skirt upwards. Thin peach panties descended over matching suspenders and stockings and pooled around her ankles. Bent across her desk the twin globes of her bottom cheeks jutted like great white moons. Alberto peeled apart the flesh to gaze on the winking star of her arsehole. Below it, the gaping pink purse of her pussy bubbled with juice.

He ran the glans of his cock up and down the bum crevice and fingered the wet lips of her overflowing honeypot. He gave her left buttock a soft enquiring slap.

'Yes!' she snapped. 'Smack me. Oh! Smack me hard!'

Broad strong hands descended in measured blows. Left, right, then left again, turning the creamy globes into quivering spheres of crimson.

'YES, YES!' she yelled. 'Now put it in.'

Alberto obeyed. It was more than his job was worth to do otherwise.

Gossamer thrust her big beautiful buttocks backwards into his crotch, spearing herself on his stiff tool. Oh, it was heaven. The interview with dishy Kelvin had turned her on. It was a pity he was such a wimp. She'd bet he'd only have half the stamina of Alberto.

She came once and slowed her thrusting, content to pace herself now the first tide of desire had washed over her. Alberto could stay hard for as long as she wanted, he wouldn't dare come till she said so. She thanked the day she had landed this job, if only for the perks. 'Perks spelt P-R-I-C-K-S,' she told herself, jamming back onto his rearing organ and laughing out loud.

Alberto muttered, '*Mamma*,' and began to gently diddle her clit, the agitation of his fingers in her cleft pushing her into the path of her next wave of pleasure.

'Oh gosh, oh gosh,' she cried, jerking her head from side to side, the flailing locks of her hair lashing down onto the yellow folder which had occupied her attention that morning.

The file marked 'Glass'.

Chapter 3

In his head, Tom Glass was sitting in the kitchen of his parents' house in Manchester marvelling at the slim white legs of his brother's fiancée as her babydoll nightie rode up her thighs.

'There you are, Tommy,' said Rosemary as she set a cup of tea on the table in front of him. She ruffled his uncombed mop of black hair affectionately, as if she were petting a dog. 'Rosie—'

'Yes, Tommy?'

'Do you know how old I am?'

She stopped in the act of cracking eggs into a bowl. 'Of course - you're seventeen.'

'I'm two months away from having the vote. Three months off going to university. Old enough to get married and have kids.'

'Yes?' There was confusion in her large brown eyes.

'Old enough not to be called Tommy. Call me Tom, call me Thomas, but please don't call me Tommy. OK?'

'I'm sorry, Tommy - Tom! I didn't know you felt like that. It's just that everyone—'

'Quite. Everyone around here wants me to stay in short pants and be cute little Tommy. It reinforces their own sense of worth - I've read about it. Mum even wanted me to be a pageboy at your wedding—'

'That was a joke. She didn't mean it.'

'It was indicative of her underlying feelings, Rosie. No one round here wants me to grow up.'

'Tommy, that's unfair.' Rosemary had abandoned the eggs and taken a seat at the table beside Tom. This was important. 'Oops, I said it again, I'm sorry. But look, Jack's on your side.'

'Jack's the worst. He wants me to be a little brother for ever. Someone he can impress, someone he can beat.'

'What do you mean?' Rosemary was agitated now.

'I mean he's got everything round here. He's got a job, he's got a car, he's got money. He's got you.'

'Me?'

'Absolutely. He's got a girl with great legs sleeping in his bed every other night at his parents' home and they aren't even married yet.'

'I didn't know you were such a puritan.'

'I'm no puritan, Rosie, but I don't appreciate you two hammering the mattress all night long in the room next door when I'm not even allowed out till closing time.'

'You're jealous, Tommy.'

'You bet I'm jealous. Two years past the age of consent and no luck and there's my brother making love to the most gorgeous woman in the city night after night about three feet away.'

'Oh God, Tommy, I'm sorry. I never thought. I mean, we - can you really hear?'

'Yes.'

'I'm embarrassed. We try and keep the noise down.'

There was a pause in the conversation. The boy's dark brooding eyes were boring into hers and she had to look away. 'Do you really think I'm gorgeous?'

'Utterly.'

'And you think I've got great legs?'

'I love the way you move. You're like a dancer.'

'You're a bit of a smooth-talker, Tom Glass.'

'That's better. I like it when you call me Tom.'

He was smiling now and it was as if the sun had come out.

'I don't believe you're as shy with the girls as you make out.'

'I've hardly ever kissed one.'

'Oh, come on!'

'It's true.'

'You must have.'

'Not properly. It's been a fiasco so far.'

'Well, for God's sake, we can soon fix that.'

Rosie leaned forward and placed a hand on the back of Tom's neck. The nightie rode higher. Her lips were soft as satin and her breath was sweet. He let her hold her mouth to his, resisting the urge to devour her. A small pointed tongue suddenly slipped between his lips.

'Oh,' he murmured as she explored his mouth. Still he did not respond.

'You can kiss me back, Tom,' she said, 'it's all right. I won't bite. Oh, that's nice.'

And it was. His tongue was in her mouth and she was sucking on it, eager to teach her pupil some of the skills she practised at night in the room next to his.

'You mustn't sit there like a block of wood, you know. Put your arms around me.'

She was on the bench beside him now and the nightie was almost up to her groin. Her body heat flowed into him through two thin layers of clothing.

'Wow,' she said, disengaging her lips. 'You see, Tom, you can kiss very well.' Her face was flushed and her eyes were dancing. The soft pressure of her left breast on his chest was burning a hole through his pyjamas.

'I'm not sure, Rosie.' Bashful, he looked down - to the creamy flesh of her thighs exposed nearly to her hips. A wisp of fair brown hair nosed into view beneath the embroidered pink hem. He lowered his mouth to hers.

Without thinking she leaned into him, mouth wide, breasts thrusting, her hands beneath his pyjama jacket to grasp his muscular torso. His hands too began to wander, pulling the pink babydoll confection up to her waist and closing over the hot smooth flesh of her buttocks.

'Oh Tom!' she squealed as he pulled her onto his lap and her legs automatically scissored around his waist, pressing her most intimate folds against a column of flesh that rose vertically from his crotch.

As she realised what she was doing she tried to pull away but it was too late. Somehow her wriggling and squirming only managed to lodge the head of the biggest, smoothest, firmest penis she had ever encountered into the wet and hungry mouth between her thighs.

'Oh God!' she yelled as this irresistible cock invaded her, miraculously unaided it seemed, and Tom's strong hands on her hips drove her down its whole length. She rose and fell on the delicious spike, her tongue down his throat, her fingers twined in his hair. The word 'damn' echoed somewhere in her head even as her first climax bubbled in her loins.

Tom did little. There was no need. The woman was like a wind-up toy - turn the key and watch her go. The beauty of it was that she had turned the key all by herself...

Tom opened his eyes with a start. A Matisse goldfish swam on the wall in front of him and by the side of his bed sat a plump nurse with an anxious look on her pretty face. As for Rosemary...

'By God, Eve, I can remember.'

'Oh, Mr Glass, how wonderful.' She squeezed his hand.

'I dreamt I was in my parents' house in Manchester. I can see them all - mum and dad and my brother Jack.'

And the girl who was nearly my sister-in-law, he added silently. He could remember every moment of the day he'd fucked her. Fucked her all over the house. In the kitchen, in his bedroom, in all the bedrooms, in the living-room on the rug by the fire - which was where Jack found them on his return from work. He'd had her every way by then, from the front, from the back, between her tits and down her throat. She'd swallowed his spunk like a parched pilgrim, he recalled.

That's what she'd been doing when Jack walked in - licking come juice from the swollen head of his penis as she lay between his spread thighs. Not that he'd seen Jack make his famous entrance because he'd had his face buried in the slippery folds of Rosie's crotch, returning the favour she'd just done him. By that point he'd dropped the pretence that he didn't know a thing about girls and he'd been giving her his special cunt-suck: a whistle of hot breath on the clit, alternating with gentle tongue flicks and accompanied by two fingers pistoning deep into the vagina. She was coming even as she screamed out Jack's name.

'Poor Rosie,' he said out loud. 'I wonder what ever happened to her?'

Chapter 4

'Congratulations, Petra,' said Cassie Crow, as she downed a glass of red wine. 'It's good to see another woman get a grip on the reins of power.'

'It's only while Tom's out of commission,' said Petra Rosewater, Deputy Executive Officer of Glass Mountain.

They were sitting on the roof terrace of Cassie's apartment, the remains of an alfresco dinner on the table between them. The late summer sun was setting over the river in spectacular fashion. It was a fabulous view, expensively acquired. But while *Fragrant* remained the topselling women's monthly its editor could afford the best.

'Of course, you're the exception that proves the rule,' said Cassie. 'You're much too attractive to be the boss.'

'Come off it, Cassie, times have changed.'

'Says who? We're running another article next month on boardroom discrimination. If you're a woman you still only stand a chance if you look like a wet weekend. And have no tits.'

'What?'

'It's true. Thirty-eight double D spells typing pool, thirty A and buck teeth means you might make upper-echelon workhorse. Apart from me, you're the only woman I know of with a cleavage and a seat on the board.'

'Not that big a cleavage.'

Cassie laughed and speared a chunk of smelly goat's cheese.

'No one's going to overlook it, sweety-pie. The way you shake those pretty little apples I'd say you were a major distraction at any big boys' meeting.'

Petra did not dispute the point, there was no arguing with Cassie when she'd put away two gins and a bottle of wine.

'Anyway,' she said, 'I thought all this discrimination was changing. That's the point of The Primrose Court, isn't it?'

'Aha.' Cassie grinned. 'My lips are sealed.'

'Rubbish. You know something, don't you?'

Cassie busied herself pulling the ribbon off a large box of Belgian chocolates and did not reply.

Petra curbed her impatience. Cassie was a good friend but her work on the Corrections Committee of The Primrose Court was a bone of contention between the two of them. Cassie was sworn to secrecy, of course, but she enjoyed leaking snippets of information. First, though, Petra had to jump through hoops.

'Cassie, please.'

'Have a chocolate.'

'I don't want a chocolate. And you shouldn't eat them either. What happened to your diet?'

'I've got a new one. Haven't you noticed?'

'I've noticed you hoovering up cholesterol all evening, if that's what you mean.'

'And how do you think I look?'

Cassie stood up and turned around so Petra could admire her shape.

There was a lot of shape to admire. Cassie Crow was not a small woman. She was tall and eye-catching, with long shiny red hair and laughing green eyes. Her tight white slacks clung to her hips and bottom as if sprayed on and her curves, though ample, were supple and seductive. She lifted the hem of her thin blue sweater and displayed an area of tanned brown midriff.

'See?' she said, pinching the flesh between finger and thumb. 'No spare tyre.'

Petra was impressed. 'You look great,' she admitted, 'you really do. What's the secret?'

'This.' Cassie plonked a book on the table. 'It's the latest thing from the States and *Fragrant* dropped a bundle on it for serial. When it came in I insisted on guinea-pigging it myself.' Petra picked up the slim volume. The blush-pink front cover typography read: *The Come-Again Lifestyle - Discovering Your POT. The sensational multi-million-copy bestseller by Chastity Honeydew.* Filling the entire back page of the jacket was a portrait of a doll-faced young woman whose elaborate blonde coiffure was spread across a pillow. Her lips were full, luscious and parted and her eyes were closed, long eyelashes resting on a cheek as flawless as a baby's bottom. She appeared to be in the throes of ecstasy.

'Interesting,' said Petra, attempting to keep the scepticism out of her voice. She knew she had to humour Cassie if she were ever to find out who was next on the hit list of The Primrose Court.

She ran her eye over the copy on the front flap of the book. There were lots of separate lines in a big bold face preceded by asterisks:

* Discovering the way to Honeydew Heaven!
* How to calculate your revolutionary POT
* Understanding your POT chart
* Locating your POG
* Techniques and positions explained
* Satisfaction guaranteed - and how!

'It looks a bit technical,' she said.

'That's just crap,' said Cassie. 'It's like all these books. It's got one idea and the rest is window-dressing. I mean, you can't sell a one-page book, can you?'

'So what's the idea? Save me ploughing through a hundred and ninety pages.'

'OK. First you have to find your POT. Mine's eighty-one. That's the number of letters in your first name, times the month of your birth. Nine letters in Cassandra times September, the ninth month, equals eighty-one.'

'OK. I was born in August so I'd be five times eight - forty.'

Cassie frowned. 'That's not enough. If it's under fifty you have to add in the letters in your surname. In your case that's fourteen times eight, that makes one hundred and twelve. Wow, you lucky girl.'

'So?' Petra was at a loss.

'You still don't get it, do you? Let me explain in words of one syllable.'

'Please do.' Petra helped herself to more wine, Cassie was irritating the hell out of her.

'POT stands for Personal Orgasm Target. Mine is eighty-one. That means I must achieve eighty-one orgasms a calendar month.'

'Good God.' The blood drained from Petra's face.

'That's the whole thing. No diets, no aerobics, no workouts, no funny pills. Just doing it, lots. And it works, as you can see. In the office we call this "Fucking for Fitness".'

'But, eighty-one times a month. That's...'

'Two point six one comes a day in a month of thirty-one days, or two point six six averaged across a year. That's a minimum. You can do more if you want to.'

'But how? I mean, Luke left six months ago...'

'Petra, there's no need to be embarrassed. We are not talking sex here. This is not about messy relationships and faking it and finding some slut's knickers in his briefcase. This is health and fitness and personal growth.'

'You're not kidding!' Petra's voice rose an octave. 'I'll have to grow another clit to make a hundred and twelve orgasms a month!' And she reached for her wineglass.

'According to the book, there are some women who are so highly tuned they can do that in an hour. But that's a bit freakish, if you ask me.'

Cassie took her calculator out. 'In your case, I make it three point six eight a day. We're never going to get the smile off your face.'

'But I'm not doing this!'

'Come on, Petra. I need more guinea pigs. We're going to profile the first month's progress of half a dozen different women and Chastity Honeydew is going to provide a commentary. She's coming over from California to promote and part of our deal is that she writes some extra stuff for *Fragrant* readers. I've spent hours with her on the phone already, working out the details. We paid a fortune for the book. It's dynamite.'

'I don't need this, Cassie.'

'Yes, you do. You're a stressed-out female executive who can't enjoy life any more. Businesswoman X, actually - we reserve your anonymity. You're perfect for us and it's perfect for you. Trust me.'

'What will Kelvin say?'

'He'll love it. He'll be on cloud nine or wherever when you start demanding his body every night.'

'But he can't do it a hundred and twelve times a month! Besides, he's not around half the time.'

'Honey, you are so naive. *He* doesn't have to come, you do and his being away could be a big advantage.'

'Oh God.' Petra realised that somewhere along the line she had agreed and she felt an involuntary twitch between her legs. She was soaking, she realised. 'You're a terrible influence on me, Cassie Crow.'

'Darling, you certainly won't regret it. Especially when you see Philippe.'

'Who?'

'Philippe. He's my POG - Personal Orgasm Guide. He studied the method with Chastity in the States and *Fragrant* assigned him to me. He's French. You'll adore him.'

Petra gazed at Cassie in shock though, come to think of it, the existence of a 'Personal Orgasm Guide' wasn't much of a surprise. Only a hot new lover could work the kind of transformation she saw in Cassie.

'Is this Philippe due here this evening?' she said.

'At any second.'

'I'm leaving,' said Petra and stood up.

'You can't go. You need to observe the techniques. It's much better than looking at the book. Besides I need you to take the video.'

'Video.' Petra's voice was flat, she could not react to any more surprises.

'Yes. Chastity says I need to analyse my orgasms so that I can enumerate them properly. I mean, sometimes I'm not sure when one ends and another begins. So I need a video I can look at in the cold light of day. You're the only person I can trust.'

'What about this Philippe?'

Cassie laughed. 'Don't be stupid, darling, he'll have his hands full.'

Petra picked up her handbag. 'I won't take pictures of you and some toyboy having it off. I mean it, Cassie.'

'Yes, you will.'

'No.'

Cassie's jaw set firm and for a moment Petra glimpsed the resolute face that doubtless presided over *Fragrant's* editorial conferences.

'You will if you want to find out about today's meeting of the Corrections Committee,' she said.

'I've changed my mind about that. It's not important to me.'

'Forgive me, Petra, but I've always thought that anything concerning Tom Glass was *very* important to you. So why don't you sit down and I'll explain how my video camera works.'

Petra sat.

Chapter 5

'Who's Rosie?' said a low-pitched female voice, intruding on Tom's reverie of long-lost seduction. 'Tom, darling, don't tell me you've returned to the land of the living off your rocker.'

The silver-blonde vision at the door was tall and slender with an oval face and a long nose. The eyes were cool and grey and her lips and pencil-thin eyebrows arched upwards inquisitively. She was at once familiar and mysterious and she was looking at Tom much as a collector of coins regards a prized possession. Her face was bright with expectation.

'Hi there,' said Tom as emphatically as he could. He didn't know who the hell she was but she looked fabulous and at the back of his mind a small voice asked: *I wonder if I'm fucking her?*

Nurse Biscuit came to his aid. She dropped Tom's hand like a hot coal and scrambled to her feet.

'Oh, Miss Matthews,' she cried, 'it's such a thrill to see you again. Isn't it wonderful that Mr Glass has come out of his coma?'

'I dashed here straight from the studio,' said the newcomer. 'As you can see, I didn't even have time to change.'

Tom's mind was racing. He took in the fuchsia-pink summer jacket that Silver-blonde was slipping off her shoulders and noted the insignia on the breast pocket. The report of his accident in the *Dog* came back to him. This must be the Badger TV weather girl. His fiancée.

'Marianne,' he said, holding out his arms. *I must be fucking her!* he thought with glee.

'Darling,' she cried and fell into his embrace.

Nurse Biscuit edged out of the door.

'Thank God, you're all right,' murmured Marianne into Tom's neck as she gave him small perfumed kisses. 'I mean, you *are* all right, aren't you? You still have lots of wires and tubes and things sticking into you.'

She disentangled herself from him gently as if suddenly aware he was fragile.

'Well, I did fall ten storeys,' he said. 'I can't say I'm back to normal. I'm having trouble remembering things. I don't know how I fell, for example, or anything that led up to it.'

'How convenient.' The smile had slipped from Marianne's face.

'I know the papers are still stirring things but that's their business. Those bastards are out to shaft everybody.'

'Quite.' Her penetrating grey eyes had moved from his face and were now focused elsewhere on his body. He had the feeling that she was making her own assessment of the damage he had sustained.

'Why,' she asked at length, 'have you got a hard-on?'

It was a good question. The tower between his legs was plain as a pike-staff beneath the cotton sheet.

A dream bubble burst in Tom's head, bringing with it a vivid impression of Rosie's silky thighs muffling his ears and the coral pink folds of her fig in his face. But he said the only thing that was acceptable in the circumstances.

'I'm just pleased to see you, Marianne.'

'Are you really? I was beginning to think you weren't. You haven't asked one thing about me.'

It was at this point, Tom realised later, that he could have come clean. He could have told her the reason for his distracted manner. But how do you tell your fiancée that you don't recall ever seeing her before in your life? Especially when she's sitting on the side of your bed running her fingers over your thunderously erect tool.

'God, it's enormous,' said Marianne, pushing the sheet down his thighs to bring his cock and balls fully into the light. 'I don't remember ever seeing it quite so big.'

'Really?' Tom wanted to ask her precisely when she had last seen it and what they had done together. Were they a long-standing partnership joined by a well-established intimacy? Or a hot new liaison who fucked like rabbits whenever they got the chance? It was an intriguing situation.

Marianne had both hands on him now, rolling his balls in her palm and slicking his foreskin back and forth across the purple helmet of his glans. She lowered her long and graceful neck and slipped her cool lips over the burning head of his prick.

'Mmm yes,' breathed Tom and thrust his pelvis upwards into her face.

She raised her lips from his straining tool and licked him. 'Have you,' she said between licks, 'thought any more about the Black Raven arts slot?'

Tom stared at her. Her long pink tongue trailed cunningly across his knob, teasing him, promising more.

'Well?'

'I'm sorry, Marianne, I told you I was having a little trouble remembering things.'

'I don't see how you can have forgotten something so important to me, Tom. You know I've had it up to here with being a weather girl. I've got much more to give the TV world than my sunny smile and perky manner. It's like being a fucking Barbie doll. And I'm pissed off with wearing pink.'

She was getting worked up, Tom noted with alarm. Her long red fingernails were digging into the tender skin of his scrotum just this side of pain.

'What's Black Raven?'

'Black Raven, Mr Mogul, is a television company that you happen to own. They need a presenter for their new arts programme and, apart from being your wife-to-be, I'm bright, I'm beautiful and I'm sure-as-hell available.'

There was a silence after this outburst. Marianne had withdrawn her hands from Tom's loins and his cock lay twitching in frustration on his belly. He was fed up. He rather fancied wielding some of this power he was supposed to possess. Starting now.

'OK, Marianne,' he said, 'I shall talk to Black Raven within the next twenty-four hours. Your career is at the top of my agenda.' That sounded good at any rate.

'In the meantime,' he continued, noting with satisfaction a softening of her expression, 'I'd like a demonstration that you really are available. If you don't melt down my erection within the next ten minutes you can return to Badger and spend the rest of your professional life predicting ridges of high pressure.'

Marianne's face set hard and for a second Tom thought those scarlet talons of hers were about to fence for his cheek. Then she clapped a hand to her mouth and made a low gurgling sound, like the rattle of pebbles in the rushing water of a brook. It was a most seductive laugh. She probably *was* wasted on the weather.

'Very good,' she said at last. 'You really had me going for a moment. I love it when you pretend to be a ruthless tycoon. It turns me on.'

She got off the bed and kicked off her shoes, unzipped her skirt and threw it on the chair. Below the waist she wore just a scrap of thin turquoise material. The prominent mound of her pubis bulged against the cotton. She hooked her thumbs under the waistband of her panties and lowered them an inch.

'Shall I?' she breathed. 'Do you want to look, darling?' Tom's cock was beating a tattoo on his stomach in an agony of frustration. He tried to keep the impatience out of his voice.

'Time's running out, Marianne. Drop your knickers or it's back to Badger for good.'

'Oh you sod,' she said and pushed the thin strip of cotton down her thighs, laying bare the long slit of her vagina just six inches from Tom's face.

Perhaps it was the slimness of her hips or the length of her elegant body but the pouting sex delta at the junction of her smooth thighs seemed enormous. Or maybe it was because between her legs she was as hairless as a clam. At any rate, the outer lips of her pussy were unfurled to reveal a glistening succulence within and at the top of her crack her swollen clit seemed to sit up and beg. The breath caught in Tom's throat. This was a cunt in need of serious attention.

Marianne took a small step forward, pushing her pelvis into Tom's face. He flicked out his tongue. She groaned. He sank his hands into the apple-cheek rounds of her bottom and pulled her onto his mouth. She made a throaty noise as his lips found her clitoris and dropped a hand to his groin.

For two minutes there was no conversation, just moans and grunts and the rude slick-slick of fingers and tongue on slippery genitals and the agitation of Marianne's feet as they squirmed on the polished wooden floor. She came with a sharp cry on Tom's tongue and then again as he pushed a finger between her buttocks and up into her arsehole.

'Christ,' she muttered, breaking away from his embrace, 'it's no good, I've got to have it up me.'

She climbed onto the bed and straddled his loins, carefully avoiding the tubes still attached to his flesh. There was a metal hoist above the bed and she took hold of it with one hand while the other aimed his swollen member at the hungry nook between her thighs.

The hoist could have been specifically designed for this very activity. Given the nature of the exclusive medical facilities supplied by Partridge Place this would not have surprised either Tom or Marianne. But for the moment they were only concerned with the friction of cock in cunt, with the jostling of slim white thighs on muscular hairy ones and with the approaching moment of release as the spunk gathered in Tom's balls and Marianne's hairless pussy wept in anticipation.

At the door, her face pressed tight to the small crack which afforded her a perfect view, Nurse Biscuit gazed on in wonder.

And in a dark room on the floor above, a thin-lipped Dr Flint made notes in a small black book. In front of her, among a bank of television monitors, flickered the image of an ambitious TV weather girl suspended on a well-known businessman's cock.

Chapter 6

Petra was not much of an expert with a video camera.

'It doesn't matter,' said Cassie. 'Just get an establishing shot of what we're up to and then zoom in on my face when things hot up. You press this little red button here.'

Philippe was not happy about the filming. He lolled against the doorframe dressed in a purple tracksuit with a towel round his neck. Petra had often admired the size of Cassie's luxury kitchen but somehow Philippe's presence seemed to shrink the room. He was so big his head looked like it might graze the ceiling if he stood up straight. His black hair was cropped to his scalp and his jaw was square like a comic-book hero. Tortoise-shell spectacles gave him a professorial air - a professor of muscle.

'You will keep my face out of ze shot,' he said to Petra.

'Don't worry, Philippe,' said Cassie, 'this is just for my personal use. I've asked Petra to film the exercises so Chastity can provide an insight into my reactions.'

Philippe didn't look altogether mollified, thought Petra, but the mention of Chastity's name put an end to his objections.

'OK,' he said, flinging off his tracksuit to reveal an awe-inspiring physique barely contained by a canary-coloured singlet and blue jockey shorts. 'Let's get to it.'

'Don't you find him a bit intimidating?' muttered Petra as she followed Cassie out of the room but her friend did not appear to hear. It was evident she was under his spell.

Petra had expected the action to take place in Cassie's bedroom but to her surprise she found herself in another room which was kitted out as a gym. A rowing machine and an exercise bicycle stood in one corner, dusty from disuse she noted, and a large rubber mat lay on the floor. Cassie and Philippe took up positions facing one another and, to the blare of a disco beat, began what looked like a series of aerobic exercises.

'*Allez, allez!*' yelled Philippe as Cassie bounced up and down, her red hair flying and her substantial breasts jingling.

Petra aimed the camcorder and filmed a few feet. There didn't seem much point in continuing, however - surely Cassie didn't want a record of this?

Then the music slowed and the pair of them began to stretch their limbs in a languorous fashion and make balletic arabesques.

'*Ah, oui,*' growled Philippe, 'more slowly now. Ze blood it is flowing and we must listen to ze needs of ze body.'

Petra had trouble stifling a laugh but Cassie's rapt expression reminded her of her obligations. The redhead looked a trifle daft, twirling around on one foot in her bra and pants, but there was no doubt she was giving her all.

In one surprising movement Philippe seized Cassie around the waist and lifted her off the floor as if she were a two-year-old. He reversed her in mid-air and suddenly she was upside down clinging to the solid trunk of his body. Petra pressed the little red button - this was more like it.

In this position, Cassie's legs were around the Frenchman's neck and her arms encircled his waist, both of them nose to crotch in a standing *soixante-neuf*. 'How appropriate,' thought Petra, now finding her attention fully engaged.

Beyond holding a half-naked eleven-stone woman upside down, Philippe didn't appear to be doing much. But below his waist his pupil was busy and, as she glimpsed the thick wand of cock flesh that thrust from his briefs into Cassie's face, Petra felt a stab of desire. Not that there was any chance of her friend passing this particular baton - half of it was already down her throat.

Up top, Philippe was now using his mouth on the pantied crotch in his face. Petra marvelled at the way he first sucked Cassie through the material and then eased aside the sodden gusset using just his lips and tongue. Was this part of the famous Honeydew technique? she wondered, or simply innate Gallic flair? Whatever it was, she knew that it would be beyond her lover, Kelvin - more's the pity.

The pair of them had now subsided to the floor and Philippe was teasing Cassie's exposed pussy lips with his tongue, licking the length of her long, auburn-haired slit and then probing the tip into her gooey depths.

'Oh God,' Petra heard Cassie groan as she responded to this treatment. 'I'm going for my first - ah! Oh yes!' and her creamy buttocks began to quiver in Philippe's broad hands. Cassie's legs opened and closed in agitation around the Frenchman's neck. A lesser man would surely have wilted under the pincering of those strong thighs but Cassie's wild throes had no effect on his gentle lick, lick, licking along her swollen labia. 'AAH!' screamed Cassie and twitched to a climax.

They rolled apart and Petra was amazed to see that Cassie was consulting her watch and scribbling on a piece of paper.

'Have to keep a record,' she explained to Petra as she shucked off her wet panties and threw off her bra. Her breasts were full and pendulous, with long scarlet points that stood up like loganberries. Petra had never seen nipples like those before. What would they taste like? she wondered, shocked that she would think such a thing. But shock seemed an inappropriate reaction given the circumstances.

Philippe had stripped off too and was on his hands and knees, suspended above Cassie's body. Petra watched in fascination as he lowered himself till he was just inches above her and he began to move, from side to side and up and down. It took her a moment to realise that he was brushing her body with his cock, drawing the tip of his hanging member backwards and forwards across the dimpled dome of her belly. As he did so, he caressed the tips of her nipples with the great slab of his chest, occasionally pressing down on her and then pushing up to relieve the pressure. Petra wondered what it must be like to be body-kissed by a man mountain who could crush you at any moment.

Certainly Cassie liked it. She had hold of his teak-hard buttocks and was thrusting her pelvis up at him, trying to work the head of his elusive tool into the hungry hole between her legs.

'Please, please,' Petra heard her saying, 'put it in, Philippe. Fill me up and fuck me. Oh please - OH!'

Petra saw that his great cock had nosed into her bush and with one flick of his hips he was into her.

'Oh my GOD!' screamed Cassie and exploded into a flurry of jerks and twitches.

'*Deux fois*,' Philippe announced as dispassionately as a tennis umpire. 'You want to go for more? I think you are well ahead of your weekly score.'

'No, don't stop! I need at least three, maybe four!' howled Cassie, jerking her loins up at him as he held himself impassively over her.

'OK but I don't want you to overdo it,' he lectured. 'I have seen people too keen at the beginning, they end up with strained ligaments and pulled muscles.'

'Sod that, Philippe,' said Cassie. 'I think there's only one way to learn and that's on the job. Let's go for it! Oh yes!'

Philippe didn't argue further, he just swung into action as if to prove his point, pistoning his powerful cock between her legs in a blur.

Petra tried hard to record the meaningful action as requested, keeping the camera focused on Cassie's face as she moaned and howled through a succession of orgasms. But Petra's camera hand was shaking with excitement. She couldn't resist staring at Philippe's lean buttocks as they thrust and flexed and hollowed, driving his menacing cudgel of flesh up into Cassie's loins. She was mesmerized too by the sight of her friend's swollen pussy as it engulfed the big cock. Yielding yet strong, soft yet resilient, it joyfully embraced the pounding weapon.

'AAH!' yelled Cassie finally and passed out.

It took a few moments, in which time Philippe bid them *au revoir*, before Cassie was able to speak.

'Didn't I tell you, Petra? That's what I call personal training.'

'Well, he certainly pressed your little red button. It's not very romantic, though, is it?'

'My God, woman, what do you want?' Cassie sat up and reached for the glass of water Petra was offering her. 'This is lifestyle sex not romance, health and fitness not emotional dependence. We're talking work-out fucking here, perfect for today's independent woman. This way, just think of all the time you save in not having rows and pretending to be seduced and pussyfooting around before the guy gets down to your actual pussy. Mind you, there is one thing I regret.'

'Oh?'

'I wish I could get that bastard Philippe to come inside me.' Petra was astonished, though it was true that in the blur of orgasmic action she'd seen no evidence of Philippe ejaculating.

'Doesn't he ever?'

'No. Not one drop of his precious fluid does he shed. Mind you, I'm his ten p.m. appointment. He probably saves it so he can spunk off over lucky Miss Midnight. What the hell are you laughing at?'

Chapter 7

Kelvin Priest sat in bed doodling on a notepad and stroking his penis. The pad contained impressions of his interview that morning with Gossamer Hawk and his penis was similarly inspired. Kelvin was struggling to put some shape to the article he was preparing for *Nouveau*. He was not finding it easy.

Gossamer had knocked Kelvin for six. The combination of larky sixth-former and mature woman, of high-pitched giggle and low-slung cleavage, of flirtatious blonde and stern officer of the court had him in thrall. She had virtually propositioned him, had held out the image of herself stripped to the waist with the expanse of her soft perfumed bosom at the mercy of his roving hands. How he had longed to take up that proposition.

But had it been a trap? Had his natural timidity saved him from a trip downstairs to the cells? There, it was rumoured, transgressors were held in soundproofed confinement, subjected to a rigorous programme of 'attitude realignment' conducted by twenty-stone bull dykes who looked on men as an inferior subspecies.

Here, of course, lay the crux of the matter. As an enquiring journalist he should have probed more deeply, asked Gossamer searching questions about the business of The Primrose Court. How, for example, did they decide who to investigate? Who sat on the Corrections Committee? Was it really, as officially stated, an advisory body peopled by female business leaders and concerned only with self-regulation of the business community? Or was it a gang of harpies picking on their competitors and paying off old scores?

Those were the things he should have asked. Instead he had allowed her to shoot the breeze in her delicious fashion, to hypothesise about arses on girls in the street and barbarians in suits. Some of that stuff would be fine for the average *Nouveau* reader who was always in need of guidelines on how to think correctly. But Kelvin wanted to give *Nouveau* man more. He could see the heading now: 'Are we heading for a sexually correct police state? Kelvin Priest puts Prosecutor Hawk on the rack.' That would get the quiche and branflake set buzzing.

There was nothing for it, he would have to pick up the gauntlet thrown down by Gossamer and invite her out to dinner. His tool twitched in his fingers - Y-front man said yes.

He pushed the bedclothes down and looked his cock in the eye. The head was as red as a beet and the shaft pulsed in his hand. It had never looked so big. Not that it was especially large - he didn't kid himself he was spectacularly endowed. But what he had, had never been cause for complaint. It had kept Petra happy for two years and he was sure it could give Gossamer a thrill too.

Hypothetically speaking, of course.

The chug of a diesel engine in the street below alerted him to Petra's arrival. It was not an unusual situation for him to be tucked up in bed and for her to return home in a taxi. She had a big-deal job at Glass Mountain and she often worked late, and since Glass's accident she had not once shown up before midnight.

He heard the sound of her footsteps in the hall and he covered up his twitching cock and balls.

Petra burst into the room and chucked her briefcase onto a chair.

'Hello, darling,' said Kelvin, 'tough day?'

'Don't ask,' she snapped. She appeared flustered. Her lustrous dark hair, normally held under control by an assortment of bands and barrettes, was flowing loose and her pale cheeks were flushed. She was pulling at her clothes and throwing garments onto the floor. This was not her normal behaviour.

'You must be tired,' said Kelvin, wondering what the hell had got into her. 'Come to bed.'

'You bet,' said Petra, now reduced to a tiny pair of scarlet silk panties. She was not a big girl, being slim and light of foot, nevertheless she was pleasingly curved. She had high pouting breasts with nut-brown nipples and a waist Kelvin could almost span with his hands. But her hips swelled and her bottom cheeks swayed with all the womanly allure a man could want. And the neatly trimmed black muff at the fork of her thighs was bursting out of the scrap of silk that encircled her loins.

Kelvin couldn't help observing that the scarlet panties were stained a darker hue in the vee of her crotch. In fact, he would have been blind not to notice as the material was now poised an inch in front of his nose. Her hands were in his hair and her lean thighs on either side of his torso as she straddled him on the bed. His confusion was overwhelming.

'What's up, Petra? Are you all right?'

'Shut up, Kelvin. I want you to eat my pussy.'

'But, Petra, I think you—'

'Christ, Kelvin, can't you do what you're told for once?' she cried and jammed his face onto her pantied mons. 'Now, eat me out. Suck me through my panties. Oh God, that's better!'

It was the best fuck they'd had for ages, probably since the start of their romance. Not that this was a meeting of mind as well as body - one of those cosmic exchanges between lovers in which the giving is as important as the receiving. In this carnal bout the receiving was all-important to both parties.

As Petra rode on Kelvin's face she pictured herself upside down on Philippe's tongue, clinging to the Frenchman's tree-trunk of a body, her lips around his formidable baton, his fingers playing on the cheeks of her upturned arse the way he had pleasured Cassie.

It took her only moments to come and she slid from Kelvin's chest eager for more. Kelvin's generous tumescence was sympathetically received, first of all in her mouth though she didn't keep it there long - the damned thing looked as though it might go off at any second - and then where it truly belonged, up her well-juiced cunt.

It didn't last long there either but she came at the same time he did, in a long-drawn-out spiral of pleasure that radiated up her spine and down her legs as he speared his tool up, up, up into her very centre. Then he did a very surprising thing.

Even though he had just exploded inside her, he kept his cock jammed deep between her legs and gently stroked her pussy lips and clit, all the while tonguing and kissing her nipples, until she had had another orgasm - a slow deep soul-stirrer that left her floating on a cloud.

'*Troisfois*,' she murmured into his hair, her hips undulating to his rhythm.

But Kelvin didn't hear. As he mouthed the cherry pits of her nipples he dreamed of the fuller, lusher pastures of Gossamer Hawk's bosom where, for the moment at least, it was still safe to let his imagination roam.

'I'm sorry I was such a witch,' said Petra as she snuggled into Kelvin's body *post coitus*.

'I'm not complaining,' said Kelvin. 'You can stay late at the office every night if you come home like that.'

'I wasn't at the office, I had dinner at Cassie's.'

'Aha.' That explained one mystery. 'I had a phone call from Partridge Place. I wondered why they couldn't get you at work.'

'You've got a message about Tom?' Petra sat bolt upright. 'Why didn't you tell me?'

'I couldn't. I had a mouth full of pussy, remember? Don't panic, Glass is out of his coma and feeling fine.'

'Thank God.' She subsided onto the pillow, relief mingling with a series of thoughts, chief among them the news she .had finally extracted from a shagged-out Cassie. The Corrections Committee had forwarded Tom Glass's name for investigation. Petra had to let Tom know as soon as possible. Still, there wasn't much she could do about it at the moment. She put her hand on Kelvin's shrunken cock and gave it an inquisitive squeeze.

'What's got into you tonight, Petra?' he said. 'Not that I'm complaining.'

'If you must know, it's Cassie. She's made me promise to go on a new diet.'

'But you don't need a diet.'

'It's more a health regime. For *Fragrant*.' His prick was big in her hand now.

'That smelly rag.'

'Shut up and fuck me. I want it hot and hard. I want to come again.'

He put his hand between her legs. Juice was running out of her like a river. His come and hers, mixed.

'Any other orders, mistress?' he asked, four fingers inside her and churning.

'Yes, do you speak French?'

'I can say *soixante-neuf*. Will that do?'

'Parfait. Just be quick.'

Chapter 8

Tom was dreaming. But, like last time, the dream had the solidity of real life. His past life.

He was in an attic room in a large Victorian house. The dormer windows were open wide and a warm breeze puffed the flowery Habitat curtains into the cramped space, making it even smaller. Jeans, a T-shirt, a crumpled summer dress and a pair of M&S panties lay in a pool of sunlight on the rush-mat floor. He was squashed into a narrow single bed with the owner of the panties. There wasn't much room but neither of them was complaining. On the contrary.

'Aiee,' groaned Elvira, 'is too much, too much!'

Tom laughed and thrust deeper between the fabulous olive cheeks of her upturned bum. His hand was beneath her body exploring the thicket of her crotch, diddling her throbbing clit towards orgasm.

The clock on the bedside table said 11.30. Tom was supposed to be at a lecture on *As You Like It*, currently being delivered a mile down the hill in the English Department by his tutor, Lionel Slack. He didn't care. Buggering an Italian sex-pot with a bum like a ripe peach was an education in itself, possibly one with more long-term advantages. The beauty of it was that Elvira was also Professor Slack's au pair.

'Si, si!,' muttered Elvira into the sheets as Tom began to ram with urgency into the velvety pillows of her broad buttocks. 'Give it to me, Tomas. Shoot your hot spunk inside my ass!'

The real purpose of Elvira's foreign sojourn was to improve her English. That she had succeeded in broadening her bedroom vocabulary was a matter in which Tom took pride. He did not, however, kid himself that he was her only teacher.

He pushed himself up on both hands to get a good view of his thick stem see-sawing in and out of her bottom hole. The white shaft made an exciting contrast with the pink mouth of her elastic anus and the delicate sheen of her brown buttock flesh.

It was amazing to him that he could fuck her up the arse, that she would want him to do it to her that way. In truth, it was the only way she would let him penetrate her - apart from in the mouth. She had left Italy a virgin, she said, and she would return *intacta* between the legs or her father would kill her. But between the bum cheeks was another matter, she had to have some way of paying for her bedside English lessons. Besides, so Tom had concluded after a couple of visits, she just loved to be poked in the butt. It drove her wild.

'Ah, ah, ah!' she squealed, wriggling back onto his prong, trying to ram every centimetre of available cock flesh up her fundament, her own fingers now busy on her clitoris. 'Yes, yes, I'm coming! I'm coming!'

And so was Tom, there was no denying the honey-sweet suction valve between her cheeks and the fleshy kiss of her creamy moons on his belly as he pumped and banged and finally shot off deep into her hungry bowels.

'God, Elvira,' murmured Tom into the coal-black tangle of her curls now spread across the pillow, 'that was fantastico.'

She just grunted and a moment later, as Tom had anticipated, her breathing deepened and she cradled her head in her arms. Tom slipped from the bed and pulled the covers over her. She had made it clear the last time they made love that she liked to be left to recover alone in her small bed. He had pretended to be sorry about it but in fact it suited him well.

He dressed quickly and slipped down the stairs. The house was quiet. He presumed that Lionel's wife was out and the kids were at school. A good time to snoop in the Professor's study.

The study was on the first floor at the front. Tom had been there several times that summer term for tutorials and once, in his first term, for a freshmen's cocktail party. Tom knew his way about.

He knew, for example, that Lionel kept the key to the filing cabinet by his desk in a pretty china cup on the mantelpiece next to the framed photographs of his children. He opened the cabinet and soon found what he was looking for.

The Professor's study was large and well appointed. Lionel preferred to work in its airy luxury than in his stuffy room in the English Department. In a corner of its book-lined splendour stood a photocopier. From Tom's point of view, the arrangement could not have been handier. Tuesday mornings were turning out to be a piece of cake. Get up late, stroll to the Prof's, sneak in the garden door, fuck Elvira senseless, sneak into the study, find the text of last week's lecture and copy it. Simple.

It helped that Professor Slack was a creature of habit. His lectures were finely honed - as they should be, he'd been giving the same ones for nearly ten years. Now they were scripted down to each significant pause and impromptu aside. The scripts were neatly typed and filed in order, ready to be pulled out at the appointed time in the academic year. Fortunately Tom didn't have to sit and listen to them. He had discovered a short cut.

He had discovered other things of Lionel's too. For example, his mark book. It was Lionel's practice to return a student's essay after scrupulous evaluation and to record its worth in a green directory. Once returned, of course, there was no way Lionel could check that the mark on the essay and the mark in the green book remained the same. Using the red fountain pen that the Professor kept by his book - fussy old fart - it was a simple matter for Tom to subtly amend his past performances. It was surprising how many essays of Tom's improved with time. He soon had better marks than any other student on the course, despite the fact that he rarely appeared at lectures.

Tom was feeling pretty cocky today. After making his copies, he began to flick through the correspondence in the Professor's in-tray. It was boring stuff but he couldn't tear himself away. A fortnight earlier he'd come across a letter from his own father urging Professor Slack to treat him with particular sensitivity because of his feud with his elder brother. Tom had laughed at that.

Right at the bottom of the tray he struck lucky. There were seven or eight Polaroid photographs in a brown envelope. They were very explicit. Despite lousy lighting and red eye, Elvira looked pretty good, Tom thought. Good enough to set his cock twanging like a tuning fork even though the Italian minx had drained him dry less than twenty minutes earlier. Here was Elvira lying naked, playing with her bush. Elvira bending over and spreading her buttocks in invitation. Elvira holding herself open with one hand and aiming a vibrator with the other.

Then, even more interesting, there was Elvira sucking cock - taken at a distorting angle as the suckee pointed the camera downwards. Then - Good Lord - there was the suckee himself with his head on Elvira's thigh, tongue extended towards the spread lips of her honeypot. The suckee was Professor Lionel Slack.

Tom's heart hammered in his chest. The revered man of letters was dipping his nib in the Italian inkwell in the attic, just like Tom himself. And making a record of his extra-curricular activity. How bizarre.

Tom knew this discovery had to be to his advantage though quite how, as yet, was not clear.

He heard the sound of the front door opening on the floor below. Shit!

Without thinking, he pocketed a photo, one that clearly showed Lionel in contravention of his matrimonial commitments, and replaced the envelope at the bottom of the in-tray. He grabbed one of the Professor's own scholarly works on Shakespeare from the shelves and stuffed inside it the sheaf of papers he had copied. Then he marched smartly into the corridor.

At the bottom of the stairs, looking up at the sound of his descending footsteps, was a slender girl in a baggy brown school uniform. Tom knew who this was from the framed pictures on Lionel's mantelpiece - Christina, the eldest daughter. She was older than in the pictures, though. And despite the ugly shapeless clothes, it was clear from her porcelain-perfect complexion and almond eyes that she was a beauty.

'Hello,' said Tom, more heartily than he intended. 'I'm one of your father's students. The au pair let me in. I came by to get a book your father promised to lend me.'

All of this was true and he met her curious gaze with as much sincerity as he could muster. Her eyes were caramel brown and her blonde hair hung in a single braid down her back like thick rope.

'He says that one's his best.'

For a moment Tom was bemused. Then he realised she meant the book. He almost laughed out loud. She didn't suspect a thing.

'Got to rush,' he said, pushing past her still form and striding for the front door. 'I'm late for my next lecture.'

He ran down the front steps aware that those beautiful brown eyes were burning into his back.

Tom woke up suddenly. It was as if someone had flicked a switch and pitched him forward twenty years in the blink of an eye. He had reclaimed another segment of his past and the taste of it was in his mouth.

Two women stood by his bed, looking down at him. One was about forty with a tired face, wearing a light summer raincoat and holding a scuffed briefcase. The other was taller and younger with peroxide curls, pink lipstick and a sulky expression. She was dressed in a rainbow-coloured shell-suit with stripes on the sleeve - could it be some kind of uniform? She looked mean.

'Thomas Glass?' said the weary one.

'Yes?'

'I'm Inspector Claire Quartermain of the TCU and this is Sergeant Tooth. We'd like some of your time.'

'Police?'

'The TCU, Mr Glass.'

'What's that?'

'The Thought Correction Unit.'

'I still don't understand.'

'Tell him, Amy,' said the inspector and slumped into a chair.

'The Sex Police,' said the sergeant. 'You're on our list, Mr Big-shot. We're going to eat your bollocks.'

Chapter 9

'What do you mean - "eat my bollocks"? This is outrageous!' Tom used his power voice - it had worked for him so far - and reached for the alarm button by his bed. A small but firm hand captured his before he could summon help.

'There's no need to be alarmed, Mr Glass,' said Inspector Quartermain. 'Amy sometimes jumps the gun. This is only a preliminary chat so we can get to know one another.'

'I demand to see Dr Flint,' said Tom, only half mollified. Amnesiac or not, he knew these two were trouble.

'Of course you can see Dr Flint. But there's no point. We're here with her blessing. She's always most cooperative.'

The wind was now almost gone from Tom's sails. 'Well, make it quick. I'm still not feeling well.'

Claire Quartermain smiled. Her eyes were bright and quick, like those of a small rodent. Her smile did not reassure Tom in the least.

'Excellent,' she said. 'Perhaps we can start with your version of events last Friday evening. Why don't you tell us what happened?'

'I don't remember. I've just spent three days in a coma. I'm surprised Dr Flint didn't mention it.'

'So you have no recollection of how you came to be exposing yourself in the street in full view of the audience leaving a London theatre?'

'You tell me, Inspector. I trust you are investigating what seems like an obvious assault on my person. And when you find who is responsible let me know. If you don't prosecute, I'll sue.'

The policewoman seemed unimpressed.

'For someone with no memory of the events in question you seem very sure of yourself, Tom.'

'Mr Glass to you, Inspector.'

An awkward silence descended. Tom blustered on, aware he was making an enemy of this woman but unable to stop himself.

'Why do you assume that I'm in the wrong? I'm the injured party here. I fell ten storeys into the street and it's a miracle I'm alive. Now I'm stuck in hospital unable to run my business. I've lost my memory. And every day I'm pilloried in the newspapers as if I'm some filthy pervert! It's not fair!'

'Oh dear,' said the inspector, 'I can see we've got off on the wrong foot. I know how to cheer you up, though. Amy!'

The blonde sprang to attention. 'Yes, guv?'

'Get out your goodies. Let's put a smile back on Mr Glass's face.'

'Excuse me, guv, but I don't know that I want to. He is a pervert, you can see for yourself.' And Amy pointed to the sheet bunched over Tom's loins. It was not bunched sufficiently to conceal the tumescent column of flesh that reared without apology between his thighs.

How could Tom explain that since he had regained consciousness he had been in an almost permanent state of sexual arousal? That he had been plagued by sexy nurses and importunate fiancées and that his dreams had been peopled with naked, cock-happy conquests from his lurid past?

A steely hand shot out and grasped Tom's bed sheet. Claire Quartermain jerked the cover from his body and suddenly his penis was laid bare, stretching from crotch to belly button in unrepentant glory.

'Blimey,' said Amy, her features now animated, 'what a salami!'

'Precisely, Sergeant Tooth. The sausage that stopped the West End. The subversive weapon that undermined an entire business community. Exhibit number one for the prosecution in The Primrose Court, I'll be bound.'

'Oh for God's sake,' shouted Tom. 'It's my penis, you stupid harpies, and what I do with it is my own affair—'

A shriek of high-pitched laughter rang out from Amy Tooth, cutting across Tom's protest.

'My, my,' said Inspector Quartermain, 'maybe you really have lost your memory. Either that or you are sorely in need of retraining. I can see that we have a serious investigation on our hands, Sergeant. Stop tittering and do your duty.'

Tom watched in dumbfounded astonishment as Amy Tooth unzipped her hideous shell-suit from throat to navel and emerged from it like a butterfly from a chrysalis. He gulped at the sight of two grapefruit-sized breasts packed tight into a shiny gold satin brassiere that lifted and separated, offering to his fevered imagination a feast of succulence. Her creamy midriff was bared to shiny black PVC shorts, cut high on the thigh and tight across the bulge of her pouting mons veneris.

Her legs were long and fleshy, the skin of her thighs smooth and white above gleaming leather boots that encased her up to the knee. She was a cock-stiffening dream-come-true - even for a man like Tom whose cock needed no further stiffening. It jerked on his belly in salute.

Amy turned to rummage in her bag, bending at the waist to do so, thrusting out her gleaming posterior in heart-stopping provocation.

Inspector Quartermain observed Tom's interest with satisfaction. 'She's got a hell of an arse, hasn't she? I thought that might be to your taste.'

He could not deny it. The swollen hemispheres of flesh filled his vision and his exposed cock pulsed with guilty desire.

Amy straightened and turned, one hand now sheathed in a rubber surgical glove, the other holding a small plastic bottle.

'Don't be alarmed, Mr Glass,' said Inspector Quartermain. 'She's just going to take a sample.'

'A sample?' said Tom as Amy stepped up to the bed. 'What sample?'

'Tell him, Sergeant,' said Quartermain, a smile licking her thin lips.

'A sperm sample,' grunted Amy as her gloved fingers closed on the shaft of Tom's penis. 'We need a sample of your filthy, pervert's spunk. It's standard procedure, isn't it, guv?'

'Just routine,' said the inspector. 'I'd lie back and enjoy it if I were you. Sergeant Tooth is renowned for her technique.'

Amy shot the elder woman a poisonous glance and began to pump Tom's cock with no attempt at finesse. Her breasts thrust against her halter, the nipples like big buttons beneath the satin. Her mouth was set in a hard line and her eyes were fierce.

'Hey!' shouted Tom as she almost lifted him off the bed by the root.

'Pardon me, darling,' she drawled sarcastically and smacked his cock from side to side across his belly.

'Do it properly, Amy,' said Quartermain.

'Sorry, guv,' the girl said and began to massage the head of Tom's tool in earnest.

'That's better,' said the inspector. 'She does know what she's doing really, Mr Glass. She's had lots of practice.'

Amy's hand speeded up, flicking Tom's foreskin up and down the crimson glans. Her brow was furrowed with concentration and the pink tip of her tongue protruded from between her pursed lips.

Tom stared ahead at the junction of his abuser's white thighs and at the mound of her sex encased in gleaming black. He was paralysed by lust and fear.

Claire's voice broke the silence.

'She's pretty, isn't she, Tom? I bet you'd like to see her naked. Peel off those pants and get your hands on her creamy bum. Spread her legs and stick your tongue up her puss. She tastes of sea, did you know that? Some girls are sweet. Pussies made out of spun sugar and candied fruit. Like your little Petra, I bet. Amy's just the opposite. She's musky and tangy, all salt and spray. She's got a savoury cunt, haven't you, Amy? I bet you'd like to make a meal of it, Tom - Oh, I say! That's more than enough for a sample, Mr Glass, you've quite filled up the jar.'

'So what did you make of him, then?' said Claire Quartermain to Amy Tooth as they made their way along the corridor outside Tom's room.
  'He's just your average offender, guv.'
  'Average offenders don't run billion-pound businesses, Sergeant.'
  'You know what I mean. Out of his smart suit he's a pervert like all the rest.'
  'Better endowed though, wouldn't you say?'
  'I wouldn't.'
  'I see. You've had so many that size, you're blasé.'
  'Oh please, guv.'
  The inspector grabbed her subordinate by the arm and shoved her roughly towards a door marked 'Toilet. Staff only.'
  'In here,' she said, bundling the sergeant inside and locking the door. 'Strip. I want everything off.'
  'Claire, for God's sake!' cried Amy.
  'Get your tits on parade at the double, Sergeant. Now.'
  Amy fumbled at the zip of her shell-suit. Her hands were shaking as she peeled it off her trembling body.
  'You made me do it, Claire,' she protested. 'You made me jerk him off. He could have done it himself - or the nurse—'
  'What's the point of that, you little fool? I wanted to see how you would handle it. And you liked it, didn't you?'
  'No, I swear.' Amy was almost naked now, her big breasts dangling as she bent to ease the skin-tight pants over the bulging mounds of her buttocks. Claire took a nipple between finger and thumb and squeezed.
  'You adored it, Amy, you little tart. You love a big prick, don't you? For two pins you'd have stuck it in your mouth, wouldn't you?'
  'No! Layoff, Claire - you're hurting!'
  'Not until you admit you're a cock-happy nympho at heart. God, you're sopping!'
  Claire had two fingers buried deep between the girl's legs and now she forced two more fingers inside. They slid into the wetness without resistance. Her other hand continued to pull at Amy's nipple viciously. Their bodies were moulded against each other, one clothed, one naked. Amy slipped a hand beneath the other's skirt.
  'I'm sorry, Claire, I couldn't help it. I mean, with that sodding great thing in

my hands...'

'So you admit it?'

Her eyes bored into Amy's face.

'I admit his cock turned me on but the rest of him turns me off! He's a degenerate like all the rest.'

Amy's hands were now inside the inspector's knickers. The two women stood eyeball to eyeball, their fingers busy between each other's legs.

'So you're not fucking men on the side and doing me just to help your career?'

'No, Claire. Honest.'

They kissed at length, both of them shaking with passion.

'Stand up on the seat,' hissed the inspector and Amy scrambled to obey, presenting her drooling vagina at head height to her superior.

Claire spread the thick lips of the puffy pink pussy on offer and teased its length with the tip of her tongue. Her hands slid up the back of Amy's thighs to her shapely buttocks.

'Oh yes,' muttered Amy, her fingers in the other's soft brown hair, urging her to mouth her aching cunt.

The inspector began to chuckle. 'Of course, Sergeant, if you're very good to me I might let you handle Mr Glass again in the near future. When we get him in the cells.' And she pressed her mouth to Amy's vagina and went to work.

'Oh yes,' sighed Amy, on the brink of her first orgasm, 'when we get him in the cells...'

Two - Shagged Rotten
Chapter 10

Kelvin arrived at the offices of *Nouveau* feeling light-headed. He hoped it wasn't the onset of a cold or one of those inexplicable viruses that afflicted people in the summer - usually during Wimbledon fortnight, in his observation. Kelvin took some pills and examined his eyes in a small hand mirror for signs of strain. If he were honest he well knew the cause of his fatigue - sexual excess. He and Petra had been at it like rabbits most of the night and again that morning. What had got into her? he wondered. Not that he was complaining.

'No recreational drugs in the office,' said a beery voice in his ear, 'not unless you share them with me.'

Kelvin looked up guiltily into the puffy face of Ted Flinch, the editor, and quickly tipped the aspirins and mirror into his desk drawer.

'Of course,' Ted rumbled on, 'you kids know naff-all about dope. You think coke's just a sticky drink, don't you? If I said, "Give me a hit" you'd think I was asking for a punch on the nose.'

This was a familiar theme of Ted's, a survivor of many a youth trend - and the magazines that went with them. In the heyday of flower-power he had launched *Wow, Babe!*, to be followed a couple of years later by *F**k*, a journal of street cred printed in multi-coloured inks on black paper. At this point he had sold out to IBG, the magazine big boys, and had presided over a variety of offerings ever since. As he often said, at least twice a day by Kelvin's reckoning, his heart was in the sixties but his pension was in the next century. Someone on the top floor had had a good laugh when they saddled him with *Nouveau*, a politically correct magazine for the nervous nineties.

'Congratulations,' said Ted. 'You're now our chief correspondent on contemporary human relations. In old-fashioned parlance, our sex writer. Write about these.' And he dumped a bundle of thick paperbacks on Kelvin's desk.

'What's the big deal, Ted?'

'That feminist rag *Neurotica* is running a mail-order offer on female sex novels. Take a look.'

'It says on the back, "Not for sale to men."'

'Yes. That's the angle. These aren't ordinary old wanking fodder - pass the Kleenex, let's toss off in the bog, kind of thing. This is sensitive, politically aware, blessed by the sisterhood, erotic literature, for God's sake. Anyhow, it's all yours. Talk to a few women, see what they think of it. Then I want an in-depth evaluation for our readers.'

'Thanks a bunch, Ted,' said Kelvin.

'Don't sound so glum, man. Don't quote me but I bet if you can persuade a woman to actually read that mush you'll soon have her screaming for the real thing. Play your cards right and you'll shag your way to two thousand words. Speaking of shagging, I want your piece on Prosecutor Cuntface on my desk by Friday night.'

'Neanderthal,' muttered Kelvin under his breath as his boss shambled off. He wondered for the umpteenth time how Ted had ended up editing a magazine for the thinking man.

The reference to Gossamer, however, had him reaching for the phone. Despite his recent exertions with Petra, the thought of Prosecutor Hawk had his prick at a stretch to equal, he presumed, the heroes of the literary works that now adorned his desk.

Tom was still shaking when Petra arrived at the hospital.

'He's already had one lot of visitors this morning,' said Nurse Biscuit as she ushered Petra into his room, 'and I think they've tired him out. Perhaps you'd better not stay too long.'

Tom looked at this new arrival with suspicion. She had an intelligent face and there was kindness in her round brown eyes. But she wore a business suit and carried a briefcase that looked like a newer version of Claire Quartermain's. Surely this wasn't some other crazed official come to torment him?

'Who the hell are you?' he snapped.

Petra was flabbergasted. She had been thrilled to see Tom conscious, sitting up in bed, his eyes once more alive with fierce intelligence. But there was something else there, too. Surely it couldn't be fear?

33

Nurse Biscuit spoke up. 'Tom, surely you remember Miss Rosewater? She's been here every day while you've been unconscious.'

The suspicion vanished from Tom's face but his eyes bored into hers, as if looking for a clue.

'It's great to see you alive again, Tom,' said Petra. She wanted to touch him but she didn't dare.

'Leave us alone please, Eve,' he said and then he grinned in his old familiar way. 'I'll be all right with Miss Rosewater, I promise.'

The smile vanished as soon as the nurse did. Petra cleared her throat nervously. He leaned forward suddenly and grabbed her hand.

'Are you really a friend of mine?' he hissed.

His grasp was painful but she didn't want to break it. 'I like to think so,' she said. 'Why are you behaving like this? If it's a joke it's in poor taste, Tom. I've been really worried about you. So has everyone at the office.'

'Aha.' He relaxed his grip. 'So you work for me, then?'

'I'm your Deputy Executive Officer, for God's sake. Why are you asking me these things?'

'Just one more question. This is important, believe me. Are we, or have we ever been, er, lovers?'

'For crying out loud!' she shouted and smacked him round the face with her free hand. Then she froze, shocked at what she had done.

He didn't move a muscle but his cheek began to pulse scarlet as he said, 'That doesn't exactly answer my question.'

'No, damn you,' said Petra. 'We haven't, we don't and we never will. I'm sorry I hit you.'

'Oh, that's OK.' He leaned back on his pillows and grinned at her. 'It's just that I've lost my memory. Well, my recent memory. I don't even know your first name.'

'Petra.'

'Ah.' A thought stirred in his head but he remained silent.

'Look, Tom, we've got a lot of business to discuss.'

He shook his head. 'You deal with it. Use my name. Just while I get myself together.'

'Really?'

'I mean it. I'm going to trust you. But there's one thing I want you to do. Ring whoever runs Black Raven and tell them to talk to Marianne Matthews about their new arts programme.'

Petra grinned. 'So you haven't forgotten everything?'

'Marianne came to see me. She reminded me of a few things.'

'Like your forthcoming wedding?'

He didn't reply. Instead he closed his eyes and his chin settled on his chest.

'There's one more thing, Tom. I'd rather leave it but I've got no choice. The Primrose Court is investigating you for sex crimes. I think you need some advice.'

He laughed. 'It's too late.'

'What?'

'Two witches from something called the TCU were here just before you. To be honest, Petra, I feel like I've suddenly woken up in a world gone mad. I can't remember anything that's happened in the last twenty years. The best thing you can do for me is to tell me what The Primrose Court does and why there are stormtroopers marching around in PVC pants calling themselves the Sex Police.'

'OK.'

'And when you've done that, Petra Rosewater, you can explain how come Inspector Claire Quartermain says your vagina tastes like spun sugar.'

Her jaw dropped.

He grinned. 'That's what she said. I mean, how would I know? Not that I doubt it for a moment.'

She didn't hit him again. But she wanted to.

Chapter 11

Tom surreptitiously slipped the tie from his neck and slid it into his jacket pocket. A club jam-packed with expectorating punk rockers clad in leather and safety pins was not the venue in which to sport a necktie. Nor was it the place to wear a blue blazer with a college crest, rumpled grey cords and Hush Puppies. Not for the first time in the uncomfortable half-hour since he had arrived Tom wondered why he had come.

The reason was a pair of caramel brown eyes that still, a year on from his last sight of them, followed him in his dreams. The note in his pocket was mysterious - which, of course, was one reason why he had rearranged his life at short notice to stand in surroundings he found deeply disagreeable.

'Tom,' it said, 'will you meet me at the Singing Bird on Friday night? Any time after 9.30. There's a ticket in your name on the door. Please come - I need your help badly. Christina.'

The name 'Slack' had been added in brackets after 'Christina' but it had been unnecessary. Tom had often thought of the slim schoolgirl at the bottom of the stairs on his last visit to the home of Professor Slack. Almost all of those thoughts had been guilty ones.

He had sold the compromising photo of Lionel Slack to the *Sunday Skunk* and at the time it had seemed like an inspired move. He had driven a hard bargain - it had been the first real test of his negotiating skill - and the money which subsequently lay in his deposit account was earmarked to bankroll his off-campus schemes. 'Hold the front page,' remarked the newspaper executive who had signed the cheque.

'Whore Stuffed By Virgin sensation. If we can afford it, we'd better put this chiseller on the payroll.'

But the *Skunk* - 'Never scared to raise a stink!' - had gloried in its pound of flesh. 'LECHEROUS LECTURER'S DEN OF VICE!' ran the banner headline, 'Meet Professor Lionel Slack' - dirty old man of letters!'

Naturally the *Skunk* had garbled the facts. It improved the story no end to say that Elvira was one of the Professor's pupils and not his au pair. Tom, his identity masked as 'a concerned student', was quoted, claiming that the Professor 'always looks up girls' skirts in tutorials' and 'it's common knowledge that some female students leave their knickers off to gain better marks.' With the stolen photograph (judiciously cropped) as its centrepiece, accompanied by pictures of a tearful wife accosted on the doorstep by a reporter, Lionel didn't have much of a leg to stand on.

What Tom had not foreseen and what now lay at the root of his guilty conscience was the fall-out from this affair. The Professor disappeared from the university almost overnight - rumour had it that he had flown to Italy with Elvira - and the large sunny house on the green was suddenly occupied by a new Professor of English, a tight-arsed martinet whose passion was Anglo-Saxon poetry. A couple of months later Tom saw Mrs Slack in a supermarket in the city centre. She was standing in front of a shelf of baked beans with her hair in rat's tails and her blouse buttoned up wrong. It was only then that Tom realised exactly what he had done.

Now he stood in the uncomfortable surroundings of the Floating Turd - as it was known - squeezed on all sides by a leaping shouting crowd of his own age who dressed and spoke as if they came from outer space. Which they might well have done for all Tom knew. Of the cool and beautiful nymphet Christina there was no sign - until the band came on.

Tom didn't know much about music - any music - and the complexities of contemporary pop styles were a foreign language to him. This hadn't stopped him volunteering to manage his friend Sebastian's student band but he had seen that as a financial opportunity and acted accordingly. So, when five girls jumped on stage and began to thrash their instruments and shout, he took no interest in the noise they made. But he took a lot of interest in the crowd's reaction and in the band's appearance.

He spotted Christina at once, though her hair had been pulled up into spikes and was streaked with pink. She stood at the back in a torn white T-shirt and army boots, a ring gleaming in her left nostril as she banged at an electric guitar.

The other members of the group were dressed in a similar fashion though they managed to show a great deal more flesh. Tom's attention was caught - as was every other observer, he imagined - by the singer at the front of the small stage.

She was older than the others, a woman among schoolgirls. She wore a leather mini and a black halter top which displayed the body of a showgirl. Her legs were long and strong and, from Tom's vantage below the stage, they seemed to go on forever, up into the dark mystery beneath her abbreviated skirt.

Unlike the other girls, her hair flowed about her face and shoulders in a black mane. As she sang she ran her fingers through the dark mass, tossing and shaking it as she thrust her face up into the spotlight. Her features were big and exotic: a long nose, a firm jaw and broad full lips. Whatever she was singing, it came from the heart and she had the audience of scruffy, sneering kids eating out of her hand.

After the set, Tom pushed his way to the door, his ears ringing. When he'd gone in he'd shown no interest in the advertised list of performers. Now he noted that he had been watching Shani and the Shagbags. Christ, what a bloody name.

He'd assumed finding Christina would be a hassle but, at the front office, he was simply pointed towards an unmarked door which led backstage.

She met him in the corridor. Close up the eyes were as magical as before though he couldn't say the same about the rest of her.

'I saw you in the audience,' she said. 'You're a bit straight for a place like this.'

'You're not kidding. What's this all about, Christina?'

She stepped close. 'I need a favour, Tom. I know we don't really know each other but my dad always liked you and I can't think who else to ask.'

'Ask away.' Those sincere brown eyes made him feel like Judas. Whatever she wanted he knew he would help.

'We need a manager. Will you do it?'

He was struck dumb. He hadn't expected this.

'You handle The Scholars, don't you, and they're doing really well. Please, Tom.'

'But that's different. That's just student union gigs. You're in a bigger league.'

'Do you think so?'

'To be honest, Christina, I might have cloth ears but, judging by your singer, you should be top of the hit parade.'

'Hey, Tina, I like him already!' The soft voice came from just behind Tom.

Shani looked no less overwhelming up close. A loose white shirt covered her shoulders but hung open to reveal her sumptuous curves, still glistening from her on-stage exertions. Her skin was a pale *cafe au lait* and her eyes were as black as midnight.

Tom put out his hand. 'You were fantastic,' he said, doubtless it was expected of him but nevertheless it was true.

Her touch was warm and dry and she kept hold of his hand, pulling him into the band's dressing-room. The other girls were sitting around smoking. They weren't wearing many clothes.

The lead guitarist was naked, teasing her spiky red hair in front of the mirror. From the rear, the two halves of her arse were spread wide, white and firm.

The drummer was towelling her hair, naked to the waist. She made no attempt to cover her small high tits as Tom entered. The keyboard player was rolling a joint, her bare breasts dangling, the nipples long and red.

'Hey, girls,' said Shani, 'meet our new manager. He says he's going to put us on top of the charts.'

There was a silence. The lead guitarist swigged from a beer bottle and belched.

'He doesn't look old enough,' said the keyboard player. 'I suppose he's going to fuck us over like those other sleaze balls.'

'I hope he can fuck, at any rate,' said the drummer. 'The last one had no staying power.'

'Meet the Shagbags, Mr Manager,' said Shani. The dark shadow of her cleavage beckoned him. The broad swell of her hip pushed against his. 'Do you think you can handle us?'

'Come clean, doc, is he putting it on?' Claire Quartermain's voice was low-pitched and confidential. Nevertheless Madeleine Flint had no doubt that they had reached the crux of the phone call.

'I don't think so,' said Madeleine into the mouthpiece wedged between her shoulder and chin. She was using both hands on a computer keyboard and at the same time her eyes flicked backwards and forwards across a bank of monitors above her head. Dr Flint believed in making the best use of her time.

'So he really has lost his memory?' said Claire.

'It's only a partial loss and it's returning fast. As of now he can recall his entire life up to the age of twenty more vividly than he has done for years.'

'Huh.' The inspector was unimpressed. 'How long's it going to take until he remembers last Friday night?'

'I can't say. This kind of thing is unpredictable.'

'Can't you hurry him along? Give him extra elephant juice or something?'

'Claire, please.' Dr Flint introduced a hint of exasperation into her voice. 'This is strictly experimental treatment and I'm taking enough risks already. You must realise that I'm working on the cutting edge of neurological drug assistance. If he overdosed he could end up stuck in some particularly potent episode of his past.'

'Some particularly potent bonk, you mean?'

'Well, yes. Given that we are aiming to stimulate his sexual memory and use that as a trigger to recall past events and emotions. It's like asking a word processor to—'

'—search for a key phrase in a document - I know all this crap, doc, you've dinned it into me before.'

Madeleine Flint sighed loudly, she was weary of this conversation.

'So you're saying,' continued the policewoman, 'that we have to wait till he's caught up with all the fucking he's done between the ages of twenty and thirty-eight? Christ, woman, at that rate this case won't make court till next century!'

On the monitor to Madeleine's left, Tom Glass stirred feverishly on his bed. A gentle hand reached out to soothe his brow. Nurse Biscuit was at her station, a notebook and pencil in her lap.

'Be patient, Claire,' said Dr Flint. 'We're getting some excellent material. I'm going to hand him over to you stuffed and plucked, ready for the oven.'

'Thank God for that.'

'Just do me one favour. Petra Rosewater, Glass's number two, is threatening to move him.'

'What!'

'She's talking about transferring him to a neurological unit elsewhere so she can get other opinions on his condition. Can you have a word with her?'

There was silence on the line, followed by a sly chuckle. 'I'd love to,' said Inspector Quartermain.

Chapter 12

It was all very well for Tom to say he trusted her, thought Petra as she sat glumly at her desk, but there were some decisions she couldn't take on her own.

For the most part she knew what she was doing. Though the executive officers of the reporting divisions of Glass Mountain would have preferred to deal with Tom himself they accepted that, for the moment, she spoke for him. Furthermore, a lot of time was spent in figure work, reviewing performance against target, calculating growth and compiling an overview of the group's position - areas in which she specialised. Trouble-shooting the various divisions also took her time but she'd had three years' worth of experience watching Tom do it and, if she got stuck, she wasn't too proud to seek advice.

What gave Petra most concern was the new stuff. Tom's future plans. Innovations. That's what made men like him special, of course. They saw an opportunity and went for it with conviction. It needed the kind of skill and vision she didn't have.

Which is why she was staring in confusion at the document in her hand. It was an agreement from a firm of solicitors in Scotland declaring the conditions under which Glass Mountain would purchase their clients' glass-ornament business for five million pounds. At first Petra had treated the matter as a joke and had rebuffed Messrs Mitre & Gauze politely. It was when they sent her a copy of a covering letter signed by Tom and guaranteeing the deal personally 'if it's the last thing I do as Chief Executive of Glass Mountain' she began to feel uneasy.

The agreement was dated Friday 9th July - the day of Tom's accident. Harriet, his secretary, had denied preparing it for him and indeed there was no record of it on her word processor. However, they had discovered a copy of it on his desk.

By now, Petra had a sick feeling in her stomach. She couldn't credit that Tom would have any interest in a glass-ornament business but the papers in her hand told her otherwise. Maybe he knew something that she didn't. He'd played crazy but profitable hunches before. But why would he offer five million pounds for a concern that, as far as she could tell, last year turned over something less than fifty thousand?

It was almost a relief to turn her mind to other matters though her pulse quickened and her jaw set as Inspector Quartermain and a TCD sidekick walked unannounced into the room.

'Sorry to drop in on you like this,' said the policewoman.

'I'm very busy,' said Petra in a voice that even to her own ears sounded nervous and prim. 'I thought you'd finished here.'

Immediately following Tom's accident, the Metropolitan Police had invaded the penthouse, searching for clues to Tom's mysterious fall. They had soon been replaced by Claire Quartermain and her shell suited goons who had not confined themselves to the top floor.

'This a special trip to see you,' said Claire, making herself comfortable on the sofa. She kicked off her shoes and put her feet up on the low table in front of her, pushing aside a pile of computer print-outs in the process.

The sight infuriated Petra, as did the memory of what Quartermain had supposedly said about her to Tom. She decided to seize the initiative.

'I take it you've come to apologise, Inspector, for making indelicate remarks about me to Mr Glass.'

'Oh dear, did I? What did I say?'

'I cannot repeat it, Inspector, but it was highly personal and deeply insulting. In the circumstances I must ask you to state your business and leave at once.'

Claire appeared not to hear.

'It's strange but I can't remember what I said about you, Ms Rosewater.'

'You said she had a cunt that tasted like spun sugar, guv,' offered her companion with a smirk.

'But that's a compliment, my dear! Or is it not true? Thank you, Sergeant Tooth. She has a good memory for these things,' she added confidentially.

'Get out!' shouted Petra. 'Leave my office instantly, you fascist bitches!'

The moment the words were out of her mouth Petra knew she had made a mistake. Not that she cared, for the adrenaline was pumping.

'Amy,' said Quartermain in a tone of weary resignation and suddenly Petra found herself pinioned from the rear, her arms twisted up behind her in a grip of steel.

Petra's shout of protest was cut off by a gloved hand that was clamped to her mouth.

The inspector rose slowly to her feet, taking her time to put her shoes back on and smooth down her skirt. She took a position directly in front of the immobilised Petra.

'Oh dear,' she said, 'I was hoping we could have a civilised conversation and now look what you've done. However, it does give me the chance to satisfy my curiosity...'

As Petra became aware that the policewoman was undoing the buttons of her blouse she tried to struggle free, twisting her body and stamping her feet. But Amy Tooth had a hold like a vice.

'You're very pretty when you're angry,' observed Quartermain, pulling the shirt wide open and flipping the cups of Petra's white lacy bra above her breasts. 'My, my, what have we here? Oh such adorable brown nipples! That's right, shake those pretty titties - what a sight you make! I bet your Tom just creams his pinstripes whenever he looks across the boardroom table and imagines these little beauties in his face. Would you mind terribly if—'

And the inspector bowed her head to take a nipple in her mouth, first one then the other, rolling them between her lips, palpating the meat of the breast as she did so. She did it gently, knowingly, then more forcefully.

'Why, Amy, would you believe her nipples are erect? I think she must like me.'

A muffled squeal of fury escaped from Petra's captive mouth but the policewoman ignored it. She unzipped Petra's skirt as she mouthed her breasts and let it fall to the floor.

'I mustn't forget what I came here for,' she said, now pinching the hard kernels of Petra's nipples between her fingers. 'I was going to tell you politely, Ms Rosewater, but there doesn't seem much point. Get off Madeleine Flint's back. Leave Glass where he is. Don't make waves. All right?'

Claire's eyes were drilling into Petra's, expecting some kind of response. She nodded her head as best she could. This was probably the most humiliating experience of her life.

'Good,' said the policewoman, 'and now we've got the business out of the way I think I'd better check one more thing.'

The moment Petra felt the woman's hand on her hip she knew what she was going to do. She collapsed at the knees but Amy Tooth held her up as Quartermain stripped her panties down her thighs.

'I knew you'd have a pretty one,' came the awful sound of the inspector's voice as she slithered down Petra's exposed and defenceless body. 'Such a neat little muff, such gorgeous black hair. Do you trim it yourself? Or do you ask your lovers? You must have lots of lovers.'

The voice ceased its sly catalogue of degradation for a moment and Petra found herself holding her breath.

She felt the heat of Quartermain's mouth before it closed on her exposed vulva. And then a gentle, insistent exploration of her sex with lips and tongue and probing fingers. She tried to press her thighs together and repel the invader but the sergeant's leg was planted between hers from the rear, holding her open.

'Oh!' The voice was her own but she scarcely recognised it as it escaped her lips. She realised her mouth was no longer restrained, she could shout for help if she wanted to. 'Oh God,' she heard herself say softly, 'don't do that to me...'

'She's got a wicked mouth has Inspector Quartermain,' whispered Amy Tooth's voice in Petra's ear as her pelvis went into spasm on the insidious probing of Claire Quartermain's tongue.

Amy began to toy with her naked hanging breasts and Petra's hands, now free, clutched at Claire's silky brown hair, pulling her face into the fork of her body.

'I hate you,' she murmured. 'You loathsome perverted lesbian bitches. Oh, God, you're going to make me come!'

And then she began to sob silently, bracing herself against the woman behind her, her legs apart as Inspector Claire Quartermain did things to her vagina with her mouth that robbed her of her sense of self.

Afterwards they buttoned Petra's blouse and laid her on the sofa almost tenderly. She lay as if in a trance, her naked legs spread carelessly.

Amy Tooth surveyed the jewel between her thighs with a mischievous glint in her eye.

'Well, guv, what's the verdict? Sweet, is she?'

Claire grinned, her lips swollen and wet. 'Pure candy floss,' she replied.

Chapter 13

Tom woke from his dreams in the thick heat of the late afternoon. His head was leaden and his throat was parched. Eve Biscuit poured him a glass of water and he drained it in one.

'Why are you always here when I wake up?' he said. 'I'm out of danger now, Eve. You can go and save lives elsewhere.'

'I've got to keep an eye on you, Mr Glass,' she replied. 'Dr Flint's orders.'

Tom grunted. His headache intensified as he registered the ever-present thump of rock music from the next room. 'What is that bloody awful racket? It never stops.'

'That's our other celebrity patient. Luke Hailsham. He has that music on all the time.'

'Who?'

'You know. From Half Cut.'

'Is that a pop group?'

'Of course it is, Mr Glass. Everybody knows Luke Hailsham. He's in to have his vasectomy reversed. Now his wife's gone off with the kids he wants to have another lot with his new girlfriend. He says he knows you. He used to record for your record label.'

'Oh.'

'You don't remember much, do you, Mr Glass?'

'Some things, Eve, are coming back to me with crystal clarity...'

The group took him back to the flat they shared by the river. It was a large space over an old warehouse and they had the place to themselves.

'It's great,' said the drummer, whose name was Patty. 'We can make as much noise as we like.'

'And we can do what we fucking well like, too,' said Ange, the keyboard player, producing an enormous spliff.

'And what we like to do is fuck!' shouted Patty.

'Don't listen to them, they're all talk,' said Sam the lead guitarist and took hold of Tom's hand.

Shani and Christina had melted away into the darkness and it dawned on Tom that this was the real test of his ability. An initiation test alone in the dark with three smashed and randy musicians.

Sam led him to a far corner of the room. Mattresses had been laid out side by side beneath an enormous window. The stars were bright in an inky black sky and, below, the river lapped against the barges and houseboats moored on the dock.

'This is incredible,' said Tom.

'We lie here at night and get stoned,' Sam murmured. 'We take our clothes off and let the river breeze blow over us. On hot nights like this it's the coolest place in the city.'

She tugged him down to the mattress. He wasn't sure how she had managed it but she was already naked, her limbs glowing pale in the half light. Quick fingers unbuttoned his shirt.

She made him kneel up to get his trousers off and she slipped her hot lips over his cock the moment it was free. Her mouth was small and tight and his tool stuck halfway into her face. She sucked on it happily, one hand on his shaft, the other clutching his arse.

He watched the bobbing spikes of her hair and thought it was strange that she was mouthing his cock when she hadn't even kissed his lips.

There was a rustling behind him and he turned to see Ange and Patty by the bed. Ange was naked, puffing on the joint, a dark mass of hair in the delta of her crotch. Patty was pulling a thin slip over her head, her little breasts jiggling as she did so.

Tom felt somehow disconnected from his body. A woman he didn't know was lying naked between his legs, giving him the most intimate caress imaginable. And two others, it seemed, were lined up for their turn, nude and willing. He looked down the graceful bow of Sam's spine to the flaring white curve of her buttocks and ejaculated down her throat.

Sam drank his seed down then lifted her head.

'Where's that joint?' she said and Ange placed the cigarette to her sticky lips. She inhaled and held it in. Then she hooked an arm round Tom's neck and kissed him, blowing the smoke deep into his lungs. He rolled back onto the bed, his head in a spin.

The others were on him then. Ange knelt over his head pushing the soft curls of her quim into his face. He buried his hands in the firm flesh of her buttocks and, as his tongue found the satiny lips of her pussy, other hands completed the removal of his trousers.

Tom had never partied quite like this before. Not with the dope. Not with three brazen women hungry for his body. Not - as he was later to realise - when a few million pounds and a record company were at stake.

He brought Ange off in seconds it seemed and reached for Patty. He humped her on her back with his tongue down her throat and a finger on her clit. She seemed to like it. He made sure he didn't come.

He had Sam and Ange kneel on all fours in front of him. He smacked their jutting white bum cheeks with his rock-hard tool and also with his hands. He put his cock into Sam and then into Ange. He compared the velvety handshake of each pussy and toyed with their slick-wet lips and the firm buds of their clits. Then he rode Ange to a climax, pulling and clutching her big hanging breasts as he did so.

Sam complained as he lay on his back, catching his breath. 'I wanted you to come inside me. Why did you choose her?'

'Because I'm saving you up,' he heard himself say. 'I'm going to bugger your arse in a minute.'

And he did, stretching the elastic hole of her anus with his big penis, working himself in and out between her smooth white buttocks, while diddling her gaping pussy with his fingers until she howled her orgasm into the cradling arms of one of the others.

They did everything he wanted them to, everything he could think of. They kissed and sucked each other, mashing their tits and pussies together at his whim, sixty-nining in a chain, bringing themselves off tongue to quim, nipple to clit, just as he directed. He felt like a pasha in a harem. And all the time he wondered whether Shani of the midnight black eyes was out there in the darkness, watching and judging.

She appeared in the morning, bringing a mug of coffee to him as he lay on rumpled semen-stained sheets in the harsh light of day. There was no sign of his companions of the night.

'OK,' she said, 'we agree to give it a try. We know you know nothing but that's no different to the other managers we've had. At least you don't pretend you do.'

They shook hands.

'From now on, it's business,' said Shani. 'Last night was a one-off. You're never gonna screw my girls again. Agreed?'

Tom agreed.

'And in particular you won't try anything with Tina. Right?'

'Right.' What choice did he have?

Tom was feverish when he woke. It was evening now but still hot and humid. Though he had slept for most of the day he was exhausted.

Nurse Biscuit's eyes were big blue pools of concern.

'Christ, Eve, I'm having some weird dreams. It's like my life is being played back to me. I'd forgotten about those three.'

'Those three who?'

'The Shagbags. A group - you won't remember them. I'd forgotten some of the crazy things we got up to.'

'Such as?'

'I can't tell you.'

'Oh, like that, was it? Go on, I'm not a virgin, you know.' She leaned forward and took his hand. The blouse of her tunic gaped just as it had the moment he regained consciousness the day before. He looked with longing at the upper slopes of her milky white breasts, his mind and loins still afire from his memories.

She placed his hand in the neck of her shirt and smiled at him.

'Oh, Eve,' he groaned, 'you won't leave me alone in here, will you?'

'Not if you promise to tell me all about these naughty dreams of yours. If you do, I might stay with you all night.' And she bent her head so her soft breath mingled with his.

As his lips touched hers, his hand slipped deep inside her cleavage to close on the warm globes of her beautiful bosom.

Chapter 14

Kelvin was not sure exactly how he had ended up in the cells below The Primrose Court but he didn't care. He was drunk on two Negronis, a bottle of Venetian Chardonnay - and the intoxicating presence of Gossamer Hawk.

Dinner had gone well, so well that Gossamer had promised to show him round afterwards 'below stairs at the PC'. And so here he was, boozily following the Prosecutor into a meanly furnished reception area. A skinny woman in a lurid shell-suit sat behind the desk, boredom stitched across her forehead. A nasty glint shone in her small currant-black eyes when she saw Kelvin.

'Got a customer for us, have you, Prosecutor?' she asked Gossamer.

'A very special visitor, Gloria,' said Gossamer in her crystal tones. 'One of the gentlemen of the press, Mr Kelvin Priest of *Nouveau* magazine. I'd like you to give him your most particular attention.'

Had Kelvin been less tipsy or less excited by his proximity to the gorgeous Gossamer he might at this point have smelt a rat. But he smelt only T'Adore, the Prosecutor's perfume, and he smiled benignly at her as she explained she had an urgent call to make upstairs and that she was leaving him in the *very* capable hands of Sergeant Gloria Just.

The sergeant waited until the door had closed behind the silk-suited form of Gossamer before she spoke.

'Fiona,' she shouted while staring beadily into Kelvin's face, 'get your skinny arse out here. We've got a visitor. He's a VIP,' she added as a tall blonde in a skinny white top and a purple mini appeared in the doorway behind the reception desk.

The blonde was very young and very sullen but her pout of boredom was replaced by a malicious smile at the sight of Kelvin.

'Ooh,' she said, 'that's nice. We haven't had a VIP for ages.'

Kelvin grinned squiffily.

'In this office,' said the sergeant, 'VIP stands for Very Insignificant Pillock.'

'Or Very Insubstantial Penis,' said Fiona.

'He'll be a great disappointment to her highness in that case,' said the sergeant.

Puzzled, Kelvin looked from one to the other, the mist of euphoria slowly clearing from his brain.

'Let's check him in, then,' said the sergeant and suddenly the blonde was at Kelvin's side, pushing him forward.

'Hey,' he said as his wallet was pulled from his pocket and his briefcase emptied onto the desk.

'What's this?' said Sergeant Just, seizing two paperbacks of female erotica that Ted Flinch had asked him to review that morning. Her fingers eagerly flicked through the pages of - Kelvin winced as he saw the cover - *Beat Me to a Silken Pulp* by Labiella De Cruz.

Gloria Just's thin mouth set in an unforgiving line as she scanned a page. 'My God,' she cried, 'this is grade-one *filth!*'

'It's perfectly legal,' protested Kelvin. 'You can buy it in every bookshop in the land.'

'Listen to this,' said Fiona, snatching the book and reading out loud. '"As Gawain's honeyed threats flowed like molten lava through her veins and her tender wrists chafed against the iron manacles of the dungeon wall, she became aware of his burgeoning manhood throbbing against the sensitive skin of her perineum." Cor, this is hot stuff!'

'It's OK,' yelled Kelvin. 'It's politically correct - it's written by a woman!'

'So how come you're reading it? It says on the back here, "Not for sale to men." Come on, Fiona, let's book the creep.'

Suddenly Kelvin's wrists were seized and his fingers pressed onto a pad of ink.

'Get off me,' he shouted but one drunk new-man journalist was no match for two skilled and determined officers of The Primrose Court. In a trice, his jacket was stripped from his shoulders and his belt pulled from his trouser pants.

'Help!' he shouted. 'Gossamer, help - oof!'

The punch in the stomach doubled him up and Fiona slammed his head onto the desk top while Gloria handcuffed his hands behind his back.

'It's no use you shouting, pretty boy,' said the blonde. 'She's three floors up.'

'Let's gag him anyway,' said the other.

'Right - I've got just the thing.'

And, before Kelvin's shocked gaze, the blonde reached beneath her skirt and dragged her knickers down her long white thighs.

She held up the scrap of pale blue cotton. 'Have a sniff, you dirty sod,' she said, trailing the material across his face. It was warm and musky.

There was a coarse chuckle from behind Kelvin. Then a hand seized his nose and jerked his head back. As he opened his mouth to breathe, Fiona shoved the balled-up panties between his lips.

'You like doing that, don't you?' said Sergeant Just.

The blonde wrapped two-inch parcel tape around Kelvin's mouth. 'You bet,' she agreed. 'I love shoving a bit of my arse down men's throats. Not that it makes up for what they've done to women. Bastards!' And she slapped Kelvin hard on both cheeks.

Kelvin's eyes watered and he howled soundlessly into the wad of cotton, the mist of euphoria now replaced by the fog of pain and humiliation.

They took him into a cell that was as grim and depressing as any prison room of his imagination. The door seemed six inches thick, with bars on the window. The floor was of grey stone and a bare light bulb cast shadows across a sloping metal bed frame in the centre of the room. The air was chilly - the heat of summer did not permeate these walls.

They stripped him naked with relish, leaving the handcuffs in place and slicing his shirt off with a razor. Gloria did the cutting and Kelvin could tell she enjoyed it. Then Fiona began to rub talcum powder into his body, over his chest and up and down his thighs, pulling apart his buttocks to spread it into his crack, an impudent leer on her face.

The pair of them fitted him into a skintight rubber body-suit. Despite the powder and their evident expertise it took a while to get it just right, especially when they had to release his hands to fit it over his shoulders. But at last he was encased from neck to toe in the supple embrace of rubber. The weird garment had no crotch, leaving his cock and balls lewdly exposed to the open air.

They pushed him onto the bare bed and tied him across the chest with a strap. His hands were fastened above his head; his legs were bent up and apart, his feet fixed so they couldn't move. He was helpless: bound, gagged and immobile with his penis and testicles lolling obscenely between his spread thighs.

Kelvin was shocked, afraid and in pain. He told himself to get a grip. He tried to be philosophical. He reminded himself that, whatever happened, this was bloody good copy. He reckoned he was doing pretty well.

But when Gloria Just leaned between his legs with a pair of scissors he fainted dead away.

Chapter 15

It was easy to gauge how much Maeve Slack's circumstances had changed. The steps leading down to her basement flat were steep and treacherous and there was a cracked pane of glass in the door. Tom rang the bell and steeled himself for a necessary but doubtless painful encounter. The memory of Lionel's abandoned wife drifting like a lost soul around the city-centre Sainsbury's was still fresh in his mind.

So it was with relief that he viewed the elegant figure in a scarlet kimono who answered his knock, her thick brown hair tied back from her handsome face, a surprised smile on her lips.

'She'll remember you,' Christina had said. 'Go on Thursday, after lunch. Sam and Mandy will be at school. It'll be perfect.'

'Well, praise the Lord, it's Thomas Glass,' said Mrs Slack. 'Miracles will never cease.'

Tom was hesitant, his prepared speech gone from his mind. Her rich brown eyes seemed all-knowing. 'I'm sorry I haven't come before,' he said, thrusting a bunch of roses into her arms. 'I meant to,' he added, hoping that the lie didn't show.

'If you say so,' she said, taking his arm and pulling him inside.

In the narrow hallway her presence was overwhelming. She was nearly as tall as Tom and she smelt of perfume, wine and - the thought seized Tom like a caress on his cock - bare flesh. As she walked ahead of him he could see the globes of her bottom outlined against the thin silk of her robe and he knew she was naked beneath it. This was not what he had expected.

She led him to the rear of the flat and out onto a small sunbaked patio. A battered sun-lounger and two white plastic garden chairs stood by a small shaded table on which lay a bowl of fruit and the remains of a salad. Without asking, she pushed a glass of white wine into his hand and pointed to a chair. Tom sat, unable to take his eyes off her long tanned legs as she arranged herself on the sun bed. The flowers had been magically positioned in a vase on the table. He couldn't recall her doing it.

'So, why have you come to see me?' she said. 'I presume it's not solely out of concern for my welfare.'

Those brown eyes were on him, darker, more tempestuous than her daughter's. He took a large gulp of wine, this was the tricky part. 'Christina,' he began but she cut him off.

'Have you any idea, young man, how painful it is to be abandoned by both your husband and your eldest daughter within the space of six months? That's a rhetorical question, by the way, there's no need to answer it.'

'Christina hasn't abandoned you, Mrs Slack. She's very concerned.'

'Huh. If she's so concerned why isn't she here? Why isn't she at school using her God-given brains instead of dancing on a stage half naked like a little slut?'

'She says you threw her out.'

'I gave her an ultimatum. I told her if she was to continue living under my roof she had to take her A levels and steer clear of clubs and pop groups. Oh God!' She threw back her head and shouted in frustration. The rich chestnut hair fell free of restraint across her half-exposed shoulders and the rounded flesh of her bosom strained against the kimono. She looked fabulous.

She held her empty glass out to Tom and turned her fierce gaze on him as he filled it. 'Don't ever get married and have children, Tom, unless you want to be kicked in the teeth.'

'Have you considered, Mrs Slack, that Christina might be pursuing a legitimate career in the music industry? That she has the potential to be very successful in a way that might not seem obvious to you?'

'What do you mean?' Maeve's glass was empty already but her gaze was steady. Tom did not dare look away.

'I mean that this group is going to be big.'

'How do you know?' There was interest in those glittering brown eyes - and not just in what Tom was saying. 'You must be hot in that jacket and tie. Take them off, don't mind me.'

Tom got to his feet and gratefully stripped to his shirt. As he did so he gazed down the gaping ravine of her cleavage, at the plump tawny flesh spreading beneath the flimsy neckline of her robe. She caught him looking and grinned. Her lower lip was full and wet with wine.

'Tell me then,' she said, 'why my daughter is going to be a superstar.'

'I didn't say that,' Tom replied. 'I said that the group is going to be successful. The singer is going to be the superstar.'

'Really?' Her tone was not entirely sarcastic. Tom had said something that was making her reconsider matters.

'I've seen them, you know,' she continued. 'Tina made me go to some frightful dive. It wasn't my idea of entertainment. But I suppose there was something about the woman singing. I could understand why all those little boys in the crowd were coming in their pants. I just didn't want them doing it with my daughter up on the stage.'

Tom nodded sympathetically.

'What's your interest in this?' she asked.

'I'm the group's new manager. That's why I'm convinced Christina is not wasting her time. She's writing songs for Shani. We've got great plans.'

'My God.' Maeve Slack shook her head, whether in amusement or disbelief Tom couldn't make out. He pressed on.

'That's really why I've come, Mrs Slack. To say that I'm looking after Christina's welfare and that everything's looking good. I've got them a TV spot next month. You're going to be very proud of her, I promise.'

She grabbed the bottle herself this time and emptied it into her glass.

'I can see I'm destined to be publicly humiliated all over again,' she said. 'First I'm depicted to the nation as the dreary wife of the dirty professor. Now I am to be the mortified mother of a half-naked, underage Shagbag. That is the name of the group, isn't it?'

'It's a headline-grabber, Mrs Slack. Personally I think it's ghastly but you've got to get people's attention these days. Actually, I'm glad you brought up the question of Christina's age because she's not yet old enough to sign the management agreement and I wondered if you, as her parent, would be kind enough to...'

'You little shit,' she cried and knocked him off his chair with a swing of her arm that came from nowhere.

The next thing he knew she was on top of him in a whirl of perfumed silk, pummelling and smacking his face, her warm weight grinding him into the flagstones of the patio. Such was his surprise he made no attempt to fight back but raised his arms to ward off the blows. Despite the pain of her attack he registered that her kimono had burst open and that her big tawny breasts were swinging free only partially hidden by the curtain of hair that now cascaded over both of them.

She pulled his arms away from his face and pressed them down onto the stones. Her eyes blazed and her wide wine-wet mouth was inches from his as she hissed, 'Are you sleeping with my daughter?'

'No,' said Tom truthfully.

'I don't believe you.' She hit him hard across the face. Tom noted the thrust and jiggle of her tits as she did so. She hit him again.

'I swear to you I've never touched her,' he said as calmly as he could.

She hit him once more and blood from his nose fountained over the pair of them. 'Oh hell,' she said, 'now look what you've done.'

'She sounds a fierce lady,' said Nurse Biscuit as she nestled in Tom's arms in the narrow hospital bed.

'She was very passionate,' said Tom, reliving the fresh-minted moment from his past, revealed to him in his sleep just a few moments before.

His cock was a swollen baton of flesh in Eve Biscuit's hand. 'You're hard again,' she said, fondling the length of it. 'I bet you had a stiffy while she was smacking your head watching her big boobs flying everywhere.'

Tom grinned in the dark. 'I'd been stiff since the moment I walked into her flat. I'd always had the hots for her when I met her with Lionel. I'd never had a grown-up woman before; I'd only had girls my age.'

'Aha, so you did bonk her then,' said Eve, slicking Tom's foreskin back and forth across the bulging head of his tool. 'Tell me about it. Tell me all the lurid details.'

'You're not the sweet little innocent you appear to be, are you, Eve?'

'Don't be daft,' she said, 'I'm a nurse. Now just you lie still while I put this poor swollen fellow somewhere comfortable.'

The pale curve of her hip gleamed in the dark as she cocked her leg over him and aimed the head of his tool into the shadow of her loins. With a grunt of satisfaction she tucked the straining bar of his penis into the slippery mouth of her pussy and laid her body along the length of him.

'Go on,' she said, 'tell me what happened next.'

Tom cradled Eve's soft weight on his chest and did as he was told.

Chapter 16

Petra remained under the shower for an age, the water as hot as she could stand it. However, the attempt to cleanse herself of Claire Quartermain's degrading caress was not a success. Afterwards she sat on the bed in front of the mirror and spread her legs. The curling pink gash of her pussy was gaping and swollen. The inspector had called it pretty. She put a hand between her legs and began to—

'I'm *not* a lesbian,' she shouted out loud and jumped to her feet. The fact that she had come on Claire's tongue more profoundly than on any man's cock had to be simply part of the policewoman's ghastly professional skill. Or maybe the potency of her attentions was an illusion, the indecencies so effective because they had been forced on her as part of an interrogation. What she needed, she thought, was Kelvin's familiar lovemaking to reassure her. Where the hell was he anyway?

She pulled on the long T-shirt she sometimes wore to bed and made herself a sandwich. On her desk lay her briefcase and a bundle of papers she had grabbed as she had hastily quit the office. Among them was a package that Harriet had insisted she take with her. 'Don't open it here,' she'd hissed as she'd pressed it into Petra's hand.

Petra pulled the padded envelope towards her and noted with a sinking heart that it came from Mitre & Gauze, the solicitors representing Glass Tools of Glendrockit. It could only be trouble.

The object contained within was undoubtedly that. Petra had seen dummy pricks before. A boyfriend had once given her a pink plastic one and she had thrown it out unused. She had examined them once or twice in friend's houses - Cassie, for instance, had a collection. They came in all shades and shapes, with weird attachments and stupid names and Petra had never ever been tempted to do more than laugh at them. This was different.

The phallus was made of coloured glass and, to her surprise, it felt warm to the touch. As she folded her fingers round the thick stem and cradled the base in her palm, Petra felt as if she had never held such a precious object before. Its contours were life-like but somehow smoothed out so that it was aesthetically more pleasing than the real thing - and bigger. As she held it, the glass appeared to change colour, the indigo lightening and swirling within the solid shaft, paling to yellow as she traced a finger up and around the swollen head.

'Oh my,' she said, Claire Quartermain's assault quite banished from her mind, 'you're beautiful.'

The accompanying note from Mitre & Gauze informed Petra that this was a prototype product of Glass Tools, designed for the discerning connoisseur of erotica. It was intended to enhance the home as an *objet d'art* but, if required, it could be used in conjunction with a selection of specially prepared aromatic oils. The item was known as The Magic Wand.

Petra opened a small velvet-lined box and took out some small vials of liquid. They were musky and fragrant, much like any aromatherapy preparation but, in conjunction with the glowing presence of The Magic Wand itself, the fragrance sent Petra's pulse racing - and her loins throbbing.

She hardly needed lubricating, such was the state she was in already, but she anointed the Wand with a few drops of green liquid. She pushed back the chair and spread her legs, pulling the T-shirt up and over her belly.

'What's Kelvin going to think if he comes back now?' she wondered as she positioned the monster between her legs.

Then she didn't think of Kelvin any more as she pressed the length of it up inside herself, the smooth glass glans nosing between her swollen labia as if it knew its own way. 'Oh,' she moaned out loud and 'OH!' more loudly as the thing infiltrated the depths of her, filling her as completely as if it had been made to measure.

'Oh yes!' she cried, rocking the glass dildo back and forth. She held it by the balls and manipulated it inside her, marvelling in the solidity of it, at the ease with which she seemed to be able to manoeuvre it for her pleasure, at the *reliability* of this big tool in her own hands. She discovered there was a rounded protuberance at the base which thrust up to kiss her clit if she twisted just so—

'Yes!' she shouted on the crest of a sudden orgasm.

'YES!!' she cried as she rode the wave of ecstasy.

'Oh yes, yes, yes!' she murmured as she wallowed in the afterglow, falling forward onto the desk to cradle her head in her arms.

The ringing of the telephone by her side woke her from a profound sleep. It was Cassie.

'Hi, darling, how's the war?' she said.

'Huh?' was all Petra could manage.

'You sound drugged. It's OK, I'll make this short. Philippe's about to come any minute and God do I need a little workout.'

Petra was awake now. She had a pretty good idea what Cassie was going to say next and she wasn't disappointed.

'I'm just making sure you haven't forgotten about *The Come-Again Lifestyle* profile for the magazine. I've fixed it all up and Chastity's going to analyse your results. So don't neglect the regime. Three point six eight a day's your target. If I were you I'd round it up to four.'

'Cassie, I've been thinking—'

'Don't say it. You're not weaselling out on me now, Petra Rosewater.'

That had been Petra's intention. The more she'd thought about it the more she'd been turned off by the whole thing. Especially after the Claire Quartermain incident.

'Come on, darling. It's a licence to fuck and it's healthy - what could be better?'

'Look here, Cassie,' said Petra firmly. You had to be firm with Cassie or you got steamrollered. Cassie was Australian. She leaned forward to make her point and suddenly became aware of a solid, comforting feeling in her loins. The glass dildo was still buried deep inside her.

'Don't you look-here me,' Cassie was saying. 'I'm counting on you so *you'd* better be counting your comes. How many have you had since last night?'

Petra opened her mouth to tell her, once and for all, to forget the whole thing. Instead she heard herself say, 'Six.'

Cassie laughed. 'You sly bitch. See if you can manage a couple more tonight, then we can say you started yesterday.'

'But, Cassie—'

'Philippe's at the door, I've got to go. Two more tonight, darling. Go for it.'

Petra gingerly extracted the phallus from between her legs. To her amazement, it had changed colour. The swirling indigo of the shaft had been transformed into sunset orange and the great head had turned pink.

She couldn't resist. It was as if the thing was real. She plunged the plum-shaped knob into her mouth.

She gorged on the dummy penis, tasting the spice of the oil and the honey of her own juices. She thrust it down her throat till she gagged, rubbed the smooth head on the roof of her mouth, pushed the tip of her tongue into the eye of the glans.

When she took it out, the stem was a deep maroon and the head a flaming scarlet.

She looked at her watch. It was nearly seven. 'Sod Kelvin,' she said.

She put The Magic Wand to the salivating mouth of her pussy and pushed home.

Two more tonight. She'd go for it all right.

Chapter 17

Tom lay still, as instructed, on the sun-dappled flagstones and held a wadded ball of paper tissue to his nose. His head sang and he could still feel the weight of Maeve Slack's body on top of his as she pummelled him. The bruises and scratches on his arms and chest smarted. Blood congealed on his face and pooled beneath his head, matting his hair. Behind him, just out of his vision, a bee buzzed. Inside the flat he could hear the sounds of Maeve fetching water and towels. He felt unaccountably serene.

She returned and knelt down by his side. She began to clean him up, her hands no longer aggressive but tender.

'I'm not sorry,' she said. 'I must let my temper out or go mad. That's what this last year has taught me.'

'I'm the one who should apologise,' he said, which was truer than she realised - or so he hoped.

Her face was furrowed in concentration as she ministered to him. There was blood on her cheek and her mouth was turned down at the corners. Her hair fell forward, hindering her work and she had to keep brushing it back, out of her eyes. As she did so his gaze strayed to her breasts dangling loosely within her robe.

'You're lucky you still have your eyes,' she said. 'I was that mad I'd have scratched them out. Don't you want to know why?'

'I've never touched Christina,' he said.

'Maybe not but you had your way with Elvira, didn't you?'

Tom's heart skipped. Any mention of Elvira in these circumstances was alarming.

'I found her diary,' Maeve continued, placing a plaster on a cut on Tom's neck. 'Maybe the little slut didn't think anyone round here could read Italian but she was wrong. She wrote a lot about you, considering you were one of many.'

'Oh, really?'

'She suspected you knew about her affair with the teacher.'

'Who?'

'The teacher. That's what she called him. Of course it turned out to be my bastard of a husband. There, that's finished. You'll be needing a new shirt but there's still a few of Lionel's around.'

Tom began to sit up.

'You should keep your head back. Sit like this,' and she positioned him with his head in her lap. He looked up into her face, her fascinating bosom, loosely covered, looming over him.

'Did you know she was having an affair with Lionel?'

'I thought she was having an affair with me.'

'Would you have told me if you'd known?' Her eyes searched his face. 'If I'd found out I could have done something. I could have got rid of her before the papers got onto it. I've fixed things like that before.'

Her perfume was intoxicating. He could see her nipples pushing against the thin scarlet silk like fingertips.

'What I don't understand,' she said, brushing his hair off his forehead, 'is why she sent that photo to the papers.'

'You're beautiful,' said Tom, desperate to change the direction of the conversation.

Her fingers lingered on his brow. 'I'm a middle-aged woman who lost her husband to an Italian tart half her age. Do you know they've set up house in Rome? He's teaching and I bet she's fucking his students already. *Plus ca change.*'

'You mustn't think about it,' he said, catching her hand and pressing it to his lips. Her fingers tasted of antiseptic. He licked the ball of flesh at the base of her thumb. She sighed. He ran his tongue from her palm up the tiny blue veins on the inside of her wrist.

'She said you were quite inventive in bed.'

'Oh yes?'

Her eyes were laughing now as they looked down into his. 'She said you were a bit clumsy at first but you were a quick learner.'

'What else did she say?' He had his fingers in her hair, playing with the heavy curls.

She was smiling. 'I couldn't possibly tell you the other things - not on so slight an acquaintance.'

Tom had never kissed a woman when recovering from a nose bleed before.

He played it safe and tugged her head down to his, feeling her long slender neck curve beneath his fingers as she bent to offer him her parted lips.

Her mouth was like molten honey, sweet and hot. The skin of her back burned into his hands through her flimsy kimono. He ached to strip her and explore her perfumed flesh but he held back. He knew he mustn't rush at her. This was a woman to be pleasured on her own terms.

But she was eager too. She pushed her tongue to the back of his throat and ran her hands beneath his blood-soaked shirt across the planes of his chest. 'Take it off,' she ordered him. 'Take everything off. Let me see you.'

He did as he was told, kicking his shoes off and flinging his clothes onto the flagstones. She made him stand in front of her and turn round, her eyes devouring his tall rangy frame, the hard white buttocks, the lean thighs, the forest of black hair at the base of his belly. And his cock.

'I might have known Elvira wouldn't lie about that,' she said.

He stood over her and ran his hands down her back under her kimono, the flesh satin smooth to his touch. 'What do you mean?'

'She said you had a big cock and she was right.'

'Oh!' cried Tom as her hands sank into the rounds of his buttocks and her lips closed over the tender knob of his penis. He felt perilously close to coming just at the touch of her mouth. He lifted the veil of her hair so he could look at her sucking him, at the incredible sight of his long white bar of flesh disappearing between her wide red lips. She sucked him hard, hollowing her cheeks, a blue vein beating in her neck.

With his other hand he reached into the neck of her robe and drew out a plump pear-shaped breast, the long brown nipple nosing into his palm.

He hadn't intended to come in her face but he had little choice in the matter. She held his shaft in one hand and wanked him slyly, pumping and squeezing, all the time mouthing the swollen plum of his glans. He watched spellbound as she fellated him, her red lips working and her opulent tit-flesh swinging. When a long finger was insinuated between his buttocks, seeking out the sensitive pucker of his anus, he knew he was lost. As she penetrated him to the knuckle, his knees wobbled and he ejaculated into the hot cavern of her mouth.

Maeve collapsed on the sun-lounger, Tom's spunk glistening in the corner of her mouth, her legs spread carelessly. As he watched, his head still thick from the rush of orgasm, he saw her untie her robe and slide forward, presenting the open gash of her sex to him. It was clear where his duty lay.

He took his time positioning himself between her firm bronzed thighs. He admired the smooth sheen of the skin on her long legs, the slender turn of her ankles and the titillating contrast of the white flesh tones beneath her bikini line.

'You're very brown,' he said.

'I've spent a lot of time out here this summer.'

'Like this?' he said, lightly brushing his hand over her bush of chestnut-coloured pubic hair.

'No.'

'But you do go topless, don't you? Your breasts are as brown as the rest of you. It's just this fascinating triangle here that's quite white.' And he traced the line of creamy skin across her belly with the tip of his tongue. He could see a dewdrop of moisture pearling the inside of her thigh. He licked it up and she shivered involuntarily.

Her vagina was open before him like a rose in bloom, its fragrance as heady, its petals quivering in anticipation. Her outer lips were long and brown, a fascinating furl of flesh just begging to be kissed. Tom obliged.

'Oh,' said Maeve as he took her labia between his lips.

'Oh yes,' she moaned as he separated them with his tongue and pushed gently into her moist interior.

'Oh God,' she shouted as he slid his tongue up the length of her crack to tickle the throbbing pearl of her clitoris.

She twined her fingers in his hair and jammed his mouth into her crack. He had meant to tease her, to make her wait but now the juice was pouring from her like water from a tap, and she was bucking her pelvis into his bruised and battered face. Within seconds, it seemed, she was coming all over him.

She was still shivering like a jelly, her sumptuous breasts quivering on her chest, when he crawled on top of her and sank his pulsating cock into the hungry hole between her thighs.

He kissed the spunk off her lips and she sucked the cunt juice from his tongue while they fucked, feasting on each other's bodies like starving people. As they came, together, the sun-lounger collapsed, pitching them onto the stone floor and gashing Maeve's hand.

She laughed as Tom helped her bind the wound. 'You realise I won't be able to sign your contract now,' she said. 'You'll have to come back some other time.'

'How about tomorrow?' he suggested.

Chapter 18

Kelvin regained his senses to a tingling sensation on the skin of his scrotum and the drone of a woman's voice. He looked down his rubber-suited body to see Sergeant Gloria Just wiping foam from the blade of a cutthroat razor. Across the room, Fiona of the long legs and the purple mini was perched on a chair, orating the work of Labiella De Cruz.

Gloria looked up and caught Kelvin's panic-stricken stare. She smiled almost kindly.

'Don't worry,' she said, 'I'm just making you more presentable.'

Kelvin eyed the mound of hair clippings on the floor and the glint of the razor in her hand as she bent over his loins. The bloody woman was shaving his bollocks! He jerked against his bonds in fury.

'Careful,' said Gloria, 'or you might go out less of a man than when you came in.'

Kelvin froze as the razor descended. A tug of her fingers, the kiss of steel on skin and another strip of white foam was deposited into the soapy bowl at her side. In other circumstances, he might have felt a frisson of excitement at these intimate attentions. But not now - which was a pity from more than one point of view.

'What would be most helpful,' said Gloria, 'would be an erection. Could you possibly lend a hand, Fiona?'

The sound of the blonde's breathy Cockney rose in pitch and the words she was uttering suddenly began to impress themselves on Kelvin's brain.

'"More, more,' pleaded Sanctimonia whimperingly as the ground glass pressed into the sensitive skin of her womanly breasts. 'Thrash me, oh Master, until my crimson gore mingles with the copious fluids of my sensuous loins!'"

'Get off your bum, Fiona, and do something,' said Gloria. 'He's no bigger than a cocktail sausage.'

Fiona was aggrieved. 'I'm reading him his porn, aren't I? It's what turns him on.'

'Turns you on, you mean,' snapped Gloria.

Kelvin saw that what she said was true. The way Fiona squirmed in her seat, her eyes glued to the page, suggested that her interest was fully engaged. And, as he followed the curve of her legs up to the shadows below the hem of her tiny skirt, he remembered that she wore no panties. Suddenly his interest was fully engaged too.

'Blimey,' said Gloria, 'I think you may be right.'

'Told you,' said Fiona, easing forward in her chair so that her long white thighs pointed in an open vee towards Kelvin. Her mini was now a band of purple around her waist and a goatee of dark pubic hair was fully revealed in her spread crotch. Fiona, Kelvin could see, was not a natural blonde.

The silken whip fell again and again on the abraded skin of the beauteous slave. Her Master's eyes were cruel slits, glinting in the leather mask, obsidian and immutable. The tempests of orgasm echoed far off in Sanctimonia's loins as she beseeched him for more.

Fiona's free hand stroked the silky hairs of her pussy beard. Her fingers played with the loose dark lips of her opening, pulling and pinching. Kelvin was transfixed as she inserted a finger, her wetness gleaming on the knuckle as she pushed in and out. Then she had three digits inside and was rubbing the swollen peg of her clit between thumb and forefinger. This was plainly a girl who knew how to give herself a good time. By now Kelvin's penis was suitably distended.

Gossamer timed her entrance to perfection. As Fiona prepared to yield to the Labiella-inspired tempests of orgasm and Gloria wiped the last smudge of soap from the quivering tower of Kelvin's tool, the Prosecutor flung wide the door.

'Goodness gracious,' she cried. 'What on earth is going on?'

Kelvin's two tormentors jumped to their feet.

'We're preparing the prisoner,' said Gloria. 'He gave us a bit of trouble at first but now he's as sweet as pie. You can see for yourself.'

Gossamer was apoplectic. 'This man isn't a prisoner, you stupid clod. He's my special *guest*, a reporter for a magazine with a *significant* impact on the national consciousness!'

Fiona spoke up. 'He's a pervert like all the rest, Prosecutor. We found this disgusting filth in his bag.' And she held up the copy of *Beat Me to a Silken Pulp*.

Gossamer studied the volume for a moment. 'Not for sale to men,' she muttered to herself. 'Oh dear.'

She looked into Kelvin's eyes and his stomach flipped. God, she was magnificent! Surely she didn't believe in this preposterous rubbish?

'Get out of here, you two idiots,' she said. 'I shall deal with him myself.'

'Yes, Prosecutor,' they muttered and backed out of the door.

'My poor, poor darling,' cried Gossamer, rushing to the helpless Kelvin and stripping the tape from his lips. He spat the cotton gag from his mouth.

'Gossamer, thank God!' he cried in a cracked voice. 'It was ghastly!'

She found him some water and dried his mouth with the sleeve of her blouse when it dribbled down his chin.

Before he could say anything she kissed him. Gently at first, then in a hungry, deep-throated tongue-rape that thrilled him to the toes of his rubber-suited feet.

'My God, Gossamer,' he spluttered when she let him up for air.

'I'm sorry, darling, I get rather carried away when I'm with a man I find so utterly scrummy.' And she squeezed the shaft of his recently denuded penis with an enthusiasm that was almost overwhelming.

'Gossamer, you really are the most fabulous creature. I would die for you, I swear—'

'Oh good,' she said, two hands now on his twitching genitals.

'—but aren't you going to set me free?'

'I can't just yet. Sergeant Just would be suspicious.'

'Suspicious of what? For God's sake, Gossamer, I've been wrongfully imprisoned and abused!'

'Did they abuse you like this?' she asked, delicately running a finger up the underside of his shaft. 'Or like this?' She bent her head and ran her tongue lightly across the swollen helmet of his glans. The sensation was exquisite. He jerked his loins upwards, wanting to bury his burning tool in the warmth of her mouth, but his bonds restrained him.

'Don't tease me, Gossamer,' he cried. 'Set me free so I can hold you.'

But Gossamer took no notice. She stepped back from the bed frame and began to unbutton her blouse.

Kelvin's protests died in his throat as he watched her strip down to a basque of shiny black latex that offered up her big pink breasts to his hungry gaze and left bare the white dome of her belly, down to a hairless slit.

'Oh Gossamer,' he breathed.

'How do you like me?' she said, loosening her hair so it fell in a blonde cloud across her satiny shoulders and taking a step towards him.

Kelvin did not reply. The sight of those longed-for breasts soaring above him, their jutting overhang accentuated by the upthrust of the basque, was overwhelming. He longed to cup their soft weight in his hands, to bury his face in that perfumed expanse of luscious tit-flesh, to feed one by one those succulent brown nipples into his mouth... But he couldn't, he was pinned down, utterly at her mercy. He almost fountained his spunk at the thought.

She was rearranging his legs, lowering his feet so he lay flat on the bed. As he gorged his eyes on her naked hanging breasts, the rounded curves elongating as she bent over, he was aware she was refastening the bonds round his ankles. He did not fight her, the visual rape of his senses had undermined all thought of resistance.

When she was satisfied with the arrangement, she produced a bottle of baby oil and poured a handful onto his chest. She began to slick it into the rubber surface of his skin, over his torso and up and down his legs and arms, the great breasts swaying above him as she did so. She paused at his cock and balls, examining them closely. Then she lowered her head to his loins and suddenly a jolt of pain shot through his shaft.

'Ow,' yelped Kelvin.

'Sorry, darling,' said Gossamer. 'Gloria missed a hair,' and she extracted it from between her teeth. 'I can't abide any hair down there at all. Look.' And she placed a foot on the frame of the bed by Kelvin's head, displaying her pussy split in all its shaven glory.

Kelvin gazed at the shocking expanse of bare skin - the prominent pink pearl of her clitoris, the wet crinkle of her labia and the moist dark opening between - and gasped. This was the most naked vagina he had ever seen. He had never wanted anything so badly in his life.

'Please, Gossamer,' he croaked, 'please...' It was all he could manage.

Gossamer smiled. She knew what he wanted and now she was prepared to give it to him - on her own terms.

First she oiled his cock, then she climbed on top of him, her broad thighs on either side of his slim hips. She knelt up and placed the head of his throbbing tool at the mouth of her pussy, a bare inch from her wet lips.

'Now,' she said, 'let me show you how we press charges in the cells of The Primrose Court.'

It was the most sensational sex sensation Kelvin had ever had. The kiss of shaved and oiled cunt on cock was more intimate than anything he had ever felt before.

She lowered herself slowly, taking his length millimetre by millimetre into the furnace of her sex, until he was sheathed to the hilt. She sat completely still for a moment, her full weight on his loins.

Her huge breasts trembled above him, her honeyed thighs gleamed in the harsh light and her wide mouth smiled down at him. He longed to thrust his cock in and out of her creamy white belly, to devour her with his mouth, to ransack her voluptuous flesh with his hands - to *fuck* her properly, for God's sake. But he couldn't, he just had to lie back and take it.

He watched as she slid a finger into the groove of her pussy and her other hand began to pull and tweak her nipples. The colour rose in her cheeks as she pleasured herself, her breath shortening and her breasts heaving. She came twice before she even moved her hips in any kind of motion that might bring him release. When she came, he felt a fluttering inside her, a delicate beating of butterfly wings against his weeping penis - but it was not enough to bring him off.

'Mmm,' sighed Gossamer as she fell forward on top of him and settled her flesh on the oil-slick slipperiness of his rubber embrace. 'This is heaven, darling. I could go on like this all night, couldn't you?'

Kelvin wasn't sure, but he had a feeling he was going to find out.

Chapter 19

Tom took the stairs to the flat above the warehouse three at a time. He had some good news for Shani and the girls. He couldn't wait to tell them how he planned to land a record deal.

The key to it was Maeve Slack. She was a generous woman, generous with her body, her wine and her time. For the past two weeks they had spent most afternoons in bed together. Between bouts of energetic lovemaking she had listened to his schemes to get the Shagbags off the ground - and to his frustrations as each plan came adrift. He told her how difficult it was to get through to the people that counted. He had a tape of Shani and the girls but he couldn't get anyone important to listen to it.

'I know Chas Cross,' Maeve told him during one languorous siesta. Though she was on the point of burying his impatient cock between her wet red lips, Tom stopped her. Chas Cross was the boss of Euphoria, an independent label which had minted money in the days before punk with a table of dreamy singer-songwriters. Euphoria was now off the pace, Tom knew that much. He also knew that Chas Cross was a laid-back maverick who might see the potential in Shani - if only Tom could get his attention.

'You're kidding,' he said.

Maeve grinned at him, her mouth poised over his cock, her lingers moving on the white stem.

'Lionel taught him at Fleetmore. He stood up for him over some drugs fuss and stopped him being sent down. His mother was very grateful. I've kept in touch.'

'Maeve, you're a bloody marvel,' he'd said, plunging his straining tool into her

60

face. 'Just get me his home phone number.'

That had been ten days ago. Since then he'd phoned Cross nightly. Most of the time the phone was engaged. The time he spoke to Cross it was after midnight. Tom played, the Lionel Slack card at once and introduced himself as the student manager of a band. Cross was polite, Tom kept it short but rang again the next night and the night after that. On the fourth night Cross picked up the phone and said, 'Hi Tom,' but he turned down Tom's requests to listen to the tape of the Shagbags himself. 'Send it 'to the office,' he said, 'Phil will give it a spin.' Tom told him he'd already sent two copies and got no response. 'Too bad,' said Cross. It sounded like he meant it.

Tom changed tack after that. He rang every night, between one and five in the morning, but he dropped the direct sell. He asked Cross's advice, discussed the record business in general and bitched about Euphoria's competitors. Cross was unfailingly good-humoured - and always wide awake. In his shoes, Tom would have been neither.

On the seventh night Cross asked Tom why he had stopped pitching his group. Tom told him he was waiting till Euphoria came begging.

And now, if things went according to plan, they would do just that.

The door to the flat wasn't locked which didn't surprise Tom. It never was. The big loft looked unoccupied. There were clothes and unwashed plates and stage gear everywhere; it smelt of stale food and perfume and dope. He picked his way through mattresses, past the makeshift hanging wardrobe bulging with unpressed clothes, heading for the far corner of the open space. Here there was a more conventional layout, a corridor with small rooms leading off it - a kitchen, a bathroom and bedrooms.

This, he knew, was Shani's area. It was her he really wanted to talk to.

Through the half-open door he saw her long coffee-coloured legs, stretched out on the white sheet of a bed. He stopped to one side of the door, suddenly transformed into intruder - and voyeur.

He knew at once she was not alone. There were sounds in the air. Soft feminine sighs, a low-pitched giggle, a sudden intake of breath. Shani was making love - and her partner was not a man.

Tom wasn't altogether surprised. Unlike the others she did not have male hangers-on. And there was something aggressive about her that went beyond attitude. She was possessive about the girls in her band, that was clear, her black impenetrable eyes following them as they flirted with their admirers. Like the leader of a pack, she was formidable.

He stepped closer, peering through the doorjamb, hidden from the couple on the bed.

He should have expected the other girl to be Christina but he hadn't and it was a shock. She looked small and vulnerable in Shani's arms, her thin white limbs glowing pale in the bigger woman's dark embrace. And though she looked defenceless, she was certainly not reluctant.

Their heads lay side by side on the pillow, their lips glued together in an endless kiss. Clothes lay crumpled on the floor but neither girl was naked. Shani wore panties and a thin black bra; the curve of her left breast bulging against its constraint as she lay on her side. Her fingers were picking at the ribbons of a peach camisole, laying bare the alabaster swell of Tina's delicate bosom. As the small pink nub of a nipple came into view Shani covered it with her mouth and Tina held her close, eyes tight shut, shivering with passion.

Tom was shivering too. He leaned against the doorway, hoping the hammering of his heart could not be heard. He felt, stupidly, betrayed - not only because he wanted these women for himself but because he could imagine with what horror Maeve might view the proceedings. And had he not promised her he would look after her estranged daughter? Yet here he was watching her being devoured by a predatory lesbian - and enjoying every second.

Shani's hand was in Tina's panties, Tom could see her fingers moving beneath the thin peach silk, a match to the camisole which was now off her slim shoulders. Shani lifted her head from Tina's breast, leaving the nipple swollen and red and wet. She put her face to the younger girl's and pushed a long pink tongue into her mouth. Tina sucked on it, moving her hips now to the rhythm of the singer's hand between her legs. She put her own hand on the outside of the material and pressed Shani's fingers harder into her. They broke the kiss, Tina was breathing hard. Shani pulled her hand away and stripped the panties down the girl's thighs.

'Hurry,' sighed Tina, kicking the flimsy garment from her foot and displaying to Tom the candy-pink split of her open-mouthed pussy, wisps of fine blonde hair curling on the apex of her mound, the spread lips wet and eager. Then the thrilling sight was blotted from his view by the dark shape of Shani's head as she plunged between Tina's legs, her glossy black locks covering the girl's slim white thighs.

Tom shut his eyes and leaned his head against the wall. It was wrong of him to watch, he knew, he was trespassing on a private moment of significance. This performance, however, was not to be scorned. Shani made love like she sang - with passion and commitment. He opened his eyes again.

The women had shifted position. Tina was on her back, her knees lifted, her thighs spread, her bottom on the edge of the bed. Shani was on her knees on the floor, her head dipping to Tina's crotch, her hands roaming the flesh of her lover's supine body. Her *cafe au lait* skin glistened in the morning sunlight as she worked, her brown fingers now pressing hard into the girl's inner thigh, leaving pink fingerprints on the white skin. Her broad rear jutted towards the doorway, the black panties cutting into the flesh of her spread buttocks. As she sucked and kissed the younger girl, her back hollowed and her arse swayed. She was eating the girl alive.

There was a low keening in the air which rose to a sob. Tina's hand was pressed to her mouth, as if she were trying to suppress the sound, but the rush of orgasm was now upon her and she was screaming through her fingers at a pitch that threatened to shatter glass. Shani was remorseless. Her arms were a band of steel around the girl's thighs and her mouth was locked to her vagina. At last the high-pitched cry cracked and broke into sobs. Tina reached down to pull Shani into her arms and the pair of them lay on the bed in a shuddering embrace.

There was silence. Tom wanted to move his position but he didn't dare. Then the girls began to whisper.

'I love you,' he heard Tina say and the singer mumbled something into her ear.

'No,' said Tina, 'please not now.'

'That's tough,' said Shani, 'because you got no choice,' and she got off the bed and walked towards the door. Tom had no idea what he would have done if she had taken a pace further but she didn't. She stood in front of a chest of drawers and pulled something from it. Then she unhooked her bra, spilling forth her big brown breasts, the nipples a bluish black, the dark circles of her areolae gleaming. She stepped out of her panties and dried herself with them between her legs. The thick black hair of her pussy was cropped short and the deep crease of her cunt split was fully on view. Then she strapped on the dummy penis.

Tom wondered later why he hadn't come in his pants - or maybe he had. His entire crotch seemed soaked yet his cock was as hard as a rock. As his shell-shocked brain devoured the incredible sight before him he wondered if it would ever go down again.

Despite her protests, Tina's eyes were wide with excitement as Shani returned to the bed. Shani found cream and Tina rubbed it onto the pink plastic truncheon thrusting from Shani's crotch.

'It's so big,' she said, anointing the gleaming tip. 'I'll never take all that.'

But she did and Tom could see that she loved the sensation as it disappeared up her hungry little snatch. From his position by the door he could savour every nuance of this unusual coupling: woman on woman, brown skin on white, heavy breasts crushed against swollen strawberry buds, black locks mingling with blonde - and the glistening dark ovals of Shani's buttocks rising and falling between Tina's slender white thighs, driving the plastic monster home to cries of mingled delight.

Tom had never seen two women making love before and the sight of it thrilled him to the core. It also gave him an idea.

The women sang their way to orgasm. One voice low and guttural, the other sweet and high-pitched. They balanced each other, the notes spiralling up the scale in harmony they fucked each other to ecstasy.

They were making so much noise there was little need of Tom to take precautions, nevertheless he tiptoed away. What he had to say to Shani could wait, in any case it needed refining in the light of what had just occurred to him. Right now he had to see Maeve urgently. Unless he buried his rock hard erection between her willing thighs soon he felt it would be with him for ever.

However, he didn't intend telling her how he had acquired such a passionate need.

As he closed the door of the flat behind him the women sang on, their duet far from its conclusion.

Chapter 20

Once Tom had sold his big idea to Shani he knew things would go according to plan. He'd always known she was ambitious but not until he'd seen her standing over Tina - that big pink dildo thrusting like a weapon from her loins, a fierce intensity burning in her face - had he realised that she was also ruthless. She had simply nodded when he explained what he wanted her to do. She didn't like it but she would do it. And God help him if it didn't work.

By a stroke of luck the Shagbags had landed a spot on a local TV magazine show *Newspoint Sou'-Sou' West* - the keyboard player's brother worked on the show as a researcher. Tom knew that no one would take any notice of a poxy three minutes on regional late-afternoon telly but that didn't matter. What did matter was what the papers would say the next morning. His original contact on the *Sunday Skunk* had now moved to the daily version. Tom made the call.

To Tom's way of thinking, Shani and the girls put on a sensational performance. The song was one of Christina's, moody and mellow and - the way Shani put it over - very sexy. Of course, Tom couldn't look at her without imagining the raw passion which she had displayed when making love. He pictured her big black-nippled breasts quivering and the broad ovals of her buttocks undulating as she thrust between Tina's pale thighs. The image had haunted his thoughts for days.

For the performance, Tom had insisted that Tina abandon her punk uniform. So now she wore a thin white shift that left her arms and shoulders bare and flowed around her long coltish body. She had also dropped the pretence that she could play the guitar, so now she stood to the side of the stage mouthing the chorus harmony into a microphone. To Tom's eye, she looked like a virgin sacrifice.

As the number moved to its climax, Shani took hold of Tina and pulled her to the centre of the stage. The contrast between them was exciting: the voluptuous black woman in leather side by side with the slim blonde maiden. They were singing into the same mike so their mouths were close. As Shani hit her last note she closed her lips over Tina's, holding the girl tight in an uninhibited kiss.

For Tina, there was no escape. Surprise flickered in her liquid brown eyes and then they closed as she surrendered to her lover's embrace. 'Soul Kissing' was the name of the song and that's what they did, mouths locked, tongues entwined, the bootlace thin strap of Tina's dress falling off her shoulder as Shani's arms crushed her with uncompromising fervour. Behind them the Shagbags played on into the fadeout and the producer held the shot tight on the two women eating each other alive before someone elbowed him in the ribs and he cut to a traffic report.

Tom had the next morning's edition of the *Daily Skunk* delivered to Chas Cross by messenger, together with another tape of Shani and the girls. On a slow news day, the paper had run a photo of Shani and Tina with their tongues down each other's throats across half the front page above the heading SHAGGED ROTTEN! The article read:

Move over Johnny Rotten! Punk rock moved into a new era yesterday when girl-group Shani and the Shagbags flaunted their deviant sexuality on television. Soon after two of their number kissed and pawed each other before an audience of millions, a spokesperson for the group said, 'We're taking music away from politics and putting it back where it belongs - in the bedroom. And if the bed is shared by two women, so what? We're not ashamed to say it's OK if girls want to shag each other. In fact, it's great!'

More followed inside, including the revelation that Tina was the runaway daughter of Professor Lionel Slack who had himself fled the country when he had been caught with his hand up his female students' skirts the previous year. There were provocative pictures of Shani, showing a ravine of glistening cleavage, and a shot of Tina which made her look about ten. A sanctimonious leader comment complained of falling standards of moral guidance provided by teachers. What pleased Tom most however was the reporter's conclusion:

If this kind of behaviour is designed to attract attention to the group's music, there is really no need for it. In the *Skunk's* opinion Shani is the most sensational new singing talent we have produced in years and her material is as strong as her voice. Our advice to these ambitious young women is - drop the stunts and get down to the recording studio. Quick!

As far as Tom was concerned, it couldn't have been better if he had written the copy himself.

It had the desired effect. The phone call he had been hoping for came at midday.

'All right, Tom,' said Chas Cross, 'exactly what kind of a deal are you looking for?'

Three - Arse for Art's Sake
Chapter 21

Cassie Crow had no doubt that *The Come-Again Lifestyle* was going to be a raging success. The kids at *Fragrant* were pulling out all the stops on the extracts and she had the book publishers - what a sad sack of wimps they were -

eating out of her hand. And Chastity Honeydew, the author, was due to fly in shortly from California to provide an exclusive interview and oversee the volunteer profiles.

Just one thing was bothering her - her own *Come-Again* regime. Under Philippe's gloriously rigid tutelage she had been busting her targets but for the past week the Frenchman had been ducking appointments. First he claimed to have a cold and now to have damaged his back.

'How?' she had demanded on receiving the news. 'You're built like a brick shithouse - don't tell me your plunger's bust.' When sincerely annoyed, Cassie's New South Wales origins tended to show.

The long and the short of it was that Cassie had been robbed of her very personal trainer and had to fall back on her own resources to make her targets. This had proved difficult. Though she womanfully massaged and kneaded, probed and stroked - with a full battery of sex aids - she found wanking hard work. She needed that ridiculous sausage of flesh that all males, no matter how cretinous, carried with them wherever they went. But what she did not need was the whole baggage of personal politics that inevitably accompanied the sausage. 'Gimme the toad without the whole,' was her philosophy these days.

Many times she had flicked through her bulging Filofax and lifted the phone to call some past or would-be lover and then thought better of it. She didn't have the time or the emotional energy. Damn that fornicating Frenchman!

Cassie was churning the situation over in her head as she jogged round the pond in the park. Philippe had insisted on early morning exercise as part of the regime and she had kept it up. She might be failing her POT but she was damned if she was going to develop one.

It was a beautiful day - an azure blue sky, a low sun slanting through the leaves, ducks and moorhens afloat on the green water without a care in the world. The air was clean and pure - except around a bench occupied by two scruffy erks who were chain-smoking in a toxic haze.

'Hey, this is a smoke-free zone,' yelled Cassie as she passed them for a second time. 'Why don't you stick your head in the oven? It's quicker,' she said on the third. Until a year ago Cassie had been a sixty-a-day girl and she had all the zeal of a convert.

Now she had their full attention. She could feel their eyes on the pump of her sun-browned thighs, on the twinkle of her buttocks in her tiny white shorts, on the rise and fall of her bosom as she bounded along the path. One of them, she noticed, was broad and muscular with tattoos on his bare arms, the other was blond, skinny and very young. The first had piercing blue eyes and the blond's were a liquid brown - she saw this when she plumped herself down between them at the end of her fourth circuit.

'Hi, guys,' she said. 'Great morning, isn't it?'

The one with blue eyes said something in a Glaswegian accent that took her a moment to decipher. Unscrambled, it was revealed as 'A great morning to fuck your big arse.'

She looked back at him steadily. 'Why don't you then?' she said.

He grinned, his teeth were big and white and his lips petal pink. Cassie's heart was pounding - and not just from her exertions.

He placed a large gnarled hand on her right breast and squeezed her tit. 'Give us a kiss,' he said but by the time she realised that's what it was his tongue was halfway down her throat.

She clung to his muscular torso, sucking on him. He pulled her T-shirt from her waistband and up to her neck. 'Let's see what you've got,' he muttered, yanking her sports bra upwards and spilling her big white breasts out into the sunlight.

'Bloody hell!' whispered the blond boy, his eyes out on stalks at this fabulous display. His Adam's apple bobbed in his long thin neck as he spoke.

'Touch me,' she said to him. 'Feel my tits. Pinch my nipples. Go on.'

As the boy's shaking hands closed on her, she shivered. This was more like it! She was acting like a mad slut and she didn't care.

The one with blue eyes was looking over to the other side of the pond. A middle-aged woman with a dog was slowly moving in their direction. She hadn't seen them yet.

Blue-eyes pulled the T-shirt down over her quivering tits, Blondie's fingers still cupping the big globes.

'You're a crazy bitch,' the Scot said. 'What's your game?'

Cassie had a hand in each of their laps, searching out the outline of their genitals beneath the denim of their jeans. There's a sausage to each cretin, she reminded herself as she found two taut bulges. Big sausages too.

'Take me somewhere and fuck me,' she said. 'You know you want to.' There was no doubt about that. Blondie's cock was twitching beneath her fingers. It would be fun to make him come in his pants if it wasn't such a waste.

'Let's take her with us, Jimbo,' said the blond boy. 'Please.'

Jimbo reflected for a moment. Cassie scratched a long nail across the hard baton of flesh trapped against his thigh.

'OK,' he said at last. 'We'll take her to the house.'

'What house?' she said, a note of caution sounding for the first time in her head.

'It's just by here, we're doing it up. The owner should have left by now so we'll be OK.'

Jimbo made her walk in front of them as they left the park and he kept up a commentary for the benefit of his young companion.

'She's a big lass, this one. Classy though. You're in for a treat. Look at those legs, Ally, firm and strong - I bet they could squeeze the life out of a man. What a way to go, eh?'

'Fantastic!' cried Ally. Cassie wondered if he was a virgin. 'She's got a good cunt on her too, you can tell by the gap at the top of her legs. If it's too wide then she'll be slack, no friction on your dick, you see. But that looks just about right, not too tight to strangle your tackle and broad enough in the hips to give you a good ride.'

'And her arse, Jimbo! Fantastic.'

Cassie swung her hips in an exaggerated fashion.

'Too right, chummy. I can't wait to climb on board.'

Cassie thrilled to the sound of these half-baked crudities. What arrogant pigs they were! If they didn't give her what she wanted maybe she'd hand them over to Claire Quartermain. Not that the TCD would bother with proles like these two.

They stopped in front of a terraced house festooned with scaffolding. The front door was open and a grizzled giant of about sixty was mixing plaster in a bucket.

'Where you bin?' he said when he caught sight of Jimbo and Ally. 'Mrs Shackleton wanted to talk to you but she had to go.' He addressed the Scot but his eyes were on Cassie.

'Good,' said Jimbo. 'This is Mrs Smith,' he added. 'She's come to look at how we're getting on. She's thinking of having a loft extension, aren't you, Mrs Smith?' He shot Cassie a meaningful look.

'That's right,' she said, playing along. 'Can I go in?' and she strode up the garden path without waiting for a reply. Jimbo and Ally fell in behind her, leaving the bemused giant to continue with his plaster.

'Don't worry about him,' said Jimbo, directing her up the stairs with a hand on her bottom, 'he's as thick as two short planks.'

On the walk to the house Cassie had worried about being ravished in a building site. It was one thing to have two eager roughs between your thighs in the heat of the moment, but quite another to spend the rest of the day pulling splinters out of your bum. She need not have worried. From what she could see the loft space was in building chaos, but the rest of the house was obviously lived in - presumably by Mrs Shackleton.

'In here,' said Jimbo, opening a door on the first-floor landing and pushing Cassie into a large and comfortable bedroom. The big bed dominated the space, the cream bedspread and blue duvet calling out to be tumbled on. But the two men were all over Cassie already, Ally grinding his pelvis into her buttocks and Jimbo pulling her tits into the open. They showed all the signs of wanting to fuck her standing up.

'Put me on the bed,' she ordered as their hands plucked at her clothes. God, it was marvellous to be stripped naked by these two horny brutes! She didn't make it easy for them, only lifting her arms when she feared they would tear her T-shirt from her body.

The three of them toppled onto the bed. There were four hands and two mouths upon her, Jimbo's unshaven chin was rough on the tender skin of her breasts. She shivered with pleasure. She'd never had two men at her before. She was going to savour every moment.

The men had their cocks out now. The stiff poles of flesh were rubbing against her hips and belly. Maybe now was the time to impose some order.

'I want the boy first,' she said firmly, pushing Jimbo away. The Scot backed off, seeing the sense in what she said.

Ally's tool stood out from his body, the long pink shaft pulsing, the helmet a blood-engorged purple. It was obvious he might explode at any moment.

Cassie spread her legs for him and threaded the quivering member inside her. She was running with juice. It was like plunging a brush into a glue pot. He sank down on her and stuck fast. She scissored her thighs over his back, holding him deep inside.

His tongue was in her mouth and his fingers were everywhere, exploring the satin opulence of her nakedness. They fluttered from her hips to her bottom cheeks to the rounds of her bosom flattened against his bony chest. He thrust his pelvis against her, sending the long needle of his penis deep into her hungry vagina. 'Oh!' she heard herself cry. 'Oh, yes please.'

But he couldn't last long enough for her. Not that she cared for she pushed his slim body from her almost before he had finished spunking and reached for her other lover.

Jimbo bulled into her without mercy, taking his broad stubby cock all the way back and then plunging into her again, his strong hands ransacking the cheeks of her arse, using them as a lever to thrust and power his lust into her. He didn't keep going long either but that didn't matter to Cassie. She shrieked as he shot deep inside her, taking her over the edge.

She lay back on the pillows between the two of them while they recovered. She held a limp cock in each hand and her big breasts heaved in time with her short breaths. Ally was gazing with longing at her swollen raspberry nipples and she pulled his head down to suckle at her chest. His penis was once more erect.

'What now, lover?' she said to Jimbo, whose thick cock was also showing signs of recovery.

'I'm going to teach my young friend here how to suck pussy,' he replied, sliding down Cassie's body until his head rested on her upper thigh. He ran an exploratory finger through her auburn-haired bush and between her swollen pink labia. The touch was surprisingly gentle and sent an electric tingle echoing through her loins.

'Now see here,' he said to a wide-eyed Ally, 'this is what's called the clitoris and if you just tickle here with your tongue, like this...'

'Oh yes,' muttered Cassie between clenched teeth, regretting some of her earlier disparaging thoughts about the male sex. Maybe these cretins knew a thing or two after all.

Chapter 22

For a smart woman, Marianne Matthews was sometimes a bit slow on the uptake. And so, when she once said to a girlfriend, 'To me, sex is just a tool,' and the friend burst out laughing, Marianne was perplexed. To her, sex *was* just a tool, a means to an end. True, she often enjoyed it and she subscribed to the theory that regular orgasm was good for the health, like a daily bowel movement, but she didn't much like doing it unless she had good reason.

For one thing, it was often inconvenient. Why spend hours selecting an outfit, putting on make-up, arranging the hair just so - when five minutes of furious body contact with a man with no appreciation of these things left you looking like an unmade bed? For two pins, Marianne wouldn't have bothered in the first place - especially when it left you riding the lift in the Black Raven Television skyscraper with what felt like half a pint of spunk running out of your knickers.

But there were always reasons why she had to spread her legs for a man. She wasn't so fabulously good-looking or intellectually devious that the important doors in life would open for her otherwise. She was a pretty girl with a throaty voice and slim hips who came from a middle-class home in Ruislip. Her father was an overweight accountant with a firm hand on the till who had lectured her about self-sufficiency even as he refused to help her with her maths homework. The young Marianne knew that if she was to have a flat in Knightsbridge, a wardrobe full of designer clothes and a red Mercedes runabout then she would have to stand on her own two feet. Or lie on her back.

Of late she had lain down much less frequently and, another gratifying factor in her recent success, with more attractive patrons. When she had first stepped out from drama school (daddy had paid for that - 'And it's the thing I'm paying for,' he'd told her) she'd wasted a lot of time bonking the wrong types: penniless actors and seedy directors who lost interest once their cocks had crowed. She'd had to fall back on one of her father's colleagues for the deposit on her mortgage. And though Uncle Harry was pasty and gross he was pitifully generous - he had no choice, Marianne would have had no qualms about telling her father. Then she bedded a senior producer at the BBC, earned some exposure on children's programmes and she was on her way.

Her capture of Tom Glass last year after a TV awards dinner was her crowning achievement - she'd given him a blow-job behind a potted palm in the hotel ballroom and then refused his calls for a week. It had been a high-risk strategy but it had paid off and now she only had to foreclose on his promise of marriage and she could start thinking in terms of mansions in the country, custom-made Versace outfits and a Ferrari or two in the garage.

So why was it she had allowed Gerald Gin-sling, or whatever his name was, Head of Arts Production at Black Rave to put her over his executive desk and mess up her fine silk underwear? Though he was slim and stylish, with clever lips and hands, it couldn't have been his sex appeal - she knew herself too well. There had to be another reason. Such as insurance.

The fact was that this bloody accident of Tom's had thrown all her plans into the melting pot. Every time she went to see him, first at the hospital and now at this country nursing home, she had the feeling he didn't know who she was. They made love, of course - these days he was randier than ever - but there was something funny about him. And about that blonde slut of a nurse who was always by his side, her cow eyes following his every move. Marianne knew what that look meant. And though she didn't much care if Tom fucked her fat arse to pass the time, she did care if her rich and powerful fiancé had conveniently forgotten his existing commitments.

Even more worrying, suppose he was brain-damaged? He could turn into a cabbage at any time. And if he became a vegetable before she popped a wedding certificate into her deposit box then she really would need some insurance.

She took a paper tissue from her handbag and dabbed at a dribble of spunk beneath her skirt. God, that Gerald had been a bull! Her pussy was still throbbing with the size of him.

She couldn't deny that Tom had kept his promise to put in a word for her with Black Raven. When Marianne had first encountered Gerald the previous week he was obviously unhappy about it. As a decisive young executive with a mind of his own he didn't like to be told what to do. Yet the word had come down from on high: the Badger TV weather girl had to be taken seriously. And as an ambitious young executive who knew where his next expenses cheque was coming from, he did as he was told. It didn't stop him being snotty.

'You do realise that *Gravitas* is an *arts* programme, don't you, Miss Matthews? It's not a sing-song for kiddywinkies or a weather forecast. This is an eyewitness report of cultural trench warfare. A bulletin from the cutting edge. Who's in, who's out, what's hot, what's going to define the aesthetic map for the thinking man and woman in the weeks ahead. Forgive me, Miss Matthews, but it seems to me that we need someone with more *weight* than your CV suggests you possess.'

Marianne had smiled at him. She had a very effective smile. 'I'd heard you were thinking of Henrietta Suckling,' she said throatily.

'In my opinion, Henry has just the right mixture of intellectual credibility and professional skill to cut across boundaries and subject the arts community to the microscope of rigorous critical scrutiny.'

'If you ask me,' said Marianne, though he hadn't, 'she's been around the block too many times. And if you want weight just look at her thighs. Mine, as you can see, are half the size.'

Maybe that was the point at which sex crept into the interview. Marianne should not really have played the sex card, it was unnecessary. On the other hand it was all she knew and it worked. Gerald's pale blue eyes had dropped to her lap and her long slender legs. They had strayed there on a regular basis throughout that first meeting. Nevertheless he had continued to do his best to resist her.

'Really, Miss Matthews, don't you think those kind of personal observations are a trifle *de trop?* We are appealing to the life of the intellect here. We need a presenter who can command respect from every corner of the aesthetic spectrum.'

'So why choose one who's best known for chocolate commercials? Look, Gerald,' and here Marianne leaned forward to place a small elegant hand on his knee, 'it seems to me that you need a fresh approach. You want fast finger-on-the-pulse stuff with lots of action and - I hate to say it - sex appeal. Henrietta was great in her day but her tits have gone.'

'What!' Gerald was outraged.

'It's true. Don't say you haven't noticed. Her neck's got all scrawny and her boobs have slipped. Look at her on screen.'

Gerald regarded her with a tight little smile. 'You're a tough cookie, aren't you, Miss Matthews?'

Marianne grinned. She liked her qualities to be recognised. She took a folder from her briefcase. 'I thought you might like to see a few of my ideas. Issues, discussion topics, studio guests - that kind of thing.'

Gerald meekly took the folder. Somehow they were going to proceed on her agenda. 'Just don't forget, Gerald, if you want youth, drive, ideas - and tits that are self-supporting - that's what I'm selling. Right?'

And Gerald, his eyes now glued to the points of her nipples pressing through the cornflower blue silk of her blouse, muttered, 'Absolutely.'

That had been a week ago and things had moved on swiftly from then. Marianne had taken part in a studio run-through and been introduced to the company hierarchy. How much was down to Tom and how much to her own charms she wasn't sure but she knew she was in. Lunch and the afternoon session with Gerald had confirmed it. It hadn't been absolutely necessary to let him stick his big penis into the hairless clam between her legs but she suspected that she owed him one. Wherever else he might now be inserting his truncheon she'd bet it wasn't between the plump thighs of Henrietta Suckling - not any more.

Actually, fucking Gerald had passed an enjoyable hour, considering it wasn't one of her favourite pastimes. She'd sat on the edge of his vast desk and he'd knelt at her feet, licking upwards from her toes, nibbling and tickling the soft skin on the inside of her long white thighs.

He'd gasped in awe at the sight of her denuded pussy, the pretty pink lips spread invitingly, the candied interior bubbling with juice.

'How divine,' he'd cried and Marianne had quickly jammed his lips down into her crotch before he could embark on one of his claptrappy speeches about worship and goddesses. He'd worshipped at the sticky shrine all right, drinking down her juice and licking her from clit to anus and back again until she screamed and came on his face until she felt quite faint.

Even though she'd had enough by then, she could hardly refuse him the pleasure of revealing what lay behind the big bulge in the trousers of his Paul

Smith suit. To be truthful, she'd been quite impressed by the sight of the swollen shaft he'd pulled from his pants and pressed into her small hand. She'd taken the big red head between her lips and sucked on it a bit to show willing. And when he'd shot off unexpectedly she'd swallowed all his come juice as fast as she could to avoid tasting it, even though it was something she never did. Now she was the presenter of *Gravitas*, Black Raven's flagship arts programme, she knew she could hardly afford to appear squeamish.

Since Gerald had come so unexpectedly without the benefit of sliding his tool into the hairless nook between her long legs and since she'd promised him, more or less, that she wouldn't leave until he'd done so, she let him strip her to the waist and suck on her firm pear-shaped breasts until her pointy nipples stuck up like bright red thumbs. To hurry things along, she'd placed his thickening tool between her soft white orbs and rubbed and rocked him till it looked like he was about to shoot all over her chest. In fact he was keen to do it but she'd said 'No, next time, right now I want it up my cunt!' which was really just for his benefit, to get him worked up he'd put it in her and get it over quickly.

In fact it had taken quite a while, he must have been holding back, savouring this unique opportunity, and so she'd had to talk to him a lot, whispering a string of obscenities into his ear about how she loved big cocks, especially *his* big cock, he could put it in her any time he liked, up her pussy and her mouth and between her tits and maybe if he was good, and she was sure he would be, up her arsehole which would be *so* tight around his fat cock that he'd spunk spunk and spunk inside her. And then he had and she'd come off again too, just to keep him company, and here she was leaning against the lift door with that same spunk dribbling down her legs, wondering how she was ever going to make it to the street to find a taxi.

'Excuse me, *mademoiselle*, but are you all right? You are looking very pale.'

The man was looming over her, his chest as broad as the door, it seemed, threatening to burst out of his jacket and tie. He wore tortoise-shell spectacles and an expression of touching concern. But it was his French accent that instantly captivated Marianne, wiping all thought of Gerald from her mind.

How wonderful it would be, she thought, to collapse into those big strong arms. So that's what she did.

Chapter 23

Cassie was delighted. Thanks to the efforts of her two lusty builders she had made up her arrears on the Honeydew regime and, so she calculated, was now turning her orgasm account into the black. If she could just manage a few more decent comes then she'd be ahead of schedule.

Jimbo and Ally, however, were running out of steam. Their cocks were limp and their faces were drained. Given half a chance, Cassie could see, they'd pull up the duvet and go to sleep. Well, she wasn't having any of that. It was time to be a little more inventive.

'Give me your hand,' she said to Jimbo. He looked at her glassy-eyed but did not protest as she placed his hairy paw between her legs.

'Look, Mrs,' he said, 'it's been great but Ally and I should be getting back to work.'

'Not yet,' she said, 'you wouldn't want to miss this.' And she daubed Jimbo's fingers in the goo that was running from her overflowing hole.

'Miss what?' said Ally, eyeing the slick motion of his friend's fingers on her slippery flesh.

'Well...' Cassie looked as demure as she could in the circumstances. 'I'm a bit embarrassed to say.'

'What is it?' Ally's cock was up now. It looked a little raw and tender but it was the penis of an eighteen-year-old sex-obsessed youth. Something mysterious and horny was going on and Ally's cock wanted in. Whatever it was.

Cassie leaned over to Jimbo and whispered in his ear. 'You're a right randy cow, aren't you?' he muttered but a large grin was already spreading across his face.

'What do you think?' she said, her free hand now pulling the thick barrel of Jimbo's tool. 'Are you up to it?'

He didn't answer in so many words but instead hauled her on top of him, crushing the length of her against his muscular frame and pushing his tongue down her throat.'

'What's going on?' demanded Ally, but they were too busy to answer him.

As they kissed, Cassie positioned Jimbo's swollen cock between her legs, driving the fat shaft deep into her hot and hungry vagina. And Jimbo's square builder's hands were on her big satiny buttocks, pulling the firm cheeks apart.

Ally gazed in awe at the bulging bottom flesh and the pink star of her anus so obscenely revealed to him.

'It's all yours, son,' said Jimbo. 'Put your cock up her arse... She wants you to.'

Between the great rounds of Cassie's bottom her rear hole seemed to pucker in invitation. At the base of the buttock divide Ally could see the root of Jimbo's pulsing tool, his testicles rolling between his hairy thighs as he plumbed the depths of her vagina. A strangled croak came from Ally's lips. He had never seen anything so rude in his life.

'What are you waiting for?' said Jimbo gruffly, circling Cassie's rear dimple with a blunt finger. He sank the digit in to the first knuckle and the pale moons of her bottom seemed to convulse at the sensation. 'Look, she's dying for it.'

'Please,' said Cassie, 'I want you both together. Put it in me, Ally. Hurry!'

Ally did as he was told. He was clumsy and in truth the position was difficult but Cassie didn't care. She was coming like clockwork now, even as he rubbed spit into her arse crack and the head of his tool bobbed between her cheeks. She'd not bum-fucked much before, only with an Australian boyfriend years back and he'd been a brute with a cock like a cucumber. This was different. Ally's penis was long but thin and the moment his glans rubbed against her she seemed to suck it directly into her bowels.

It was a strange feeling at first, uncomfortable rather than painful. Then his cock was all the way in and his weight was upon her, crushing her into the man beneath. It was as if an electric circuit had been completed, sending a current of sexual energy zinging through the three of them.

They fell into a natural rhythm, Jimbo's thick prick thrusting Cassie back onto Ally's thin tool which in turn pushed her back down onto Jimbo. They fell onto their sides and fucked on without a pause, the men's cocks fencing with each other within her guts, their hands fondling and squeezing and stroking her shameless flesh. She lost count of the number of times she came. It was bliss.

They didn't pause when the bedside telephone rang. They didn't even break stride when the door burst open and the giant plasterer stood over them, his big face beet red. He stared at them for fully a minute, literally struck dumb.

Ally couldn't hold out any longer. With a cry he thrust and twitched and rolled over onto his back, and lay as still as a log.

A great hand descended on him, yanking him from the bed and dumping him on the floor.

'That's Mrs Shackleton on the phone,' said the giant. 'You deal with her while I take over.'

Up to this point Cassie had hardly registered the fourth party's presence. Now she was aware that this Neanderthal brute was stripping off his clothes.

'Hey,' she said somewhat feebly, trying to pull herself away from Jimbo. But the builder's arms were round her like a vice and his loins were still buffeting hers.

'We were just warming her up for you, Doug,' she heard Jimbo say as the bed suddenly sagged from the weight of another human being - a very large human being. 'Honest.' But it seemed Doug wasn't interested in recriminations at present. He was interested in making up for lost time.

Cassie was plucked from Jimbo's embrace and rolled onto her back. Her eyes bulged as she took in the vast naked frame looming over her. He was covered in hair and from the hearth rug of his belly thrust a penis that turned her mouth to ashes. Forget cucumbers, this man-mountain had a baseball bat.

Ally picked up the phone by the bed.

'What's your real name, Mrs Smith?' Doug said as he pushed a finger as big as a carrot between the tender lips of her weeping pussy.

'Cassie,' she whispered.

'There's no problem, Mrs Shackleton,' said Ally into receiver.

'Well, Cassie, I'm sorry to tell you but I'm about to change your life.'

'Oh no.'

'Oh yes,' Doug said, lining up his outsize member. The head lodged between her legs like a ruby-red tennis ball. 'I'm going to ruin you for other men.' And he pushed his tennis ball home.

Cassie cried out, on the brink of the biggest orgasm of her life.

'I promise you, Mrs Shackleton,' said Ally, 'there's no slacking on the job. I guarantee we're giving it everything we've got.'

Chapter 24

Professionally speaking, Philippe was immune to feminine charm. In the course of his work as a trainer in the Honeydew technique he had attended to dozens of women in the most intimate of situations. All of these clients were monied and groomed, and many of them were very personable indeed. He laboured over their waxed and pampered bodies, bringing them to the peak of physical condition through the power of orgasm. Without fail, the clients fell in love with him, or at least with his magnificent physique, his skilful fingers, his magic tongue - and the glorious *baguette* between his legs which urged them towards their Personal Orgasm Targets so divinely. But at the end of each session, resisting every blandishment, Philippe would simply tuck away his breadstick and disappear as swiftly as a glass of *vin rouge* down a *routier's* throat. For the women he left behind, lying glassy-eyed in post-orgasmic stupor, he had no further thought until the next session.

But Philippe was not a Honeydew trainer every waking moment of his life. In fact, despite what he had been telling his ever-demanding clients like Cassie Crow, he was currently taking time off to pursue one or two other possibilities of employment. Extraordinary as it may sound, shagging gorgeous women all day long was not this Frenchman's preferred way to make a living.

And so, when he encountered Marianne Matthews in the lift of the Black Raven TV building, he was not thinking like a professional in orgasm achievement. In the unfamiliar surroundings of the TV HQ - where he had hopes of making a career change - he was in a susceptible state of mind. He noticed that the slim blonde with endless legs and slate-grey eyes was supporting herself against the door. She seemed distracted and the distress in her face was clear. Philippe was surprised to find himself asking if she was all right. Then, as the lift hit the ground floor and the doors opened, somehow she was propelled into his arms. He held her fast.

He virtually carried her into the street and it seemed only natural for him to climb into the taxi alongside her. When they arrived at her flat he made her lie on the sofa while he poured her a brandy and ran her a bath. He wouldn't let her, do a thing - he even stripped off her clothes and put her in the soapy water. It was strange, they'd hardly exchanged ten words and they'd known each other less than forty minutes, but this behaviour seemed entirely acceptable. Of course, ministering to naked beauties in need was Philippe's stock in trade, but this situation was different. This beauty wasn't paying him and he was looking after her because he wanted to. As he soaped her high, pointed breasts he felt a glow of satisfaction.

When he'd undressed her he'd noticed the signs of recent love-making on her body - the fresh bruising on her apple-cheeked buttocks, her red distended nipples, and the goo that had dried on her thighs and was still seeping from her intriguingly shaved pussy. These things didn't bother him, though they made him curious. Any man would have been curious.

'Philippe,' she said. She had a delightful voice, he thought, low and throaty, so unlike the shrill harpies who usually laid siege to his body. 'I can't believe I'm letting you do this to me.'

'Relax,' he said. 'My vocation is tending to the needs of the body. You should consider me as a doctor. Your personal doctor.'

She giggled and her breasts shook. Philippe, who had seen as many quivering knockers in the past year as the director of the *Folies Bergere*, was mesmerised by this delicious exhibition.

'You've washed that breast three times, *doctor*. Don't forget the other one.'

Philippe found himself blushing. He never blushed - something extraordinary must be happening to him. He was also massively erect, with seminal fluid leaking from his swollen glans into the cotton of his briefs. As a Honeydew practitioner he had come to regard his penis as just another fitness aid - like a set of weights or an exercise cycle. These days he never had an orgasm with women and he achieved erection only by a trained effort of will. But right now he felt as if he might shoot off at any moment. Amazing!

'You are a very beautiful woman,' he heard himself say.

She sipped her brandy and rested her head on the side of the bath. 'Tell me more,' she said and closed her eyes...

The alcohol and the warm water made her drowsy. The Frenchman's wonderful voice ravished her senses like an orchestra in full flow.

Yoo are a vair byootifool wooman. I wursheep yore boday... Men had said these things to her before but not in fractured English with all the intensity of a Jacques Brel song.

Wiz yore pairmishun I keess yoo ere on ze and... zen on ze arm like zis...

Marianne was in heaven. She had just nailed down the job of her dreams and in a few minutes, she had no doubt, she would be nailed herself by a new lover. A French lover, what's more.

...and on ze nick... and on yore leely wite trote - formidable!

She'd had an Italian once, a film director who'd mangled an aria from Tosca before 'auditioning' her in his hotel suite. But naturally the fat bastard hadn't cast her.

...and zee teets, so firrm, so jolie, I keess zem all ovair like zis...

And there'd been any number of anally retentive Englishmen, dry-as-toast Scots and drunken Celts. All of them more in love with themselves than her. Not to mention the married German director who'd made her pay the hotel bill on their one weekend together and pocketed the receipt.

...and zees wundairful neeples... so peenk, so adorable, zay stand up like

leetle soldjairs...

But now she was going to have a real French lover.

I keess yore leeps... mmm... yoo taste like champagne... At last a man of her own choosing whom she would fuck for fun not advancement.

Ze watair eez getting colt, cherie. Shall we go into zee bedroom?

Philippe deposited her, swathed in a large towel, on the bed next door, carrying her as easily as if she were a small child. She watched with wide eyes as he undressed, awestruck at the incredible physique that was unveiled before her.

Philippe was used to women's eyes on his body, particularly those of his Honeydew clients. He would feel their hot and greedy glances on his skin, crawling across his mighty pectorals, up his thighs and down his belly. Cannibal stares, hungry for his flesh, they devoured him wherever he went.

But now, unbuckling his trouser belt, he felt only pride under the searchlight of Marianne's curiosity. For once he wanted a woman as much as she wanted him. It was a new experience. He let his trousers fall.

'Oh my God,' muttered Marianne beneath her breath. Philippe made Arnold Schwarzenegger look like a stick of celery.

Naturally her gaze was locked on Philippe's crotch, where the head of his penis stuck up above the waistband of his bulging underpants. The straining white cotton was wet with juice and the protruding glans was purple with desire.

For me, thought Marianne. *He's in that state all because of me!* She extended a slender arm and yanked down the elastic waist of his briefs.

His liberated tool branched upwards from his loins as firm and solid as the bough of a tree. She grasped it with both hands and fed the glistening head between her lips.

Philippe grunted with surprise as she thrust as much of him as she could into her face. He tried to switch his mind into Honeydew mode and think objectively, to observe the nature of physical response when the body is aroused. To consider the reactions of nerve endings as merely connections in an electric circuit. To analyse cold-bloodedly the cause and effect of sexual stimuli...

But it was no good. The sight of that mop of silver-blonde hair bobbing against his belly, the knowledge that this elegant grey-eyed beauty was gorging on his cock and the feel of her hot lips on his pulsating stem was too much. With a howl of joy he shot a river of spunk straight down her throat. It was the first time he'd come inside a woman for nearly a year.

Marianne clamped her mouth over him tight as he exploded, drinking down his cream, determined not to miss a drop. She reflected that this was the second time that day she'd swallowed a man's load. Maybe she was getting to like it after all. Today was turning out to be full of surprises.

But the best surprise of all was yet to come for Marianne Matthews, the girl who regarded sex as one of life's necessary evils. When Philippe pressed his dark-cropped head into the fork of her slender thighs she discovered she was in the hands - and tongue and lips - of a cunnilingual expert. She was already on her way to her first orgasm when the phone rang.

'I have a call for you from Gerald Goldring,' said a bored female voice.

Gerald who? wondered Marianne as small ripples of sensation flickered through her belly. Oh *him* - the other guy she'd sucked off today. Her new boss.

'Hello, darling,' came his oily voice down the line. 'I've been thinking we ought to meet up tonight.'

'Why?' said Marianne, pulling Philippe's face closer into her crotch.

'I've been telling Sir Charles Mastiff what a find you are and he's desperate to meet you. Eight o'clock at The Mount Morris Grand. He keeps a suite there when he's in town.'

Philippe's tongue was like a warm and friendly snake. It was deep inside her, titillating all the pleasure points on the way to ecstasy.

'Sorry, Gerald, I can't. I'm not working tonight for anybody.'

A note of anger crept into Gerald's polished tone. 'Look, Marianne, Sir Charles is the man who allocates the budget. I've told him how sensational you are in all *sorts* of ways. No one says no to Sir Charles.'

'Tom Glass might,' said Marianne, getting irritated now. 'My husband-to-be, if you recall.' Why couldn't this prat get off the phone and let her concentrate on what Philippe was now doing to her clit?

'Well, Glass might indeed but I hear he's off his trolley and out of commission. Get real, Marianne, you can't afford to say no. Your contract's not signed yet.'

Marianne breathed an anguished sigh, the rising tide of excitement suspended for a moment. Philippe sensed her change of mood. He kissed her thigh gently and ran a comforting hand up her spine.

'OK,' she said, 'I'll see you there.' She twitched her pelvis in the Frenchman's face, urging him to resume his caresses. He began to eat her out in earnest.

'Excellent,' brayed Gerald. 'By the way, I hope you haven't forgotten your promise.'

'What?' Why wouldn't this idiot hang up? She couldn't hold back much longer.

'Your pretty little arse, my darling. I'm on fire already just thinking about it. You'll let me fuck it, won't you?'

'Oh God!' shrieked Marianne as the riptide of orgasm raced through her. 'Oh yes, yes, YES!'

'I'll look forward to it then,' said Gerald and hung up.

Philippe crawled up the bed and wrapped her in his arms. He rocked her gently and stroked her hair while she recovered her breath. By reflex she put her hand on his penis. It was like an iron bar stretching across his belly. 'So you're engaged to be married,' he said softly.

'Philippe, darling,' she said, absent-mindedly stroking his shaft, 'before we get carried away, I think we should have a serious talk.'

Chapter 25

Whatever the rumours, and the tabloids were full of them, Tom Glass had not come off his trolley - though sometimes he felt as if he might. It was nearly a month now since he had fallen into the street and lost control of his life. And though he was getting back to normal he knew the whole process was taking too long. He was still unable to run his business empire and he was the subject of some kind of crazy prosecution by the fanatic females of the Sex Police.

Thank God for Eve, he thought for the umpteenth time as he sipped his afternoon tea on the patio of Spilling Grange. She had devoted herself to him completely since his accident, sleeping by his side at the hospital in London and accompanying him to this luxurious nursing home in the Leicestershire countryside.

In front of him stretched a green expanse of lawn laid out with croquet hoops and beyond lay a meadow full of grazing sheep where bunnies romped at twilight. Around the old house curved a rippling trout stream which meandered away into thick woods crisscrossed with sun-dappled paths ideal for the strolling convalescent with a few hours to kill. It was idyllic but Tom wasn't fooled. Sooner or later each path came to a halt at the fence, ten foot high and topped with barbed wire. Guards with dogs patrolled at night. Every visitor was checked in and out at a security barrier. This was Spandau Spilling and Tom was Rudolf Hess.

So thank God for Eve, he said to himself again as he watched her walk across the lawn, a spray of freshly gathered wild flowers in her hand. She was a tall, sturdy girl and she looked good in a country setting. The starched white blouse of her nurse's uniform was stretched tight across her jiggling bust and her strong firm thighs undulated beneath the navy blue of her skirt as she strode towards him. He knew, from the memories that had returned to him, that he wouldn't have fancied her in his past life. He would have dismissed her as too big and gauche, not 'sophisticated' enough for him. But now he knew better. He appreciated every glorious inch.

Of course it was all bound up in his returning memories. The process of reclaiming his past was somehow all about sex. Each snapshot of his personal history framed a woman in his bed or on the floor or in the garden or, well, almost anywhere. And not just one woman, either, there had been many, in all sorts of combinations. And each of these encounters had plunged him back in time as if on some erotic Tardis. The dreams had seemed more real than the first time around - if that were possible. He didn't understand it. He found it frightening. Particularly because he didn't much like the person who was revealed to him this way. He told Eve as much, each time he woke from a trip into his past. He'd cling to her and confess and she'd absolve him with her understanding words, her loving smile and her magnificent, opulent body. Thank God indeed for Eve.

'Oh Tom,' she said as she arranged her posy of flowers amongst the tea-time crockery. 'Look at you!'

He realised she was looking at his crotch. He grinned a sheepish grin. His cock was sticking out of the fly of his pyjamas, the stalk stiff, the helmet gleaming red. 'You've been thinking about your old girlfriends again, haven't you?'

'No,' he said truthfully, 'I've been thinking about you. Come here.'

'Oh no, Tom, not now,' she protested even as she stepped close enough to his chair for him to slide his hand up her smooth thigh.

'You're not wearing any knickers,' he said, parting the fluffy hair of her bush with his fingers and exploring the frill of her labia.

'You asked me not to.' She gave a little moan as his fingers circled her clitoris.

'Why not?' He lifted the hem of her skirt with his other hand so he could see her pussy as he toyed with it.

'So you could feel me any time, you said.'

Her cunt was like a flower, he thought, lifting its head to the sun and opening its petals. Her fragrance filled his nostrils. 'You're not wearing a bra either, are you?'

'You know I'm not. You forbade me. So you can watch my tits bounce, you said.' His fingers were sticky with her juice now. They made a squidgy sound as he slipped them in and out of her slick vagina.

'I was watching them sway as you walked towards me across the field. They seem to move about of their own accord. As if they've got a life of their own.'

'They're too big.' She was rocking backwards and forwards from the hips, as if trying to capture his entire hand in her snatch. He held his fingers still and watched her movements quicken.

'Take them out,' he said. 'Take off your blouse so I can see them properly.'

'Oh no, Tom, please. Someone might be watching.' Despite her protests her fingers were already unfastening the buttons. She slipped the blouse from her shoulders and dropped it on the floor. 'There. Satisfied?'

They probably were too big, Tom reflected, even for her substantial build. The huge white globes quivered in the sunlight, slung halfway to her waist. What made them seem even larger was the smallness of her nipples, tiny rose-pink buttons thrusting out from the centre of the dimpled saucers of her areolae.

'I think they're magnificent,' said Tom, his voice hoarse with desire. 'Play with them for me.'

'Tom!'

'Lift them up and squeeze them. Wobble them around. You know what I like, Eve.'

She did indeed. Her cheeks flushed bright pink but she did as she was told. She shivered her shoulders and set the great tits dancing from side to side. She took a breast in each hand, cupping them, lifting the weight of flesh upwards and then letting them fall in a pink and white shimmer. Without being asked, she lifted first one breast, then the other to her mouth, bending her head so that she could suck and tease the tiny nipple into a scarlet point. And all the while her pelvis thrust back and forth as she humped shamelessly on Tom's fingers.

'God, Tom Glass, you're a beast,' she hissed, pinching her nipples with her fingers. 'You really bring out the tart in me.' Her bottom lip was swollen and her eyes were half shut.

Her thick fair hair had come loose from its ponytail and now danced around her head in a blonde cloud.

'You're no tart,' he said. 'You're a magnificent, horny woman. You do it because you love it, don't you?'

'Oh yes,' she cried as he leant forward and placed his lips over her vagina. She thrust her loins onto his mouth. A plump buttock in each hand, he lapped at her eager cunt. She ground herself to ecstasy on his face, moaning, 'Oh yes indeed oh gosh oh Christ YES!!'

The orgasm slowly drained away leaving her weak and delirious. She rested her weight on his shoulders, his head still buried beneath her skirt. She felt exhausted and light-headed - especially as she knew she'd have little time to recover before he'd want to bury his burning erection somewhere in her tingling body.

She supposed he was right, she did love it. But she knew she was indeed a tart. After all, someone - not Tom - was paying her.

Chapter 26

'They're at it like rabbits down there, guv,' said Sergeant Amy Tooth as she looked towards the rear of Spilling Grange from a window in the west wing.

Inspector Claire Quartermain stood up from her seat across the desk from Dr Madeleine Flint and joined her junior colleague.

'My, my,' she said as she took in the sight of Nurse Eve Biscuit wriggling half naked on the fingers of patient Tom Glass, 'they don't care, do they?'

'They think they're on their own,' said Dr Flint.

'Obviously,' said Claire.

'Cor, look at those knockers swing,' enthused Amy. 'If she belts him round the head with those he'll never get his memory back.'

'That'll do,' said Claire, administering a severe pinch to her subordinate's left buttock out of Madeleine's sight. 'Though that would be a nasty setback, wouldn't it, doctor? All of this is taking long enough as it is.'

The doctor's mouth compressed to a thin line. 'As you know, Inspector, you cannot accelerate the healing process.'

'Can't you?' The policewoman turned to face her. 'I thought that's exactly what you were doing. You said you could speed up his recovery with your wonder drug. You promised me you'd slip him some extra.'

Madeleine Flint sighed. 'I did increase the dosage, it's true, but I'm not sure the result isn't counterproductive.'

'What do you mean?'

'I mean that the more he takes, the more he remembers.

Instead of just recalling the significant sexual moments of his life and using them as stepping stones to recovery, he's now reliving many insignificant encounters as well.'

Claire Quartermain cursed. 'You mean he now remembers every time he got his leg over with one of his pop singers fifteen years ago?'

'Not every time.'

'Just as well, eh, guv?' said Amy. 'We'll be drawing our pensions by the time he's finished otherwise.'

Claire shot her a look of pure venom. It was all very well for Amy to laugh, she didn't have Gossamer Hawk breathing down her neck. Yesterday's meeting with the Prosecutor was too fresh an encounter for Claire to find the present situation amusing.

Gossamer had laid matters on the line. The recently established Primrose Court had not found universal favour - which wasn't much of a surprise in Claire's opinion, though she did not venture it. Too many of its victims had been nonentities: middle managers with wandering palms, dinosaurs on the verge of retirement who weren't worth reforming, and so on. What was required, according to Gossamer, was the public vilification of a youthful captain of industry. Put a man like Glass in the dock, she had said, and you put The Primrose Court on the map.

As things stood they could probably stitch Glass up with no problems. However there was no point in bringing to book a politically incorrect business mogul when he had no memory of his crimes. 'We're not Stalinists,' Gossamer had said when Claire had ventured to suggest that it didn't matter what Glass remembered. 'We must expose the whole man in all his ghastly chauvinism and force him to recant. Then we'll make a real impact on the male bastions of power.'

This kind of talk made Claire uncomfortable. She was just a pragmatic policewoman and she'd go a long way to avoid starry-eyed idealists like Gossamer. Unfortunately Gossamer had a lot of clout. A zealot with power - just who you didn't want for a boss. And right now she was demanding Tom Glass's nuts on a platter.

'So how much does he remember now?' said Claire to Madeleine.

The doctor consulted her notes. 'He's just taken over Chas Cross's company, Euphoria, and become a millionaire at the age of twenty-four.'

'Blimey,' said Amy, 'how did he manage that?'

'Shani and the Shagbags had six number ones in a year and two platinum albums. Euphoria had been in trouble and the company had such desperate cash-flow problems they couldn't pay Glass his royalties on time. Cross let Glass buy him out.'

'With his own money?' said Claire.

'Basically, yes. The real story was that Cross suddenly lost his grip. He became besotted with one of the Shagbags and his business went to pot. Glass took advantage. Here's Nurse Biscuit's report.'

Madeleine pushed a folder across the desk. 'You could also look at the videos.'

'What videos?' said Amy.

'We've got recording equipment in his room. So far there's about five hundred hours of material. We can use it to corroborate Nurse Biscuit's testimony and vice versa.'

'I wouldn't mind looking at some of those videos,' said Claire.

'I see no objection provided they are logged out.' Madeleine pointed to a bookcase overflowing with cassettes. 'They're completely unedited. You'll have to fast forward through a lot of, er, activity between Glass and Nurse Biscuit.'

'Of course,' said Claire. 'We'll ignore all that, won't we, Amy? It's of absolutely no interest to us at all.'

Downstairs, in Tom Glass's room, Nurse Eve Biscuit was oiling her big breasts unaware that a concealed camera was watching her every move.

Tom was watching too as she slowly poured aromatic flower essence onto the upturned jellies of her chest and smoothed the lotion into every pore. Tom stood by the bed, breathing hard, his cock twitching in impatience as Eve's little fingers teased her nipples to firm peaks and smoothed under and over the big rounds, setting the flesh wobbling deliciously.

'Now you,' she said, beckoning him closer and slicking the lubricant up and down the broad spear of his distended penis.

He straddled her chest and laid his cock in the valley between her pink and glistening mountains. She grasped one in each hand and folded the warm flesh over his aching member, squeezing her bosom in from the sides until his barrel was completely enveloped. He braced himself on hands and began to shaft up and down that delightful passage. On the upthrust his empurpled glans speared up from her cleavage and she bobbed her head to lick the gaping eye of the shiny helmet before it slid back down her slippery valley.

The ritual of the tit-fuck was well established between the pair of them.

As they amused each other in this fashion they talked. It wasn't uplifting conversation - in a general sense, that is, though they found it stimulating. It concerned the pleasure they took in each other's body - the shape, the size, the feel, and so forth. Comparisons were made with others and, in particular, their suitability for the precise activity in which they were engaged. Dr Madeleine Flint, it was agreed, would be too slender of bosom to provide much comfort for a lusty tool like Tom's; and Eve's last boyfriend, so she said, had been so diminutive that his cock would have been lost forever had they ever tried to do it this way.

As ever, when discussing the matter, Tom would conclude that Eve provided the most exquisite, the most perfect and probably the most unbeatable tit-fuck in the entire world. This comment always pleased Eve and led her to greater activity with her hands and tongue. The whispered endearments became more obscene and less coherent. Soon, in fact, Tom was unable to utter anything at all beyond 'Ooh' and 'Oh yes' and finally, 'I'm coming', at which point he inundated her face and neck and chest with a river of spunk.

As always, Eve rubbed the cream from his cock lovingly into her tits, soothing the abused flesh, laughing up at him with a sparkle in her eye. And a hunger, too, for it was her turn now and she was savouring what she would have him do to her next.

And, unknown to them both, the camera in the ceiling recorded every thrilling moment.

Chapter 27

Marianne arrived at The Mount Morris Grand in disarray. Her face was flushed, her silver-blonde mane was uncombed and her clinging black jersey sheath plainly showed that beneath it she wore no underwear. Nevertheless she looked fabulous, she had the air of a well-fucked woman - which she was. Every eye in the cocktail lounge turned in her direction as she made her way to the table occupied by Gerald and a lean, craggy-faced gentleman in a dinner jacket - Sir Charles Mastiff. He elected to kiss her hand while Gerald summoned a flunky to pour her champagne. Most of the bottle had gone already, she noticed, but then she *was* half an hour late.

'*Salut*,' she gurgled and drained her glass in one thirsty gulp.

'Welcome,' said Mastiff in a bottomless gravelly voice, his deep-set gaze boring into hers in an unnerving fashion. 'Congratulations, Gerald,' he continued without taking his eyes off Marianne, 'I can see at once that I have underestimated the potential of *Gravitas*. The nation will embrace arty-farty chit-chat as never before just for the chance to look at Miss Matthews.'

Marianne grinned happily at him and stifled a burp. The alcohol had gone straight to her head and she felt suddenly and deliriously happy. The reason for that was the wonderful French boy waiting for her at home, whose caresses had made her rather late. Sex, of course, not being of great importance to her, the impact he had made on her in bed that afternoon had been significant. He was some kind of physical trainer, she had discovered, who had studied a new method of keeping fit through orgasm. My God, if this was the result she was all for it. It had been hell leaving him behind, she even felt a slight pang of guilt in saying she had to attend an important business meeting and wouldn't be back till late.

And now she was here, in opulent surroundings, being feted by two handsome men who were about to buy her a most expensive dinner. And then - well, no doubt they would want to take her dress off and subject her to all sorts of physical indignities. But that was show business and Marianne had her career to think of. At heart, she was a practical girl and the practical thing was to just get on with it.

'Can we eat soon?' she said to her two admiring companions. 'I'm famished.'

The meal passed in a dream. Marianne ordered lots of bitty things like caviar and asparagus while the men made serious selections across four courses. Her appetite was assuaged by two quickly eaten bread rolls and so she picked at her food. Though she knew where the evening was destined to end, she wasn't sure about this bit. She suspected her role was to look decorative while Gerald pitched his pet projects at his chairman.

She noticed, as did Sir Charles Mastiff - she could tell by the set of his jaw - that each of Gerald's schemes was more obscure than the last and involved an expensive overseas trip.

'There's the most fabulous little theatre company on the South Pacific island of Kitongu,' brayed Gerald. 'Every year the indigenous population has a festival of arts taking a landmark work of western culture and adapting it to their own traditions. Last year they performed the complete Ring Cycle in grass skirts and coconut shells. This year, so I'm told, they're doing a stage version of *The Magic Mountain* in a full-size native war canoe. I was thinking that Marianne and I might embark on a little scouting mission to evaluate the possibility of a half-hour *Gravitas* special.'

Marianne was filled with horror. Though the thought of a jolly in the South Seas was appealing, big-mouth Gerald was not the companion she would choose. She stepped in swiftly. 'Wouldn't that be a little extravagant? And Mann has such little relevance to the aesthetic agenda of women today.'

Gerald shot her a glance of pure venom but she had the chairman's attention and that was what she was after.

'So what do you think would be of relevance?' asked Sir Charles.

Marianne said the first thing that came into her head. 'Orgasms.'

She had their attention now all right. She continued, inspiration striking as she seized her moment. 'There's a book about to come out here which tells you how to keep fit by having more orgasms. I think we should interview the author, examine her method, talk to people who've tried it - you know the sort of thing.'

'But that's not art,' howled Gerald. 'That's women's-page crap journalism. We'd lose all our intellectual credibility!'

'And get a top-ten rating, I shouldn't wonder,' said Mastiff, his face alight, 'especially if Marianne presents it in that dress. This is the kind of creative input I like.'

Marianne beamed. 'It's all very hush-hush at present,' she said, 'but I've got an inside track to the author.'

The hunky Philippe and his magic tongue, she thought to herself.

'Well, stay on it.'

You bet!

'And keep me posted.'

Gerald opened his mouth, no doubt to pour scorn, but Mastiff cut him off. 'Don't say another word about it, Gerald. You've made a brilliant appointment in this young lady and she's told me all I need to know. I'm very pleased with the pair of you.'

He snapped his fingers at the head waiter, 'Coffee and champagne in my suite now, please.' He turned to Marianne. 'You don't mind if we trespass some more on your time, do you? I think we need to take this matter of the orgasm a little further.'

'Whatever you say, Sir Charles,' said Marianne, taking his arm as they left the restaurant, 'I'm all yours.'

It was a short journey to Mastiff's suite but an eventful one. By the time Marianne stepped through the door the dress was half off her back. The television executives completed the process and pushed her straight into the bedroom.

'Are you sure this programme isn't called *Grab My Ass?*'; she protested but there was no response. The time for joking was over.

She lay on the bed face down, stark naked, listening to the slither and click of two men swiftly pulling off their clothes. Whatever their disagreements over programme policy, the pair knew how to work in concert when it came to poking pussy.

'Kneel up,' barked a voice, 'get on your hands and knees.'

Marianne did as she was told, aware of the spectacle she made with her bum pointing up invitingly and her breasts hanging down like ripe fruit. For a woman who didn't much like sex she couldn't wait for their hands to close on her hot and eager body. It had to be Philippe's fault. What he had done to her that afternoon had her senses singing. Not that she wanted to think about Philippe just at the moment.

'I say!' whispered Sir Charles. 'What a fabulous figure.'

'Indeed, sir.' Gerald's voice sounded tight. 'Fabulous.'

'Exquisite.'

'Graceful.'

'Oh, for God's sake,' the voice was Marianne's, 'cut the crap and fuck me, please.'

'Look, she's trembling, Gerald. Do you think she's cold?'

'I think she's hot for it, sir. She's trembling because she's horny.'

'Please,' yelled Marianne, 'please! Oh!'

There were hands on her now, delicately touching her, smoothing over her curves, gently caressing her limbs, stroking her flanks. The bastards must have done this before.

'Fine tits, Gerald. I find the way they elongate in this position very satisfying.'

'Quite, sir. And if you slap them just a little, like this, and set them rippling back and forth...'

'Oh, marvellous!'

Marianne made a grab for Gerald's cock, which was bobbing before her face. But Gerald stepped away and a hand crashed down on her right buttock with a smack.

'Stay still!' hissed Sir Charles and he hit the other buttock just as hard. To her surprise, as the pain faded a warm glow seemed to spread through her loins. She was dripping wet between the legs.

'Please, please, please!' she heard herself moaning. She was rubbing her thighs together now, trying to ease the itch in her hungry pussy, undulating her whole frame, aware her tits were swinging and her arse was gaping and that she was making an obscene display of herself. She couldn't help it.

They had closed in on her now, pressing their hairy male nakedness against her yielding softness. She could feel their cocks rubbing against her arms and legs, their hanging balls brushing against her. Their pungent man-smell, of sweat and cologne, enveloped her. Two mouths were on her as well, kissing her back, her neck, her dangling breasts. It was glorious. She was squealing out loud with pleasure as her thighs juddered together.

Fingers pinched her nipples knowingly and a hand probed her arse crack, wetting her anal pucker with the juice that was slicking her thighs.

'Put it in, put it in,' she moaned over and over. 'Both of you. Together. Put it in.'

One of them shut her up by thrusting the thick head of his penis between her lips. She swallowed him to the root, her nose buried in the coarse hair of his belly. She could feel his hands in the thick mop of her hair pulling her into him.

Then something hot and very big pressed into the dimpled hole between her arse cheeks. She recognised that bull's pizzle of a cock. She squirmed and clenched her buttocks round it. It was her own fault, she'd fired Gerald up with the prospect of shagging her arse and now he was going to do it.

His hand slapped her bottom again, once, twice, on each side, urging her to keep still. She couldn't for she was already twitching with orgasm. Then the big thing was lodged in her bum and she was coming full spate, thrusting back down on it with a mouthful of cock at the other end and her tits swinging like church bells on Christmas morning.

They skipped the coffee - it had gone cold - and opened the champagne. Then the two men changed ends. After Gerald, she took Sir Charles up her arse without a murmur. The men poured more champagne and moved her around on the bed like a rag doll. She lost track of what they asked her to do but she didn't say no. This was business after all.

She kept count of the number of times she came, however. Now she was doing a programme on the orgasm regime it seemed appropriate.

Chapter 28

The video wasn't the best quality Amy Tooth had ever seen but the sound was good, which was probably the most important thing. She plumped the cushions on the sofa and delved into the second layer of her box of chocolates. By her side Claire Quartermain sipped from a long gin and tonic and stroked Amy's bare thigh. The sergeant was nude from the waist down. So far this had been a pretty entertaining evening.

On screen it was past midnight in Tom Glass's bedroom. Moonlight from a high window illuminated two people on the bed. Perspiration glistened on Tom's forehead as Eve Biscuit pulled his head down to the comfort of her soft bare chest. He had just made fierce and energetic love to her, as if slaking a terrible thirst. Amy bit on a hazelnut crunch and Claire lit a cigarette. They had enjoyed the fun and games but now it was time for business.

'How did you end up with Euphoria?' Eve's voice was little more than a whisper. 'Pop-group managers don't normally run record companies, do they?'

'No, they don't.' Tom chuckled. 'I guess I was lucky.'

'It couldn't just be luck.'

'I suppose not. Chas came to me before Christmas at the end of the first year and said the royalties were going to be late. He said Euphoria had short-term difficulties which were eating up the cash and that it took time to collect money from overseas sales. I asked for a statement, so I could see exactly how much we were talking about. It was a hell of a lot. As far as I could tell it was a straight accounting, he hadn't tried to stitch me up. The problem was that he didn't have the money at that moment.

'Frankly, I was worried. I knew more than he thought I did because I had a girlfriend in his accounts department.'

'Aha.'

'What do you mean, aha?'

'Because there's always a woman. That's how you remember, isn't it?'

'That's true.'

'So, what was she like? Give me all the filthy details.'

'Eve, I think you've got the most prurient mind I've ever come across in a woman.'

'But you like me for it, don't you?'

'Oh for Christ's sake,' muttered Claire as the figures on screen moved into a clinch, 'get on with it.'

'You want me to fast forward?' said Amy. 'Personally I think it's rather sweet.'

'Spare me,' said Claire. '"Ooh look, I think they're going to wait until he's coughed" the details.'

It was true. The two heads on screen had separated and Tom was speaking once more.

'Meredith was American and very ambitious. She didn't like the way the department was run. She thought it was sloppy and un-businesslike but she couldn't do much about it. She reported to Robert, the Company Secretary, who was a founder member of Euphoria. In other words, Robert had been at school with Chas and they were tight. She'd tried to seduce Chas and failed but she pulled Robert for a while before he got married and when I met her she was thinking of going back to the States. So you can see that she was a bit of a loose cannon. She also had a big mouth.

'So when Chas spoke to me I already knew from Meredith that the figures from the US were a disaster, that Chas had borrowed a ton of cash to build a studio in the Caribbean which had hardly returned a cent of investment and that his distributor in Japan had just gone belly-up owing Euphoria a fortune. Really it was Shani and the Shagbags who were keeping the business afloat and if Chas paid us what he owed in royalties he'd have no money left for anything else.

'I told Chas I could sue and he said it would take years to come to court and I'd have nothing in the meantime, was that what I wanted? He said he was only asking for six months' grace.

'I said I wanted a deal and I'd settle for a fat slice of the company. He laughed and said I was naive. I said I wasn't and I'd trade in something he really wanted.'

'What was that?'

'Tina.'

'What?'

'He was mad about her. The way she looked so cool and virginal and wrote all these passionate songs for Shani. He thought the other members of the group were complete slags and that Tina was some kind of symbol of purity. He was besotted.'

'And he agreed to hand over his company for the privilege of getting her into bed?'

'Yes.'

'And you arranged it?'

'Yes.'

'Oh, Tom. That's disgraceful.'

'I know.'

'It makes you no better than a pimp!'

'I'm not proud of myself, Eve.'

'How did you manage it?'

'I wouldn't want to shock you.'

'Go on, lover, try.'

'You're asking for it, Eve, aren't you?'

Claire groaned. 'Don't tell me he's going to fuck her again.'

'Looks like it, guv,' said Amy, her eyes glued to the sight of Tom kneeling over the pneumatic nurse, his stiff penis casting a long shadow over her belly.

'Time for the intermission, I suppose,' said the inspector, sliding to the floor and prising apart Amy's thighs. 'Pass those chocolates over here.'

'What are you up to?' said Amy, handing over the box. Claire contemplated the girl's spread legs - the pretty brown muff and the glistening pussy lips peeking through the curls. She selected a coffee cream.

'Ooh!' squealed Amy as something small and hard was pushed into the mouth of her vagina. 'Ooh, Claire, you sexy witch,' she grunted as the inspector's tongue quested inside her after the chocolate.

On the screen Tom's lean buttocks were rising and falling between Eve's quivering thighs. Between his legs could be glimpsed a dark knot of hair and the rolling purse of his ball-sac. His face was buried in the nurse's hair as his hands ransacked the gleaming white pillows of her breasts.

Amy's mouth was fixed in an O of excitement as she watched the lusty fucking. Her pussy gaped in an O of ecstasy as Claire rimmed it with her tongue and flicked a chocolate-stained tongue-tip across her swollen clit.

'Just remember, my sweet Tooth,' said Claire, as she paused in her delightful task, 'you're not the only one around here who likes a soft centre.'

Chapter 29

Petra was feeling pretty good - the Honeydew fitness routine had put a spring in her step and a twinkle in her eye. In fact, she was a real convert.

'My,' said Cassie with a sly note in her voice as she reviewed Petra's results, 'I wouldn't have thought Kelvin had it in him.'

But it was no thanks to Kelvin that Petra had achieved her POT every day for a month. And there were no new names in Petra's personal organiser - unless you could count The Magic Wand. The glass dildo had put Petra to sleep every night with a smile on her lips and woken her in the morning with an urge to plunge its smooth glowing head between her thighs at least once - maybe twice - before breakfast. It was the most entrancing thing she had ever owned - the ultimate sex object. She was in love.

Truth be told, it had taken her mind off Kelvin and the sudden deterioration of their relationship. Petra felt guilty because it had started the night she had first wanked herself to exhaustion with the Wand. Kelvin had been out late, so late that when he'd returned he'd bedded down in the spare room so as not to disturb her - or so he said. He'd stayed out late the next night and the night after that. Soon the late nights and the spare room had become a pattern.

Petra thought it was funny how quickly the new regime had become established; obviously it must have suited them both. She would leave the office around ten or eleven at night and go straight to bed with a sandwich, a glass of wine - and the Wand. It would often be one or two in the morning before she fell asleep, usually with the glass tool still buried in her sated pussy. She didn't care to speculate on what Kelvin might be up to. They rarely saw each other and at weekends they found reasons not to be together. His reason, like hers, was called 'work' but she had no doubt - if she were to force the truth out of him - it might be better termed 'another woman'.

On the morning Cassie congratulated Petra on her Honeydew endeavours and made her sly remarks about Kelvin's prowess, Petra put down the phone and marched into the spare room.

It was neat - that surprised her. Like most new men, on the domestic front Kelvin was pretty much old school and Petra did most of the clearing up around the flat. She had expected chaos but the bed was made, his clothes were hung tidily and folded in drawers and, on the table by the window, pencils and paper were squared away by the side of the word processor. Even the wastepaper basket was empty. This was not at all like Kelvin. As a journalist, it was an article of faith that his working papers were in unfathomable disarray.

This orderliness made it easy for Petra to spot the clues to Kelvin's new way of life. On the bookshelf above the table were a row of paperbacks with uniform luminous green spines. Petra was surprised to see that they were porn books designed for female readers. And hanging up in the wardrobe was a weird all-in-one garment of black rubber. She took the smooth membrane between thumb and forefinger - it felt like loose skin. She shivered. She noted that the article had a cutaway crotch. Kinky.

Of course she checked for the obvious things: dirty shirts with lipstick stains, love letters hidden at the back of a drawer, female trinkets under the bed - not that she really thought Kelvin would dare bring a lover back to the flat. She found nothing.

When she left she took with her one of the erotic books - maybe it would provide some clue to Kelvin's mysterious conduct. On the other hand, she wasn't holding her breath.

She looked at the book on the train up to Spilling Grange. In a tightly packed carriage full of men she would have felt embarrassed to be seen reading *Cold Stone, Warm Flesh* by Morticia Chekhov. However, she had selected her first-class accommodation with care. It contained only one other person, evidently a businesswoman like herself, dressed in a severely cut navy-blue suit, making notes on a foolscap pad. Holding the book so the cover could not be seen, Petra began to read.

By the end of the first chapter the naive young heroine, Deliciosa, had fallen into the hands of the cruel but charismatic Thaddeus who took her back to the family castle. By page thirty he had introduced her to the delights of the old schoolroom and caned her bare bum, by forty-five he had flogged her in the ancestral hall and on seventy he was heating up meat skewers in the kitchen to pierce her nipples.

'Yuk,' said Petra out loud and the woman opposite looked at her keenly through her black-rimmed spectacles.

Petra found it hard to believe Kelvin was turned on by this stuff. Surely he didn't want to stick red-hot skewers into *her* nipples? Evidently not. Whatever he was sticking where these days, it wasn't into her. She flicked on through the pages.

On page ninety-five Deliciosa, now pierced, degraded and rendered multi-orgasmic, was introduced to Thaddeus's former governess, an imperious female with horn-rimmed spectacles whose first words to her were—

'Take off your knickers!'

Petra's head jerked up, she could have sworn she had actually heard the words. The woman opposite was grinning at her.

'Take off your knickers,' she repeated, 'that's what someone always says to the heroine in those books.'

'Oh,' said Petra. 'You're right.'

'Of course. And the silly girl goes around bare-arsed for the rest of the story. You can imagine what happens then.'

'Quite.' Petra nodded, not wanting to appear ignorant.

'So now you can put the book away and talk to me. If you'd like to, that is.'

Behind the spectacles the stranger's eyes were almond-shaped and hazel-hued. She had a wide curving mouth that tugged upwards at the corners. She didn't look kind but she did look interesting. Petra was surprised to find she did not resent being bullied like this. She put the book into her briefcase.

'What do you want to talk about?' she asked.

'Your pretty little cunt, of course.'

The woman's smile was still in place but Petra felt as if she had just been doused in cold water. 'You can't talk to me like that!' she spluttered.

'Why not? If you don't like it you can go and sit somewhere else.'

'I could report you.'

'You could but there's no point - who'd believe you? Anyway who's reading pornography around here? Not me. If I were a man, of course, I'd never get away with saying something like that. But, then, if I were a man I wouldn't dare.'

Petra stared at her, aghast. There was no arguing with what she said.

'So, take off your knickers and hand them over,' continued the woman. 'Unless you're not wearing any.'

'Of course I'm wearing knickers.'

'What colour?'

'White.' Why did she say that?

'How sweet. Let me see.' It was the recent encounter with Inspector Quartermain, Petra later reasoned, that caused her to comply. That all-too-vivid scene had been replayed frequently on nights she had cuddled up with only the Wand for company. The woman opposite her had the same mocking arrogance of the inspector and the same confidence that her will would prevail.

Petra stood unsteadily, supporting herself with one hand as the train rushed on. With the other hand she raised the skirt of her short summer dress.

'Oh yes,' said the woman, leaning forward to gaze at Petra's bare white thighs, 'you're quite a curvy little thing, aren't you?'

The hem of Petra's skirt had now reached the vee of her pantied crotch and her hand shook as she lifted it the last few inches to reveal herself.

'White indeed,' said the woman, 'I rather hoped you'd be lying so I could punish you. Never mind, I'll find some other reason.'

'What?' Petra couldn't believe she was doing this.

'Take them off quickly.' The voice was harsh. 'Show me your cunt, slut, and hurry up.'

The words hit Petra like blows to the face. She fumbled her panties down her thighs and fell back onto her seat to slip them over her shoes.

'Who said you could sit down? Stand up at once!' hissed her tormentor and Petra jumped to her feet, her panties now in her hand. The woman snatched them from her and pressed them to her lips.

'They're soaking wet,' she pronounced with a hoarse laugh. 'You delicious little baggage. My, are we going to have fun! Now, let me have a good look at you...'

And as the train rushed onwards Petra held her dress high and eased her feet apart. Maybe she was going crazy but she couldn't help herself. The woman leaned forward till her mouth was an inch from the impudent curls of the exposed pussy. Her eyes were on Petra's most intimate secrets like a torch beam at midnight and her breath caressed Petra's itching clitoris like a warm breeze off a summer sea.

'Oh God, oh God, oh God,' she moaned softly.

Though her persecutor had not even touched her, Petra knew she was about to come.

Chapter 30

When Tom offered Chas the use of Christina's beautiful bod in exchange for a stake in Euphoria, he had no idea how was going to deliver. But the gleam in Cross's eye told that somehow he had to find a way.

The outcome was a surprisingly formal dinner party in Shani's luxurious Chelsea flat. It was not the kind of place Tom had envisaged for the singer but she was not a predictable woman. The rooms were large, the ceilings were high, and the windows were wide. An interior designer had doubtless been at work but the effect was personal - warm, luxurious, seductive.

Shani was in Tom's confidence - she had to be. She'd laughed when he'd told her about her conversation with Chas.'

'I can fix Tina,' she'd said, 'but why should I? What's in it for me?'

'Power. And a bigger slice of the cake. We'd be in a unique position, for God's sake - we'd control our own record company.'

'OK,' she'd said, fixing him with her snake-charmer stare. 'Just don't fuck me over, white boy. I'm a witch, remember?' Tom knew that well enough. He'd seen it in the way she hypnotised her audience and manipulated the girls in the group. And in the way she cast a spell over Tina.

After dinner Shani led her guests into the living room. There were only three of them - Chas, Tina and Tom.

'Why have I got to be there?' Tom had asked Shani

'Because Tina wants you to be,' had been the reply. 'Besides, don't you want to watch?'

Right now he was watching Shani kiss Tina beneath the mistletoe. It was a week before Christmas and all of them, he realised with a cock-stiffening jolt, were game for an early present.

Tina wore a black cocktail dress that finished at mid-thigh and was held up by two thin straps. Her blonde mane was piled high baring the long white stem of her neck. The pale flesh of her shoulders gleamed like porcelain. Shani turned her to face the two men and she obeyed like a puppet, her eyes cast down. One strap was off her shoulder. She made no move to replace it.

'Who's first?' Shani whispered into her ear.

To his surprise, Tina said softly, 'Tom.'

Her big brown eyes bored into his as she kissed him, her mouth wide and wet, her tongue darting inside him like a little fish. In his arms she was light and slender but the flesh of her back was warm to his touch. She wound an arm round his neck and pulled him down onto a large soft sofa. Somehow her dress had fallen to her waist and one small perfectly curved breast was in his hand.

Tom was at a loss. This was surely not what was intended.

But the nipple was big like a nut in his palm and his other hand was on the full curve of her buttocks beneath her skirt. If she wore panties, they were so small as to be undetectable.

He managed to turn her head so he could look back into the room, expecting to see a very unhappy Chas.

But Chas was far from discontented. He and Shani were locked in each other's arms beneath the mistletoe and his hands were roving the seat of her scarlet stretch pants. As Tom watched, her loose silk blouse was detached from her shoulders and fluttered to the floor.

Tom was troubled. Events were marching on seemingly out of control - Tina's small hand was now inside his jeans wrapped around the stem of his rampant tool - and he was possibly on the brink of blowing the biggest deal of his life.

Tina had his cock out now and had slipped the knob into the hot little furnace of her mouth. She bobbed her head up and down on it eagerly and reached between his legs to palm his balls. From the way she handled him Tom knew she was not experienced in the activity. On the other hand, enthusiasm was intoxicating. At any second he was liable shoot down her throat.

She took her lips from him just in time and sat back on her haunches between his legs. His purple cock wagged in her face, glistening with spit. She grinned up at him. 'Is this what my mother used to do to you?' she said, mischief dancing her eyes.

Fortunately he didn't have to answer for, at that moment, a big black nipple was thrust between his lips as Shani smothered him. Her midnight mane of hair fell around him and his hands closed on her pneumatic flesh. He heard a squeal and a cry from Tina but he couldn't see what was happening for the lights had gone out. However he could guess. There was a moan in the darkness nearby and a sticky kissing sound. Shani lay rigid and unmoving on top of him, his cock in her hand and her tit still in his face. It was as if she was waiting for something to happen.

'God, Tina,' came Chas's voice in the darkness, followed by scuffling, slippery noises.

'Oh, oh, oh.' That was a female voice, small and tender.

'Do you like that?'

'Oh yes.'

'And that?'

'Please, Chas, please...'

'And this?'

'OH!'

On top of Tom, Shani's body began to shake. For a moment he wondered if she were upset. A foolish thought, he realised, as he recognised a fit of silent laughter. On the floor now there were unmistakable sounds: of flesh colliding in ascending rhythm, of complementary moans and sighs and of sticky in-out noises as cock cleaved cunt.

Shani was moving off Tom, pulling him by the hand. They left the room as silently as they could - not that it mattered as Chas and Tina were rattling the furniture. Nothing less than an earthquake would have shaken them out of their stride.

In the hall the pair of them could not contain themselves. Shani pushed Tom into the nearest room and they sobbed their laughter into the covers of a large bed.

Tom recovered first and looked at Shani's long gleaming body quivering beside him. All she wore was a leather corset which lifted her big coffee-coloured tits and left bare the forested tangle of her pussy mound. In the forest her long madder-hued cunt lips gaped and gleamed. Tom's cock still jutted from his jeans, wet and eager and in no mood for merriment.

He slid it into her in one, covering her mouth with his, hugging her sumptuous body tight. At once the laughter died in her throat and the coal-black eyes burned into his. She fought him for a second or two, as if by reflex. Then her long limbs relaxed and a yellow flame, like a distant candle, flickered deep in her pupils. Her loins moved with his and her mouth opened and she drew him in.

She was hot and sweet and intoxicating and, much as he wanted to, he couldn't last long. Fortunately she was primed too. They convulsed and came in succession, him first and then her, swallowing the stiff sword of his cock with her voracious loins, her pelvis dancing against him.

She pushed him off her at once.

'There's millions of guys in the world who'd pay a fortune to do what you've just done,' she said.

'Not forgetting the girls.'

'Them too.'

From the next room there came a high-pitched moan.

'Tina's just tuning up,' said Shani.

'I didn't realise she could be so enthusiastic,' said Tom sliding his hand up a soft-sheened thigh.

'Oh, I did,' said Shani, opening her legs to allow him access.

Tom had no reason to doubt it.

Chapter 31

Petra knew her behaviour was shameful. Standing there on the train, holding her dress high to reveal her nude pussy mound to a complete stranger - that was shameful. Shameful and glorious. She couldn't help herself.

The dark woman simply stared at her bared pubis and Petra came. The strength melted from her legs and she hung on to the luggage rack with her free hand as her pelvis jerked convulsively. She could feel the petals of her cunt opening before the woman's penetrating gaze. She could smell the perfume of her own excitement thick in the air. And she danced like a puppet and orgasmed in the woman's face.

The sound of the carriage door sliding open broke their spell. Petra fell back onto the seat in a confused and blushing heap, pulling her skirt hastily down her thighs.

'Good morning, ladies,' came the sound of a cheerful voice. 'I trust you are enjoying the journey on this delightful morning. May I remind you there is a buffet car on this service, providing a variety of delicacies - though I would recommend from personal experience that you steer clear of the croissants.'

Petra stared at the tall youth in uniform as though he were a man from Mars. The intrusion of everyday reality into this fantasy journey was hard for her to take. Her companion, on the other hand, was not fazed for a moment.

'I suppose you'd like to see my ticket, Inspector.'

'I would indeed, madam, though I'd prefer to be called Phil. We're user friendly these days, especially to attractive ladies travelling in first class.'

The woman flashed Phil a smile as she flashed her ticket. She looked positively flirtatious.

Petra reached for her handbag but the dark woman suddenly grasped her hand, preventing her from opening it.

'It's all right, darling,' she said to Petra, 'I've got yours here.' And she held out her other hand to the railway inspector.

Phil looked bemused as he took the white scrap of material from her. Petra froze, rigid with panic. She knew what he held in his hand.

'Bloody hell,' he said as he unfolded Petra's tiny panties. Then, bonhomie instantly replaced by suspicion, he demanded, 'What's your game then?'

'Just a little user-friendly fun,' said the woman. 'My friend's lost her ticket but she can show you something else instead.'

Petra said nothing, the other woman was in control. She could feel the juice seeping out of her onto the seat beneath her bare buttocks.

Phil was turning the panties over in his hand. He fingered the damp gusset.

'Wet, aren't they?' said the woman. 'She can't help having such a juicy quim. Would you like to look at it?'

Phil was speechless now but the bulge in the grey serge of his trousers was unmistakable and spoke volumes.

The woman had removed Petra's bag from her lap and was looking at her. Petra knew what she was expected to do - and she did it.

'There!' cried the woman in triumph as Petra slowly pulled her skirt up her thighs. Her little black bush, framing two pink-frilled pussy lips, sprang into view. 'Isn't that a pretty sight?'

Loquacious Phil was lost for words. Just a grunt issued from his dry throat but his appreciation of Petra's charms was obvious.

'Perhaps you'd like a closer inspection, *Inspector?* Why don't you spread your legs, my dear, and let the gentleman have a good look.'

Petra did as she was told, sliding forward on the seat and parting her thighs. Both her inner and outer lips were on full view and at the top of her glistening sex-furrow her impatient clitoris throbbed.

'Play with yourself,' came the order and Petra obeyed. She drew her fingers through her muff, fluffing out the silky hair. She ran a slim index finger around the edge of her gaping hole and up to the pearl of her clit. She nudged it with her varnished nail and her whole pelvis rippled in response. Breath hissed between her teeth. She stroked herself again.

'Put your fingers in.' She did so, one then two. Then the whole of her hand as she rubbed the nub of her clit, ramming her knuckles into her juicy slot and moaning out loud. She couldn't have stopped herself from coming if the entire railway inspectorate had entered the carriage.

'She's a complete slut, isn't she, Phil?' said the dark woman, amusement and contempt in her voice. 'Have you seen enough yet? Or is there something else my friend can do for you?'

Petra hoped there was. Her hand was still between her legs, gently fingering her labia, keeping her raging desire on the boil. Her eyes were on Phil's flushed face - and on the swelling at his crotch. He looked as if he might burst out of his trousers at any minute.

Finally he spoke. 'By Christ, I've got to fuck her!' he growled, and took a step towards Petra's enticing form.

The dark woman seized his arm and held him back. 'Don't touch her,' she hissed. 'I want to look at you first.'

To Petra's surprise, he obeyed her. At the woman's bidding he stripped down to brief blue jockey shorts that barely contained his excitement. Beneath his uniform his tall sinewy body bore the remains of a Mediterranean tan and his stomach was as flat as a board.

'My, we're in luck,' said the woman and pulled his briefs to his knees.

Petra gave an involuntary moan as his cock sprang into view. It was sparsely haired and thick, the flaming-red head gleaming with excitement. For two pins, she would have sunk it between her legs at once. But that was not permitted. Yet.

'Not bad,' said the orchestrator of this bizarre occasion. She peered closely at the bobbing organ through her spectacles and, taking a pencil from her jacket pocket, she used it to lift his heavy scrotum. 'Turn round,' she commanded and the two women surveyed his bronzed back and the tight white moons of his buttocks.

'Do you want him?' the woman said to Petra.

She nodded, her eyes bright.

'Very well. But you'll both have to do what I say.'

She made Petra take off her dress and allowed Phil to fill his hands with her small swaying breasts. She positioned their bodies to her liking, with him standing and Petra in his arms, her legs scissored round his waist, her hands holding on to the luggage rack. Thus, wrapped around each other in a hurtling train, the two of them made intimate acquaintance.

The dark woman took charge of their genitals, pressing the plum of his stiff tool into the hungry vagina suspended above it. And then feeding the fat length of him inside her.

The weight of Petra's body drove her down onto Phil's broad penis. He stretched her wide and she howled as she sat on him, bumping and shifting with the rush of the train. His mouth was on her upturned breasts and his hands held her up by her arse cheeks, his fingers curling into the crack of her behind. Petra felt helpless, suspended in mid air, balancing on a stranger's cock, hanging on to the rail above her lest he should be thrown off his feet by a sudden jolt.

It was incredible. Every judder and shake of the train rubbed their sex membranes together and sent electric thrills jolting down to their nerve ends.

Below them, the choreographer of this erotic *pas de deux* sat making notes. Petra looked down in amazement to see the woman peering intently at their writhing bodies and jotting things on her pad. What the hell was she doing?

But Petra was no longer capable of rational thought. Her body was one mass of sensation. The difficulty of sustaining the position had delayed her satisfaction long enough - and she guessed her partner felt the same way too. He thrust up into her with carnal intent and bit down on her nipple. As a finger pushed at the dimple of her anus and then sank in to the second knuckle she squealed and rubbed her belly furiously against his. If only he would reach round and diddle her clit...

And then she felt something hard and slim nose into the gap between their lunging loins. With remarkable accuracy it approached the hood of her clitoris and applied the exact point of pressure that she required. Petra looked down and saw the dark-haired woman leaning close to their lunging bodies. With one hand she appeared to be groping between Phil's legs - fondling his balls maybe from the way he was now bucking into her. And with the other she was poking the tip of a pencil onto Petra's aching, yearning clit.

'AAH!' Petra's squeal of ecstasy was drowned out by a shout from Phil that reverberated throughout the carriage.

'Oh God!' he yelled again as he emptied his balls into her and the two of them collapsed onto the floor. At that precise moment, the train began to slow down.

'Oh shit, I'm late!' cried Phil as he disentangled himself and scrabbled frantically for his clothes. 'You're two wild women, I've got to say that,' he added, grinning from ear to ear and hopping into his trousers. Suddenly he grabbed Petra's hand. 'Just tell me one thing, darling - did the train move for you?' And he backed out of the door laughing, his good humour quite restored.

Chapter 32

On arrival at Spilling Grange, Petra accepted the offer of a drink with alacrity. The ice shook in the tumbler as she gulped a generous gin and tonic poured for her by the ever-solicitous Nurse Biscuit.

'Is there a problem, Petra?' asked Tom. 'You look a bit frazzled this morning.' He himself looked a picture of health, lounging in a deck chair on the sun-dappled lawn.

'No problem, Tom,' said Petra as emphatically as she could. What else could she say?

The truth was she had just experienced the train ride of her life and she was still in shock at her own behaviour. She had never done anything quite so outrageous before as fucking a total stranger on a train. But it wasn't so much the hip-hugging pelvic dance on Phil's thick cock that disturbed her, it was the way she had allowed the dark-haired woman to manipulate her, the fact that she had positively gloried in handing over to another person the responsibility for her own insatiable libido.

Well, at least she had solved one mystery about her erotic companion. Her identity. And that was as bizarre a coincidence as any she had ever come across. As they parted the woman had handed Petra a business card with a sardonic smile. It read: Morticia Chekhov, Author and Purveyor of the Erotic Arts. So now Petra was the proud possessor of an authentically autographed and spunk-stained pornographic novel. She intended to put it back on Kelvin's shelf as soon as possible. Let him work it out.

'Another drink, Petra? You look as if you're about to eat the glass.'

'Perhaps you'd like a shower,' suggested Eve Biscuit

'Oh yes,' Petra said at once. The expression 'travel worn' hardly covered how she felt.

Under the splash of warm water she began to feel better. But her mind was still in turmoil and two quick gins hadn't helped. She stepped out of the shower stall and felt giddy. She subsided onto a stool and buried her head in a towel.

'Are you all right, Miss Rosewater?' Nurse Biscuit was at the door, concern on her pretty face.

Petra opened her mouth to say, 'I'm fine' but nothing came out.

The nurse took over, gently towelling her dry, providing a bathrobe and producing a hairdryer. In seconds, it seemed, Petra found herself sitting in front of a dressing table. The small room also contained an easy chair, a portable television and a bed. As Eve dried her hair she said, 'This is where I sleep. It's right next to Mr Glass so I can keep an eye on him at night.'

Petra glanced quizzically at the voluptuous blonde nurse. Who was she kidding? She spent most of her nights in Tom's bed, it was well known.

The bathrobe was open almost to Petra's nipples and Eve's eyes in the mirror were on her breasts. More specifically, they were on the raw marks of Phil's ardent attentions. The nurse put down the hairdryer to examine them.

'That looks sore,' she said. 'How did you do it?'

Petra was caught by surprise. 'My boyfriend,' she said hastily, 'he's very passionate.'

'I can see that,' said Eve, opening a jar of ointment. 'The marks are very recent.'

'Yes. They are.'

There was a silence as Eve began to rub the cream into Petra's abraded tits. Her fingers were soothing and supple. The bathrobe fell to Petra's waist as Eve sought and found further sore spots. Her nipples were red and swollen. There were bite marks on the undercurves of her high pointed breasts.

'Ooh,' cried Petra.

'Did that hurt?'

'No, not exactly.' It was the opposite, in fact. Petra's flesh was singing, her nerves still jangling from her adventures on the train, from ceaseless application of the Wand, from her constant search for orgasmic release in the cause of Honeydew heaven...

'Oh yes,' she moaned between closed lips as Eve found a sensitive spot on the back of her neck.

'Stand up,' said the nurse and Petra obeyed without a thought, presenting herself nude, every square inch of her sensitive flesh alert to Eve's ministrations.

The nurse found the marks of rough fingers on Petra's bottom cheeks. She saw the fresh bruises on her inner thighs. She noted that her labia were puffed and swollen. 'I can guess what you've been up to, Miss Rosewater,' she said. 'You took a lover on the train, didn't you?'

Petra nodded. Eve was rubbing cream into her bum now and she found herself pushing her arse cheeks back onto the girl's hand. She couldn't help it. It felt delicious.

'I suspected something like that when you turned up all wobbly at the knees, with your hair messed up,' said Eve. 'But I knew for sure when I picked up your clothes while you were in the shower.'

Petra looked at her blankly.

'There were no knickers.'

'He must have kept them,' said Petra.

'How romantic. Was he handsome?'

'Very.' It was true. Phil had been a hunk. She'd been lucky. The mood she'd been in she'd have shagged Quasimodo.

'Are you going to see him again?'

'I hope not,' said Petra, aghast at the thought.

'You're a bit stiff across the shoulders,' said Eve. 'Would you like me to massage you? I know what I'm doing.'

Petra had no doubt of that. As she lay face down on the bed, Eve busied around fetching what she needed and soon those strong knowing fingers were working their magic across Petra's shoulders. She felt as if she were in a dream. So it was a few moments before she identified the weighty kiss of flesh across her back that was not generated by Eve Biscuit's hands. She turned her head to look at Eve and her heart thudded in shock. The nurse was bending over her stark naked. Petra was in receipt of a double massage, from Eve's hands and from the biggest pair of breasts she had ever seen.

'My God, Eve, do you ever massage men?'

'Only the ones I really like.'

'I bet they like it too.'

Eve giggled and smacked Petra on the rump. 'Turn over, Miss Rosewater, and let me do the other side.'

Petra had never before contemplated the fleshy opulence of one of her own gender. Until recently she had not taken any interest in women in a sexual sense. But from Claire Quartermain to the woman on the train, the next step was obviously meant to be someone like Eve Biscuit.

As the curvaceous nurse stood over her, massaging her limbs, Petra felt she understood for the first time the lure of a woman's body. Watching all that glorious nude flesh on the move, the thrust and swing of the girl's big bosom, the curve of the hip and the dome of the belly as it sloped down to the mystery of her pubic delta, Petra reacted as she imagined a man might. First she wanted to explore all that tumbling creaminess - to roam those big bouncing hills, to explore the winding curves, to lose herself in the secret nooks and crannies of Eve's generous flesh. And then, if only she had the Wand to hand, she'd fuck her stupid.

'Oh, Eve,' she breathed as the nurse worked on her upper thigh, the little finger of her left hand a millimetre away from the pouting lips of her yearning pussy. 'That's so good!'

Nurse Biscuit smiled. 'Would you like a body hug, Miss Rosewater? It's my speciality.'

Petra nodded. She'd have agreed to anything.

The nurse mounted the bed and straddled Petra's thighs. For a moment she loomed over the supine woman, the cloud of her fair hair and the rounded mass of her sumptuous body blocking out the light from the window. Then she slowly lowered herself on top of Petra. She covered her like a silky blanket of warm flesh: the big breasts crushing against the smaller woman's chest, the firm columns of her thighs capturing Petra's slim ones, her entire body cleaving to Petra in an incredible all-over embrace.

'My God,' whispered Petra, her arms automatically folding around the other woman's back, accepting the soft weight. 'Oh Eve,' she muttered into the nurse's neck as she felt, for the first time, the pressure of another woman's belly on hers.

Eve was wriggling now, searching for the right connection between their forms, taking the weight off Petra's chest but increasing it on her pubic bone until - 'Oh!' cried Petra in surprise - their vaginal slits were joined in an open-mouthed kiss.

Petra swooned. It was too much - the heat, the gin, the incredible body rub. And now this, the feel of another woman between her thighs, pressing her cunt into hers, their clits rubbing together, rushing them both towards an orgasm of unique intensity. What a day for Honeydew, she thought as her loins rippled to the first thrill.

She found she was kissing Eve Biscuit like a lustful male, her tongue halfway down her throat, her hands palming and stroking the silky globes of the other's swollen teats where they stuck out between their heaving bodies. 'Oh Eve, oh Eve,' she muttered over and over like a mantra, as her lips flicked over the sweet curve of the other's neck and her hands found the girl's nipple - big and fat and rubbery in her fingers.

Eve had set up a masterful rhythm now: rolling her pelvis down and across Petra's, driving their hungry pussies together, marching them to the summit of their first come. A high-pitched squeal rose from both throats as they reached their destination together.

Outside, on the lawn, a discordant yet thrilling sound roused Tom Glass from sun-baked slumber. These days, the once nervy hard-edged business tycoon tended to drift off into a sensuous reverie in any spare moment - and, between shagging his delicious medical attendant, there were plenty of those.

He came to his senses fast, the noise from the room next to his reaching a crescendo. He knew at once what it was, though he could hardly believe his ears. The sound of Eve's excitement was a familiar one but this was even more intense than usual. What was she up to?

Tom stepped slyly into Eve's room, expecting to find her pleasuring herself and fully intending to give her a helping hand. What he did not expect to see was another woman in her arms on the small bed, the two of them quite nude, their loins dancing in tandem as the insistent cries of female orgasm echoed around the small space. Tom had quite forgotten about his visitor but now, as he took in the implication of the dark hair tangled in Eve's blonde mane, the slim arm clasped tightly around her neck and the small feet with their wriggling, scarlet-painted toes scrabbling against the bedsheet, Tom remembered Petra.

He had been erect already, of course. But if it had been anatomically possible, this realisation would have put another six inches on his straining, throbbing tool. Petra, his petite and curvy deputy, with her air of ever-vigilant efficiency, who gave the impression she kept a clipboard between her legs - he couldn't believe it. And yet here she was in a position that clearly revealed she kept something much more interesting in that location.

The two women had not noticed him, their pleasure was too exclusive. He approached the bed as if sleep-walking, his eyes fixed on the apex of their splayed legs where the rivers of their gratification mingled. Above were the pale swollen moons of Eve's shaking arse cheeks, the deep shadow bisecting the smooth spheres pointing down to the brown-tufted maw he knew so well. And beneath that, winking and gaping, thrusting upwards like a thirsty mouth at a water fountain, was the pretty pussy slit of Petra Rosewater, framed by the succulent flesh of her trim but well-rounded thighs and buttocks.

The line that ran from the base of the blonde girl's spine down to the bedsheet, encompassing two arseholes, two cunts and a myriad of dizzying possibilities, hypnotised Tom. He fell to his knees and leant forward as close as he could. The scent of female excitement was overwhelming and the proximity of their abandon intoxicating. He could see their labia rubbing together, the slippery folds of skin clinging and sucking as they kissed. And, deeper, in the heart of their connection, he could glimpse the two clitorises - Eve's small and pink, Petra's longer, redder - glued together, keeping the women on a never-ending roundabout of sensual pleasure.

Tom knew it was rude - an inexcusable breach of sexual etiquette - but without previously announcing his presence he thrust his face into the double-cunted fissure of flesh in front of him and began to slake his thirst.

Later, when the afternoon had come and gone and the two women were lying in Tom's arms, Petra said, 'That's the most enjoyable business meeting I've ever attended.'

Eve rolled over onto her back and stretched. The three of them were sprawled across two mattresses on the floor - hospital beds not being wide enough for the afternoon's activities. 'Is that what happens at business meetings,' she said. 'I've often wondered.'

Tom said nothing, he was still in a reverie of sexual intoxication. The impact of these two different but equally delicious women had rendered him incapable of idle speech. He still savoured in particular the look of horror and of expectation on Petra's face when she had finally registered his presence - and that had not been for some while after he had begun lapping her delicious cunt. Since then he had been forced to revise his opinion of his colleague. She was a perfectionist at everything she did and she did much more than he had suspected.

'I came up here for a reason,' she was saying.

Tom nodded and idly stroked her silky smooth hip.

'I don't think the police are interested in finding out about your accident,' she continued. 'Quartermain just wants to nail you for sex crimes. It's up to us to find out who pushed you off the balcony.'

'We've talked about this before, Petra.'

'I know.' She was sitting up now, her face earnest, her pouting breasts shaking as she made her point. 'But now you remember so much more of your life, can you think of anyone who might want to kill you?'

'No.' Really those little tits were quite delicious.

'But you must have made enemies. People in your past who might bear a grudge.'

'No.' He'd never have imagined he was still capable but his cock was suddenly at full stretch. Again.

'Don't be stupid, Tom,' said Eve. 'Present company excepted, what about every woman you've ever slept with?' Tom gave it some thought.

Rosie, Elvira, Shani, the Shagbags, Maeve - Christ, yes, she'd skin him alive! Every one of them had a motive - and that's all he could remember so far. Good God.

Suddenly his erection had disappeared.

Four - Banged Up
Chapter 33

Throughout the summer, as the business community relaxed and dreamt of weekends in the country and buckets of brandy sours on foreign beaches, The Primrose Court continued its work. There could be no relaxation for those who toiled in its name: they were women with a mission. Officially, this was to purge the male establishment of its outmoded attitudes. Unofficially, as Gossamer Hawk often remarked, it was to take the prick out of his pinstripes and replace him with, well, a woman like her.

Overnight, it seemed, many prominent company men took hasty vacations or long weekends or fell prey to their first illness in years. And when they returned to their offices they were paler and softer than before - in manner, rather than appearance. 'The old bastard's lost his balls,' was said often in ladies' loos throughout the City when some long-feared despot was heard to say 'please' twice in the same sentence.

These were the kind of men who had never been known to bother with common civility unless it were to their advantage; captains of the company ship, they cracked the whip from dawn to dusk. But now the office galley-slaves were showered with enquiries about their health and told that those urgent figures for the chairman could wait till tomorrow, or next week, or whenever convenient. In the past, the meaning of this kind of conduct had always been clear - the boss wanted to get his leg over. And once that had been achieved it was back to the oars for the slave in question, though doubtless she then rowed with a silver chain around her neck.

The consequence, in many cases, was that businesses went soft, like their executives. Without the mad-eyed fanatic on bridge, driving the crew on at speeds they didn't know possible, the ship tended to drift without direction. And the consequence of this failure was inevitable - a change of leadership. Many new captains were appointed that summer. They were youthful, vigorous, efficient and they soon got their ships back on course. From the galley-slaves' point of view nothing much had changed. Apart from one thing - the new captains were all female.

'It's not right,' said a well-upholstered blonde to her friend as she applied lipstick at the end of the working day. 'Charlie Kite could be a beast but you knew where you were with him.' Her friend nodded. They both knew where the blonde had been with Kite - on his office chesterfield every Friday night. Now his office was the domain of the new boss, a Ms Snippy with an MBA and a wardrobe of white blouses that tied at the neck in a bow. The old leather chesterfield had been replaced by a glass table and a bank of computers. It was funny how she missed the smelly old thing, the blonde mused as she finished her make-up - both the sofa *and* her former lord and master.

And in the basement of The Primrose Court the hard work of executive retraining ground on.

'Mr Kite, I would like you to cast your mind back to the evening of Saturday April thirtieth.'

'Why?'

'Do you remember what you were doing?'

'No. It had been a bloody awful week, I can tell you that. We'd had the auditors in and we were fighting off a hostile bid from DungCo. I should imagine I got pissed.'

'You were watching the Eurovision Song Contest.'

'If you say so. That's not a crime these days, is it?'

'Perhaps you recall the Latvian entry?'

'Oh, vividly. It was called "Boom-bang-a-bang-ski".'

'There's no need to be sarcastic, Mr Kite. In fact it was called "My Love is as Wild as a Sheep" and sung by two young men with leather trousers and long hair.'

'Fascinating. Is the tax-payer really footing the bill for this ridiculous charade?'

'Do you remember saying, "Get those two heart-throbs. I bet they're up to their ears in Latvian pussy"?'

'So?'

'Are you not aware that a sexist comment of that nature is a category B crime of conscience?'

'*If* I said it.'

'Are you denying it? We have a witness.'

'Who?'

'Your wife.'

'What!'

'Her statement says that after dinner, which you ate while watching the television, you made crude and derogatory remarks at the contestants in the song contest. When the Irish entrant sang, "I'll Come Running Back" you said, "With those knockers, darling, you'll get a black eye", and at the German entry, "*Ich Liebe Dich*", you shouted out, "You can suck my *Dich* any time, *Fraulein*".'

'I just told you, I was drunk.'

'So you admit these offences.'

'No, I do not.'

'You maintain that your wife is lying then.'

'She was drunk, too.'

'Not so drunk I don't remember your piggish behaviour.'

'Veronica! What are you doing here? Is this a trick? Where are you?'

'She's in the observation booth, Mr Kite. She can see you but you can't see her.'

'This is outrageous! Hey, what are you doing with those wires?'

'I'm fastening electrodes to your testicles. As you show no remorse of any kind, it is time for your retraining to begin. Mrs Kite, would you like to press the red button on the console in front of you?'

'This one?'

'Veronica, don't you dare - aah!'

'That's the one. It seems to be working.'

'What's this little clock thing?'

'That's the discomfort dial, Mrs Kite. If you turn it to the left you increase the intensity of the correction.'

'Like this?'

'AAH!'

Excellent, Mrs Kite, you seem to have mastered the technology already. Now, I believe we asked you to prepare questions for your husband that you think are relevant to our line of enquiry.'

'There's rather a lot of them, I'm afraid.'

'Don't worry about that, Mrs Kite, we have all night.'

'Oh Christ.'

'Shut up, Charles, and listen to me for once. Tell me about your trip to Paris with that bitch Tricia Markham.'

'Honestly, Veronica, I don't recall—'

'You remember Tricia, Charles - the PA with eyes like a cow and udders to match. Was she a good shag?'

'Please, Veronica - aahh!'

'Better than me?'

'AAAHH!'

'Mrs Kite, would you object if I put my hand on your husband's penis? We find that, in conjunction with the pain, a little pleasurable stimulation is conducive to reprogramming an offender's thought processes.'

'Go ahead but I'd wear a glove if I were you, you don't know where it's been. Does she, Charles?'

'AAAAHHHH!'

These methods were effective for most subjects though there were some for whom the approach was counterproductive. At their weekly progress meeting Gossamer Hawk and Claire Quartermain often discounted action against executives with certain proclivities.

'There's no point in bringing him in,' said Claire, looking at the file Gossamer had just handed her. 'He pays through the nose for this kind of treatment in Shepherd's Market every week. Why give it to him for free?'

'Oh drat,' said Gossamer with unusual emphasis. 'You'd better shop him to the tabloids, then. We have to shift the old turd somehow.'

Claire made a note. She was aware that, beneath the Prosecutor's habitual delicacy of manner, impatience was seething. Suddenly there was an outburst.

'Our work is just not proceeding fast enough, Claire. British business is still stuffed full of antediluvian old farts who think a woman's place is on her back with her knickers round her ankles.'

'There's a lot fewer than there were, Prosecutor. We've got the City running scared.'

'Not scared enough. Not the big boys. We've replaced some ageing middle men but we haven't touched the real tycoons.'

Oh dear. Claire knew where this was going - Tom Glass. She tried to head Gossamer off.

'We're making progress in the Glass investigation. It won't be much longer. Dr Flint says—'

'I don't give a flying fig about Dr Flint,' yelled Gossamer, puce in the face. 'That man's made a monkey out of her, Inspector, and I want him arrested. Let's see how he responds to our kind of medicine. I want him in the cells by tonight.'

Claire grinned at her superior. This was more like it. She couldn't wait to tell Amy Tooth.

Chapter 34

Kelvin knew he was onto the biggest story of his life. A scoop that was too hot for *Nouveau* - and too expensive, for that matter. He'd flog it to the *Rabbit* or the *Dog* or the *Sunday Skunk* in return for a ton of cash - or possibly a job. He'd make that prick Ted Flinch curse the day he'd given him the boot. Which he had done, some three weeks previously, when Kelvin had abandoned the struggle to reconcile the demands of days at the office and nights with Gossamer Hawk. Now his full-time devotion was to the cruel Gossamer while he planned the coup that would relaunch his career.

So, for the moment, Kelvin was keeping his head down. Literally. Right now his head was down below the desk of Naomi Picket, Opposition spokesperson on Gender Discrimination and senior member of the Corrections Committee of The Primrose Court. Kelvin was gently tonguing her quim. For such an aggressive woman she had a dainty little mollusc between her legs, prettily petalled and tasting of the sea. His tongue burrowed into the heart of her open oyster as his arms circled the substantial cushions of her buttocks and his nose rubbed against the tiny pearl at the apex of her slit.

He heard the quick intake of her breath as he pleasured her, coaxing her to her four o'clock orgasm. 'A small indulgence in a life of self-sacrifice,' she'd said, without discernible irony, on the first occasion Gossamer had sent him round. 'It improves the taste of my afternoon ciggy.'

Kelvin had no doubt it did. After he'd finished between her legs she would smoke two cigarettes on the trot. On one memorable occasion she'd smoked three, it had taken her that long to recover from his attentions. Now when she ordered him beneath the desk, she'd say, 'I want a three-fag come this afternoon, slave. You'll not get off your knees otherwise.'

It gave Kelvin a perverse pleasure to be called 'slave', to wear a collar and chain around his neck, to drink water from a bowl in the kitchen downstairs like a dog. It answered a need in him that Petra had never fed. To give up, for a few hours each day, the responsibility of being uncertain, insecure Kelvin Priest and to be the property of strong women like Gossamer Hawk and Naomi Picket was bliss. What's more, it was going to make his name.

The phone rang on the desk, the bell reverberating through the wood. As Naomi's hand descended on his head Kelvin anticipated her needs and relaxed his pressure on her throbbing genitals. The journey to orgasm could wait.

'Lord Swankie, how delightful to hear from you,' said La Picket in her smarmiest tones. She was like a chameleon, Kelvin had observed, able to trim her accent and demeanour to suit her audience. If she hadn't been a politician she could have taken the West End stage by storm.

Lord James Swankie was the chairman of a family-owned bank whose female employees never rose above the rank of counter clerk and were obliged to wear low-cut cerise blouses and matching mini-skirts over fishnet tights. Lord Jim himself had a well-publicised liking for field sports and blondes of an age half their bust size. As far as Kelvin knew, he had not so far come to the attention of Inspector Claire Quartermain of the TCU. Beneath the desk he nuzzled the peachy skin of Naomi's inner thigh and pricked up his ears.

'Now now, my lord,' Naomi was saying, 'you know very well it would not be wise for you and I to be seen in public.'

From her point of view Kelvin knew this to be true, her party colleagues would be aghast to find her socialising with a traditional chauvinist like Swankie. He, on the other hand, was happy to be seen with a pretty woman anywhere. What lay between her ears was of no account to him in comparison with what lay between her legs.

And what lay between Naomi Picket's legs was a delicacy to be savoured. Kelvin began to lap the long curling pussy lips, sucking first one, then the other, into his mouth. At first the hand on his head threatened to push him away and then it slipped to his neck and hugged him to her crotch. He began to French-kiss her cunt like a departing lover.

'Look, make it six-thirty here this evening,' said Naomi, wriggling in her seat, keen now to concentrate on her pleasure. She put the phone down with a bang. 'I wonder what that old lecher would have said if I'd told him I was being sucked off under the desk. What do you think, slave?'

Kelvin knew better than to answer. Instead he pushed two fingers into the long slippery tunnel of her cunt and circled her clit with the point of his tongue. Her breath was expelled from her lungs with a hiss like a steam kettle as she began to boil over. It wasn't always men, Kelvin reflected as he manipulated her soft perfumed pussy, who were predictable in matters of sex.

It was risky - God knows what The Primrose Court harpies would do to him if he were caught - but Kelvin knew he had to take a chance. He hid in the downstairs sitting room to witness the meeting between Naomi and Lord James Swankie.

He guessed she would receive him there. It was a small room at the back of the house with a sofa and comfortable chairs where Naomi liked to relax with a drink after office hours. On occasions she had relaxed there with Kelvin's cock in her quim but he suspected she preferred the head-under-the-desk routine. He didn't mind much either way, in the service of Gossamer Hawk he was content simply to satisfy.

He hid beneath a small circular table whose mahogany top had been scarred by the careless use of hot cups and discarded cigarette ends. As a consequence it was now covered by a thick woven cloth with a fringe that fell right down to the floor. Provided he didn't sneeze, Kelvin thought he was pretty safe hiding beneath it. Naomi had dismissed him, as usual, after he had performed his afternoon service and she had no idea he was still in the house.

Just as he was checking his cassette recorder he heard voices at the door. He hoped his luck was in - it was too late to back out now.

Lord James Swankie, it was evident, had turned up in a merry mood. He accepted a drink with alacrity and requested another before Naomi joined him on the sofa - Kelvin assumed they were sitting on the sofa from the direction of their voices.

'I must say,' boomed Swankie, 'that I thought this malarkey of yours was a bit steep when you lot put the arm on me last year. But now I've seen what's happened to some of my pals I think it was worth it.'

'I'm so glad you take a positive point of view, my lord.'

'*Oh*, I'm always positive. What's life if you can't have a bit of fun? All the money in the world's no good if you can't persuade a pretty totty to put your dick in her mouth.'

'Quite.'

'I don't shock you, young woman?'

'This is a private conversation, my lord.'

'I don't care about that, though I dare say you do. I've considered spilling the beans about our arrangement, you know.'

'Really? There wouldn't be much point. As I'm sure you're aware, we're empowered to levy severe fines for corporate misbehaviour. You would simply end up paying much more. And the personal inconvenience that you and the members of your board might suffer during the investigation—'

'*Oh* quite,' Swankie cut her off. 'I only said I'd considered it.'

Kelvin was agog. He knew he'd been onto something and here was confirmation. Swankie had bought off the court and the TCU!

'Besides, in time I expect it to be an accepted part of our policy to issue licences to businesses which will ensure their on-going integrity.'

Swankie laughed. 'Licences to fuck around you mean - a licence to lust! That's rich. Give us another drink, there's a good girl. I adore the way you stick your arse out when you bend down to get the bottle.'

Kelvin held his breath. To address Naomi Picket in this fashion was to risk disfigurement. Emasculation at the very least.

Naomi chuckled. 'You don't disappoint, do you, my lord? You're nothing but a penis in a suit.'

'I can soon remove the suit, my dear.'

'Give me the cheque.'

'Give me the licence.'

There was a rustling sound, as of paper exchanging hands.

'Isn't it usual to shake hands on a deal, my lord?'

'I intend to shake more than that, my dear. Why don't you slip out of your skirt so we can celebrate our arrangement we did last year.'

'Jim, you know that was a mistake. I swore to myself it would never happen again.'

'And I swore that it was worth the entire sum of money I paid you at the time. Drop your drawers, girl. A hundred grand buys me something, surely.'

There came more rustling noises, this time of clothing being removed.

'Satisfied?' asked Naomi.

'Not yet. Turn round. My, my - I declare you've got a little larger than last year. I like it, mind you. There's nothing beats a big bum in suspenders.'

'You're an old traditionalist, Jim. And though that's not a point of view I hold, I can appreciate any set of deeply held beliefs.'

'Appreciate this then, you big-arsed trollop!'

There was a smack, followed by a squeal and then silence. Silence as in an absence of speech but not of movement. There was slithering and scuffing, a hiss of breath and a rhythmic deep-throated moan. Kelvin was transfixed. He had the information he needed and he knew he must keep cool. The last thing he should do was to lift the cloth which concealed him and peek.

Kelvin peeked.

Lord Swankie was a virile man of late middle years. At present his virility rose from the fly of his handmade charcoal suit and disappeared between Naomi Picket's pink lips. She was gumming the fat knob of his pulsating cock with admirable skill at the same time as she fondled the bulging sac of his testicles.

'Enough!' he barked suddenly and threw her face down over his knees. At first she laughed as he smacked the wobbling rounds of her fair white bottom then, as the flesh turned a flaming scarlet, she burst into tears.

Kelvin was rigid with shock. This was the most extraordinary thing he had ever seen. How he wished there was some way he could have filmed the events that unfolded before him in that stuffy little room as his cock wept into his pants and the mismatched twosome in front of him ran the gamut of carnal pleasures.

Without visual evidence, he reflected as the lush nude figure of the Opposition spokesperson for Gender Discrimination prostrated herself on all fours to allow the notorious reprobate Lord James Swankie to penetrate the pretty pink dimple of her anus, nobody would believe him.

Chapter 35

A little of a person, Cassie Crow well knew, could go a long way. Particularly when that person was unutterably gorgeous, indisputably talented and unconscionably rich. And was sitting in your office, behind your desk, having hijacked your entire magazine. It had been two days since Chastity Honeydew and her entourage had entered the offices of *Fragrant* - 'The indispensable lifestyle bible for the independent woman that is YOU' - and Cassie had never spent a longer forty-eight hours.

Chastity had materialised in the building almost unnoticed, such was the pandemonium caused by the prior arrival of four muscle-bound young men in shorts, sweatshirts and mirrored sun-glasses. Jogging in formation, they swept at speed past the arm-flapping receptionist on the front desk. Her screech of protest alerted the magazine staff but there was little they could do to eject these bronzed hulks as they took up strategic positions along the corridor and barked into walkie-talkies.

'It's wet-dream time,' muttered Rita the production editor, 'we've been invaded by the Chippendales.'

At that moment a much smaller figure in a baggy zip-up jacket and a baseball cap trotted along the corridor right into Cassie's office.

Cassie was dialling the emergency services as the intruder pulled off the cap and a mane of golden hair spilled down her back.

'Hiya, Cass,' said the blonde one, shucking the baggy jacket off her shoulders and stepping out of loose training pants. Chastity Honeydew emerged like a sunburst: her toothy smile gleaming from ear to ear, the upthrust of her bosom straining her lemon singlet, her to-die-for legs showcased in tiny white shorts. She looked about nineteen years old, the picture of California-girl perfection. At that moment, deep down, the entire staff of *Fragrant* wanted to wring her slender, unlined, flawless neck.

They hadn't, of course. They had fawned over her as if she were visiting royalty, which she was in a manner of speaking. She and 'her people', as she referred to them, at once commandeered Cassie's office, leaving Cassie herself to the small spare desk she had intended for her visiting American contributor. Chastity's boys filled the fridge with organically purified water, installed their own fax and word-processor and rigged up a satellite TV outside Cassie's office which was permanently tuned to CNN.

Cassie had thought that she and Chastity would be working side by side, preparing the orgasm-regime profiles and other features for the special Honeydew issue. But Chastity wasn't playing. 'Give all the stuff to Randy,' she said to Cassie when she produced the copy she had prepared, 'I'll go through it later.' Then the five Americans had barricaded themselves in Cassie's room.

By the end of day two Cassie was tearing her hair. She was homeless in her own office. What's more, she watched with increasing anxiety as her staff were summoned, one by one, into Chastity's presence. They emerged with dopey smiles on their faces as if they'd been brainwashed.

'What's going on?' she demanded of Rita. 'What the fuck are they doing in there?'

'Fuck is what they're doing,' said Rita, dragging on her cigarette. 'What did you expect?'

Cassie's face was a mask of rage. 'I expect loyalty and support. I expect to be told what's happening. I don't expect my magazine to go down the toilet in five minutes just because some blonde witch from LA turns up with an army of toyboys.'

Rita raised an eyebrow. Cassie's fury was not a new phenomenon to her. 'You invited her, darling. You blew a load of money on a book about bonking and now she's here doing it you start complaining. You've only yourself to blame.'

Cassie could see the logic in this but she wasn't in the mood to appreciate it. 'Do you mean they are actually fucking? Fucking my staff in my office?'

Rita laughed. 'She doesn't call it that, of course. She's reviewing everyone's standing vis-à-vis their orgasm targets. You know the whole shtick - you started it off. And, surprise surprise, Chastity is recommending everyone to have more orgasms. That's where the Chippendales come in.'

'Oh my God.'

'Don't knock it. Amanda in Sales has just had a stiffie between her legs for the first time since the Silver Jubilee. As far as she's concerned this is the next best thing to the Second Coming. Of course, as far as she's concerned, it *is* the Second Coming.'

'Knock it off, Rita.' Cassie scowled at her. 'As far as *I'm* concerned it isn't funny.'

'Chastity doesn't think it's funny either. She's dead serious. She's a single-issue fanatic on the subject of female orgasm. She told me my cough would clear up if had more of them. I said I was looking forward to the day when they sold them in packets of twenty. She didn't laugh.'

And neither did Cassie. She was considering smacking the smirk off her editor's red lips when one of the Honeydew men entered the room. He was carrying a clipboard and he consulted his notes before addressing Rita.

'Are you ready for your treatment, Ms Lawrence?'

'You bet, Randy.'

'If you'd care to step this way, you're next in line for the treatment centre.'

Cassie stifled a snort of displeasure. Rita grinned and stubbed out her cigarette.

'That's great, Randy, but I've got a better idea. My flat's just round the corner and I've got all the equipment you need right there.'

'Well, I don't know if Chastity would be happy—'

'Of course she would. I've already talked to her about it. She wants me to give you a home-cooked dinner and show you a good time in a foreign city.'

'Provided you show her a good time first,' muttered Cassie, heading for the door. This was getting to be more than she could stand. If even Rita was defecting to the enemy she was really on her own.

Behind her she heard the boy say, 'OK but please call me Rhett.'

'Why?'

'Because that's my name.'

'If you insist,' said Rita, 'but I'll never remember it.'

It was ten o'clock at night and the building was almost deserted. As far as Cassie could tell, all of the magazine staff had gone home but the invaders from LA remained in her office. She was getting fed up with waiting them out. She wanted them to clear off so she could snoop around and see what evidence remained of their activities. However, this was getting ridiculous. She decided to barge in, on the pretext of saying goodnight. It *was* her office after all.

She strode down the corridor and into the workspace outside her room. Her assistant had long gone but the television was still there, a man in a brown suit was addressing the empty room on pork-belly prices. Fortunately the volume had been turned right down.

Cassie paused with her hand on the door to her office. Then, changing her mind, she leant over her assistant's desk and peeped behind a propped-up notice board through the glass panelling into the room beyond. When she saw what was going on, she was glad she had taken this precaution.

There were three people behind the glass: Chastity and two of her boys. Between them they wore hardly a stitch. Chastity was bending over Cassie's desk, the top of her bowed blonde head pointing directly at Cassie. Behind her, spearing his cock into her outthrust rump was boy number one. His face was set in a rictus of concentration as he gazed down at the taut and creamy buttocks buffeting his flat belly. Reclining on the sofa, paging through the *Herald Tribune*, was boy number two. He wore a small white towel around his waist. Every so often he yawned. Chastity lifted her head. Her voice could be clearly heard above the drone of the television.'

'Hey, Carter,' she said, 'get cranking, I'm gonna need you in a moment.'

The man on the sofa sighed and flipped the towel from his loins, revealing to Cassie's prurient gaze a slumbering serpent coiled on his thigh. He took the lazy member in one hand and began to pull on it without enthusiasm, his eyes never leaving the sports section.'

Cassie sighed too and her heart thumped in her chest. Amidst this acrimony and politicking, she had neglected her own fitness-training and now she was reminded of all those orgasms she had yet to achieve. She was dreading the moment when she had to reveal the failings of her own regime to Chastity.

'Ooh, yeah!' yelled the blonde suddenly, shimmying her buttocks back into the loins of the boy behind her with a burst of energy. 'Gimme, gimme, Troy. Go for it now!'

The boy's face was a picture of concentration as he gazed down at Chastity's spread buttocks and his penis plunging to and fro in her gaping pussy mouth. His big hands gripped her hips tight, sweat dripping from his brow onto her bobbing arse as he gave her his all.

'Yeah, yeah!' implored Chastity, raising her upper body from the desk top, her impossibly round breasts swinging free, her blonde hair cascading over her bronzed shoulders. 'Gimme all you got, baby. Sock me with your sugar-stick!'

The boy on the sofa had now diddled his tool to an impressive length though Cassie noted that it was still only semi-erect. For the first time he looked at the copulating couple on the desk. With an expression of complete indifference, he began to fold away his paper.

'Go for it, baby, go for it!' yelled Chastity. 'Do it! Take me there! Gimme the big one now!'

The boy at her rear was beet red in the face. As he twitched into orgasm his great body became rigid, every tendon straining. He looked like an Olympic weightlifter attempting a world record. Then he spasmed his last and slumped forward across the golden form beneath him. He had gone for the big one.

And missed.

'Oh SHIT!' screamed Chastity. 'I never got there! Get off me, you great ox!'

Troy pulled himself away from her, his face now that of a little boy on the verge of tears. 'God, I'm sorry, Chastity. I thought we were together, I thought—'

'Shut your moronic mouth and get lost,' hissed his employer. 'Carter, bring your dick over here, you're on.'

With a weary sigh, the boy on the sofa strode over to the desk, his half-hard penis swinging in front of him. The blonde grabbed it and tugged him towards her by the root. His broad frame loomed over her as she laid her forehead on his gleaming pectorals and pressed the soft swellings of her chest into the hardness of his torso.

In a little-girl voice she said, 'You won't let me down, will you, Carter?'

'Of course not, baby,' he replied and brushed the top of her head with his lips. In her small hands his big penis was now at full stretch, the helmet a shiny scarlet. She ran a blush-pink nail along the underside of his shaft and it jumped at her touch. She parked her bottom on the edge of the desk and pulled him into position between her spread thighs.

Troy sat on the sofa, his head in his hands, his tool snail-like between the bronzed slabs of his thighs.

Outside Cassie gazed on, not sure what to make of this bizarre scene. But, as she watched Carter run the head of his big stalk up the length of Chastity's pouting split, her body began to throb to its own rhythm. Without thinking, she dragged her knickers down her thighs and jammed her hand between her legs. Watching that bitch Chastity getting it had made her wet. Very wet. She was on the brink of coming already.

The sound of footsteps made her look round in panic. The last of Chastity's boys stood there, a box of pizzas in his ham-like fist, his eyes bulging at the sight of her.

'Ms Crow?' he said. 'Are you all right?'

Cassie was still bent over the desk in the position she had adopted to peer through the glass. Her skirt was above her waist, her panties round her ankles and her large fleshy rump was thrust towards the newcomer. Her fingers, though stilled by his presence, were wedged in her throbbing pussy.

'I work with Ms Honeydew,' he said.

'I know.' Cassie removed her hand from between her legs and began to clamber off the desk.

'I'm Randy,' he continued in embarrassment.

'Thank God for that,' said Cassie, removing the pizzas from his grasp and placing those big hands on the soft, quivering cheeks of her arse. 'So am I.'

Chapter 36

It was a first, Cassie knew, and probably a last. She had never arrived at work at six-thirty before but today it had been necessary to beat the opposition. She sat at her assistant's desk in the solitude of the empty office suite and nursed a cup of tea in front of the television. Thanks to Randy, she felt better. The warm glow of his attentions the previous night had not yet faded from her loins. He had also done wonders for her orgasm chart. Though her POT was still well down at least she would be able to demonstrate to Chastity some recent activity.

Cassie was a secret fan of breakfast television. The marketing people had once told her that a significant proportion of *Fragrant* readers tuned in every morning, so she felt an obligation to watch. At any rate that was her excuse for ogling the soapy-smooth Irish presenters and the tanned hunks who urged the bleary-eyed world to work out on the way to work. And today, more than ever, she had cause to wet her panties at the invitation to tug on the Lycra and flex her pees. For the hunk in a leopard skin jumpsuit, his wedding tackle on display like a vacuum-packed lunch, was known to Cassie. She had unpacked that lunchbox and munched on his sausage many times. She was hungry for him still.

Philippe.

So that was why the rat had never resumed her sessions and had fobbed off all her approaches. Obviously he had not been suffering from a bad back after all. He'd been planning a change of career.

'OK, everybody,' said Philippe on the TV screen as the producer closed in on his pumping thighs, 'imagine you 'ave something 'ard and firm between your buttocks.'

'You bet,' breathed Cassie.

'Imagine you 'ave a *citron*. Now squeeze that wiz your buttocks,' purred the Frenchman. The camera framed his lean tight buns as he demonstrated. '*Qui, oui*, squeeze that *citron* for me!'

Cassie squeezed her *citron*. She felt good, like she always did with Philippe. What a shame she now had to share him with an audience of five million. The dirty, *dirty* rat!

Marianne Matthews also squeezed her *citron* while Philippe strutted his stuff. It gave her enormous satisfaction to watch him flex his fabulous frame as Badger TV's new fitness guru. This was in some measure because she had made the necessary introductions - 'my parting gift to Badger' she called it - but mostly because their affair still burned white-hot.

Philippe gyrated his muscle-packed butt on the bedroom television as Marianne ground the heel of her hand into her pubic bone. The pressure tugged the flesh of her pussy up and down, stretching her clit, tickling her all-but-sated nerve ends. The room smelt of last night's fucking and now the aroma of her present excitement thickened the atmosphere still further.

Pump pump went Philippe's tight bum on the small screen and *pump pump* went Marianne's silky buttocks on the bed sheet. She pushed two fingers between the swollen frills of her labia into the hot swamp of her cunt. She was in a fever and couldn't help herself - just as she hadn't been able to help herself last night. She had intended Philippe to have a good night's rest and had sworn to herself she would leave his irresistible body alone. Somehow it hadn't worked out like that. At two in the morning she'd had her ankles round his ears and when the alarm had gone at four to get him to the studio he'd had to remove his beautiful cock from halfway down her throat.

And now here she was, inspired by the sight of her lover on television, wanking her raw and swollen pussy to yet another orgasm.

'*Formidable*,' said the pink-suited TV presenter. 'Thank you, Monsieur Muscles. All the ladies will be rushing out to buy lemons after that.'

Let them, thought Marianne, pinching her clit between thumb and forefinger. *Just so long as I can keep his banana.*

Chastity Honeydew removed her spectacles from the bridge of her nose and tossed them onto the desk. She stared up at the ceiling for a moment before fixing Cassie with her milky-blue eyes. She sighed. It was an expression of profound disappointment.

'Well, Cassie,' she said at length, a furrow of displeasure on her flawless forehead, 'it hurts me to say it, but I suspected as much.'

She tapped the notebook she had been reading. 'Your POT results are pitiful, the worst I've seen in months. I can see now why your operation here is on the skids.'

Cassie's jaw dropped, she had expected personal vilification but to condemn *Fragrant* was like threatening her own child. 'I beg your pardon,' she said.

'Just look at this outfit, Cass. Low morale, no motivation, poor time-keeping. I mean, it's eight-thirty in the morning and where is everybody?'

Cassie opened her mouth to tell her that office hours began at nine but Chastity had already moved on.

'I've worked on magazines in New York and I tell you, sister, they make this set-up look like amateur night. Remember *Pink Pajamas?* The hottest rag in the Big Apple when you were still learning how to sharpen a pencil. I doubled its circulation in five months. Believe me, Cass, I've seen pros in action and this bunch you've got working for you couldn't cut it in a kindergarten.'

'So how come our circulation has just hit half a million and I'm the Women's Magazine Editor of the Year?' said Cassie with acid in her voice.

Maybe Chastity did not hear, at any rate she did not answer. There were other things on her mind. 'Take a good look at yourself. You're the boss - at present anyway - but you mooch around here like you haven't had a big one for a month. And when I look at your results, I see that you haven't. OK, there's a few ups on your graph here and there, and you obviously made some kind of effort last night for which I am grateful, but basically there's zilch. I mean, it explains why you look so terrible and all. But you started off so well. What happened? Did you forget to change the batteries in your vibrator?'

During this speech Cassie considered murder, maybe she could glue up Chastity's lips and nostrils and let her suffocate on her own wind. Instead she said, 'My Personal Orgasm Guide quit. I don't seem to have got on very well without him.'

The furrow on the flawless brow lengthened and something approaching concern flickered in the milky-blue eyes.

'Shit, honey, you should have said. We'd have got you another.'

'I kept hoping he'd come back. He was - he is - a bit special.'

'Do I know him? What's his name?'

'Philippe.'

'*Philippe?*' Chastity looked thunderstruck. 'French guy built like a young Arnie Schwarzenegger? With a *schlong* like a jumbo *bratwurst?*'

'I like to think of it as a loaf of French bread.'

'Whatever. Something you can make a regular meal out of. And your meal ticket ran off. Poor you.'

Cassie was amazed to find that Chastity was holding her hand. The gesture was so unexpected she began to cry.

'Hey, come on, sister,' said the American and she produced a handful of paper tissues from somewhere to stem the flow.

'I remember that guy,' she said as Cassie mopped up. 'I trained him personally out in LA. Though, believe me, he didn't need much training. He had complete control of his body and could keep it up for hours. And he knew all the little places where a woman likes to be...'

The milky-blue eyes began to cloud with nostalgia and other emotions. She reached for the tissues herself.

'I thought he'd gone back to France. He left about a year ago. I tell you, Cass, it's been a bloody year since he went.'

'Really?' Cassie was rapt. This conversation had taken an unexpected turn. Having let slip her own guard she was interested in any admission Chastity might make. She opened her mind to the possibility that she might come to like the bitch after all.

'You see, Cass, I believe in the Honeydew method. It's my life's work. Healthy living through orgasm, that's my philosophy. By the way, my next book's called *Multiple Orgasms, Multiple Choices*, it's about freedom and liberty and all that stuff - do you like it?'

'Fabulous.'

'So, you see, I'm a business, I got commitments, I got turnover to generate through books and seminars and spreading the Honeydew philosophy all over the world. So how do you think it would be if it got round that Chastity Honeydew couldn't come any more?'

'*What?*'

'You see. You're shocked. You've gone white.'

'You mean you can't have an orgasm?'

'Haven't had one for a year.'

The implications of what she had witnessed in her office last night flashed through Cassie's mind. It was true, Chastity had not come, despite the efforts of her trained studs.

Chastity sighed a heartfelt sigh.

'I shouldn't tell you, Cassie, but I need to tell someone. I haven't got my rocks off since that Frenchman packed up his breadstick and left me last year.'

An idea dawned. 'Would you like to meet Philippe again?'

Chastity pursed her pretty pink lips in a wan smile. 'Sometimes I think that if I could just get into his pants one more time the lights would go on again. You know, that I'd be OK after that.'

'Right,' said Cassie, getting to her feet with renewed energy. 'You and I are going to pay a visit to a certain television studio tomorrow morning.'

'What for?'

'It's a surprise. Just bring the boys with you.'

'Why?'

'I want to go in with all goons blazing.'

'I don't get it.'

'Never mind. Just remember I'm doing you a big favour and I want something in return.'

'What's that?'

'I want my office back.'

Unaware of the fate awaiting him, Philippe pushed open the door to Marianne's bedroom, dropping with fatigue. He had been awake half the night making love and up before dawn to give his all to his new job. Then he had made straight for the gym - keeping himself in shape was now more important than ever. He had been longing for the moment when he could pitch face down onto the soft mattress and bury his face in the pillows and allow sleep to descend on him like a soft warm blanket...

'Darling.' The husky voice was in his ear and Marianne's fingers were on his back, plucking at his shirt like little mice. 'You can't go to bed with all your clothes on. Let me help you.'

'No, no, *cherie*,' he murmured. 'Just leave me. I'm so *fatigue*...'

'Philippe, I insist. At least let me take your jeans off. Lift your hips, that's right. Oho! I thought you said you were sleepy.'

'Marianne, please.'

'My, my, look at this. I swear that's a part of you that never sleeps. I bet I know where he'd like to go.'

'No, *cherie*, no.'

'Oh yes, my darling, *yes!*'

Chapter 37

'Here we are, Miss Rosewater, the best table for you, as promised. May I bring you an aperitif?'

'Make it a mineral water, Josef. I've got to keep a clear head.'

Petra Rosewater had thought hard about this lunch meeting. Her intention was to establish some kind of ascendancy over her guest and so she had selected the venue with care (a converted boathouse overlooking the river packed with media trendies) and had power dressed for the occasion (a white silk suit with padded shoulders, buttoned to the throat). Her plan was to take the bull by the horns - or the dyke by the dugs, as she'd said to Harriet when she'd left the office. She was lunching Inspector Claire Quartermain and she was scared shitless.

'Petra, my dear, what a delightful place!'

Petra stood shakily and allowed her cheeks to be bussed by a vision of summer sunshine in a pink and cream dress with a scooped neck and short sleeves. Claire Quartermain's arms were tanned and her hair fell onto her shoulders in loose brown curls. The lines of weariness around her eyes and mouth were crinkled into a smile and, most terrifying of all, she was wearing lipstick. The waiter's eyes caressed her shapely hips as he eased her into her chair.

'You must have some clout to get a table here,' continued the policewoman. 'I hear it's all the rage.'

'Tom has the clout,' said Petra. 'He put money in the business.'

'How philanthropic of him. Cheers!' And she drained a tumbler full of fizzing clear liquid a-chink with crushed ice. 'I hope you don't mind, I ordered a cocktail on my way in. Delicious.'

'It looks it,' said Petra whose best intentions were evaporating as fast as her Perrier.

'Here, taste.' Claire pressed the glass into Petra's hand. It bore the clear pink imprint of the policewoman's lips. Petra pressed her own to the other side of the glass and the liquid bubbled down her throat like iced nectar.

'Waiter,' said Claire to the alert Josef, 'you'd better fetch a couple of these at the double. And bring the menu and wine list while you're at it.' Petra still had the cocktail glass in her hand. She took another gulp. Already things seemed to have slipped from her control.

'Look, Inspector—'

'Claire.'

'Look, Claire, the reason I've asked you here is to discuss Tom's accident.'

Josef returned with the drinks and fussed. Petra could have done without the recitation of the day's specials but Claire was agog. She made him repeat the list so she could fix the details in her mind. Petra ploughed on.

'I think I've got some idea who he saw that night. It was a secret meeting that he didn't discuss with any of us.'

'I think I'll have guinea fowl, they say this chef is very good with game. Shall we have some wine?'

'If you like.'

'I'd prefer red. How about a beaujolais? That's not too heavy.'

'OK.'

'I rather like the look of the St Amour. What do you think?'

'Please, order what you like.' Petra was fast realising that there was no point in trying to talk seriously to the inspector until she had eaten. Or maybe the woman was deliberately trying to put her off. In which case she was succeeding.

'I'll have the same,' she said to Josef as he hovered, pencil poised. *What the hell*, she thought and drained her cocktail.

The wine was a success. They ordered a second bottle to go with the cheese. Petra watched Claire lick a runny dollop of brie from the side of her thumb. Her long pink tongue scooped up the creamy cheese with relish. *She's like a cat*, thought Petra, *lithe and sensual and clever. With sharp claws.*

Claire caught Petra looking at her. Her hazel eyes flashed and she grinned. One silky lock of hair had fallen across her face and she pushed it away absent-mindedly as she said: 'So who was he meeting on the night he fell off the balcony?'

Petra put down her wineglass and took a deep breath. 'Whoever it was they represented a company called Glass Tools of Glendrockit.'

'Tell me more,' said Claire as she speared the bleu d' Auvergne. And Petra told her.

'So,' said Claire, still chewing, 'he bought this company without telling anybody about it and then took a dive over the balcony with a pair of knickers on his head.'

'I think he was drugged and then pushed.'

'By the person he'd just promised to pay five million quid? Wouldn't that scupper the deal?'

'It doesn't look like it. He signed an agreement that's binding. I've been trying to get out of it ever since.'

'Has he got the authority to do that?'

'Yes. He owns the company, he can act on his own without reference to shareholders.'

'I see. And what do these Glass Tools people say?'

'They say, "Where's our cheque?" Through their solicitors, that is. I haven't met anyone from the company and there's no such place as Glendrockit as far as I can tell, not unless it's in the Cayman Islands.'

'An off-shore shell company, you mean?'

'Yes. I thought you ought to know about this as it puts Tom in a better light, doesn't it?'

Claire raised an eyebrow and said nothing. Obviously she didn't agree.

'I suppose our best hope is still that he recovers his memory. I keep hoping every time I see him that he'll be back to normal. Have you talked to him recently?'

Claire grinned. 'I saw him last night. When we took him into custody.'

Petra screamed. The noise was involuntary, as was the jerk she gave to the tablecloth which caused the half-full bottle of beaujolais to somersault into her lap.

Petra wept in the ladies' loo. She had wasted her time sucking up to the Quartermain bitch when Tom was already in jail. The policewoman had made her look like a complete fool. And her white silk suit was ruined.

There was a knock on the door. 'Come out, Petra,' said Claire.

'Go away,' said Petra.

'There's no point in you sitting in there.'

'Sod off,' shouted Petra drunkenly.

'Now now, calm down. It wasn't my idea to arrest Tom, you know. I just obey orders like everybody else.'

'The Nuremberg defence.'

'It's true. Open up.'

'What are you going to do? Rape me like last time? Fuck off, you Nazi.'

'Don't be daft, Petra. Look, I've got a car upstairs, you'll be home in twenty minutes. Maybe we can rescue that suit.'

'Was it really not your idea to put Tom in jail?'

'Prosecutor Hawk's express command. Honest.'

The door swung open. A bedraggled Petra was slumped on the toilet seat.

'Come on, darling,' said Claire with her sweetest, most ominous smile. 'Let me get you home and out of those wet things.'

Chapter 38

Outside The Primrose Court the August sun was shining. It was a perfect summer's afternoon. Inside, in the basement, there was no light or warmth. In the darkness of Tom Glass's meagre cell it could just as well have been December.

Tom drew the thin blanket around his bare shoulders and shivered. The room was damp, the bed was hard and there were chains around his ankles. A tap dripped into a bucket somewhere out of sight. His stomach grumbled and his bladder ached. No one had come near him for fifteen hours - not since they'd thrown him in here at midnight.

He'd always feared it would come to this. His ordeal was just beginning.

A key turned in the lock and a shaft of blue artificial light from the corridor fell on his face. He blinked as a tall figure entered, carrying a tray. The aroma of hot tea ravished his senses.

'Bet you thought we'd forgotten you,' said a nasal Cockney voice. 'We 'adn't, we was just leavin' you to stew.'

Tom pulled himself into a sitting position, the chains on his feet clinking as he did so. His visitor had now turned on the light and he could see she was more of a girl than a woman, a thin streak with ragged blonde hair and a sulky face stretched into a malicious grin. He was conscious that beneath his blanket he was stark-naked.

The girl poured tea into a mug and set it on the floor by the bed. Tom reached for it. 'Thank you,' he said.

The girl grasped the blanket and pulled it off his body. Her small eyes gleamed as she took in his broad chest, flat stomach, lean thighs - and fat sausage of a cock. Tom sipped his tea, there wasn't much else he could do.

'You're a cool customer,' she said, 'I'll give you that. Some people go bananas when they first come in here. Scream night long. Wet themselves and everything. Then we give hell.'

'Really,' said Tom. He couldn't help noticing that she was wearing a skirt no longer than a pelmet.

'Of course, they're in here to suffer anyway so it gets them off to a good start. The sooner they suffer, the sooner they realise the error of their ways. And get out.'

'I see,' said Tom. The little witch really had the most fabulous legs.

'The way you're going, mate, I reckon you'll be in here a very long time.'

'I doubt it. There's been a serious miscarriage of justice. I expect that heads will soon roll, from top to bottom. I'd be interested to know your name.'

'Fiona.'

'Just Fiona?'

'Constable Fiona Maybe. As in maybe I'll be nice to you and maybe I won't.' And she took hold of his testicles and squeezed.

Later, in the dark, Tom willed himself to go to sleep. His bladder was now empty, his stomach full - and his face was covered in dried juice from Fiona's pussy. She'd made him suck her off before she'd let him pee. And after he'd eaten bread and cheese she'd shackled his hands and left him with no means of relieving the bone-hard erection that throbbed between his thighs. He was used to regular sexual release. His body ached for the abundant flesh of Eve Biscuit.

At present his mind was filled with images of Constable Fiona Maybe - of long pale legs and a loose-lipped cunt and a sulky face with an evil grin. And Fiona was just the advance guard, he realised, the storm troopers would be following on behind. He would need all his strength. He willed himself to sleep.

Tom dreamed of New York. Of an apartment on the Upper East Side overlooking Central Park where the winter sunlight sparkled on the crystal goblet in his hand and picked out every crest and cavity of the Jackson Pollock canvas on the wall. And glistened on the auburn tresses of his colleague and lover, Meredith Rich, sitting by his side.

Opposite them reclined their host, the owner of this luxurious apartment where servants glided across polished mahogany floors like phantoms and the walls were adorned with enough priceless modern art to furnish a small museum. Ralph Simons raised his brandy glass to Tom and Meredith in salute.

'OK,' he said, 'you finally wore me out. You got a deal.'

Tom wanted to shout with joy. He'd been trying to nail down the old sod and his TV company for six months. Instead he stood and held out his hand. Simons grasped it in strong bony fingers and clapped him on the back.

'I tell you, Tom,' said Simons, 'I wouldn't dream of getting into bed with you guys if it wasn't for Meredith.'

'I'm glad she finally won you over,' said Tom, beaming at the tall redhead. 'She's pretty persuasive, isn't she?'

'Yes, sir.' Simons ignored the slender hand she was proffering and slid his arm around her waist. 'I'm already thinking of changing my mind so she can persuade me all over again.'

Tom laughed but it rang a little hollow. He knew the kind of persuading Meredith had been up to and he was far from happy about it.

Simons had pulled the girl into his arms and was kissing her enthusiastically. One hand was on her back, rucking up the peach silk of her blouse, the other dug into the rounded flesh of her buttocks through her skirt. She disengaged her lips for a moment.

'Take it easy with my clothes, Ralph,' she said. 'You don't have to tear the paper to get at the present.'

Ralph relaxed his grip. 'Hey, that's smart. That's what I like about you, Meredith, you not only got a great ass you got brains.' And he laughed.

Tom's face ached from the effort of holding his smile in place. He wanted to kick the bastard in the nuts but Meredith's hazel eyes were flashing him an unmistakable message: Don't blow it now.

'OK then, little lady,' boomed Ralph, 'take off the gift-wrapping yourself.' He sat back in his chair with a smirk his face. 'I bet Tom appreciates a striptease as much as I do.'

'Come on, Ralph,' said Tom, 'a joke's a joke.'

'It's OK, Tom,' Meredith cut it. 'I don't mind entering the spirit of the occasion.' She pulled her blouse from her skirt with one hand and kicked off a shoe. 'Get up on the table,' commanded Ralph, 'and make it sexy.'

She made it as sexy as she could, considering she wasn't dressed for the activity. She quickly peeled off her blouse and skirt and winter tights and posed in a silk half-slip and matching panties. Her nipples were clear points beneath the slip and her knickers were caught in the cleft of her bottom. She stood above them, her face a mask of indifference, and let them look.

'Take off the rest,' said Ralph.

She pulled the slip over her head and flung it at him, her bare breasts shimmying. He caught the material and held it to his face, inhaling her perfume.

'Now the panties,' he said, his eyes big as he watched her tug the gusset free of the chestnut curls of her pussy. He snatched the garment and pressed it to his nose. 'You smell hot,' he said.

'You make me hot,' she said, 'you filthy old goat.'

'Ain't I just?' He reached up and ran his hand into her crotch. His fingers probed her damp bush, seeking the entrance to her vagina.

Tom was frozen with horror and lust. Meredith had told him that Simons was a disgusting old lecher - now he was seeing for himself.

'Hey, Tom,' Ralph said, one hand busy between Meredith's legs, the other prying apart her buttocks, 'pay attention - I'm warmin' her up for you.'

Tom looked at Ralph without comprehension. He had been debating whether to slip away and leave the pair of them to it.

Ralph's beady glare was fixed on him, even as he palpated Meredith's tender flesh. 'Take your pants off, son, and show an old boy how it's done.'

'But... I...' he was at a loss.

'Come on, baby,' said Meredith, holding out her hand. 'Ralph wants to watch us make love.'

'No,' said Tom. 'Definitely, no.'

'I don't think you mean that, son.'

'Please.' There was a note of desperation in her voice.

'Look, partner, you want this deal, don't you?'

What choice did he have?

He unzipped his pants...

Tom woke in the dark, shivering not with cold but with lust. His stiff cock sawed against the blanket in frustration. His memory of that day in New York was crystal clear in his mind. He could taste the honey of Meredith's breath on his lips, feel the taut kiss of her belly on his - and see the gargoyle grin on Ralph Simons' face as he watched the pair of them fuck for his personal pleasure.

It was not an occasion that any man was likely to forget - and yet Tom had forgotten it from the date of his fall until now. His pulse quickened. It had been eight, no - seven - years ago. It was much later than his dreams of Shani and Tina and Chas Cross. Maybe this time his memory was really coming back!

His mind turned to the events of seven years ago, when he had broken into the cable TV business, the adorable Meredith Rich by his side. His penis twitched in anguish on his belly. How he could do with Meredith's adorable touch right now!

Chapter 39

Petra cursed her foolishness many times over as the police car cut a swathe through the West End traffic on its way to her Primrose Hill flat. The burly blonde driver in a TCD shell-suit - not, thank God, the awful Sergeant Tooth - squealed corners on two wheels and zigzagged through oncoming vehicles, siren screaming, as if answering an SOS.

'This is an emergency after all,' said Claire Quartermain, taking possession of Petra's hand and squeezing it in a supposedly reassuring fashion. 'There's no time to lose if we're to save that suit.'

Petra said nothing. She was drunk and she was scared. She had stupidly put herself at the mercy of the one person in London she should have avoided - the ghastly lesbian who now held Tom Glass under lock and key. She held her thighs together as tightly as she could and willed herself to resist the forthcoming ordeal. But she knew it would be no good. Already she could feel her excitement lubricating her vagina.

Claire bundled Petra into her flat and dismissed the driver. 'Help me, darling,' she said to Petra as she began to unbutton the spoiled jacket of the suit. Like a robot, Petra stepped out of her skirt and handed it over. Then she retreated to her bedroom.

She stripped off her remaining clothes and crawled naked into bed. Her head was spinning and her body was quivering. Outside she heard the sounds of cupboards opening and water running.

Her bedroom door opened.

'I've done the best I can with your suit,' said Claire. 'I'm afraid it's never going to be the same.'

'It doesn't matter,' said Petra. 'It was my fault.'

'I had the impression it was mine. I shouldn't have sprung the news about Tom on you like that. I'm sorry.'

'What's going to happen to him?'

'There'll be a trial.'

'A show trial, you mean.'

Claire shrugged and sat on the bed. 'Let me be your friend.'

'I can't trust you.'

'No? What would you say if I told you this may work out to your advantage?'

'How could it?'

'See? You're curious.'

'I am not. Take your hands off me please.'

'But you're shaking and you're cold. Let me hold you.'

'Please, Claire. Oh—'

The kiss lasted a long time. At first Petra struggled then she tried a different kind of resistance and flopped like a spineless doll. Then she found herself kissing back, pushing her tongue deep into Claire's hot mouth. *Spineless*, she thought to herself as the policewoman reached for her breasts, *that just about sums me up.*

Claire sucked her nipples to swollen points.

'Bite them,' Petra heard herself say, 'bite them hard. Ooh yes!'

'You're a real livewire, aren't you, darling?' said the other, stripping the bedclothes from Petra's nude body.

Petra grabbed Claire's hand and thrust it between her legs. 'I hate you,' she said, pressing the fingers into her hairy mound, 'you're making me behave like this.'

Claire pulled her hand away. Her fingers were wet. 'You're on heat, woman,' she said. 'Bring yourself off. I want to watch.'

Petra pulled her knees back to her chest and used both hands, spreading herself and stroking the pink stalk of her clitoris with her left and thrusting four fingers of her right deep into her vaginal tunnel.

Claire leaned over her to drink in the view. Petra fancied she could feel the policewoman's eyes burning into her most intimate flesh as she manipulated herself. What she was doing was crazy, obscene, degrading. Yet she yearned to exhibit her weeping cunt to Claire, to finger and fondle her tingling flesh, to share her most secret parts and revel in the hot flush of shame. She couldn't help it.

'OH!' The cry broke from her throat like a surfacing bubble, to be followed by more bubbles of ecstasy as her hips writhed and her arse shook and her fingers moved in a blur. 'OH YES!' she shouted at the moment of release.

'Oh yes,' said Claire as she removed the now-still hands and replaced them with her warm lips, rimming the labial frill of Petra's hungry vagina and pushing her tongue inside as deep as it would go. She cupped the bowl of Petra's suspended buttocks and drank the juices which ran from her steaming sex. She bathed her with her lips and tongue until the intensity of the self-pleasuring faded and Petra yearned for more.

Then Claire stood and stripped. The summer dress was thrown carelessly to the floor, followed by her brassiere. She retained her white panties which were cut high on the hip. Through the thin cotton could be seen the brown hair of her pubic beard. Her breasts were full and pink and they jutted out to the sides of her body - to Petra's eyes they looked huge as they hung over her. The areolae were as big as saucers with small dark nipples like cherry stones. Petra buried her face in the soft globes and sucked like a starving puppy.

Claire insinuated a lean thigh between Petra's legs and ground her pelvis down onto the younger woman's pubis. Petra answered the pressure, buffeting her loins back into the policewoman's pantied mons. The two of them set up rhythm, pushing, jostling, squeezing their pliant flesh together, lost in a whirl of lust.

Petra came first, Claire made sure of it, pushing a hand between their bodies to finger the brunette's throbbing clit, bringing her to the edge. And over it.

'Oh, Claire!' she sobbed into the policewoman's neck and bit down hard. Claire squealed with the pain and the thrill of it and smacked the taut sphere of Petra's right buttock.

'You little bitch,' she said, fingering her wound, 'you've drawn blood.'

'I'm sorry, Claire. Punish me. Beat me. Please.'

The policewoman needed no encouragement, throwing the wriggling woman over her knees and smacking her arse cheeks until they glowed crimson. Petra twisted and turned under the blows, tears flowing from her eyes to match the river of her excitement running from her burning cunt.

'Harder, harder!' she moaned, surprising herself with the intensity of her passion. And as she squirmed under the blows, the smack of cruel hand on yielding buttock echoing through the room, her thoughts turned to the strange novels of Morticia Chekhov. Maybe they weren't so outlandish as she had first thought.

Later, after Petra had recovered, they returned to their earlier conversation.

'I know this may be unpalatable to you,' said Claire, 'but you do stand to gain if Glass is successfully prosecuted.'

'What do you mean?'

'You could end up running his business. This whole thing is about replacing men with women, don't you see?'

'But I couldn't.'

'Why not? You're doing the job already. And if you don't, they'll find some other smart cow to put in his place.'

'But he's done nothing wrong! It's his company!'

'Then put yourself in a position to help him if the worst comes to the worst. Do you know anyone with connections to The Primrose Court?'

'Cassie Crow, I suppose.'

'There you are. And I can put in a word for you too. Maybe.'

'What do you mean "maybe"?'

'Put it like this, Petra, there's a hole between my legs which needs plugging. With your face.'

Petra grinned. She had a better idea. She showed Claire The Magic Wand.

Claire turned the strange glass object over in her hand. 'My, my,' she said, a flush of appreciation on her cheeks.

As she examined the Wand, Petra slid her hand into the policewoman's sopping knickers.

'This is made by Glass Tools of Glendrockit,' she said, her fingers roving the hairy jewel of the other's capacious, loose-lipped cunt. 'Would you like me to show you how it works?'

Claire grunted as Petra located her clit. The policewoman's fingers were wrapped tight around the Wand's glowing shaft and her eyes were smoky with want.

'Then you can use it on me,' continued Petra, stroking and tickling Claire's jumping flesh.

'Mm, yes!'

'We'll have a fabulous time.'

'For God's sake, woman, put it up me!'

'If you promise to let me see Tom.'

'OK.'

'Soon. Do you promise?'

'Yes, *yes!* Just put it in and shag me silly. *Now!*'

Petra was a good citizen. She was very happy to obey an officer of the law.

Chapter 40

It was late afternoon by the time Tom and Meredith left Ralph Simons' penthouse and returned to their hotel. It had been a lengthy session. Tom supported Meredith around the waist as they approached the door of their suite in the Bluestone Towers.

'God, I can't wait to get under a shower,' she said. 'I feel like I've been swimming in spunk.'

'Who would have thought the old goat had so much juice in him?' whispered Tom into her ear. He felt high on sex and success.

'It's OK for you - it wasn't your ass he spunked over,' said Meredith.

This was true. For a finale to his orgy of voyeurism, Simons had made Meredith kneel between Tom's legs and take his cock in her mouth. Then he'd pulled a gnarled but virile penis from his pants and shot off all over her beautiful derriere. Tom hadn't been able to prevent himself spunking down her throat at the same time.

'Just think,' he said as he ushered her into the palatial sitting room that had been their home for the past week, 'you'll be able to tell your grandchildren you once got it at both ends from two millionaires.'

She stopped in the middle of pulling her clothes off. 'Sometimes you disgust me, Glass.'

'Sounds like you could do with a drink. How about some champagne to toast the deal of the decade?'

'No,' she said. 'I want a shower, coffee and bed - on my own. Ring room service if you want to be useful.'

Tom watched her sumptuous white buttocks wink at him as she strode to the bathroom. He ordered the coffee and followed her; there was a serious point to be made.

He perched on the side of the bath while she stood beneath the teeming water.

'What's it going to take to persuade you to stay here and keep that old lecher sweet while the deal goes through?'

She considered the matter as she soaped her voluptuous body. Tom watched the lather glisten on the gentle dome of her belly and gather in the luxurious vee of curls in her crotch.

'I'd settle for a piece of jewellery,' she said, holding out her left hand. 'Like a ring on my third finger.'

His eyes focused on the big wet globes of her breasts while his brain took in the implications of her words. He said nothing.

Meredith sighed. 'It's OK, Tom, I'm only joking. Why would I want to marry a man who'd sell my ass to Ralph Simons? Just give me a cheque.'

'Ten grand?' said Tom quickly.

'Make it twenty. It's a high-class ass.'

Tom did not disagree.

The phone rang in the sitting room. It was Simons. 'Are you alone?' he said.

'Yes, why?'

'There's a restaurant round the corner called The Blue Rhinoceros - meet me at the bar in ten minutes. Just you.'

Tom was pissed. He'd had more than he could stand of the old villain for one day.

'I'm sorry, Ralph, Meredith and I have other plans and I can't just—'

'Hey, *partner*, remember I haven't signed the contract yet. Be there in ten minutes. Alone.' And he hung up.

Tom pushed through the crush of people waiting to check their coats in the foyer of The Blue Rhinoceros. He was fifteen minutes late - a small rebellion but the best he could do.

He found Ralph Simons in the crowded bar. He was wearing a white tuxedo and sipping what looked like a very large Scotch. When he saw Tom his face split into a melon-sized grin.

'Hey, Tommy,' he shouted above the din, gripping Tom round the shoulders, 'whatdya think of this place?'

'Busy,' said Tom.

'Of course it is. It's the hottest place in the city. Swifty Levine and Marian Mortadella eat here every night. Howdja like the decor?'

Tom followed the direction of Ralph's gesticulating arm and took in a vast dining room whose domed roof was painted to resemble some kind of African plain. The kind populated by leaping green wildebeest, scarlet lions and, surprise surprise, blue rhinoceroses.

'I say gimme a steak house any day,' continued Simons. 'Here it's third-world food at first-world prices. You pay fifty bucks for a burnt red pepper and a baby olive, whatever that is. But I'm old-fashioned, you're gonna love it. Especially when you see your date.'

'My date?'

'Here she comes now. Ain't that a fabulous-looking woman?'

Tom couldn't deny it. The olive-skinned, almond-eyed beauty seemed to float through the crush towards them. Heads turned and conversations halted along her route. She was tall, nearly six foot Tom guessed, and the mountain of black ringlets piled high on her head, cascading down her slender neck set her high above the crowd. She wore the kind of black dress designed to make headlines at film premieres and charity galas; so cunningly cut away and cinched together across acres of gleaming flesh that it gave the impression she was both fully dressed and stark-naked at the same time.

In his ear Ralph said, 'May I present the Senior Vice-President of the Simons Corporation. Tom Glass, meet my daughter, Laura.'

Tom's head was spinning. He was seated at a table opposite Laura Simons, trying hard not to stare at her breasts. This was difficult because he had nothing to distract him from their impossible pneumatic thrust, artfully displayed beneath a whisper of black chiffon. Ralph had long gone - to the opera, he said - urging them to get better acquainted and not to talk business. Frankly Tom would have been happy to talk anything at all but each of his overtures was met with a monosyllabic response. All that remained was for him to sit in silence, magnetised by the shift and fall of his companion's near-naked bosom every time she breathed.

'Look,' she said suddenly, her coal-black eyes sparking into life, 'this wasn't my idea you know.'

'What wasn't?'

'This whole ritzy dinner shtick. Me sitting here like dog-meat and you ogling my tits.'

'It wasn't my idea either.'

'And if that's all you wanna do, jerk-off, you can go down Times Square and stick money in the slots.'

'I think there's some kind of misunderstanding here.'

'No there isn't. You're just some tourist thrill-seeker. I wonder what kind of hold you've got on my father to make him pimp for you, that's all.'

'Please, Miss Simons, I don't know what you're talking about. I can only suggest that if you find my company so objectionable we should terminate the evening immediately.'

She grinned at him suddenly. She had a big mouth, wide and fleshy with full pouting lips. The kind that would look good, the thought popped into Tom's head unbidden, poised above his stiff cock.

'You speak real la-di-da, Mr Glass. I guess it's because you're a Brit.'

'I guess,' said Tom, unnerved by what looked like another mood swing. 'Look, you don't like me and I don't like you, so let's go.'

'Where you gonna take me? If my father found out we split early I'd catch hell. There's a lowlife bar across the street - how about that?'

'I'm not going anywhere with you in that dress. You'll start a riot.'

She got to her feet, the bosom moving fractionally later than the rest of her. A man at the next table choked on a mouthful of pancetta.

'It's OK,' she said, 'I'll keep my coat on.'

They made their way out slowly, their early departure observed by every eye in the room. Laura giggled as they stood by the desk waiting for their bill.

'You know what they're all thinking, don't you?' she whispered into his ear. 'They think we're so hot for each other we're going home to ball our eyes out.'

It was true. Tom could see it in the faces of the men as their greedy glances crawled all over Laura's spectacular frame. The women were smirking at him, exchanging knowing remarks with each other. Suddenly he realised why - he was massively and very obviously erect.

Laura patted the bulge in his pants and said, 'Let's skip the bar and go back to my place. We wouldn't want to disappoint the people, now would we?'

Tom grunted his agreement. He wasn't capable of speech.

Chapter 41

Philippe emerged from the studios of Badger Television breathed in the fresh morning air. Life felt good. He escaped from a world where he was nothing but a paid gigolo and had discovered a new existence as a national fitness guru - and heart-throb. He had a sack of fan mail to prove it. And he also had Marianne, a woman who touched him as no other could. He knew he owed his spot at Badger to her and he was determined to make her happy, even if he died trying. Which he might, since she demanded the kind of lovemaking he was not accustomed to giving. Here was a woman who wanted every ounce of his precious sap. Ah well, there were sacrifices to be made in every sphere of existence.

As he reached his car, he realised he was not alone. He was flanked by two large men, almost as big as he was. Two others appeared in front of him. For once he was outmuscled - what the hell was going on?

The appearance of the voluptuous redhead did not exactly explain matters.

'Good morning, Philippe,' said Cassie. 'I believe we have an appointment.'

'Madame Crow, what are you doing here?'

'You abandoned me, you rat. You owe me a few sessions - about six weeks' worth.'

Philippe's brain was working overtime. He had always liked Cassie, she wasn't as much of a screaming neurotic as most of his other Honeydew clients. Could he have misjudged her? 'But, Cassie, that is in the past. I no longer practise as a personal trainer.'

'One more session, Philippe. That's all I want.'

For a moment Philippe wavered. Cassie did look rather fetching with the morning breeze fluttering through her loose auburn curls and the sharp points of her big breasts pressing against the weave of her tight sweater. The tall Australian had always been most responsive, he recalled.

'I'm sorry, madame, but I have resigned from the Honeydew programme.'

'Not yet you haven't, buster.'

The blonde woman appeared from nowhere, from behind one of the musclemen, probably. The sight of her froze the Frenchman with fear, like the touch of a pistol in the small of his back. A lot had happened to him in the year since he had last looked into those milky-blue eyes but his newfound confidence was wiped away in an instant.

Chastity curled an arm round his neck and drew his head down to place her lips on his. She pushed her tongue into his mouth and held him close. The embrace went on for some time. When she stepped away from him, the coveted breadstick in his pants was rigid. Chastity placed a proprietorial hand upon the bulge.

'Let's go and have breakfast,' she said.

When they reached her hotel, Chastity dismissed her boys. 'You did not need to bring your gorillas to fetch me,' said Philippe. 'I would have accepted your invitation, Chastity.'

'Would you? You ran away without saying goodbye, as I recall. I got the impression you didn't like me any more.'

Philippe looked out of the window at the tree tops of Hyde Park, though his mind was far away, reliving his life in California a year earlier. How could he explain that Chastity had overwhelmed him like a drug? That he had been compelled to escape before he was hooked forever - and turned into a zombie like all her other studs.

He shrugged. 'I did not want to be a Stepford man,' he said at last.

Cassie laughed and pulled her sweater over her head. She wore a black brassiere with transparent cups. Her long red nipples were very obvious.

'Good for you,' she said. 'But you owe us both, Philippe. I suggest you pay up and we'll let bygones be bygones.'

'Great idea,' said Chastity, kicking off her shoes and unbuckling her jeans.

Philippe's eyes bulged as the two women in front of him stripped. In his professional life, he had had vast experience of women and the display of their bodies. It was rare for him to react as other men might. But this was different. He had particular sympathy for Cassie, she seemed to be on his side. And her big creamy body with its mane of red hair was an undeniable turn-on, particularly when set beside the gold blonde nudity of his mentor, Chastity Honeydew. As the two of them pulled off their clothes to reveal their sumptuous fuckable flesh the Frenchman's cock threatened to explode.

In a flurry of shimmering breasts and bouncing buttocks the women were on him. They dragged him into the bedroom, pulling the clothes from his athletic frame as they went. For once, Philippe was not in charge. As the soft weight of Chastity's buttocks settled on his chest and her blonde-fuzzed pussy inched towards his face, he smiled. He was about to be raped. Resistance was useless - he might as well lie back and enjoy it.

In the vee of Philippe's tree-trunk thighs, Cassie laid claim to his magnificent prick. It thrust up between her hands in a white tower of tumescence capped with a ruby-red head so broad it almost didn't fit in her mouth. She was in heaven as she gorged on the beautiful monster. She fed on it like a lollipop, running her tongue from base to tip, gumming the glans and rubbing the knob against her soft upper palate.

Cassie was aware of the significance of the moment for her partner in crime. It seemed that Chastity's career as a sex guru hinged on stuffing Philippe's big engine up her twat and riding it to satisfaction. In the circumstances maybe she should give the American first crack. Maybe.

Above her, Cassie heard the intake of breath as Chastity ground her pussy into the Frenchman's face and she hesitated no longer. She too had her needs and now was no time to hang back. Faint heart, after all, never got fucked. Cassie swung her leg over Philippe's pelvis and pushed the length of him up into her aching slot.

The three of them went at it like one mad, sex-crazed beast; the two women riding the giant Frenchman, Chastity's fingers in his hair cradling his face in her crotch, Cassie's arms round Chastity's body, squeezing the soft fruits of those perfect California tits in her hands as Philippe's Eiffel Tower of a tool speared up into her belly.

Cassie screamed as she came and fell off her supine lover onto the bed, a warm glow of contentment singing through her veins. As she caught her breath she watched Chastity writhing on top of Philippe, her face set in a rictus of frustration that was familiar to Cassie from her observations of two nights ago. But this time Cassie was in a position to help out.

She smacked Chastity round the face, sending the blonde tresses flying. It was a satisfying moment. The American gaped at her in shock and bewilderment until Cassie took her hand and placed it on Philippe's cock. The instant Chastity's fingers closed around the tumescent organ the tension seemed to drain from her face. Cassie helped her shift her body backwards, down the Frenchman's gleaming muscular torso, to the staff of salvation that thrust upwards from his crotch.

'Thank you, Cass,' muttered the American as Cassie pointed the big, plum-like head into the wet opening between her legs.

'My pleasure,' muttered Cassie as she smoothed the juices from Chastity's pussy around the glans and down the shaft of the Frenchman's formidable baton. She savoured the feel of their hot pulsing genitals, the nobility of her actions swelling her breast. 'You can do the same for me some day,' she said as she eased the swollen knob into the mouth of Chastity's yearning cunt.

The American sat down slowly on Philippe's weapon, muttering to herself as she took the stiff shaft deep inside her. Her face was slack, her eyes open but unseeing, her mouth agape, the lower lip full and wet.

'Oh Philippe,' she whispered, 'how I've missed you, you dirty French fucker.'

His hands were on her body now, meeting round her waist as he thrust her down onto his pelvis.

'Ah!' she screamed, the breath rushing from her body. He lifted her up and slammed her down again. 'Oh yes!' she cried as he lifted and dropped her again and again on his mighty cock, using her body like a great masturbating fist.

'Oh God!' she shrieked as her first orgasm in a year burst upon her, racking her body with sensation, sending her peachy tits flying and her hair whirling and her hips undulating on the incredible invading penis of Monsieur Muscles.

Chapter 42

Laura's place was a ten-minute cab ride away across the wintery city. Despite the perishing cold, Tom's cock remained as stiff as a pike-staff throughout the journey. Perhaps that was because Laura had her warm fingers wrapped around it the entire time.

Her house was on three storeys close to the East River. Inside it was full of dark polished wood and chintzy drapes and Victorian prints. The atmosphere was almost European. Tom would have commented on this but the direction the evening was heading did not allow for it. In any case, he didn't want to talk to this peculiar woman - he wanted to fuck her.

They kissed for the first time in the small vestibule. As he had suspected, her wide flexible mouth was made for pleasure. Beneath his coat his penis was standing stiff outside his trousers, just as she had arranged it in the taxi. As she explored his mouth with her agile tongue she pulled his balls into the open. She examined his genitals in the dark as if she were a blind woman reading Braille. He kept his hands to himself and let her have her way. Eventually she took her mouth from his and pushed his coat off his shoulders.

'Come upstairs,' she said.

He followed her up the steep stairway, the split skirt of her dress swaying in front of him, displaying the lean lines of her legs with every step. Near the top he caught her by the ankle.

'Stop,' he said and she obeyed. 'Pull your skirt up,' he said.

She looked over her shoulder at him and grinned slyly.

'You look pretty funny standing there with your dick out,' she said, hitching her skirt up over her rear.

She wore sheer black tights with a cutaway seat and the olive ovals of her exquisite bottom pouted at him in exotic invitation. He fought the urge to bury his face in their satin perfection.

'Aren't you cold going around like that?' he said.

She bent over, resting her elbows on the top of the stairs. 'I find ways of warming up,' she said.

He smacked the delectable hemisphere of her left buttock, the sound echoing round the small space.

'Yes,' she said, 'like that.'

He smacked the other cheek, harder this time, leaving the clear imprint of his palm on the pale flesh. She sucked in her breath with a hiss and stuck her bottom out further.

He took a buttock in each hand and gently pulled her open. The circlet of her arse was a nut-brown whorl and the rear of her vaginal purse was hairless, the lips long and madder-hued. He ran his tongue the length of her crack, sucking those long lips into his mouth, then sliding back up again to tickle the bulls-eye of her anus.

'Oh,' she murmured.

He tongued her arsehole thoroughly and then brought the bursting head of his tool up to lodge between the olive globes of her bum cheeks. If she had protested at this point he would have retreated. She said nothing but laid her head flat on the stair. Her spread behind nuzzled back against his straining penis, rubbing and inflaming him.

He poked the head of his tool into her behind without ceremony.

'Ah!' she cried but did not flinch.

The broad glans stuck in the tight ring but he pushed slowly in. She met him on the outthrust, arching her back and bracing her legs. She raised her head up, the riot of black curls tumbling down her back. Now he was in her to the hilt.

'Do it to me,' she hissed as his fingers found the knot of curls at the head of her pussy and pushed down into her slit. He fondled the slippery lips of her labia as he began to fuck her arse.

He was determined to make it last, to savour every moment of this bizarre coupling on a staircase in a strange city. He wanted to make Laura come and come again, to thrust in and out of her bottom and play with her clit until she couldn't take any more. Then he'd roll her over and plug her pussy and play with those big tits that had tormented him earlier. He wanted to flood Laura with a riot of sensation and an ocean of sperm.

He smacked her buttocks some more as she convulsed beneath him in her third or fourth orgasm. Then he exploded deep inside the magic tunnel of her incredible derriere. The funny thing was, he didn't even like her.

The light shining directly into his eyes wrenched him from sleep. At once the pain and discomfort came flooding back. 'Look at the dirty bastard,' said a voice Tom couldn't quite place, 'he's got a hard-on.'

'He's always got a hard-on,' said another - Fiona, Tom was sure about that.

'I bet he's having another of his sex dreams. Reliving the good old days when he fucked over every female he could get his hands on. Isn't that right, Mr Pervert?'

The torch wavered as his persecutor smacked a hand across the barrel of his exposed tool. Tom caught a glimpse of peroxide hair and beady eyes. Sergeant Amy Tooth. He might have known.

She smacked him again, harder this time and he couldn't suppress a grunt of pain. Amy Tooth's cruel voluptuous mouth split into a grin.

'You've had kid-glove treatment up to now, Mr Glass, but that's about to change. I want a full confession of your sex crimes or I'm taking the gloves off.'

Tom said nothing though his heart hammered in his ribs and his cock twitched on his belly. He was determined not to tell this bitch a thing. Particularly not about Laura.

They crawled up the remaining stairs to her bedroom, not able to walk. They collapsed on the bed and he tore the remains of her dress from her body.

'Bang goes five thousand bucks,' she said.

'Who cares?' he said placing his head reverently between her spectacular breasts. 'I'll buy you a dozen more.'

'What would I have to do to earn them?' She slicked his foreskin up and down his prick.

'I'll think of a few things.' He sucked a thick chocolate-brown nipple between his lips.

'Don't think,' she said, 'let's just do.'

And they did.

The phone woke them at eight in the morning. Laura stretched a slender olive-brown arm across Tom to answer it. In the morning light her skin was as flawless as an infant's. She looked as if she had slept for twelve hours as opposed to three or four. He kissed her throat and she turned a lazy soot-black eye on him. His cock came instantly erect as she spoke into the phone.

'The joint stinks, daddy, but it didn't matter.'

Tom wasn't listening to what she was saying. He pulled her on top of him, his hands sinking into the satin-soft swell of her hips, his mouth caressing the delicate stem of her neck.

'I gotta tell you I cursed you for over an hour...'

He nudged the tip of his tool into the groove of her sex.

'...but I've been thanking you ever since.'

He slid up her in one smooth movement and she settled onto him with an imperceptible sigh.

'You were right, daddy. You always are. Oh!'

His hands were toying with her fabulous bum, cupping and separating the globes, ringing the honeyed circlet of her anus with a fingertip.

'You'd better talk to him yourself, daddy.'

He had one hand in her bush now, seeking her tiny pulsing clit. She held the phone to his head and the unmistakable voice of Ralph Simons filled his ears.

'Say, Tom, you're not married, are you?'

'No, I'm not.' What was the crazy old coot on about?

'A businessman ought to be married. You ought to settle down, son. Have a family.'

Laura began to kiss the corner of his mouth and the sharp points of her breasts burned into his chest as her belly rubbed against his. It was hard to concentrate on what Ralph was saying.

'My daughter loves England. Why don't you take her back with you? Just while I'm studying the contract.'

'But we have a deal, Ralph. You don't need to study the contract, just sign it!'

Laura was becoming agitated now, breathing hard into his shoulder, little shudders rippling through her as she ground her pubis into his.

'Things have changed, Tommy. We're not talking business now, we're talking family merger. Think about it, son.'

And Tom did think about it as Laura came in heaves and pants, her sinuous body slithering on top of his, her passion picking him up and sweeping him away into a shaking, quaking orgasm that rocked him to his bones.

It was a ridiculous idea. Quite insane. But there was something about this perverse and elegant beauty now slumbering on his chest that had turned Tom upside down. Maybe her father wasn't so crazy after all.

Chapter 43

The hostility rose from Amy Tooth like steam as she showed Petra into the cramped meeting room on the ground floor of The Primrose Court. Petra avoided the policewoman's belligerent gaze as she took her seat and waited for Tom. Claire had warned her that she would not be made welcome.'

Tom's appearance, however, wiped all other concerns from her mind. His face was drawn and hollow-eyed and his hands were shackled behind his back.

'Is that necessary?' demanded Petra of the blonde warder who ushered him in.

'Sorry, love,' she said. 'Sergeant Tooth's orders. She had a shit-fit when she heard he was allowed a visit. I daren't take 'em off.' And she slipped out of the room before Petra could protest further.

Petra wrapped her arms around Tom and hugged him tight. His body twitched and jumped in her embrace.

'You've got a fever,' she said.

'It's sexual frustration,' he whispered in her ear. Beneath the baggy grey jogging pants he wore she felt the solid bulge of an erection bump against her hip. 'You know how I've been since the accident. Those harpies work me up but won't give any relief.'

'You poor man!' She stroked the bulge.

'It's OK. I'm not telling them anything. Ooh!' He flinched at her touch.

'What's the matter?'

'The Tooth woman singed the hair off my balls with a cigarette lighter.'

'What!'

'I'm a bit sore in places but don't take your hand away. If we sit down would you mind just fondling me a little?'

'Wouldn't my mouth be better? I mean, if you're sensitive down there.'

'God, Petra, don't you tease me too.'

'Don't worry. I'm going to suck you dry.'

'You're an angel.'

'I'm just being practical. I want to talk to a man who can think straight not someone with his brains in his balls.'

'I don't fucking believe it!'

The big globes of Meredith's breasts were shaking with passion and Tom couldn't take his eyes off them. He hadn't been able to take his eyes off them ten minutes earlier when she'd bounced to orgasm on his penis but now they wobbled with a different kind of emotion. Anger. Disbelief. The lust for revenge. He'd just told her that he'd married Laura Simons three days ago in Las Vegas.

She came at him with a champagne bottle, 130 pounds of nude and spitting fury. Her hair flew around her head in an auburn tangle and her tit flesh quivered as she aimed blows at his head. She looked magnificent. He took the force of the bottle on his arms and crushed her to him. She bit his neck.

He had known there would be no easy way to break the news to Meredith but he guessed that fucking her first had not been the most politic. The trouble was, she had been begging for it and she was too damned gorgeous to resist.

'Bastard! Bastard!' she spat into his face. 'How could you leave me here to flash my butt at Simons for two weeks while you're off shagging his daughter? How could you do it?'

Tom didn't answer. He should have told her at once that he'd fallen for Laura but she would never have consented to stick around and keep the old boy happy under those circumstances.

'And how could you breeze in here and take me to bed without mentioning that you married her?'

'I'm sorry, Meredith. I'm a bastard, I know. But I had to have you one last time.'

'You utter sod. I'll kill you for this.'

'Are you sure she said that?'

'Positive. I remember a lot more now, Petra. And the more I remember, the more suspects there are.'

Tom was looking less haggard already. The tension had eased from his face in direct proportion to the amount of spunk that had erupted from his balls. And there had been plenty of that, Petra could still taste it. She ran a friendly finger along the length of his shaft. Even detumescent he was an impressive size.

Their conversation followed on from one instigated at Spilling Grange in the rare quiet moments of a threesome with Eve. As they'd established, it seemed that every woman Tom had ever bedded in his past had grounds for pursuing a grudge against him. And now here was Meredith.

'What about your wife?' said Petra.

'Who?'

'This Laura person. I never knew you had a wife. I've worked with you for three years, Tom, and there's never been any mention of wives or ex-wives. Just fiancées. Like Marianne.'

'Oh yes. The one with the voice.'

'Yes, that one. My God, Tom, you're incredible. No wonder women are lining up to kill you.'

'Do you think Marianne might have pushed me then?'

'No. I think she's a little gold-digger who'll leave you alone now she's got her job at Black Raven. There's someone else though who deserves some decent treatment from you.'

'I know.' In her hand, Tom's cock suddenly swelled. 'I think about Eve all the time.'

Petra gave the thickening shaft a squeeze. 'You'd like her to be doing this to you, wouldn't you?'

Tom gave a sheepish grin, his red-tipped shaft bounding shamelessly in her hand.

'Close your eyes. Imagine Eve's here, with her big titties in your hands—'

'Oh yes!'

'—her wet mouth on yours—'

'Yes, yes!'

'—and her tight warm pussy round your cock!'

As Petra pumped the big tool in her fist, her other hand stole under her skirt. She wouldn't mind a little fun with the blonde nurse herself. Putting her head up her skirt and baring that pretty pink pussy and sliding her tongue up and down the plump-lipped notch. Sixty-nining with Eve on a bed and feeling those big succulent breasts press like hot pillows into her stomach as the nurse kissed her cunt and licked her clit and made her—

'OH!' yelled Tom.

'Oh yes!' screamed Petra.

—come...

Petra removed her hand from beneath her skirt, the fingers sticky with pussy juice; her other hand was sticky with spunk.

Shame flooded over her. She couldn't believe she had behaved like this in such a place! But Tom's smiling face washed away all other emotions. She was glad for his sake they had done it. She'd bring him off again if they got the chance. The poor man didn't have much else to look forward to - apart from his trial.

Five - Tried and Found Wanton
Chapter 44

'Makes you sick, doesn't it?' said the woman next to Marianne. They were standing in an overcrowded bookshop in the City, observing an author's signing session. Marianne had already conducted her interview for *Gravitas* with the man of the moment, Edward Timberland, author of *Uncaging the Beast*. Now she was watching a phenomenon she had thought extinct, a writer receiving homage from an adoring public.

'I love you, man,' said a youth in an anorak as he hesitantly pushed forward his copy of *Beast* for signature. The author, a rugged blond giant in a plaid shirt, rose to his feet and embraced the boy to applause from the queue, which now snaked out onto the pavement and round the block.

'Puke,' said Marianne's neighbour with a yawn of distaste, 'I've got another four days of this. Cystitis would be preferable.'

Marianne looked at her more closely. She couldn't have been much over twenty-five but she wore the world-weary air of one ten years older. She had remarkably pretty features, with beech-brown eyes and a neat turned-up nose, but her hair was in a tangle, her blouse was creased and her fingernails were bitten to the quick.

'I work for the publisher,' she said in response to Marianne's unspoken question. 'I'm handling Tree-Top Ted's publicity. God help me.'

'Surely it can't be that bad? He's a great success.'

'That's easy for you to say. You don't have to be by his side every waking hour - which includes a dawn work-out in the park so he can commune with nature. Not to mention fighting off his weedy fans. Would you believe that inside every one of these nerds there's a caveman trying to get out?'

Marianne surveyed the crush of admirers pushing around the table where Ted was autographing copies. They were all ages, some greying and flabby, others pink with adolescent acne. They wore grungy T-shirts and grubby jeans and suits shiny with daily use. Apart from the bulky copies of Ted's book clutched in their hands they had just one thing in common. They were all male.

'Just look,' said the publicist, 'two hundred men standing right in front of me and I don't fancy any of them.'

Marianne could see her point. Amongst the sea of squints, naff beards and receding hairlines there wasn't a face which stirred a flicker of interest in Marianne's libido. Except one...

'What about Ted? You're glued to his side all day, couldn't you stick a little closer at night?'

The girl shot Marianne the kind of look that suggested she'd hit a nerve. 'What's the point? His whole philosophy is based on conserving his vital juices.'

'I know,' said Marianne. 'What a waste.'

Marianne had Gerald Goldring to thank for the addition of Ted Timberland to her first *Gravitas* programme. It was officially listed as 'an investigation into the sexual self-help phenomenon' but known throughout Black Raven as 'the wankers' special'. At first Marianne had resisted Ted's inclusion on proprietorial grounds - i.e. she hadn't thought of it herself. The influence of Chastity Honeydew - whose cooperation had somehow been guaranteed by Philippe was, she maintained, sufficient to sustain the entire programme. But when Gerald had told her about Ted she had made a graceful retreat, earning approbation from Charles Mastiff as a 'team-player'.

What attracted Marianne's interest in Ted's beliefs was not his assertion that inside every bloodless, pre-programmed modern man there was a wild, hairy savage longing to ride into the sunset with a naked woman slung across his back. She was also indifferent to his all-male breast-beating session in the woods when accountants and dentists threw off their uniforms of conformity and straddled tree trunks starkers, howling at the moon. As far as she was concerned guys on their own could freeze their balls off and behave like prats provided she wasn't obliged to attend. Which she wouldn't be, since her very female presence - so the Timberland philosophy went - would threaten the essential male fluids from which derived man's strength.

It was this aspect of Ted's thinking that intrigued Marianne. He believed that man drew mental and physical inspiration from hoarding his sex juices. His was a no-spunking regime. No sticky patches on the sheets, no sodden wads of

Kleenex in the toilet bowl, no stained men's magazines under the bed. More to the point, there was no shooting off down a woman's throat or over her shaking tits or even - incredible to think - deep within the tight warm suction-valve of her pussy.

In Marianne's observation, this was a mode of behaviour completely foreign to every man she had ever known. Except Philippe. He had told her that, for the year before he had met her, he had conserved his sperm. Nowadays, of course, with his happiness in her hands, Philippe's juice spurted like oil from a well. 'It's fortunate you used to bank it, darling,' she'd say as she coaxed another gusher from his loins, 'you must have been saving it all up for me.'

The notion of Ted and his acolytes conserving their essential juices fascinated Marianne - intellectually, that is. She was not, after all, much interested in sex. But from the point of view of the presenter of *Gravitas*, there was no doubt the Timberland philosophy represented a rigorous intellectual challenge.

She took up the gauntlet with Gerald.

'So you've turned into a tree-hugger, have you?' she said as they stood in the queue in the Black Raven canteen. 'I can just see you out there under the stars in your loincloth dancing in the embers of the camp fire.'

'Ha, ha,' he said without mirth. 'I've had all this from my wife. You'll belt up if you know what's good for you, Marianne.' And he plonked a low-fat yoghurt on his tray with some venom.

'And what does she say about the spunk conservation part of the new lifestyle?'

'As far as she's concerned I've been practising the Timberland regime since Whitney was born and she's three. Satisfied?'

'Regularly, darling, but it doesn't sound as if you are.' They were through the check-out now, searching for an empty table. 'We'd better not sit next to the researcher with the tits, you'll only get uncomfortable.'

Gerald scowled at her but followed the sway of her slim hips in her tight black mini to the corner of a crowded table by the window. They squeezed in beside a crew of technicians with hairy arms and beery bellies who looked at her with undisguised lust.

'This should suit you,' said Marianne, the length of thigh hard against Gerald's, 'you can empathise with your fellow apes.'

'Shut up,' he hissed.

She was amused to see the anger boiling in his eyes. Their faces were inches apart.

'I'm sorry we're so squashed up,' she said. 'Do tell me if female proximity is threatening the retention of your male essence.'

'If you keep this up, Marianne, I'm going to smack your behind,' he whispered.

'I'd rather you buggered it. You're good at that.' She smiled at him sweetly, noting the flush on his cheeks. 'Of course, now you're a tree-hugger you wouldn't be able to go all the way and spunk off up my bottom, would you?'

'Marianne, please!' His whisper was fierce and attracted sidelong glances from around the table.

'I'm sorry, Gerald, I'm only trying to get things clear from an intellectual perspective. I mean, theoretically, would you be allowed to stick your penis into my arse provided you didn't actually come?'

He was staring down at his salad, refusing to look at her.

'I mean, is it the fluid retention that's the real issue? Or are you prohibited from actually handling me?'

He forked beansprouts into his mouth, his face and neck beet red.

'As you're only a beginner maybe you're allowed partial penetration. You could put your lovely big cock halfway up my bum. Or my pussy. Or between my titties and I could lick it a little. I promise I wouldn't swallow any juice you leaked.'

He made a strangled sound, as if he were choking.

'And if you did come in my mouth then I'd kiss you and give it all back and you wouldn't lose a drop...'

Fortunately for him, Gerald's squeal of frustration was drowned by the squeak of chairs and rattle of cutlery as the technicians rose as one from the table. As they left, one of them bent over and said to Gerald. 'I'd give her one sharpish, if I were you, mate. Or would you like us to do it for you?'

'Oafs,' snapped Marianne as they wandered off chortling. 'Mind you, if I went off with them I reckon I'd soon be bathing in spunk. They say that sperm is very good for the skin. I could rub it into my breasts and my thighs—'

He grabbed her by both arms and shook her. 'Shut up, Marianne!' he hissed. 'Shut up!'

She fell across him, giggling into his neck, one hand dropping into his lap where it closed on a big solid bulge tenting out his trousers.

'I'm sorry, Gerald,' she whispered. 'I'm only teasing. There's no need to get so worked up. My, you're *huge* down there - would it help if I just squeezed—'

Suddenly he froze, his eyes bulging and his mouth working soundlessly. His pelvis was jumping and twitching against her hand and she leaned all her soft weight into his body as he lost control.

Laughter gurgled from her lips like water over pebbles. 'Oh dear, Gerald, you're all wet. Don't tell me you've lost some of your essential oils.'

'You bitch,' he breathed into the silver-blonde locks that fell over his face, 'you complete and utter bitch. I really am going to tan your arse now.'

She snuggled into his body and licked his ear. 'Go on, Gerald, agree you lost the argument.'

'Never.'

'Come on, the evidence is dripping down your leg!'

'So what? You didn't play fair.'

'Admit one thing then - a woman is much nicer to hug than a tree.'

He said nothing but his arms were tight around Marianne's delectable body. She wondered if Tree-Top Ted would be more of a challenge.

Chapter 45

'So? What do you think?' Cassie's voice was tense, expectant. The special Honeydew issue of *Fragrant* was in Petra's hands and the editor was desperate for a reaction.

'It looks fabulous,' said Petra with as much genuine enthusiasm as she could muster. 'The front photo is just right.' The full face of a winsome beauty with plucked eyebrows stared out of the page, her eyelids half lowered, the tips of two squeaky white teeth biting into her swollen lower lip. The effect was of an exquisite nymphet struggling to stem the rising tide of onrushing ecstasy, or - so it occurred to Petra - a schoolgirl about to wet herself with exam stress. She did not share this last thought with Cassie.

'I love these headlines,' she said. '"The Big O Eight Days A Week", "How To Double Your Targets In Love" - that should shift a few copies.'

Cassie wasn't satisfied. 'But what do you think of your profile? Businesswoman X, that's you. You're top of the POTs, you've beaten your target by about seventy orgasms a month. That's phenomenal.'

'Is it?'

'Are you kidding, Petra? Six comes a day, rain or shine, that's amazing. No wonder you're the boss of a multinational corporation. You're living proof of the power of the orgasm. The ultimate vindication of the Honeydew theory!'

As Cassie's voice rose in jubilation Petra's face fell.

'What's the matter, Petra? I thought you'd be pleased.'

Petra slumped onto the sofa in Cassie's living room. 'I'm sorry, Cassie, it's just that this is all crap.' She dropped the magazine onto the table in front of her. 'This makes out that I'm wonderwoman, taking control of my life, running a business, enjoying fantastic sex - it's completely false. Thank God I'm not identifiable.'

Cassie stood over her, her face hard. 'You didn't make up those results, did you? If that got out I'd be in deep trouble.'

'No, no, it's all true. It's just that—' She started to sob and an alarmed Cassie sat next to her and put her arms around her heaving shoulders. It was a minute or two before Petra felt composed enough to speak.

'You see? I'm going to pieces. The truth is I've been so worried about Tom and bound up with his situation that I've not actually been running the business. I've employed someone else to cover for me.'

'Who?'

Petra gave her a tear-stained grin. 'A man called Charles Kite. The Primrose Court had him removed as Chief Executive of Stamp & Marne and demoted him to office administrator. I rescued him from a life counting hand towels and loo rolls. He's a complete bully but brilliant.'

'Well done you. I always say delegation is the key to good management.'

'Then there's Kelvin. He moved into another room and we have no relationship at all. I haven't seen him for weeks.'

'So he's got nothing to do with your amazing results?'

'No, but they're correct, I swear to you.'

Cassie got up and fetched the wine bottle. She topped the glasses on the table and waited. It was a long wait.

'Cassie, what would you say if I told you I was a lesbian?'

'Holy shit!' Cassie's hand flew to her mouth. 'I mean, how come?'

Petra told her about the incident with Inspector Quartermain and Sergeant Tooth in her office, then about Morticia Chekhov on the train and Eve Biscuit at Spilling Grange and, finally, of the afternoon in bed with Claire.

Cassie sipped her wine and looked thoughtful. 'I can see why your results were so good, you sexy thing, but I'm not sure that it demonstrates you're an out-and-out lesbo. Fifty-seven per cent of women feel good about the idea of sex with another woman and not all of them are gay. After all, you do seem to like a bit of cock as well.'

Petra thought about that and it appeared to cheer her up. 'Of course,' she said, 'I haven't told you the real reason I scored so heavily.' She picked up her bag and reached inside. 'It's this.'

Cassie took the glass dildo in her hands and held it as if it were a sacred object. It glowed in her grasp, warming her fingers, a mist of swirling colour rising up the thick smooth shaft.

'My God,' was all she could say.

'Meet The Magic Wand,' said Petra. 'He's the real man in my life.'

'I've got to have him,' breathed Cassie, squirming her bottom into the cushions of the sofa.

'That can be arranged - at a price.'

Cassie looked up. There was a sparkle in Petra's eyes and a grin on her lips as she said, 'Where do you stand, Cassie? Are you among the fifty-seven per cent?'

'Are you propositioning me?'

'Why not? You started all this when you made me take a video of you having sex.'

Cassie giggled. She remembered it had been a turn-on having Petra watch her with Philippe.

'I was fascinated by your nipples,' said Petra, 'all long and red like loganberries. I wanted them in my mouth but would never have dared to ask you. Then.'

'I see,' said Cassie and pulled her thin cashmere sweater up over her jutting breasts. The white cups of her brassiere seemed enormous. Petra put her hand on one and squeezed.

'Be gentle with me,' said Cassie as Petra tugged the bra cup over the bulging breast and a big white globe of flesh tumbled into her palm.

'No chance,' she said. 'It's about time we got to grips with *your* orgasm targets.'

Chapter 46

On the afternoon that Tom heard from New York that Ralph Simons had been ousted as President of the Simons Corporation he rang a detective agency.

'I want someone with a video camera. Someone discreet, and experienced. I want them here in half an hour, if not sooner.'

'Blimey, Mr Glass,' said a young woman's voice, 'they're out.'

'Can *you* use a video camera?'

'I suppose so.'

'I'll pick you up in half an hour or you can tell Mr Dazzle I'm closing the account.'

As a result he found himself driving home with a blonde in a loose cheesecloth shirt and a denim skirt cut off at mid-thigh. Roxy looked about fourteen.

'Shouldn't you be at school?' he said.

She guffawed, making a lot of noise for a small person. 'You must be joking, I left ages ago. I'm not as green as I look, Mr Glass, honest.' And she gave him the benefit of a bubble grin, revealing two rows of perfectly white teeth and wrinkling the freckled skin on the bridge of her turned-up nose. Tom was not convinced but said nothing.

He parked a street away from his house and led her to the garden gate. There was a four-year-old Saab standing in front of the garage with a tennis racket and cage of balls on the back seat. He made her video it.'

'I'll go through the kitchen door,' he explained. 'You wait outside and follow me when I tell you.'

The back door was locked but he had a key. He'd been carrying it around for weeks, waiting for just this set of circumstances. He went through the empty kitchen and into the hall. He listened. From above came cries and moans. They were the sounds he had anticipated but nevertheless they set the hairs itching on the back of his neck. It was the sound of his wife making love.

He ushered Roxy up the stairs, the camera whirring, recording their progress. Tom crept into the spare room next to the bedroom and the girl followed. They moved silently though the precaution was unnecessary for Laura, as Tom well knew, took her pleasures noisily.

'OH BABY, OH BABY, OH BABY!' she was yelling. 'Take me there, sugar, *pleeese!*'

Tom locked the door behind them and placed a chair against the wall adjoining the bedroom. He indicated to the girl that she should stand on it. Then he pulled aside the curtain on the mirror in front of her and watched her pretty mouth fall open as she stared into the room next door and saw the naked man and woman on the bed.

The two-way mirror was a toy he had installed years earlier and he'd had a certain amount of fun out of it in his bachelor days. Now he was going to use it to record the extra-curricular activities of his wife.

Laura and a broad muscular man were entwined on the white sheets. They made a handsome couple. It occurred to Tom that they would make excellent models for an upmarket sex manual. Here they were in the missionary position, for example; she was cradling his thrusting pelvis in the vee of her outspread thighs, one hand clutching the compact flesh of his pumping buttocks, the other stroking his neck with agitated fingers; he was driving into her in measured strokes, his fingers on the flattened bowl of her breast, his face buried in her neck.

Laura's black hair whipped across the pillow as her body shook in orgasm and her cries, formless shouts of ecstasy, could plainly be heard through the wall.

The man must have come too for, after a moment, the pair disentangled themselves and lay side by side on the bed.

'Get their faces,' hissed Tom and Roxy obliged. The bed head was against the wall and she had to stand on tiptoe on her chair and aim the camera downwards to capture features.

Her rounded bottom beneath her short skirt was on a level with Tom's face. Her legs were bare and brown. A schoolgirl's legs, Tom thought.

Then the doorbell rang and Roxy looked at him. He shrugged. The man on the bed next door - Ray, Laura's tennis coach, Tom informed Roxy - lazily got to his feet and padded to the window. Then, stark-naked, he left the room.

After he'd gone Laura pulled on a pair of tiny white pants and a robe. Tom didn't recognise it. It was black and gauzy and almost completely transparent. Her big breasts and the treacle-dark cones of her nipples were clearly visible beneath it. The girl filmed her, the tip of her small pink tongue protruding over her bottom lip as she concentrated.

The bedroom door opened and Ray returned with another younger man. He was lean and tall and wore tennis whites. He had a sandy shock of hair that flopped over his forehead. He held out a big hand to Laura as if to shake hers and she laughed and pressed it to her left breast over the flimsy garment she wore. Tom could imagine the silky warmth in the boy's hand, the wonderful weight of flesh and the imprint of the hard nipple in his palm. He groaned.

'Are you all right?' said Roxy, her voice full of concern. 'This must be terrible for you.'

'I'm fine,' hissed Tom. 'Just get it on film.' But he felt far from fine. There was nausea in the pit of his stomach and his cock was twisted in his pants. He eased it straight, hoping the girl wouldn't notice. How could he feel sick and turned on at the same time?

Next door Ray had produced a bottle of Scotch. Laura and the boy used tooth glasses from the bathroom and Ray drank from the bottle. The three stood close together, as if they were chatting in a crowd at a cocktail party. They looked awkward and there was much unnecessary laughter. Ray slid his arm round Laura's waist and kissed her. His cock was flying like a flag, the bared helmet a flaming red.

After a bit Laura pulled her mouth away from Ray and offered it to the boy.

He dived at her, plunging his tongue down her throat. As he kissed her Ray pulled the robe open to her waist, baring her tits, cupping and mauling them in his hands. The boy broke off the kiss to fondle her breasts as well. Then Ray took the whisky bottle and sprinkled drops on her puckered brown nipples. She laughed. The men took turns in licking the spirit off.

Things appeared to heat up from that point. The two males became overeager, crushing her between them as they grabbed and pawed her silky, opulent flesh. She let them do as they liked for a minute or two, the three of them still standing, groping and kissing and laughing. The robe was off her by now, pooled in a heap on the floor, and Ray was tugging at her tiny knickers, sliding his fingers under the waistband to paddle with the flesh of her bum.

She tore herself away from them and walked to the big easy chair in the window alcove. She leaned over from the waist and placed her hands on the arms of the chair. Then she bent her knees and waggled her bottom at them. The white cotton of her knickers stretched tight over the rotund globes of her buttocks.

'Female apes show their arses like that,' muttered Roxy, 'I've seen 'em at the zoo. Guaranteed to get the fellers going.'

Too true, thought Tom as he watched the tall boy impatiently tug his singlet over his head and kick off his shorts and jockstrap. Like his body, his penis was thin and long, it stood up against his belly, the tip covering his navel.

Laura reached behind her and eased the material of her panties off her bottom cheeks until her knickers were just a line of white in the divide of her shapely bottom. She pulled the strip tight, exaggerating the outthrust of her arse, defining the pouting bulge of her pussy.

Tom wondered how long it would take before they cut short the teasing and fell on her. He was almost of a mind to go in there and show them how it should be done.

The thin boy couldn't wait any longer. He tore the flimsy material from her rear and covered Laura like a dog on a bitch. His big spade-like hands grappled beneath her to catch her hanging tits and his buttock cheeks hollowed as he pistoned into her full steam.

It was over in a flash - jab, jab, jab and he was finished.

'I thought so,' said Roxy. 'Just like an animal. No staying power.'

Ray was at Laura now, on his knees in the crook of her outthrust rear, feeling between her legs for the slippery warm of her opening and then guiding his stiff tool up and in. She leaned her head back as he pressed against the cushions of her buttocks and the two of them kissed, a long probing embrace.

'That's more like it,' said Roxy, obviously lost in the drama of the moment.

The pair were fucking in a steady rhythm now, savouring every nuance of their pleasure. The boy stood over them, eyes wide and - Tom was impressed - half erect once more. The copulating pair looked up at him and Laura said something Tom didn't catch. The boy moved closer and Laura craned her long neck to capture the tip of his tool in her mouth.

It was fully erect now and she bobbed her head on it but the position was too difficult - the chair was in the way. They retreated and, to Tom's shock and excitement, Ray put an arm around his waist.

'Oh yes,' whispered Roxy. The boy turned to the man on his knees as he steadily buffeted his loins against the soft buttocks of the woman. For a moment Ray contemplated the long wet wand of flesh swaying in his face, then he wrapped his fingers round the shaft and plunged the glans between his lips.

'Oh *yes*,' said Roxy.

Ray had one hand hidden beneath Laura's body, at work between her legs, the other cupped and explored the thin boy's sandy-haired balls. He licked and loved the long white shaft of his cock from stem to stern and then took as much of it in his mouth as he could. Ray was obviously skilled at more leisure activities than tennis.

Laura thought so too, Tom could see that. She was watching over her shoulder as Ray sucked the boy. Her eyes were half shut and smoky with desire. Tom knew that look well. She was only just getting going. It looked like being a long afternoon.

Chapter 47

Marianne felt like screaming. The *Gravitas* special was just days away and suddenly it looked as if the whole package might come apart at the seams. That morning Chastity had threatened to pull out of the programme - she was objecting to the inclusion of Edward Timberland. First Marianne, then Gerald and finally Sir Charles, had failed to appease her.

In desperation Marianne had cancelled dinner with Philippe and sent him off to talk Chastity round - if she didn't listen to him then all was lost. What cheesed Marianne off was that she had scarcely seen Philippe all week and she had promised herself a truly romantic evening with her lover. She had put champagne on ice, bought a new apricot silk teddy and changed the sheets. As she faced the prospect of an evening alone she was well and truly fed up.

Another complication now fuelled her ire. She'd had a call from Sonja, Timberland's publicity lady, to say that Ted was talking of withdrawing from the programme.

'Why?'

'He doesn't want to appear in the studio with Chastity Honeydew.'

'For God's sake!' Marianne was furious, what was wrong with these bloody authors? 'He's always known she's going to be in it,' she wailed.

'Yes, but he's developed a phobia about her. He thinks her book's better displayed in the shops than his. And when he saw her plastered all over my copy of *Fragrant* he went ape. Do you want to come over here and talk to him yourself? Please say yes, Marianne, he's driving me up the wall!'

Sonja let Marianne into Ted's hotel suite. The elegant Edwardian lounge was littered with incongruous paraphernalia. Copies of *Uncaging the Beast* were piled on every face, a set of weights and a ski machine blocked off one corner of the room and a pair of muddy running shoes sat in the middle of the Turkish rug. The remains of a very rare steak was congealing on a room-service trolley and a half-empty bottle of bourbon stood on the coffee table. Of Tree-Top Ted there was no sign.

'He's in the bedroom,' said Sonja. 'Sulking.'

As she spoke, a door to her left swung open and crashed back on its hinges. The great author loomed in the doorframe wearing shorts, trainers and a T-shirt. He stared at Marianne with a mad glint in his eye.

'I'm outta here,' he boomed. 'Don't none of you bitches try to stop me!' And he dashed across the room and out into the corridor without a backward glance.

Marianne blinked in alarm. 'Shouldn't you follow him?' she said to Sonja. 'I thought you dogged his every footstep. You might lose him.'

The publicity girl shrugged. 'Chance would be a fine thing.' She delved into her handbag. 'At least I can have a cigarette while he's gone.'

Marianne was peeved. 'What am I supposed to do? I've rearranged my entire evening to talk to your author and he's just run out on me. Literally.'

Sonja grinned at her unperturbed, a blue plume of smoke already curling from her lips. 'Don't worry, darling, he'll be back to mummy all too soon - he's lost without the hired help. Sit down and have a drink. We can swap stories of glamorous media life. Didn't you once read the weather on TV?'

In another hotel suite in another part of town, more authorial fur was being stroked. The fur in question was the delicious blonde fleece situated between the bronzed and perfect thighs of Chastity Honeydew. The stroker was Philippe. They lay on the king-sized bed, their naked bodies slick with the sweat of sexual exertion. Chastity pressed the Frenchman's hand tight to the base of her dimpled belly and said: 'More!'

Even as his fingers insinuated themselves into the soft wet folds of her yearning fig, Philippe shook his head. 'This is unfair of you, Chastity. You asked me to test some of your physical reflexes and in return you agreed to appear on my friend's television programme. We have a bargain, *n'est-ce pas?*'

'Sure thing. I guess I just need a little reassurance that everything is in working order.'

'But you swore to me it was! You said you could have the orgasms now.'

'And how, sugar.'

'So why don't you play with one of your boy-toys? And you should keep your promise to go on the television programme of my friend.'

Chastity chuckled and ran her free hand across the muscled expanse of his chest. She let it fall onto his thigh, where it came to rest just an inch away from his limp baton of pleasure.

'Tell me about your friend,' she said.

Philippe sighed. 'What can I say? She is *magnifique*. I am in love. It is a *coup defoudre*.'

Somehow Chastity's finger had found its way into the warm nook between the underside of his shaft and the swell of his balls. She stroked him lightly.

'So why are you here then?' she asked.

'To make sure you keep your deal, Chastity. This is business.'

'No question,' she said, running the tip of her finger along the underside of his shaft. The sleepy weapon was beginning to raise its head. She tickled it under its chin.

He had two fingers buried to the knuckle in her pussy. She was no longer pressing them to her pleasure zone, they seemed to have lodged there of their own accord.

'Swear to me you will keep your word, Chastity.'

'Mmm, if you keep doing that I will.'

'So there will be no more talk of pulling out?'

His penis had swollen in her hand. She smoothed a finger around the rim of his glans.

'I won't mention it again,' she said, lying back and spreading her long bronzed legs. 'You must love her very much.'

'Oh yes,' breathed Philippe, sliding between her thighs, cock rubbing against her silken flesh. 'There is nothing I would not do for her.'

'Obviously,' muttered Chastity as the head of his French prick plunged between her wet labia and filled her to the hilt.

Sonja's prediction was accurate. Ted reappeared in the room half an hour later, his clothes and hair wet with summer rain, his face red. Marianne was unsure whether he'd run around the park or simply jogged to the pub. One thing was certain, his breath stank of alcohol. Which was OK by her, she and Sonja had hit the bourbon with gusto in his absence.

'Still here?' he roared. 'God save me from city-smart females polluting my airspace and drinking my booze.'

'Now, now, Ted,' said Sonja. 'The Whimsical Press is paying your hotel bill.'

He appeared not to hear but attacked the door of the fridge as if he might tear it off its hinges. He seized a bottle of Arctic Fox beer and slammed the top against the mahogany writing desk, sending the cap spinning across the carpet and splintering the wood.

He took a long draught and fixed Marianne with his mad-man's stare. 'If you think I'm getting up on television with that Californian nympho you've got your head up your sweet ass, sister.'

Marianne could not deny she was intimidated. This hulking drunken bear was a different proposition to the smooth blond charmer she had met the day before. However, her programme - indeed her new career as a TV arts presenter - was at stake. She decided to take the bear by the balls.

'Why are you afraid of her, Ted? Is she too much of a challenge for you?'

He laughed without mirth. 'She's a sperm-sucker, that's what she is. A floozy with a snatch between her legs. A thief of men's strength like all you painted Delilahs.'

'Oh God, he's off,' muttered Sonja, topping up her glass.

Marianne got to her feet.

'Why don't you come on my programme and say that, Ted?'

His reply was so vehement, spittle sprayed into her face. 'Because I refuse to promote the work of a whore.'

'But she'll be promoting your work too. Especially if we show the interview with you first.'

He hesitated and Marianne carried on.

'To be honest, Ted, it might do you a lot of harm to pull out now. All my journalist friends will be very curious.'

His eyes narrowed. 'Tell them you've come up against a man of principle for a change.'

Marianne smiled sweetly. 'I could say you behaved like a big prick because you've only got a little one.'

Behind her Sonja snorted into her drink.

Ted's jaw dropped and a growl of rage burst from his throat. Marianne ignored him.

'I've also heard that you prefer boys to girls. Of course, I wouldn't *want* to repeat that.'

Ted's face turned puce and the growl turned into a yelp of incoherence. He bunched his great fist and took a pace towards Marianne. She stood her ground.

'What I *will* tell everybody if you pull out is that you aren't capable of expressing yourself on camera.'

It was as if she had delivered a kung-fu kick to his chest. He staggered back. The blood drained from his face. The ham-like fist unfolded. He placed the beer bottle carefully on the table and walked slowly to his bedroom.

'I'll see you at the studio, Miss Matthews,' he said and closed the door behind him.

'Bloody hell,' said Sonja, 'you were wasted on the weather.'

Chapter 48

'I'm sorry, Mr Glass,' said Roxy, 'I can't hold the camera steady any more - my arms are tired.'

It wasn't just that, Tom could see. She was shivering all over as if in a high fever and her denimed pelvis, on a level with Tom's face, was making tiny thrusts backwards and forwards in mid-air. He had no doubt what she was in need of.

He took the camera from her and put it on the floor. She made no move to get off the chair but stood there quivering, her eyes big with wonder as she gazed at the threesome next door.

Tom lifted the hem of her skirt to her waist. She wore pretty cotton panties embroidered with tiny white daisies around the waistband. In the vee of her legs the material was dark with her juices and clung wetly to the mound of her sex. The aroma of a woman on heat met Tom's nostrils as he moved in close to her, so close that her undulating mons almost brushed his lips.

'Please,' she whimpered in a small voice. He wasn't sure whether she meant him or the entwined lovers next door. In any case, though his heart was hammering beneath his ribs and his cock was pulsing in his pants, he made her wait. He wanted to savour the sight of this teenage wet-dream dancing with helpless desire.

He tugged her skirt off, pulling the elasticated waist over her hips. For a small girl they were rounded and womanly, as was her bottom. He contemplated her from the rear. Her buttocks were full and firm, threatening to burst from the tight pink panties as she squirmed on the chair before him. He yanked her knickers down without ceremony, savouring the sight of the wet gusset clinging to the folds of her moist pussy. She placed a hand on his shoulder to steady herself as she stepped out of them. It remained there, her small fingers finding the nape of his neck and pulling him softly, maybe unconsciously, towards her naked sex.

Still he made her wait, unbuttoning her shirt to gaze on her small freckled breasts, their nipples carnation pink and sticking up like little pegs. He reached up and felt them, the soft hot flesh seeming to glow in his hand.

'Oh,' she murmured, 'oh blimey.'

He turned and looked through the mirror. The threesome had changed position. Ray now sat in the chair and Laura was sitting on his loins with her back to him. In the double vee of their spread thighs could be seen the lolling pouch of his testicles and the root of his shaft spearing up between the spread lips of her vagina. She had a hand in the knot of hair at the base of her belly and was rubbing and stroking her clit.

The thin boy stood in front of them, presenting his genitals for stimulation. Laura was sucking his balls, taking them in turns into her mouth. Ray was licking his ruby-red glans and pumping the shaft of his cock with dexterity.

Tom turned back to Roxy. He traced his tongue at snail-like pace up the insides of her thighs, which were wet with her excitement. She shuffled her feet apart and made little mewing sounds as he approached her weeping pussy. The hand on the back of his neck was more insistent now, he could feel the sharp pressure of her fingertips as her agitation grew to boiling point.

The lips of her quim were pink and puffy beneath a down of hair. He blew on the curly wisps and her whole body shook. He extended his tongue tip and slyly insinuated it into the blonde bush, touching her sex for the first time. She squealed as if stung by an electric current and yanked his head into her crotch with both hands.

He held her bottom cheeks as he worked his tongue into her vagina. He licked her from north to south and back again, squeezing that pliant bum flesh as he did so, savouring the youthful succulence of her cunt and arse.

She was breathing heavily now, both her hands entangled in his hair, her hips undulating to an urgent rhythm as he pleasured her. He transferred juice from her sex to his and ran it round the tiny circlet between her bottom cheeks.

'Oh, oh,' she cried as he kissed her pussy in earnest, finding her clit with his lips and breaching her anus with his finger.

Then she was coming off all over his face, flooding his mouth with salty juices, and jumping and hopping on the chair so hard that Tom had a vision of them both toppling over and crashing through the wall into the bedroom door just as Laura came to a climax on Ray's cock and thin boy fountained his spunk down the tennis coach's throat.

'It didn't happen, though, did it? I presume you got out of there undetected.' Petra's second visit with Tom was fast running out but she couldn't resist pressing him for the prurient details of his latest recollection.

'We waited till they got going again and slipped out of the house the way we came in. I took Roxy straight to a hotel and she pulled my clothes off in the lift. We almost didn't make it to the room in time.'

Petra smiled. 'At least that's one of your lovers who didn't end up wanting to kill you.'

'True, but her mother threatened to cut my balls off if I saw Roxy again and the agency complained that I'd ruined their YTS trainee because she was refusing to sit in the office and answer the phone. Mind you, she was wasted. She'd have made a brilliant film technician, the stuff she took of LA was perfect.'

'So that's why I've never heard of Laura,' said Petra. 'You split up.'

'Once I'd got the goods on her she went without a murmur. She packed up and returned to the States. Swearing vengeance, of course.'

'Of course. We'll add her to the list of suspects. It's getting longer by the minute.'

Tom looked unperturbed, he grinned at Petra. 'Everything's coming back quickly now. I reckon I've only got a three-year gap.' Even in the drab confines of The Primrose Court meeting room, his optimism shone through. Petra didn't want to dampen it but there were important things to discuss.

'You know you won't be properly represented at this trial, don't you?'

'I still don't understand why not.'

'It's because it's not really a trial. It's an arrangement on behalf of the New Leaf campaign for policing business practice. It's not subject to the normal procedures of the justice system.'

'It's a kangaroo court run by harpies bent on seizing control of businesses and humiliating the male sex into the bargain. I've gathered that much.'

'Well, at least they can't jail you, they can only disbar you from directorships, demote you and seize assets.'

'Christ, Petra, tell me some good news.'

'A female representative of the business community can speak on your behalf at the hearing. I've only just found out.'

'Really? Thank God for that.'

'We have to decide who it's going to be. Oh Tom, please don't look at me like that!'

'Why not? There's only one candidate. You will say yes, won't you, Petra?'

Petra didn't say anything. She knew she had no choice.

Chapter 49

The courtroom was a small, circular room with no windows, panelled in oak. On a dais at one end was the Judge's chair and, around the perimeter of the room, sat the members the Corrections Committee. In the well of the court a table had been placed for the Prosecutor and in the very centre, in the blazing focus of a pair of spotlights, stood the accused, former captain of industry, darling of the gossip columns self-made billionaire, Tom Glass.

Tom forced himself to stand tall, to breathe calmly, to prevent any sign of the emotion that boiled within appearing on his face. He was uncomfortable in the clothes they had made him wear - flimsy pyjamas a size too small for his tall frame. He was acutely conscious that he wore underwear and his genitals bulged against the tight cotton. *Let the bitches look*, he thought in defiance and set his features in a mask of cold contempt.

He was the only man in the room. In the glare of the light it was hard to make out the features of the tormentors who surrounded him. Many of them wore masks, probably women he knew and had dealt with in business. Now they came to watch his humiliation, preserving the secrets of their identity. *Well fuck them*, he thought. And the thought was appropriate for, beneath this charade of justice and the fear like a weight on his chest, was the raw presence of sex.

As Tom's eyes became accustomed to the gloom he could make out the shapes around him: rounded, curved, dressed to kill. Below the tables in front of them he could see the gleam of slender legs and hear the slither of nylon as thigh kissed thigh. Their scent was rich in his nostrils, an expensive amalgam of designer perfume overlaying something more earthy. He knew that particular scent well, the smell of women on heat. These chic pampered females had turned out to see his most intimate secrets laid bare and the prospect was turning them on.

The Judge's gavel rang loud in the confined space. She was a well-preserved blonde of indeterminate years. Her features were soft and pretty but her voice had a ring of Scottish steel.

'I formally state that the proceedings in this court are empowered by the self-regulatory body of the business community of the City of London and, as such, are not subject to the common law of the land. In other words, the prisoner may like to note, we play by the rules that I choose to impose.'

'So it's a complete farce,' said Tom with some vehemence. He hadn't meant to say anything but the words had spilled out of their own accord.

'Shh, Tom,' whispered a voice behind him. Petra. Thank God he had one ally.

The Judge was glaring at him, her pale curving lips set in a thin line of disapproval. 'One of the rules I impose, Mr Glass, is that the accused says nothing unless he is asked a direct question. I am quite capable of rendering you incapable of speech and I won't hesitate to do so. I believe Ms Petra Rosewater has volunteered to say something on your behalf at the appropriate time, is that so?'

'Yes.'

'Yes, *madam.*'

'Yes, madam.'

'Very well. You'll get a turn at some point. Now let's get on with it. Prosecutor Hawk.'

It was the first time Tom had set eyes on Gossamer Hawk and he boggled at the statuesque blonde who now confronted him. Her tall, curvaceous figure had been squeezed into a floor-length gown of black velvet with a swirling cape and upturned collar. Her lips were a slash of crimson, the same shade as her long, sharp fingernails - one of which quivered an inch from his face as she struck a pose worthy of the wicked queen in *Snow White*. If it hadn't been that Gossamer was blonde the resemblance would have been remarkable, thought Tom. Apart from the bosom, of course.

Gossamer's cleavage was unmissable. Behind the curve of her outthrust arm, the exposed swell of her two incredible breasts was framed in a décolletage so extreme that it was a wonder her dress remained in place. The magnificent alabaster globes pushed out against the velvet, white on black, a mesmerising display of fleshy temptation. Tom was stunned.

'Lecher!' she screamed at him. 'Traducer of innocence! Immoral, shameless wrecker of lives! I'm going to strip life bare and expose to the court the detestable foundations of your worldly success - which is nothing less than a barbarous assault on the female sex!'

Tom heard the words but was hardly able to make sense of them such was the volume and intensity with which they were delivered - and the incongruous sight of those two shivering orbs thrust beneath his nose. The creamy flesh danced before him and his eyes feasted on the hypnotic display. Could it be that the skin tones of her left breast, just at the point where black velvet cupped and enfolded, were shading to pink? Was this the delectable rim of her areola peeking into view?

'Madam,' screamed Gossamer in theatrical outrage, 'observe the foul beast! He's staring at my tits!'

Barely suppressed sniggers came from the shadowy figures observing the entertainment. Tom smiled.

Crash! came the sound of the Judge's gavel, silencing levity.

'Sergeant!' barked the Judge and Amy Tooth strode forward. Gone was the ghastly Sex Police shell-suit. She wore a black PVC basque, fishnet stockings and thigh-high leather boots. She grinned into Tom's face and kicked him in the stomach as hard as she could.

There was a collective intake of breath as Tom pitched forward onto the floor and one high-pitched cry of anguish which, had Tom heard it, he would have identified as coming from his sole supporter, Petra Rosewater. But Tom was lost in private agony, doubled up on the floor, the breath knocked clean out of his body, a whistling in his ears and bile in his throat.

'Get him on his feet,' ordered the Judge and Amy Tooth doused him with a bucket of water. Assisted by Sergeant Gloria Just, she hauled him upright.

'You'd better put him in irons, Sergeant,' said the Judge. 'I can see he's going to be trouble.'

As the two officers of the Sex Police shackled his feet to bolts in the floor and his thin wet clothes clung to his shaking frame, Tom's spirits sank to their lowest ebb. The court, as he had always suspected, would offer him no justice. It had the power to strip him of his company, his wealth, his future in business and send him out into the world a ruined man. But first there was this public ordeal which had only just begun - a piece of vengeful theatre whose drama was his pain and shame and utter humiliation.

It was with numbness in his veins, as if he had been injected with an emotional anaesthetic, that he listened to the Prosecutor's opening statement. Her contention that his discovery, naked and aroused, in the street by a departing audience of play-goers was the culmination of years of depravity made no impact on him. Her argument that his business morality should be measured by the deficiencies of his personal life passed him by. So too her declared intention to trace the threads of chauvinism and sexism that had led him to base his success on the exploitation of women. His entire sexual history, it seemed, was to be dragged out in court and held up as evidence of his culpability. *So what?* thought Tom.

But when the principal witness for the prosecution entered the room, the anaesthetic ceased to work.

Eve Biscuit took her place in the spotlight, head bowed and refusing to meet Tom's eye.

If Tom had ever nurtured a hope of deliverance, it died at that moment.

Chapter 50

Cassie led Petra to a dark corner of a pub two streets from The Primrose Court. The younger woman was shaking so much Cassie had to support her round the waist.

'Put that inside you,' she said, pressing a glass into Petra's hand. The triple brandy disappeared in one swallow. 'That's all you're having. You'll need your wits about you tomorrow.'

Petra stared at her wide-eyed with torment. 'Is it always like that?' she said. 'Why didn't you warn me?'

Cassie did not reply. There was no way to warn someone about a trial at The Primrose Court.

Eve Biscuit had given her testimony in a monotone, staring at the floor. She looked up just once, when Tom said to her, 'Eve - how could you?'

Her eyes filled with tears and her soft swollen lips quivered.

'Gag him,' said the Judge and Amy Tooth and Gloria Just advanced on him.

He'd fought them then and reinforcements had arrived, beefy women with ham-like thighs and melon-sized breasts jiggling in their PVC corsets. Petra was aware that the members of the Corrections Committee around her in the gloom were relishing the action. Tom pushed Sergeant Just onto her back and ripped Amy Tooth's bodice so that one creamy breast bounded free to shake and shiver in the harsh light as they struggled. Then the big women arrived and pinned Tom's arms behind his back, bending them up and twisting them so that at any moment Petra expected to hear the crack of bone.

Amy forced a rubber ball into Tom's mouth with relish and Gloria secured it with a leather thong, lodging the bung deep in the angle of his jaw.

Petra found herself on her feet. 'Madam, I protest!' she shouted. 'It's inhuman to tie him up like that! He might suffocate.'

'Silence!' snapped the Judge. 'Or I'll gag you too. It's Ms Rosewater, isn't it?'

'Yes, madam.'

'Obviously you didn't pay attention to my opening remarks. This is not the Old Bailey or even the local magistrates' court. The accused has no rights here beyond those I choose to bestow on him. The same goes for his representative, so I'd advise you to keep silent.'

'But—'

'Rest assured, Ms Rosewater, if he turns blue I shall remove the gag. There is no satisfaction, even to me, in trying a corpse. Now let's press on.'

And so Petra had been forced to watch in silence as the case was advanced against her employer and mentor. Gossamer Hawk put her histrionics to one side and proceeded methodically, with the aid of Eve Biscuit's testimony and video evidence, to lay bare Tom's duplicitous love life. Despite herself, Petra was fascinated. She knew nothing about his teenage seduction of his brother's fiancée or of his affair with his university professor's au pair which had resulted in his tutor fleeing the country.

Dr Madeleine Flint testified as to the nature of Tom's memory loss and confirmed that Nurse Biscuit had been assigned night and day to his care - with the express purpose of encouraging him to reveal his sexual history in detail. Almost all of these conversations had been captured on camera.

Television monitors on the tables before the Corrections Committee now relayed the tender moments of pillow talk between Tom and Eve. Petra was appalled but she watched and listened all the same.

Most of all, though, Petra watched Tom. He had his back to her, with his arms pinioned behind him - Gloria Just had tied his forearms together for good measure - and his feet were shackled to the floor some eighteen inches apart. The thin cotton clothing had dried on his body and was moulded to his back. It clung to the hard contours of his thighs and buttocks like a second skin. His head was held high and was looking upwards, beyond the lights that beat down on him, off into the vaulting darkness.

Petra followed his gaze and saw to her surprise that there was a gallery above their heads. It was packed with female spectators. They hung over the balcony, their eyes glued to the proceedings below. The trial of Tom Glass was the most popular spectacle in town.

The afternoon drew to a close. So dramatic had been the testimony, so prurient the detail of one man's love life, the day seemed to have been transmitted in fast-forward time. Petra listened as Gossamer Hawk probed with relish Tom's takeover of Euphoria Records.

'So you see, madam, that by offering Chas Cross the nubile body of a teenage girl - whose mother and father, incidentally, he had separately exploited and betrayed - the prisoner Glass was able to take control of a leading record company of the day. If I may, madam, I would like to request an adjournment until tomorrow. Then I shall embark on Thomas Glass's abuse of his new position to systematically defraud Shani and the Shagbags of their royalty income and of the copyright to their own songs.'

'Very well, Prosecutor,' said the Judge, 'I think we've all had enough excitement for one day. Sergeant Tooth, you can take the prisoner down.' She paused and looked meaningfully at Tom. 'And when I say "take him down" I mean it in every sense.'

For a moment Petra did not understand but as Amy Tooth unbolted Tom's foot, he turned towards her and she gasped. Outlined in his prison pyjamas was a monumental erection, every bulge and ridge in his straining tool clearly visible under the harsh lights.

Then, up in the gallery, Petra noticed a small dark woman with a long nose. Between the railings of the balcony she could see that the woman's thighs were spread and her skirt was hitched up to her waist, exposing a nude and hairy pussy which she was blatantly fingering. The woman next to her, a large brunette with soft curly hair, was offering the same display, her sex fully on show, the labia long and wet as she played with them. Petra was shocked that these women had come here for such a purpose - to flaunt their nudity and to masturbate in front of Tom. Perhaps to excite him so much that he would lose control and be punished.

Amy Tooth swung her hand and cracked Tom across the cheek as hard as she could. Gloria Just kicked him violently on the knee and he pitched forward onto his face.

The pair of them flipped him over onto his back and Amy yanked the pyjamas down to his knees. His big cock was thrust weeping into the light, the foreskin peeled back to reveal a gleaming head purple with blood and frustration. Amy lifted a slim jackbooted foot and held it poised for a moment over the twitching bar of flesh that jutted from Tom's loins. Then she ground it down.

Gouts of spunk shot from his shaft, spattering over the floor and glistening on the black leather boots of the harpies of the Sex Police.

Around the room, the spectating, masturbating women sighed in unison.

Chapter 51

Fiona looked at Tom's supper tray and said, 'You ought to eat more than that, you know. You've got to keep your strength up.'

Tom gazed right through her as if he hadn't heard a word - which was true enough. Since Amy Tooth had walked all over him with her jackboots, a ringing noise had been reverberating through his head like a fire alarm.

With a tut-tut of contempt, Fiona removed the tray and stalked off, leaving her bruised and bedraggled prisoner to the solitude of his bare cell.

Tom shook his head from side to side, as if trying to dislodge water from his ears, but the noise rang on. He closed his eyes and the sound whistled through his entire body like a great wind, blowing with it memories of the day's events. The humiliation of his ordeal in The Primrose Court burned within him. It was not so much the beating, the exposure of his body or the shame of his final incontinence that hurt. Even the betrayal by Eve Biscuit was something he knew, in time, he could harden himself to.

It was the sudden certainty that had taken root in his mind as he had listened to the litany of his so-called sex crimes - the certainty that, in a weird and twisted way, Prosecutor Hawk was right. He *was* all those things she accused him of being - a moral degenerate, a selfish manipulator of women, an empire-builder fuelled only by greed and self-gratification. That most of his victims - if they could be called that - were fair game and had a thirst for sensual pleasure as profound as his own, was no excuse. He swore to himself that, however he emerged from this ordeal, he would police his future behaviour himself.

He threw himself on his mean bed and, with the wind still rushing through the corridors of his mind, succumbed to sleep.

The Chief Executive's penthouse was on the tenth storey of the Glass Mountain building. During the week Tom lived above the shop, as it were. It was very convenient. Personal visitors used a separate entrance and were rushed to the top floor in an express elevator.

The door buzzer took Tom by surprise. It was nearly nine in the evening and he'd just come upstairs from the office. Everyone else had long gone. Even the cleaners had finished their stint.

'Tom, it's Christina,' said the voice through the intercom. For a moment he couldn't think who that could be. He hadn't seen Tina for many years. Not since Chas Cross had spirited her away to his island in the Bahamas and the Shagbags split up. He pressed the button to let her in.

She'd changed somewhat. Her face was fuller, her figure too. But her eyes were the same caramel brown and her hair, now cut to her jaw, the same lustrous blonde. A pretty teenager had blossomed into a lovely woman.

Tom began to say as much but was frozen to the spot when another figure stepped out of the lift.

If anything, Shani had changed less than Tina. She wore a smart white business suit and carried a briefcase. Below the hem of the short skirt, her long legs were as thrilling as ever. Their *cafe au lait* sheen set Tom's heart thumping as of old.

Numb with shock, Tom ushered his unexpected guests into his spacious living room. The sun was going down and light flooded through the glass wall which gave onto the balcony. It was so bright the breathtaking view over the City streets and down to the river was blotted out.

'Would you like a drink?' he asked.

'No,' said Shani. 'We've come for a business meeting.'

'Oh,' said Tom. Their business together was done with years ago.

Temporarily blinded by the sun, Tom could not see clearly what Shani was doing as she set her briefcase on a low coffee table and opened it. She picked something out of the case and pointed it in his direction. The light glinted on metal and Tom knew exactly what she held in her hand. It was a gun.

'Don't say anything, Tom,' said Shani's low mellifluous voice. 'I don't want to shoot you but if I get angry I might.'

'What is there to get angry about, Shani?' Tom was sincerely puzzled and sincerely afraid. 'The lawyers finished business ages ago. You both agreed to the settlement.'

'That was then,' said Shani. 'We've had time to think about it and we think you owe us a bit more. Now shut up and do what I tell you. Take your clothes off.'

'But, Shani—'

'Do it,' she hissed, a red spark flickering in her midnight black eyes. Tom's stomach turned over. He began to unbutton his shirt.

Naked, with a pistol pointing at his stomach, Tom had never felt so vulnerable - or so small.

Shani laughed. 'Memory plays funny tricks, I guess. When I last looked between your legs things were built on a different scale. You'd better give him the stuff, Tina.'

Tom watched with alarm as Tina took a surgical cuff and hypodermic syringe from the briefcase. 'Don't worry,' she said as she tied off his arm and made him bend it. 'I know how to handle this. Just keep still.'

Tom would have thrust her aside but for the thought of the mad glint in

Shani's eyes and the little gun shaking in her fist. He said nothing as the needle sank into his flesh.

Within seconds, it seemed, he felt a glow seep through his veins. A drowsy, soppy glow like the effect of a hot bath and a large gin. Suddenly the tension and stiffness had gone from his body. He felt weak and rubbery and relaxed. 'Wow,' he heard himself say, far off, as if he were someone else.

'That's better, isn't it?' said Shani, and when he looked into her face this time he didn't see rage and resentment but a ripe, tempting sensuality. Those black eyes seemed to be brimming with carnal promise. He ached to kiss her dark full lips as he had once done. She had been incandescent in bed, it came back to him vividly.

'Look at him now,' said Tina and he realised she was gazing at his cock. It reared up from his loins as eager and stiff as a teenager's.

'Then let's get on with it,' said Shani.

Tom sat in a daze as the two women spread a plastic sheet on the floor. Shani removed her jacket and pulled on a thin cotton overall and rubber gloves. Tina hauled him to his feet and he realised as Shani rushed to help that he could hardly move a muscle of his own volition. With some difficulty they laid him on his back on the sheet.

Tina rubbed ointment into his penis. Her fingers were like flames on his skin as she smoothed it in and the sensation was exquisite. His big erection bounded in her hands, by far the most frisky part of his body.

Then it was Shani's turn. From a plastic bag she took lumps of what looked like clay, a soft and malleable material that she moulded around his loins. Soon his genitals were completely encased in the stuff. The women looked at him with satisfaction. He grinned back stupidly. He couldn't help it.

'It will take an hour to dry,' said Shani. 'In the meantime, we need your signature.'

Tina took some papers and a pen from the case. Somewhere in Tom's confused head a red alert sounded.

The last thing he must do, he knew, was sign anything.

Shani propped him up and pulled the table close so that he could reach the papers. On his belly the congealed mass of gunk was drying on his tumescent cock. She took care not to move his lower body.

'I... won't,' he said carefully, his tongue thick and useless in his mouth.

'Oh yes, you will,' said Shani and lowered her lips to his. She kissed him gently, like a soft summer breeze. The smell of her, rich and intoxicating, filled his nostrils.

'You'll sign for us,' said Tina smoothing a small slender hand across his chest, leaving a trail of tingling sparks in its wake.

Together they worked on his heightened senses, every touch and caress sending a crackle of electricity through his frame. He had never felt so sensually alive - and yet so helpless. Then Shani produced a feather. Each touch was like a lick of fire. Exquisite torture.

'Sign,' said Shani.

'No,' said Tom, his mind and body in turmoil. When they put the pen in his hand they couldn't make him grip.

'We'll spend the night with you,' said Shani. 'You can have us together. We'll do anything you want.'

A memory bubble burst in his head: Shani's glistening brown body lying on a bed, her black hair on a pillow tangled with Tina's blonde tresses, the sight of Shani strapping a pink dildo to her dark loins, the pair of them crying out in endless singing climax.

Tom's resistance broke. He signed. They took the dried gunk from off his loins, carefully cutting the mould away with a gleaming scalpel. He lost no blood, just a few hairs, and his cock stood up free, flaming pink and as stiff as an hour before.

Laughing, they produced stockings and suspenders and a camera. They put the underwear on him with some difficulty, and posed him on the sofa. Tom tried hard to spoil the shots but he was helpless. He couldn't even remove the vacant grin from his face.

Tina stripped to her knickers and posed with him in some of the pictures. He noticed she kept her face out of the frame. Then she took her panties off and put them on his head. Shani clicked away, with Tina naked by her side, Tom gazed at the fluffy bush between the blonde's legs and cursed the pair of them. He was being set up and he had no control over events at all. On his belly his rock-hard cock throbbed in torment. They took lots of close-ups.

Then, worst of all, they ignored him. Tina put her clothes on and Shani cleared away the plastic sheet and took off her overall and gloves. Tina disappeared and returned after some time with two mugs of tea. She did not offer Tom anything. He lay on the sofa with stockings on his legs and Tina's knickers on his head. She didn't even bother to retrieve them.'

So they weren't paying him any attention when he escaped. He'd been aware that the paralysis of his limbs was coming to an end. He wondered if he should make a grab for the gun but it was on the table just by Tina. He didn't think he'd manage to claim it. He wasn't sure he had the strength to do any more than make a run for it.

He thought that if he could get into the lift then he'd be whisked down to the street. Maybe he could raise the security guard from the office entrance next door in time to apprehend the women when they followed him. At least that way he'd have a witness. What the hell, it was worth a try. He didn't really think they'd shoot him.

He ran for it, springing off the sofa, lunging for the door, stepping out into the dark. But his bearings were awry and the instructions from his brain somehow became scrambled. He knew he'd blown it even as he lurched through the wrong door, onto the balcony and over the edge.

And now, as he tumbled through the night air, past the windows of his own office building, down into the street below - he remembered nothing...

Chapter 52

'Oh no,' wailed Petra as she opened the front door of her flat.

'Oh yes,' said Kelvin, taking her by the arm and leading into the kitchen. The table was laid and pans bubbled on the hob. A bottle of rich red wine stood on the table. Kelvin poured two glasses.

Petra looked at it all in dismay. Another night - almost any night during the previous three months in fact - she would have welcomed a domestic evening with Kelvin. But not tonight, not after the traumas of The Primrose Court.

'We have to talk,' said Kelvin, pressing the glass into her hand.

'Yes but not now. I don't have time. I've got to prepare a defence for Tom Glass.'

Kelvin beamed at her, that familiar lop-sided grin suddenly taking her breath away. It had been a long time since she had seen it.

'That's why we must talk,' he said. 'I have his defence right here.' And he held up an audio cassette with a grin of triumph.

The two voices echoed around the little kitchen. There was a lot of background hiss but the words they spoke and the sounds they made were plain. Petra sipped her wine and the rosy encroachment of intoxication was enhanced by the wonder of Kelvin's revelation.

The first voice was male, a confident northern foghorn.

'By gum, Harmony, you're a handsome woman for your age.'

'You're not so bad yourself, Mr Oates.' The second was female and more refined, possibly from Edinburgh. Petra sucked in her breath - she knew that voice all too well.

'You've got better tits on you than lasses half your age. And your arse isn't bad either.'

'Do you have to be so coarse, Bill?'

'I do when I'm with you, your ladyship. It brings out the gamekeeper in me. Tell you what, if you let me spunk off between those big knockers of yours, I'll bung another ten grand into your fighting fund.'

'That's a disgusting suggestion. I've never heard of such a thing.'

'Come, come, Harmony, don't tell me your Archie hasn't put his sword in that scabbard from time to time.'

'What a man does to his wife is another matter entirely. Besides it's a messy business.'

'OK, I'll up the price. Ten grand a tit.'

'Really, Bill - ooh!'

'You like that, don't you? My second wife liked having her pussy lips pinched too. She had long ones like you.'

'Bill, please! Do stop talking and get on with it, if you insist.'

'Well, I do insist. And so would you if you had agreed to pay nigh on half a million for the privilege of not being harassed and put upon by a crew of silly bitches who want to stop a man running his business how he chooses. I don't hold with it and well you know it.'

'Bill, don't get excited.'

'I'll get excited how I like from now on. I've paid for it and you conniving, money-grubbing witches from The Petticoat Court or whatever you call it are not going to stop me!'

A rasping cough, followed by loud panting and spluttering, interrupted the dialogue.

'Bill Oates has got a heart condition and he must be twenty stone,' said Kelvin. 'He almost flattened me when he got into bed.'

'What do you mean?' asked Petra.

'I was underneath. Ssh, now listen.'

'Are you all right, Bill?'

'Yes, lass, I'm OK now. Thank God for you, that's what I say. You might come over as a tight-arsed lesbian like the others but I know better.'

'Do you now?' She giggled - Petra found it a disturbing sound - and there was a silence, interrupted by bumps and slithers, as of bodies moving on sheets.

'You see, underneath you're just a horny Scottish cow who likes a big prick.'

'Oh yes! Put it in me please, Bill.'

'All in good time, girl. First it's going between these handsome tits, we agreed.'

'And you'll pay an extra twenty.'

'I shan't but the board of Oversell Supermarkets will. As their nominated representative in secret negotiations for a licence from The Primrose Court, I should be failing in duty if I did not insist on my pound of flesh. In your case my darling, *many* pounds.'

'How repulsive!' said Petra with vehemence.

'Yes, he's truly disgusting,' said Kelvin. 'He's just the kind of sexist pig The Primrose Court was created to stamp out.'

'Not him. Her. Lady Harmony Sharp. She's the mean spirited judge at Tom's trial. But you know that, don't you?'

Kelvin nodded, satisfaction etched into his features.

'Oh Kelvin, how I've missed you!' She knocked over her wineglass in her rush to fold him in her arms. The wine dropped unheeded onto the floor as they kissed long and hard.

He sat on the small wicker settee in the corner of the kitchen and pulled her down into his lap. He began to unbutton the jacket of her dark suit.

'How on earth did you get that recording, Kelvin? What have you been up to?'

He held her jacket and her blouse open and bent to kiss the pale flesh of her breasts just above the scalloped edge of her white lace brassiere.

'Stop, Kelvin! No, I don't mean it really but tell me, please what's going on?'

'OK.' He lifted his head from her bosom, now bare in his hands, the nipples dark and hard as he fingered them.

'I've been undercover, on the trail of a real story. Now I've got it. The tape you've heard is not the only one. I can prove that The Primrose Court is running a racket. The hierarchy - Gossamer Hawk, Lady Harmony Sharp, Naomi Picket - they're like the mafia. They're selling protection from the Sex Police.'

'You mean the licence that Bill Oates spoke about? The half a million pounds?'

'That's right.' Kelvin removed Petra's jacket and blouse and laid them on the side table. Her bra joined the pile. 'Of course they still want to drive the dinosaurs in pinstripes - that's what Gossamer calls them - out of the boardroom but they're also milking companies for serious money.'

'It's a scandal!' said Petra as Kelvin moved her off his lap and knelt on the floor to remove her shoes. 'Do you think Tom could have bought his way out? Why is he being persecuted when that pig Bill Oates gets off?'

Kelvin had unzipped Petra's skirt and was now drawing it down her slim gleaming thighs. She lifted her bottom to allow him access and sat down again without regard for his actions, her mind focused elsewhere.

'Tom Glass is too big a fish,' he said. 'He's a fabulously wealthy, high-profile captain of industry. He's a trophy, not a cash cow. If The Primrose Court can bring him down they're made.'

Kelvin contemplated the slim but curvaceous figure of Petra as she sat in front of him. Just the thin scrap of white lace across her loins now remained between her and total nudity. He took his glass of wine from the table behind him and toasted her near-naked perfection.

'What are you going to do with your story?' she said, taking the glass from him and raising it to her lips.

'First I thought I'd sell it to the highest bidder. The *Dog* or the *Rabbit* would pay me a fortune. But they'd exploit it to the hilt and me with it. And after the fuss had died down I'd be on my own. I don't fancy spending the rest of my life dodging the hit-women of the Sex Police. They'd peel my dick like a banana and eat my balls on toast, just to start with.'

'So?'

'So then I thought I should be more subtle - use the information as a lever. Maybe get The Primrose Court to toe the line.'

'But how, Kelvin? As you say, they'll eat you alive.'

'They won't eat Tom Glass alive, not when you've got off tomorrow. He'll be untouchable and he's powerful. With this information he can break up the mafia, get some sensible men on the Corrections Committee. And some women like you.'

'Me?'

'That's right. Women who are smart, honest and don't have a vendetta against the opposite sex.'

Petra grinned at him, the realisation that there was a way out fizzing through her veins like liquid joy. She dipped a finger in the glass and anointed the saucers of her areolae with wine.

'Lick it off,' she commanded. He did so, nuzzling his head into her chest, taking her hard little nipples between his lips.

'How should I play it tomorrow?' she asked as she cradled him to her.

'See the Judge before the court resumes. Give her that tape. I've got a transcript for you, too. Tell her that unless she calls the trial off at once, copies will go to the press.'

'I thought you didn't want that?'

He sat back on his haunches and placed his hands on her knees. 'Ted Flinch of *Nouveau* is in on it. We fell out and I was going to go for the big bucks but... as you know I've had second thoughts. To be honest, he put me on the story in the first place. He'll front for me, if necessary, and the IBG lawyers are shit-hot.'

Petra thought for a moment, considering her plan of action. 'I'll take Cassie,' she said. 'We'll have Tom Glass free by lunch. I never knew you had it in you, Kelvin.'

He pushed her knees apart and gazed with longing on the smooth lines of her spread thighs, right up to the lacy triangle stretched over the bulge of her mons. He hooked a finger into the strip of material where it disappeared below her seat into the crack of her buttocks. She shivered in anticipation, but there was one more thing she had to know.

'Just how did you find out all this red-hot information, Kelvin?'

He pulled the thin strip of lace to one side, laying bare the black knot of hair and the pink puffy lips of her excited pussy. He feasted his eyes.

'I can't possibly reveal the tricks of my trade,' he said. 'But I can demonstrate one of my most effective investigative techniques.'

And he lowered his mouth to her wet, throbbing sex.

Chapter 53

Tom was no longer used to crowds. He slipped away from celebrations at Glass Mountain as soon as he decently could. He knew nearly everyone, of course, they were his own hand-picked staff but it was hard to step from solitary confinement into a room containing hundreds of well-wishers all desperate to shake his hand. Apart from anything else he had a couple of things to take care of.

As he slid out of the door he caught Petra's eye. She was on the far side of the room surrounded by people, a champagne glass in her hand. When she realised he was leaving she made as if to press through the throng towards him. He held up his hand and indicated that she should remain. She'd done enough for him already today. In fact, she was a miracle-worker.'

He stepped into his office and, for a moment, was stunned to see another man sitting at his desk, barking into the phone. Then he remembered who it was. Charles Kite, the disgraced executive whom Petra had rehabilitated. Well, thank God; someone was taking care of business amidst the chaos. Tom backed out of the room and found an empty office down the corridor.

The people at Black Raven refused to call Marianne to the phone. They explained that she was busy preparing for a *Gravitas* special. Tom left her a message instead. It said: 'The wedding's off. There's a cheque in the post. Good luck in the job. Love, Tom.' It was a bit curt perhaps but he was sure the size of the cheque would assuage any hurt feelings.

His next task was not so easy to accomplish. He called Partridge Place and Spilling Grange without success. Then he spoke to Inspector Claire Quartermain and found her surprisingly cooperative.

They'd kept his Porsche in pristine condition in the basement garage. The engine fired at first asking and the car purred as he swung onto the City roads and headed across town.

It was one of those narrow, west London streets full of five-year-old Sunnys and Cortinas and builder's muck. The houses were turn-of-the-century terraced, always in need of repair. Green mould clogged the gutters, plastic wheelie-bins occupied the front gardens and satellite dishes sprouted beneath the eaves.

The woman on the first floor looked with half an eye as the sparkling white Porsche manoeuvred into a tight space between an overflowing skip and a rusty motorbike. Porsches were not common in this street and other eyes watched with keen curiosity. The woman turned away, not much interested. Nothing interested her at the moment.

So she did not see the tall man with a shock of dark hair get out of the car and head purposefully for her front gate. She ignored the sounds from downstairs, one of the other tenants would see to it. Nobody would be visiting her.

But she couldn't ignore the knocking at her door. It was loud and insistent. Maybe if she stayed completely silent whoever it was would give up.

The door burst open.

'Eve, thank God, I've found you.'

The sight of Tom Glass in her room, the man she had betrayed and caused to be beaten, persecuted and publicly humiliated was too much for Eve Biscuit. She fainted.

She came round and found herself lying on the bed. Tom was dabbing at her forehead with a wet flannel. When she opened her eyes he smiled.

'I'm sorry,' she said.

'I should hope so too. You're the nurse, you're not meant to faint.'

'I don't mean that. I mean—'

'Ssh,' he shut her up with a kiss. It lasted some while. Time enough for them to cling together and drink from each other's mouths as if they were dying of thirst.

'But—' she began as they pulled apart.

'Don't say anything, Eve. Not just now. I know they forced you to do it but now I'm free and so are you. It's all over.' And he stretched out beside her on the narrow bed and kissed her again.

'Actually,' he said as he pulled her T-shirt from the waist of her jeans and eased it upwards over the satin-smooth skin of her stomach, 'I was hoping that this was the beginning.'

'Of what? Ooh.' His hands were on her breasts through the thin cups of her brassiere. She reached behind her back to undo the fastening.

'Well,' he said, 'I've had some painful weeks of deprivation. I've been bullied and beaten up and deprived of - these...'

Her big beautiful breasts were bare in his hands now and he stroked them with reverence, savouring the rolling weight of their familiar mass.

'God, I've missed your kind of nursing, Eve,' he breathed as he lowered his mouth to take a stiff puckered nipple between his lips.

'So that's what you're after,' she said, feeding her breast to him and stroking the hair from his brow.

He lifted his head. 'That's not all,' he said, his fingers now busy at the zip on her jeans and tugging the thick denim over her hips. She found herself clawing at his belt.

'What else then?'

Her jeans were down her thighs now, her knickers too. They hung from one foot then dropped to the floor.

'I need round the clock care. Twenty-four-hour personal attendance.'

His shirt was unbuttoned, his trousers kicked off, his briefs yanked down to spill his cock and balls into her groping hands.

'You don't want a nurse,' she panted as, breathless with want, she jammed the big purple head of his penis into the welcoming mouth of her vagina.

His hands reached beneath her, found the full creamy smooth orbs of her buttocks, and thrust.

'OH!' she cried.

His pulsing tool was deep within her, her legs wrapped around his waist, their bodies wedged together in the small space as close as they could get. Their hips undulated together, their pelvises danced, their pubic bones rub-rub-rubbed in urgent need.

She unglued her lips from his. 'You don't want a nurse,' she repeated, 'you want a body slave.'

'Could be,' he said, now slowing the pace and spearing into her deliberately. 'What I'm really after is a wife.'

Eve went rigid. There was a rising tide in her veins and bells began to hammer in her head.

'You've got a wife,' she breathed, 'or will have. Haven't you forgotten Marianne?'

'I sacked her today.' His cock thrust faster and faster now, driving them to the edge. 'The situation's vacant.'

'Oh God,' she groaned, as the first ripples of orgasm washed over her.

'So will you take the job?' he whispered.

Her loins spasmed out of control as the wave broke and carried her away and the words came tumbling in a stream from her lips.

He smiled as he came too, the sounds of her excitement echoing from far off.

'Yes oh yes oh yes,' she cried. 'Yes, Tom, YES!'

Chapter 54

Petra was euphoric as she took her place amongst the audience in the Black Raven studio. So far it had been a fabulous day.

That morning the confrontation with the Judge at The Primrose Court had gone more smoothly than she could have hoped for. As the first echoes of Kelvin's secret recording rang round her office, Lady Harmony Sharp's face was a picture. Disbelief, outrage, embarrassment - these were all evident but one other emotion burned brightest of all. Fear.

Judge Sharp turned Tom loose at once, even before she marched into court and abandoned the proceedings. The tumult of surprise and disappointment from the spectators overrode even the Judge's gavel. Gossamer Hawk's face turned to thunder and Petra laughed out loud. She knew that later, when she heard the reason for this unexpected reverse, Prosecutor Hawk would also wear the face of fear.

The afternoon party at Glass Mountain had not been planned but there was no way to contain the explosion of excitement once Tom's appearance lit the fuse. Even the most disgruntled employee was keen to piss the day away, glass in hand, and contemplate the future now it was evident the boss was free, sane and eager to get back to business.

Petra had not worried when Tom slipped out of the celebrations but later, when his car was reported missing and he could not be found, she'd become anxious. Then he called her and they talked for quite a while. He'd finished by making her a suggestion that still made her smile. She'd said yes, how could she refuse? No one had ever asked her to be a best man before...

Now Petra sat in the invited *Gravitas* audience between her lover and her best friend, though (she realised with a forbidden frisson) the terms might equally well be applied to them both. Her body shivered with excitement. Kelvin had come back to her like a knight in shining armour to rescue her from peril and like a demon lover equipped with new skills to drive her wild - as he had done most of last night. She squeezed his thigh and grinned at Cassie on her other side. She was going to remember this day for the rest of her life.

The programme began with an introduction by Marianne dressed in her clinging black sheath dress that emphasised as much as it concealed. The topic was sexual self-help. There was a school of thought, headed by Gerald Goldring, that held that such subject matter was unworthy of a flagship arts programme like *Gravitas*. But the prospect of some decent viewing figures had long ago swayed all judgements. After all, what was the point of having a sexy new presenter like Marianne if you weren't going to talk about sex?

So Marianne began the lead-in to two filmed segments (of authors Timberland and Honeydew) which was then to be followed by the meat of the programme - the studio discussion.

'There's no doubt we have sex on the brain,' she said in her sly gurgle of a voice. 'Magazines, newspapers, even television programmes like this, are full of sexual material. Our bookshelves are packed with advice on how-to, when-to, and what-to-do-when-I-don't-want-to. But are we actually doing it at all? Our programme tonight is about two gurus of contemporary sexuality and their directly opposed philosophies. Their books are battling it out at the very top of the bestseller lists and they will shortly be in the studio to fight it out in person - though not literally of course, we hope. This is what they had to say when I spoke to them earlier in the week.'

'Hunk-ee,' breathed Cassie in appreciation as the rugged blue-eyed face of Edward Timberland beamed out of the TV monitor just in front of them. 'He's a beaut.'

'Relax,' muttered Petra. 'He's the one who doesn't believe in doing it.'

'Be quiet,' came an impatient whisper from the other side of the central aisle. Petra had noticed earlier that the audience was divided. Around her the watchers were for the most part female - smart attractive women brimming with purpose. Across the aisle the seats were packed with men, a nondescript bunch of all ages, none of whom had caught Petra's eye. It was this section that sat, rapt, as Ted Timberland espoused the virtues of self-reliance, life in the raw and semen-retention.

'Shit a brick,' muttered Cassie, 'don't ask me to date one those guys.'

'Will you please be quiet,' said the same voice as before, an obnoxious authoritarian bray. It came from a diminutive, pinstriped figure who was glaring at them in the semi-darkness.

'That little pipsqueak's getting on my tits,' said Cassie.

'Ignore him,' said Petra. 'Look, here's Chastity.' There was a murmur of approval from the women as the blonde Californian, dressed in work-out clothes of skintight Lycra, appeared on screen. At the same time, Petra became aware of a hiss of loathing from across the aisle.

'Jezebel,' cried the pinstriped one as Chastity began to describe the pivotal role of the orgasm in her work-out regime.

'Painted whore!' shouted a hairy giant in an anorak.

The men were shushed energetically by the women and some of Chastity's pearls of wisdom were lost in the commotion.

Kelvin chuckled. 'I see we're in for a lively studio discussion.'

Petra squeezed his hand in contentment, in her present mood she didn't mind one bit.

'Are you sure you want to watch this?' said Tom as Eve got out of bed to turn on the television. Her rear view was delectable, the pale ovals of her buttocks flexing and shifting as she moved. And when she bent down to pick up the remote control Tom longed to freeze-frame her in that position, just so he could savour the flowing outthrust of her hips, the swollen curve of her cheeks - and the pouting lips of her pink pussy smiling up at him in flagrant invitation. Though they had done little apart from feast on each other's flesh from the moment he had arrived, he was hungry for her again.

'Of course I want to watch it,' she said as she turned back to the bed, her big breasts billowing, the blonde thatch between her thighs winking at him. Really, the view from the front was just as intoxicating.

'OK,' said Tom as she climbed into the small bed beside him. 'Just as long as I never hear you say, at any time in our future life, that on the night of our engagement I made you watch my ex-fiancée on TV.'

She laughed and snuggled into his arms. 'She's got nothing to do with it. I want to watch Chastity Honeydew. I'm thinking of doing her regime.'

Tom groaned. 'If you're going on some celery-and-wheat-germ diet with daily aerobics the wedding's off. Now I'm at liberty I want to enjoy life, I don't want some fitness fascist in my bed.'

Eve slid a companionable hand around Tom's erection and gently slipped the foreskin back and forth across the glans. 'That's a pity,' she said, 'because I'm relying on you for support.'

'Hey, Fiona.' Gloria Just was sitting at the reception desk in the basement of The Primrose Court, flicking through the newspaper.

Fiona had her head buried in her book. She looked up.

'Your favourite writer is on the telly,' said Gloria.

'Who?'

'"Morticia Chekhov, author of *The Piercing of Patsy Punishment* takes part in a discussion about sexual self-help techniques" - that's what it says here.'

'Ooh!' A squeal of excitement broke from Fiona's lips. 'That's the one I'm reading now!'

'I know that, you dozy slut, that's why I mentioned it. The programme's just started.'

'Quick, let's watch it in the day room. There's nothing going on here.'

'Too true,' said Gloria. It was a quiet night in the cells. In fact it wasn't much fun at all now Tom Glass had gone.

She followed Fiona out of the door, watching the twitch of her mini-skirt and the eager swish of her long thin legs as she raced ahead. Quite why she was in such a rush Gloria couldn't fathom. It wasn't as if she had much to learn about sexual self-help. The way the girl practised, she had to be an expert already.

Chapter 55

In the Black Raven studio, Marianne Matthews' moment had come. As the cameras closed in on her sparkling grey eyes and sumptuous smiling mouth, she bubbled with excitement. The stage-fright that had beset her before transmission had melted into her blood, giving her a transfusion of energy. This was her first important programme, she was chairing a live discussion on a hot topic and the studio was buzzing. She just knew this was going to be a night to remember.

There were four guests on the platform with her. On her right, the women: Chastity and the novelist Morticia Chekhov. On her left, the men: poet Garnet O'Dread and Ted Timberland. The warring writers sat out on opposing flanks, facing their supporters; Marianne was in the middle, orchestrating the discussion - such as it was. Each of the speakers confined themselves to statements of their position that allowed little room for dialogue.

'To be honest with you,' Garnet was saying, 'I find nothing of any interest whatsoever in either of these books. And the idea that they address pertinent issues of our time is frankly laughable.' Marianne smiled at him warmly and urged him to continue - which he did, rubbishing all parties in his deadpan Irish drone as was his habit. He was on every arty-farty talk show going, his function being to stick the knife into the subject in question from a position of moral and intellectual superiority. It was a very successful pose. He never went out of fashion.

'But Garnet,' said Marianne, deciding to throw a spanner in the works, 'where do you stand personally on sex?'

'Basically I think that the trophy-hunting philosophy in sexual matters, be it in collecting orgasms or in stockpiling a semen bank—'

'That's not what I meant,' interrupted Marianne. 'What I meant was, do you do it?'

There was a pause. For the first time in broadcasting history, the Irish poet was silent.

'Perhaps I should put my cards on the table,' continued Marianne. 'I, personally, do it lots, and if I haven't got a partner I'll do it on my own. So what do *you* do?'

Garnet looked from side to side, his eyes spinning in his head like marbles. It was evident that he hoped, for once, to hear the sound of someone else's voice. It did not come.

'Well, I, er... I think this is a rather personal matter.'

'Surely not in the context of our discussion,' said Marianne. 'I'm sure everyone in our audience would be prepared to state their position.' She turned to the audience. 'Wouldn't you?'

The shout of 'Yes' was deafening.

'You see.' She smiled at him in triumph. 'Come on, Garnet. You wouldn't want your reticence to be misinterpreted as intellectual cowardice, would you?'

The blood drained from the poet's face. 'If you must know,' he spat at her, 'I abhor all matters to do with the procreative process. I think that sexual behaviour is the curse of creation and I *personally* would be happy to see the human race die out with my generation. I particularly detest pretty perfumed women with their breasts loose and bare under tight dresses who try and pollute the purity of my thought processes.'

'Like me, you mean?'

'Yes, yes. Just like you. Look at yourself, all flirty-flirty eyes and swishy-swishy legs and your nipples poking through your, dress. You're *disgusting!*'

Marianne glowed with inner satisfaction. She'd got the little bastard. She gave the camera her sultriest smile as she said, 'Now I think we know where Garnet O'Dread is coming from. The great poet has just revealed himself to be a complete wanker.'

'Gosh,' said Eve, 'she's brilliant. And she's gorgeous. Why ever did you split up?'

'Because she didn't love me and I didn't love her,' said Tom. 'If you want to turn it off that's fine with me.'

'Oh no, I'm enjoying it. I want to hear what Chastity has to say. And take your hand away from there, I don't want to be distracted.'

'I'm only trying to help. I thought this was all about having lots of orgasms.'

'Well, I suppose so but, ooh, must you?'

'Yes. Slide your beautiful bum onto my lap. If we're going to watch television on the night of my liberation from a dank and dreary prison cell I'd like to put my cock somewhere warm and comfortable.'

'In here?'

'Mmm yes. That's exactly where I had in mind.'

'And what about you, Morticia, what's your preference?' Marianne had switched her attack to the novelist. She was really punching now, she thought, nobody would ever again mistake her for a weather girl after this.

Before she replied, the writer removed her horn-rimmed spectacles and met Marianne's gaze. The look in those almond-shaped eyes said that she was equal to any challenge.

'Since you ask,' said Morticia, 'I like to watch.'

'You mean you're a voyeur?'

'Oh yes. All writers are voyeurs in their way. As the author of erotic stories I like people to perform for me sexually. It gives me great pleasure. It's also excellent research.'

'And you attain orgasm just by watching other people?' asked Marianne, wondering just how far she should push things.

'Don't be silly,' replied the novelist. 'I need proper stimulation in the right quarters.'

'You mean self-stimulation.'

'Not necessarily, though I don't like other people to touch me.'

Marianne was lost but she was determined to pin this superior bitch down.

'That doesn't make sense.'

'Certainly, it does. I'll show you. Just hold this.' Morticia placed the end of a thin gold chain in Marianne's hand. It appeared to be attached to the woman's clothing. 'Now just tug it gently. Mmm - ooh - that's right. If you kept that up I assure you it would give me exquisite pleasure.'

Marianne looked at the chain in her hand. 'You mean the other end of this is attached somehow to your body?'

'That's right, my dear. It runs directly to the pins pierce my nipples.'

'Aah!' Marianne shrieked and dropped the chain. There was a gasp from the audience and some nervous laughter.

Chastity reached across Morticia and took hold of the sparkling gold links. 'Allow me, honey,' she purred, 'us sophisticated women have to stick together.'

Marianne stared glassy-eyed at the thin glinting chain which, she could now see, ran from Chastity's fingers into the dark shadows of cleavage revealed in the bodice of the writer's black jacket. In that alluring ravine shone more metal and Marianne's stomach lurched. She was turned off and turned on all at once.

But now was no time to dwell on her feelings, she had to remain in control.

'Let's get this clear,' she said. 'If Chastity pulls on that chain will it excite you sexually?'

'Oh yes!' breathed Morticia, her eyelids half shut, her bosom rising and falling as Chastity set up a gentle sawing motion on the golden thread. Marianne could picture long dark nipples, engorged and erect, skewered through with a long gold pin...

'Look at this degrading exhibition!' boomed a voice from the other side of the platform. Tree-Top Ted had broken his silence at last. 'See what corrupt and immoral behaviour these perverted females are capable of! Beware, you men, of the lascivious exhibitions of whores!'

'Hear, hear!' called out Pinstripe.

'Filthy tarts!' yelled Anorak.

Other cries of protest rose from the men in the audience while the women hissed and called out in turn.

'Belt up, wimps!' shouted a tiny blonde in front of Petra.

Her friend, a more substantial girl with freckled shoulders in a thin summer frock, pointed across the aisle and cried, 'Wankers!'

Throughout the tumult Marianne was aware that, by her side, Morticia was breathing heavily, her eyes shut, her face turned upwards, her mouth agape. Suddenly she gasped out loud, 'OH!' and 'OH - OH - OH!' in a breathy, rhythmic shout.

In the audience the commotion died. All eyes were on the novelist as she whinnied and snorted, shaking her long dark hair from side to side, her bosom rising and falling. The thin gold chain was stretched taut from her swollen cleavage to the slender hand of Chastity Honeydew. *Tug, tug*, went the chain,

'OH - OH!' cried Morticia. Then 'OHHH!' as her entire body shook and her upturned face was wreathed in beatific release. The novelist had come off on camera. She leaned over to Chastity and kissed her on the cheek.

Marianne was the first to applaud, the women in the audience followed suit.

'One up to the Honeydew technique, I believe,' she declared and turned to face Edward Timberland. 'What do you say to that, Ted?'

'Wow!' said Eve, then 'Oh gosh' as Tom's fingers strummed across her clit. 'That was the most extraordinary thing I've ever seen on... Oh, Tom, please, I'm going to—' His fingers worked purposefully in the opening of her slit. In the hot oven of her vagina, his big penis pulsed. '—come again!'

'Wow!' said Fiona, transfixed by the celestial smile on the face of Morticia Chekhov as the novelist writhed in orgasm on the small TV screen. Around her, her colleagues sniggered. Amy Tooth and Claire Quartermain had joined them. Claire had her hand between Amy's legs, openly palming the bulge of her pussy.

'After you with that book, Fiona,' said Gloria.

'I've never seen that on TV before,' said Claire.

Fiona gazed dreamily at the screen. 'Does anyone know where I can have my nipples pierced?'

Chapter 56

When the question-and-answer session got under way, Cassie was on her feet in a trice.

'Mr Timberland - is it true you believe all women are nymphomaniacs?'

Ted beamed at Cassie. It was about time he got a chance to strut his stuff.

'The way I see it, ma'am,' he drawled, his blue eyes twinkling with folksy bonhomie, 'is that at heart all women are pure and faultless. I believe that their nurturing, caring dispositions, if left to develop naturally, predispose them to become the handmaidens and helpmates of men - as used to be the case. Look at any primitive society. The men hunt, protect, impose order - the women obey.

But now, on the verge of the twenty-first century, so-called education has disrupted the harmony of the sexes. Women have ambitions, they have careers *and* families, they aspire to the top jobs in finance, in industry and in government. They paint their faces and show their legs and, like Eve in the Garden of Eden, seduce men into temptation. And men prostrate themselves before them and are *raped*. They are deprived of their place at the head of the table! Robbed of the essential spermatic elixir that is the very fountain of their strength!

'So, my pretty auburn-tressed friend, in my opinion the women of today are *all* nymphomaniacs!'

'Who *is* this fuckwit?' said Amy Tooth.

'He can't be allowed to get away with that,' said Gloria Just.

'Heaven help him if Prosecutor Hawk hears any of this,' said Claire Quartermain.

'Don't worry, Inspector,' came clear, girlish tones from the back of the room, 'I'm taking note of every word.'

A fat bald man in a rumpled suit read his question from a slip of paper.

'Miss Honeydew, I have a press cutting from the *San Francisco Examiner* which quotes extensively from your lecture on female masturbation techniques to the *Screw You* symposium on sexuality. It is dated July 1968. Would you care to tell us exactly how old you are and how many times your body parts have been remodelled by plastic surgeons to cheat the passage of time?'

There was an intake of breath from the female audience.

'Sneaky,' muttered Petra to Cassie.

'Don't worry, she'll handle it,' said Cassie.

And she did.

'Hey, slap-head,' replied Chastity, 'you think you're so smart, I tell you, you ought to go see a surgeon yourself. Take a slice off your belly and stick it on your dick for a start.'

'Answer the question,' roared the hairy man in the anorak.

'Sure,' said the blonde one, rising to her feet. 'See my neck, look at my hands - where are the wrinkles and liver spots? Nowhere, man - take a good look.' Everybody did, the cameras panned in for close-ups. She shucked off her pink jacket and stuck her chest out. The big globes of her pneumatic breasts thrust tight against the thin pink cotton of her T-shirt. 'See, no bra to keep up the boobies. They're as pert and firm as when I was eighteen and that's a few summers back, I agree. I swear to you I've never been under the knife and I don't go to no Swiss clinic and chew on bull's balls or whatever. You wanna know my secret?'

'Yes!' From the women.

'You know it already. It's in my book, it's my philosophy of life, it keeps me young. It's orgasm. I come a lot, as often as I can, every day of my life. And you guys ought to do the same before you get even uglier than you are already!'

'Isn't she inspirational?' said Eve.

She was on all fours on the bed now, her head pointed at the television, her thighs on either side of Tom's torso, her arse in his face.

He had his hands on her creamy smooth bottom cheeks and his tongue in the divide between. She wriggled with excitement under his ministrations.

'Tom?'

'Mmm?'

'You wouldn't want my bum to go all flabby and my tits to droop, would you?'

He took his lips from her wet and succulent groove. 'Of course not, darling, but you can't beat age.'

'Chastity Honeydew can! You haven't been listening, have you?'

'I've been preoccupied, darling. What do you have to do?'

She grinned to herself and thrust her broad bottom backwards into his face. 'Just what you're doing to me right now, Tom. Promise you won't stop.'

Tom did not reply, he couldn't. From Eve's point of view that was just fine.

In the studio control room Gerald Goldring was having kittens.

'We have to finish it,' he wailed. 'It's getting out of control.'

'Keep calm,' said Sir Charles Mastiff. 'We'll grab a few headlines with this. We'll get double the figures for the Cup Final!'

'But that bloody woman had an orgasm on screen! We'll be banned! Prosecuted! The switchboard's under siege already!'

'Good show. Controversy is the lifeblood of the arts, don't you know that? Get a grip, Gerry.'

Gerald tried. He looked at the scenes on the monitors. Half the audience were on their feet, jeering at each other. A small blonde was in the aisle with her skirt hiked to her waist, waggling her bottom at the hairy man in the anorak.

'See,' he cried. 'That blonde piece is taunting them!'

'Lovely bum,' said Mastiff.

'It's obscene!'

'Can't be. This is the arts slot.'

'There's going to be a riot!'

'I don't think so, Gerry. More likely an orgy.'

'What!' Goldring's voice leapt two octaves. He studied the monitors. The hairy man had grabbed the blonde and her friend with freckled shoulders had come to her aid. The friend had freckled breasts too. The straps on her dress had snapped and two round and gleaming orbs with cherry-red nipples were wobbling free. And being crushed in Anorak's big hand as his mouth closed on the freckled one's lips and the blonde pulled his trousers to his knees.

'My God, Charles, they're tearing each other's clothes off!'

'Fantastic! I'm going downstairs to join in the fun, you keep the cameras rolling. This is ground-breaking television, Gerry. See you at the awards dinner!'

Chapter 57

Maybe Charles Mastiff had second sight or perhaps his reading of the situation was based simply on a prurient instinct for sexual indulgence. At any rate, he was right. The potential riot was becoming an actual orgy.

The mutual antipathy between the two sections of the audience was fuelled by sex, though not necessarily by desire. Although deep down, as deep as they could suppress it, the males lusted after the females, these well-groomed purposeful women were not impressed by the men. 'Yuck, what a load of nerds,' Cassie had said at the beginning of the evening and that about summed up the general view.

But when the nerds began to get stroppy, to revile the very notion of female sexual satisfaction, to proclaim the superiority of their self-control - then feminine pride was at stake.

Cassie had a big tow-headed boy trapped between the seats.

'So you don't like me, eh? My body revolts you, yes? You'll shrivel up and die if I lay a finger on you - is that it?'

'No,' he protested, trying to back away. 'It's not you. It's the principle. It's women in general.'

He tripped and fell backwards. Cassie knelt on his chest and lowered her face to an inch from his.

'I bet you've never got this close to a real woman before, have you?'

He shook his head. He was very young and his skin was as clear and unlined as an egg.

She placed her lips to his neck and licked round the sharp knob of his Adam's apple. He tasted soapy and clean. She whispered in his ear.

'Do you like my perfume? The feel of my lips on your throat? Shall I kiss you?'

He made a strangled noise that could have meant anything, but Cassie was not about to wait for permission. She kissed him long and hard, exploring his mouth with her tongue. She wriggled down his body, slid her hands under his shirt and ripped it open. His chest was broad but hairless. She scratched his nipples and he squirmed beneath her.

'Would you like to see my breasts?'

She pulled her thin cashmere sweater to her chin and yanked the cups of her bra up over her bosom. Then she leant over him, dangling the big white gourds in his shocked face. She lowered her long loganberry nipples to his lips.

'Go on, suck them. Feel my tits. Kiss them, bite them. Don't know what you're missing, do you, my little caveman?'

The boy moaned, his hands and face full of her bountiful chest. He rootled and squirmed like a puppy at his mummy's teat. Cassie delved her hand below his waist, she wasn't finished yet.

'What's this then, you naughty boy? I thought you were supposed to banish sexual thoughts. If you want to conserve your sexual juices there's no point in getting a big stiffie like this.'

She had it out in the open now, leaning back on her haunches, her big breasts on display, her hands stroking his cock and balls. His long red member thrust up awkwardly between her fingers, a tear of juice glistening in the eye.

Cassie clasped it gently, it looked as if it might go off at any second.

'You're a virgin, aren't you?' she said.

He nodded.

'Do you want to be - really?'

He shook his head. It seemed events had robbed him of the power of speech.

'Good,' said Cassie and pulled her skirt to her waist. He watched, boggle-eyed, as she dragged her panties down her thighs and wriggled out of them. Her red-tufted muff and pink pussy split were spread before him as she straddled his hips. She took his stalk and rubbed the scarlet head into the glistening opening between her thighs. The touch of her velvet flesh on his tool was like a bolt of electricity.

She sank down on him in one movement. He moaned and filled his hands with her full soft breasts. His eyes rolled up in his head and he twitched and flopped like a landed fish. And lay still.

Cassie chuckled as she lay on top of him.

He looked at her with adoration and apology. 'I'm sorry, I didn't... I mean, you didn't...'

'Ssh.' She shut him up with a kiss. 'Forget Tree-Top Ted, come home with me and *I'll* show you how to behave like a man.'

This scene, with variations, was repeated through the room. One by one, Ted Timberland's most ardent disciples were vanquished - whether by choice or by force, it mattered not.

'Let's get him,' said a slim middle-aged beauty to a teenager in jeans. The pair of them grabbed Pinstripe as he tried to run for it and the slender woman tied his hands behind his back with his tie. The teenager pulled his trousers down and rummaged in his Y-fronts.

'As limp as a lettuce,' she pronounced.

'Take your clothes off,' said the other.

The teenager was buxom and ripe. She turned and lowered her jeans, waggled her smooth golden buttocks, dragging her knickers up into her crack. 'How's that? It always gets my boyfriends going.'

'I'm not surprised,' said the other. 'He's flesh and blood after all. See.'

The girl looked over her shoulder. The woman was pumping a short stubby tool in elegant fingers. The head was broad and blood red.

'Make him shoot over my arse,' she said.

'And he can lick it off afterwards,' said the woman. 'That'll teach him to be such a dickhead.'

'No!' shouted Pinstripe and fountained a deluge of semen into the air. It splashed onto the girl's pretty bottom in a graceful arc and Pinstripe slumped to his knees.

'Get licking,' commanded the girl and buffeted her bottom into his face.

'Let's go,' said Petra to Kelvin as the action hotted up around them.

He was a little reluctant, the small blonde had Anorak's cock in her mouth and her freckled friend was sitting on his face. She really had the most fabulous breasts...

'Put your eyes back in, lover,' said Petra. 'I'll make it worth your while later.'

But they found their way barred - by Morticia Chekhov.

'Hello, my dear,' she said to Petra. 'I thought I spotted your pretty face from the platform. You're not going, are you?'

'We certainly are, Morticia. Goodbye.'

'But you haven't introduced me to your handsome companion.'

'This is Kelvin. Say hello and goodbye, Kelvin.'

'Wait.' Morticia put her hand on Petra's arm. 'I'm sure there's time for me to tell Kelvin the circumstances of our last meeting.'

'No!' Petra tried to pull her arm away but found she was held fast. Kelvin was looking on with interest. She saw his eyes resting on Morticia's enticing cleavage and the gold chain which looped down and up, its end tucked into her breast pocket.

'It was on a train, Kelvin. We got into a fascinating discussion with a ticket inspector.'

'Morticia!' squealed Petra in dismay. The hazel eyes turned in her direction. 'Well, perhaps we could stay a little while,' she said, beaten into submission.

The novelist smiled and took them both by the hand. 'Excellent. Let's find an out-of-the-way spot where we can keep an eye on these most *interesting* proceedings.'

Tree-Top Ted was apoplectic. In front of him his fans and disciples were falling prey to the painted and perfumed Jezebels who followed the whore Honeydew.

'Fight! Fight!' he roared over the heads of the scrimmaging throng, reaching for the silver flask of Big Boar bourbon in his jacket pocket.

'Repel those foul women, damn you!' he implored his followers, taking a long restorative swig of liquor before plunging into the writhing mass to pull copulating bodies apart. His reputation, his whole ethos, not to mention his battle for book sales was on the line here.

'Damnation take you!' he cried, lifting a wriggling nymph from the supine body of a naked dentist and hurling her over his shoulder. 'Honeydew - you'll burn in hell for this!'

A cameraman followed his every move.

In the day room of The Primrose Court, the events at Black Raven were under scrutiny.

'Good God,' said Gloria, 'I can't believe I'm seeing this.'

'Why doesn't someone pull the plug?' said Amy.

'Anything goes on late-night telly these days,' said Claire. 'It's probably a happening - like they used to have in the sixties,' said Fiona. 'You know, a spontaneous event.'

'Never - it's a put-up job.'

'It was probably better in rehearsal.'

A voice of authority cut through the banter.

'I don't think this is an occasion for levity,' said Gossamer Hawk.

Silence fell. On the television screen Tree-Top Ted threw a small flailing girl over his shoulder. The camera captured his blazing eyes and howling mouth.

'I think,' continued the Prosecutor, 'it's time for action. Inspector, I want an arrest. I want that man there' - on the screen Ted grabbed a naked woman by the hair - 'in the cells by midnight.'

Chapter 58

Sir Charles Mastiff surveyed the scene from the back of the studio with satisfaction. Half-naked bodies were everywhere. Women were making nude men run the gauntlet of their nubile bare-breasted bodies to regain their clothes. Not many of them made it. Other men had been tied to the seats and women were taking it in turns to excite them. Spunk flew through the air. The boldest of the women had painted themselves with it. It glistened on their thighs and buttocks.

Marianne, unsure of her role now proceedings had taken an unexpected turn, had grabbed a microphone and was conducting interviews with participants.

'She's a real trooper, that girl,' said Mastiff in admiration as he watched her quiz a lipstick-smeared merchant banker as he lay vanquished on the floor.

'I think she's brilliant,' said a dark shape in the shadows by his side, her mouth outlined in the glow of a cigarette.

'She was wasted on the weather,' said the television executive eyeing Marianne's pert bottom as she bent to thrust her microphone into a pile of wriggling bodies. 'It's imperative we have sexy girls in arts TV. It's all very well appealing to the eggheads but you've got to have something good to look at while you're discussing Schopenhauer.'

'Nice tits and bum, you mean?'

'That's putting it a bit crudely but, basically, yes.'

'Would mine do?' The dark shape moved into the light and ground her cigarette end into the floor.

'I know you,' said Sir Charles. 'You were in the green room with Timberland.'

'Sonja Sargeant. I'm handling his publicity. Actually I'm considering a change of career.' Her hands were working at the buttons on her chocolate silk blouse, pulling it open.

'I see; said Mastiff, his eyes lighting up at the big smooth mounds of flesh barely contained in the sculpted cups of her lacework brassiere.

'Not yet, you don't,' said Sonja stepping out of her skirt and revealing long flowing legs in black stockings and suspenders. Her blouse, too, fluttered to the floor and her bra followed. Her jutting dark-nippled breasts quivered before his eyes.

'What do you think?' she said. 'Give me an interview, at least.'

'Here?' he said.

'Why not?'

She took his hand and put it to her chest. The flesh was hot to his touch. The full smooth orb overflowed his palm.

'It could take a while,' he said, slipping his other hand over the curve of her hip, 'to really test your suitability.'

She said nothing to that. She already had her hand in his fly.

'I didn't realise intellectual programmes were like this,' said Eve as she knelt on the floor and rested her elbows on the side of the bed.

'You've led a sheltered life,' said Tom, kneeling behind her and anointing her rectum with a whorl of transparent jelly from a tube.

'God, look at her sucking that big cock!'

'She's not sucking cock, Eve, she's practising fellatio in the cause of art.' Tom rubbed ointment into the head of his penis and placed it in the dark divide between the cheeks of her bottom.

'That's a bit of a mouthful,' she said.

'Whichever way you look at it,' he agreed, plunging into the sweet tight tunnel of her anus.

'Oh,' she said and pushed back against him. 'God, you've got it all the way up me.'

'Does it hurt?'

'Not exactly.'

'Shall I stop?'

'Oh no.'

He found her clit with his fingers and began to tickle. 'Ooh, that's good, Tom!' And she squirmed and bucked, riding backwards and forwards on his fingers and cock in a gallop towards orgasm.

Suddenly her thrusts faltered and she began to giggle. Tom's eyes had been glued to the shiver and shake of her broad white bottom and the elastic ring of her anus stretched tight around his tool. He looked up and he chuckled too as he took in the familiar face on the television screen.

'It's funny,' he said as he resumed his thrusts, 'for years I thought Petra had a clipboard between her legs.'

'Well, you know better now, don't you?' said Eve, squirming beneath him.

'Me and ten million viewers,' said Tom and shot off deep inside her voluptuous bottom.

Petra had known Morticia would humiliate her but, of course, that's also what she wanted. She wasn't so sure about involving Kelvin, however. Things were too new this second time around. But it seemed she didn't have a choice.

They had been watching the orgy from the side but now Morticia led them to the platform where the action raged.

'Take your clothes off,' said the novelist and, with trembling fingers, Petra obeyed.

'Take his penis out,' was her next command and, without looking Kelvin in the eye, Petra did as she was told. His cock reared from his trousers, a straining bar of flesh in her hand. She clung on to it as if it were her sanity. Lust and fear boiled in her loins.

She found herself on her back on the table as Morticia positioned her to her liking. Then she was lying with her legs spread-eagled and hanging down, her pussy at just the right height for any eager male. And suddenly there were lots of those.

First came a large hairy man with a muscular torso. Petra recognised him as the man in the anorak. He seemed to have undergone a kind of religious conversion.

He groaned as he sank his big tool inside her and thrust with a purpose that had her moaning with shame and delight. He didn't last long but behind him was another ex-sperm-conserver and another behind him, his cock at the ready.

Petra took them all, she had no option. And she wouldn't have wanted it any other way. Now she had started, she didn't want to stop.

Between orgasms she looked at Kelvin. He was standing by Morticia's side, watching her intently. On his face was an expression of desire, frustration and - could it be? - pride in her performance.

As Petra gazed into his eyes, Morticia whispered to him. At her command he took a pace towards Petra, his cock thrusting up from his loins like an angry weapon. Morticia spoke to him again and Petra realised then that Kelvin, too, had fallen under the woman's spell. And somehow, even as a camera zoomed in to capture her taking Kelvin's penis deep down her throat, that made everything all right.

'I need your help,' said Chastity to Marianne as the presenter stood uncertainly behind a large shambling cameraman who was heroically capturing the scenes of lust and mayhem around him. Marianne had given up on her interviews and was contemplating giving the cameraman some hand relief - God knows the poor fellow was in need of it from the way his trousers were stretched over his bulging crotch. Being a newcomer to this kind of programme, however, she had been uncertain whether it was professional to jack off a working technician. Would the camera shake, for example? Or would it be in contravention of union rules? Marianne had always been wary of touching studio equipment lest she set off some dispute.

Chastity's request rescued her from this dilemma. The Californian sex-therapist was stripped for action. She wore a man's sports shirt, calf-high white cowboy boots with tassels and a scarlet G-string. The shirt was undone and her big tanned breasts floated ahead of her like two balloons. Her long blonde hair hung wild and loose and there was a crazy light in her eyes. This was her night of ultimate triumph.

'You're on my side, aren't you?' she said to Marianne, who nodded - what else could she do? Now was no time for debate.

'Help me get Timberland,' hissed Chastity. 'Come on!'

Ted was in the thick of the throng, separating bodies with his spade-like hands, hauling wriggling women off fallen men and heaving fornicating couples apart. Occasionally he would stop and take a swig from his flask and hurl curses at no one in particular. Then a curvaceous bottom or a bare breast would catch his eye and he'd lash out, plunging once more into the fray.

Chastity caught him from behind, leaping onto his broad back and wrapping her arms around his neck. He didn't go down. Instead he swayed unsteadily, surprised for a moment, then bent forward at the waist, pitching Chastity onto the floor. Marianne kicked him on the knee and he fell sideways. Then both women jumped on top of him.

They wrestled in a panting, wriggling heap with him yelling and cursing, his breath on fire with booze. Chastity tried to pin his arms, her bare breasts in his face, the hard stubs of her nipples rasping across his cheeks. He recognised her.

'You'll burn in hell, Honeydew,' he shouted. 'You're a corrupter of souls! An evil sex-crazed whore!'

Chastity said nothing, instead she fastened her mouth to the side of his neck and sank her sharp white teeth into the flesh.

Marianne heard his roar of anguish as she pressed her to his legs, trying to contain those hard, pumping thighs as he fought against the pressure. Her hand found his belt and she nimbly unbuckled him, pulling open his fly. He howled and bucked beneath her as she delved inside his clothing.

Chastity was wrapped tight around his torso now, sucking and licking the blood from his neck wound. His mouth found her nipple and he bit her too. Then a strangled moan rose from his throat, pitched somewhere between agony and ecstasy - Marianne had her hand on his cock.

As she had known he would be, he was vast. Tree-Top Ted had a limb worthy of his name. Marianne wrestled his trousers and shorts down his muscular thighs, baring a gnarled and mighty branch of a penis. It was as hard as teak, as brown as a nut and as erect as a cock can be when it has known no sexual relief for years on end.

Marianne knew what she had to do to complete Chastity's victory. Above her the warring writers were locked in the kind of clinch that suggested that their antipathy was on hold. There were no more screams and curses, just the licky-sucky noises of lips on flesh.

Ted was flat on his back and the two women were on top of him. Marianne knelt on his thighs and pulled Chastity backwards so her loins were poised over his. She yanked the tiny triangle of the G-string from Chastity's bulging pussy and thrust Ted's big cock between her silky smooth thighs.

It wasn't easy to make the right connection. It flashed through Marianne's head that this was what farmers did when helping recalcitrant bulls and cows. But Marianne was a resourceful woman for one who professed to care little for matters sexual. She knew what angles worked and what didn't, where and how

186

to apply a little lubrication and just what body parts to push.

'AAH!' roared Ted as his great tool was sheathed in the Honeydew cunt.

'Oh boy!' breathed Chastity as the quivering organ filled her to the limit.

'No! No!' cried Ted as the blonde lifted and plunged on top of him, the gleaming orbs of her breasts quivering, the golden mane of her hair enveloping him. And the hot, tight, incredible, long-forgotten-but-now-instantly-recalled pressure of pussy on penis teased and excited and urged him to—

'NOOO!' burst from his throat as he gushed his long-dammed desire deep into the succulent honeypot of the luscious sex goddess. And, as the flood hit her like a bolt from a geyser, Chastity was swept away in her own glorious orgasm.

Silence fell throughout the studio. For a moment, all eyes were upon the two warring writers locked in a battle of lust. Then a woman laughed and another cheered and the air was full of female yells of triumph.

Ted thrust Chastity from him and rose unsteadily to his feet. His shirt hung in rags from his bloodied chest and he was naked from the waist down. His tree trunk of a penis stood at half mast, the shaft glistening wet. From the red swollen glans trailed a string of the precious male essence he had fought so hard to conserve. And failed.

With a howl of despair, Ted lumbered towards the studio doors. He ran down the corridors, down the stairs, through the reception area and out into the night.

And straight into the arms of Inspector Claire Quartermain and an elite squad of the Sex Police.

Chapter 59

Sonja Sargeant walked into the offices of The Whimsical Press the next day with a beam on her face. Her hair was a bird's nest, there were shadows under her eyes and her blouse was crumpled. These things were par for the course, but not the smile or the light burning in her brown eyes.

'This,' she proclaimed to her assistant, 'is the first morning of the rest of my life.'

The assistant looked at her watch. 'Nearly the first afternoon,' she drawled. 'Blow-job's been screaming for you for the past hour. You'd better go and sort him out.'

'My pleasure,' said Sonja, looking for once as if she meant it. Basil Swan was a self-styled old-fashioned publisher, 'one of a dying breed' as he was fond of saying. As far as his underpaid, overworked staff were concerned, extinction could not come quick enough.

'Where the bloody hell have you been, Sonja?' he squawked when the publicist strode into his office. 'Now that Timberland's tour is over I won't have you goofing off. Have you seen your in-tray?'

'Oh fuck off, Basil,' said Sonja and lit up a cigarette.

'Hey, you can't do that. It's no smoking in this building. We'll be in trouble with the landlord. And don't be rude to me, the staff might hear. These walls are very thin.'

Sonja placed a white envelope on his desk.

'What's that?' he said.

'My resignation.'

'Not again.'

'I mean it this time, Basil. I'm out of this ghastly firm and this ghastly business. I've got a job in television.'

'Good God, have you really?'

'Black Raven TV. Senior researcher and special consultant on the book industry. Ten grand more than you pay and lots and lots of perks. So you can take your job, Basil, and stuff it.'

'Oh.' His jowls wobbled in a sulky fashion. 'You'll be working out your notice, of course. Technically it's three months—'

'Three minutes, Basil. I calculate you owe me two years' holiday. Don't kick up a fuss or I'll tell your wife your nickname around the office. And how you earned it, of course.'

'Christ, Sonja, what a little bitch you've turned out to be.'

'I've been well trained. Bye, Basil.'

'Wait, Sonja. Er, your assistant, Andrea—'

'Adriana.'

'Is she any good?'

'Hopeless. Ambitious though.'

'She's got good legs.'

'There you are then. I'm sure she'll shape up under your personal supervision.'

Basil's beady eyes twinkled. 'So be it,' he said. It paid to be a philosopher in this business - every cloud, after all, had a silver lining.

Sonja was clearing out her desk when the phone rang.

'It's the police,' said Adriana. 'About Tree-Top Ted.'

Sonja took the receiver. 'Can I help you?'

'This is the Thought Correction Unit,' said a disinterested female voice. 'We're holding a man in custody who claims he's a writer called Edward Timberland. He says you're his publishers.'

'That's true but there's been a mistake. Mr Timberland flew back to the States this morning.'

'Are you sure?'

'Certainly. He's been visiting Britain on a publicity tour but his flight left at midday today. He'll be in the air by now.'

'I see. I wonder who we've got then.'

'Frankly, officer, Mr Timberland has many devout fans who want to be like him. It's no surprise to me that some of them actually claim to *be* him.'

'I see.'

'It's probably a misguided cry for help. Don't be too hard on the imposter, will you, officer?'

Tom's guest for lunch arrived twenty minutes late. He wasn't surprised - it was a miracle she had turned up at all. Charlie Kite had moved heaven and earth to track her down at such short notice.

'I believe we've recently played our long-time-no-see scene,' he said as he rose and took her slender hand.

Tina looked steadily into his eyes. 'So you do remember?'

'It's only just come back to me.'

They sat down and faced each other across the white tablecloth. In the background the noise of the busy restaurant was faint. This was a private corner; Tom's instructions had been specific.

'Are you expecting me to apologise?' she said.

'No. I probably owe you an apology first. It was shitty of me to send that photo of your father to the papers. I never realised the trouble it would cause. I'm sorry about that.'

She shrugged and sipped from her glass. 'It didn't end up badly. Mum remarried and I have two half-brothers in Italy. They're adorable.'

'Did you - when you and Shani drugged me that night - did you mean to kill me?'

'No!' Her caramel eyes bored into his. 'Of course not. When you ran out of the room it was completely unexpected.'

'I wouldn't have fallen off the balcony if you hadn't doped me.'

'I'm sorry.'

'Aha, so you do apologise.'

'I apologise for causing your accident. I think we're quits.'

'Apart from this.'

Tom took the glass object from beneath the table and placed it on the white cloth. The dummy penis glowed, a golden honey colour.

Tina looked from the Wand to Tom's face. A smile tugged at the corner of her petal-pink lips.

'You're not trying to get out of the deal, are you?'

'I signed the contract under duress.'

'Are you intending to go back to court to prove it?'

He grinned. 'Of course not. I'm going to mass-produce this thing and sell the hell out of it. From what I've heard, it's a winner.'

Tina placed her hand upon the glass object and the colours within began to swirl.

'Do you recognise it?' she said. 'Doesn't the shape seem familiar to you?'

Tina's fingers stroked up and down the shaft and the broad, plum-shaped glans gleamed crimson.

Tom frowned as he stared at it. Pennies began to drop. 'You took a cast of my cock that night.'

'That's right, Tom, and this is the result. Isn't it beautiful?'

'Good God!'

'I'd be proud if I were you. Now every woman who's ever lusted after you can possess you. Thousands of them. That should give you a thrill.'

'It's bigger than I am.'

'I'd keep that quiet if I were you.'

They both laughed. They were still laughing when the waiters descended with food and wine. After they'd eaten, Tina put an envelope of photographs on the table.

'We needed some of them for the model of your cock,' she explained. 'We took the rest as insurance.'

'Blackmail, you mean.'

She didn't bother to deny it but pushed the pile towards him. 'I don't see any need for that now. You keep them.' Tom left them where they were.

'Tell me one thing, Tina.'

'Yes?'

'When I ran through the list of women who might want to harm me - well, there were quite a few.'

'I'm sure.'

'I'd slept with them all and somehow things had gone wrong afterwards. They all ended up hating me. But I never slept with you.'

'Perhaps you should have done.'

'Oh.'

'I always wanted you, Tom. You had everyone else - what was wrong with me?'

'But you were in love with Shani.'

'I was in love with lots of people. Including you, but you never did anything about it.'

Tom stared at her in surprise. Did she really mean that all this trouble could have been avoided if, for once, he had *not* kept his hands to himself?

'Tina, I don't know what to say.'

'It's your cue to say come with me to a hotel around the corner where we can discover what we've been missing all these years.'

Tom was tempted. The mature Tina was even lovelier than the delicious blonde nymph of fifteen years ago. Surely, after his ordeal, he was entitled to drown in those rich brown eyes, to bury his face in that thick honeyed hair, to taste the candy-pink pussy he had once glimpsed as she had lain in Shani's arms in the flat above the river?

But he hesitated. This was a test of his new mettle. Tina's full pale mouth turned down in disappointment.

'Is it true you're going to marry the nurse? The one who testified against you.'

'Yes.'

'Congratulations. In that case I suppose I'd better make do with this.'

Tom saw that she was squeezing the Wand. Her hand was wrapped tight around the shaft and from between her slim fingers thrust the big glass glans. It glowed a fiery spitting red.

In the cells of The Primrose Court another hand was stroking another penis, one no less magical in its dimensions though made of flesh and blood.

The hulking frame of the American lay stretched out on his back. He had a rubber bung wedged between his lips, an oiled wooden plug jammed deep into his rectum, two silver clamps that bit into his nipples and leather bonds on his wrists and ankles. Apart from that he was stark-naked. His erection rose from his belly like a great branch.

Gossamer pumped the big tool with quivering fingers. As she did so her huge white breasts shook above her black leather basque, the nipples sticking up like clothes pegs, the circles of her areolae the size of saucers. She fancied she could see her own incredible image mirrored in the pupils of the man beneath her.

'How many times has he come off?' she asked.

Amy Tooth raised her head from Gossamer's crotch. She was on her knees paying loving homage to her superior's thick-lipped pussy split, toying with the bush of blonde hair that fluffed from beneath the basque and plunging her tongue deep into the sugar-sweet pinkness beneath.

'Five times, so far,' she said and flicked her tongue across the ruby-red nub of the Prosecutor's trembling clit.

Gossamer speeded up her fingers on the American's trembling limb.

'Excellent,' she said. 'By the time we've finished with you, Mr Sperm-saver, there'll be none of your precious essence left.'

And the great cock spat a volley of vital male elixir high into the air, splattering the white globes of the Prosecutor's fabulous breasts.

Also by Noel Amos and available as paperbacks at AMAZON
Lust at Large
Lust on the Line
Lust on the Loose

www.ingramcontent.com/pod-product-compliance
Lightning Source LLC
Chambersburg PA
CBHW020246130626
46549CB00005B/2089